PRISONER OF FATE

When Fletcher came to Kate in the line of captives, her own vivid blue eyes met his squarely, and she refused to give him her hand.

"Do not waste your attentions on me, Sir," she said icily through gritted teeth, "for I find the likes of you beneath *my* attention!" With that she lifted her chin in the air and turned her head away in a gesture of dismissal.

"Do not dismiss me too quickly, my saucy Miss," Nick laughed as he grasped her chin and forced her face to turn toward him, eyeing her with interest.

"I wonder what it would take to make a smile cross those lovely lips and have them whisper words of love instead of spitting poison."

Kate gasped in shocked fury and swung her hand up to strike him. He easily caught it in an iron grip, twisting her arm behind her and pulling her roughly to him. Kate trembled as she felt his body hard against hers. He laughed again and brushed her lips with a kiss.

"Another time, my little spitfire," he promised haughtily as he released her and moved away.

DEFIANT DESTINY

NANCY MOULTON

AVON
PUBLISHERS OF BARD, CAMELOT, DISCUS AND FLARE BOOKS

DEFIANT DESTINY is an original publication of Avon
Books. This work has never before appeared in book form.

AVON BOOKS
A division of
The Hearst Corporation
959 Eighth Avenue
New York, New York 10019

First Avon Printing, November, 1982

To Nancy Dunker, for believing I could write this novel—and to everyone who dreams of romance

Chapter 1

Kate Prescott's anger enabled her to ignore the knot of fear in her stomach.

"Damn!" she muttered. You never knew what the Fates would decree next, no matter how carefully you tried to plan your life, she thought. How could this have happened when they were only two weeks away from New York, their destination?

Only moments before, everyone on board the British frigate *Newgate* had been summoned on deck. The battle was over. Kate could feel the ship standing dead in the water. She knew they must surrender.

As she emerged on deck with the other passengers, Kate was momentarily stunned by what she saw there. Black smoke and flames billowed from burning canvas and shattered masts and decks. Her eyes began to water, and she had to cover her mouth with her lace handkerchief to keep from choking on the acrid smoke. The crewmen who had not been shot or struck down by splintering timbers and flying metal were doing their best to tend to their bleeding and dying comrades. Others rushed to smother the hungry flames. The deck was red with blood.

Kate turned her face from the terrible scene. Her glance took in a ship closing in on their starboard side. It was a sleek, narrow-hulled corsair—the victor in the short but devastating battle.

Kate recognized its flag from talk she'd heard on board the *Newgate*. Called the Grand Union flag, it carried thirteen alternating red and white stripes, and in its canton, or corner, was the British Union Jack. The stripes represented those thirteen American colonies which dared defy Britain's rule and try for independence. The coming of spring in this year of 1776 had seen an escalation of the war between the two countries.

And Kate Prescott seemed to be in the middle of one of those war-spawned battles. The American privateer moving toward them had attacked and brilliantly outmaneuvered the *Newgate,* finally catching it in a crushing broadside, the final crippling blow. Rather than further risk the lives of his men and particularly his important passengers, the young British captain, John Douglass, had ordered their colors struck and the white flag raised.

The passengers and crewmen who were able came to stand mutely on deck to watch the two longboats dispatched from the American ship close the distance between them. No one spoke, so numbing was the reality of defeat and capture by the enemy. The only sounds were the crackling of uncontrolled flames and the moans of the wounded and dying men on deck.

Kate squared her shoulders resolutely and plucked up her courage. Well, she thought, it does no good to despair over Fate's decrees. She had learned that long ago from her father. To wallow in self-pity was to miss the opportunity to turn a situation to advantage, James Prescott often had said. All right, Father, let's see how that philosophy aids me now, Kate thought.

She glanced at Captain Douglass, whose grim expression reflected her own mood. His handsome face was lined from worry. Kate guessed him to be about thirty years old, but at this moment he looked ten years older.

He and Kate had been attracted to each other at the onset of the voyage, and their relationship had grown beyond friendly acquaintance.

Kate saw the hardened line of his square-cut jaw. She knew what he must be feeling. The Fates had dealt him a nasty hand for now, and even if his life were spared, his military career was ruined.

She heard him mutter an oath under his breath and followed his gaze out to the approaching American ship.

"Damned Fletcher!" Kate heard him murmur furiously as the grappling hooks dug into the ship's timbers and the exuberant Americans swarmed aboard. Others had whispered that name as they realized the privateer was Nick Fletcher's sleek *Sea Mist*.

So it was Nick Fletcher who had defeated them, Kate thought apprehensively. He had been the scourge of the North Atlantic for British ships since war had broken out between the colonies and Great Britain.

Nicholas Fletcher was known as a cunning and ruthless adversary, one who struck with the quick destructiveness of a lightning bolt. The British commanders, restricted in their thinking by regimentation and rules of battle, were constantly undone by Nick Fletcher's bold thinking and unorthodox maneuverings.

Paradoxically, he had a reputation for being a gentleman—indeed, a gallant—when it came to dealing with the ladies. Women dreamed of being his captive. Kate laughed to herself scornfully. She would shortly have a firsthand opportunity to find out if the tales were true or false.

Nick Fletcher was rumored to be a British nobleman, the son of a baron who had made a fortune in the textile business. Rumor had it Nick Fletcher had had a bitter falling-out with his family for some unknown reason and had come to America, where his military genius had earned him command and ownership of his own ship.

Now, as Nick Fletcher climbed aboard his newest prize, Kate carefully scrutinized him. He *was* handsome. His wavy hair was blond, streaked white by sun and sea. His face was hidden by a short, neatly trimmed yellow beard and moustache. He was broad-shouldered, narrow-hipped, and carried his six-foot frame arrogantly. He wore the dress uniform of the colonial Navy—dark blue cutaway coat with red lapels, red vest trimmed with gold buttons, dark blue breeches, and black tricorn hat. An ornately carved sword hung at his side.

But it was his eyes that held Kate's attention, for they were a vivid blue; their penetrating depth sent a shiver up her spine.

Kate reluctantly admitted that Nick Fletcher cut a dashing figure. She heard a low murmur arise among the other ladies as they whispered behind their fans, not taking their eyes from him. The sea wind whipped Kate's auburn curls around her face. The May air was warm, but she felt chilled as she watched Nick Fletcher swagger across the deck, his piercing blue eyes reflecting a sinister gleam.

At that moment Kate hated him for his smirking mouth and triumphant air. Poor John Douglass. Her glance moved to the British captain, who stood tensely at attention. His fists were clenched, his gray eyes were narrowed with rage, and it was with obvious effort that he held himself in check. Kate hoped desperately that he could control his anger. The look on Fletcher's face left not the least doubt that he would relish killing anyone foolish enough to defy him.

Nick Fletcher stopped in front of John Douglass and raised his hand in a mocking salute. Douglass returned his salute smartly.

"At ease, Captain," Nick ordered, a sneer pulling at the corners of his mouth. "So we meet again, Douglass. I always felt we were destined to come to this someday. How unfortunate for you that I am the victor."

John Douglass gritted his teeth and struggled to hold his tongue. He knew Fletcher was baiting him, and he would at least not give him the pleasure of seeing him lose his temper.

He, too, had felt they would someday meet like this. Even when they had been at school together, they had been enemies, rivals for whatever the other sought. Then there had been that nasty business about their commissions aboard the *Manchester*. Well, Douglass told himself, at least he would keep his dignity and, he hoped, his life and a chance for revenge against Fletcher.

With a flourish, Nick Fletcher graciously accepted Douglass' sword in surrender, making no effort to keep the smirk from his face.

But when he next turned toward the defeated British crew his face was serious, and there was no hint of the sneer he'd worn just a moment before.

"Men of the *Newgate*," he began in a deep, resounding voice, "I salute you. You fought well and bravely today and are to be commended."

He paused to allow his words to register. Confusion showed on many men's faces as they stared questioningly at the tall, handsome rebel before them.

"Know this. I have not the time nor the inclination to take prisoners or hamper my ship's movements towing this battered hulk to New York as a prize. Neither would I see good seamen slaughtered for the sake of expediency."

A tense silence gripped the ship. No one spoke. So many lives depended on the whim of this rebel.

"Therefore," Nick continued sternly, as his steel-blue eyes swept the assembled crew, "hear me well."

"Some of you, I know, are colonials who were impressed into service aboard this vessel. If you can prove your identity and your American background and will swear an oath of loyalty to the rebellion, you are welcome to join me and my men."

A low murmur began to sweep through the crowd of men.

"The *Newgate* will be stripped of all but the barest canvas. If the rest of you are half the seamen I think you are, you will be able to gain New York Harbor against the odds of the sea."

Heads began to nod as man turned to man to remark on this extraordinary turn of events. Some eyed Nick Fletcher suspiciously. Those who had never shown mercy themselves could not understand it in another.

Kate was as puzzled and uncertain as any of them. She would have to watch this Fletcher carefully. She suspected he more than lived up to the reputation he'd earned for being cunning and devious.

At last fifteen men stepped forward to claim the first choice Fletcher had given. They were escorted below by several of Fletcher's men to inspect the documents that would prove their identities.

Fletcher again approached Captain Douglass, who still stood grimly at attention, his jaw clenched in a hard line.

"I know it is admiralty policy to keep a special listing of those who have been forced into service, for the purpose of keeping a closer watch on them during voyages.

I would see that list, Douglass, along with your log and any documents relating to the American cause." It was a command, not a request.

Douglass started to frame an angry refusal but was cut off by Nick's sword, which had been drawn with lightning swiftness and placed against Douglass' bare throat. Fletcher's voice was low and deadly.

"I advise you to speak only when you are given permission, Captain Douglass, and then to choose your words very carefully. I admire good seamen, but I have little use for scheming conspirators such as you. I would count it as nothing to rid the world of one of your kind."

Douglass clamped his mouth shut once more and tried to conceal his relief when Fletcher withdrew his blade and sheathed it.

"Lieutenant Avery, take two men and follow good Captain Douglass below to his quarters. Bring me the list and any other documents you deem important. You know what we seek."

A handsome, dark-haired young man in an American uniform stepped forward and acknowledged Nick's order with a salute and a crisp, "Aye, aye, sir." Then, followed by two burly seamen, he motioned for Douglass to lead the way belowdecks.

The fifteen colonials came back on deck and stood in formation before Fletcher. Another of the rebel's young officers presented documents to him, while pointing out five men who would not be acceptable. They were mustered out of the group.

Kate noticed that Hensley Forbes was among those with adequate credentials. She neither liked nor trusted this small, round-shouldered man. More than once during the voyage from London she had caught his demonlike stare upon her. She'd learned his name, but little else about him; he seemed to keep to himself and generally was not liked by the other men because of his sly manner. Even now, as he was led with the others to the boats below, he furtively glanced her way, and Kate saw just the hint of a sneer curl the corner of his mouth. She looked away in disgust. Her eyes fell on Nick Fletcher, who now was turning his attention to the passengers.

The six male passengers looked worried. They were

bankers and politicians loyal to England and valuable to the British cause in America. To them, Nick gave only a cursory salute and a mockingly polite exchange of conversation. But to the ladies he was gallantry itself; he paused to bow deeply before each one, kissing each hand. Even stuffy Lady Farnsworth was visibly flustered, making a small curtsy. Her pretty daughter, Hillary, curtsied and giggled demurely behind her fan. The other two women, wives of the bankers, merely inclined their heads to acknowledge his greeting.

Kate's agitation was building. She wondered how this would affect the chances she had of succeeding in her own mission. This pompous pirate could ruin everything.

When Fletcher came to her in the line, her own vivid blue eyes met his squarely, and she refused to give him her hand.

"Do not waste your attentions on me, sir," she said icily through gritted teeth, "for I find the likes of you beneath *my* attention!" With that she lifted her chin in the air and turned her head away in a gesture of dismissal.

Complete silence prevailed as everyone's attention was drawn to her defiant figure. Fletcher was momentarily taken aback by her boldness but recovered with a laugh.

"Do not dismiss me too quickly, my saucy miss." He grasped her chin and forced her face to turn toward him, eyeing her with interest.

"I wonder what it would take to make a smile cross those lovely lips and have them whisper words of love instead of spitting poison."

Kate gasped in shocked fury and swung her hand up to strike him. He easily caught it in an iron grip, twisting her arm behind her and pulling her roughly to him. Kate trembled as she felt his body hard against hers. She frowned deeply and looked defiantly up into his cold eyes. He laughed again and brushed her lips with a kiss.

"Another time, my little spitfire," he promised haughtily as he released her and moved away, shouting orders to the remaining men who had come aboard with him.

As Kate rubbed her sore arm, she cursed herself for her actions. She was stupid to have let her anger get the best of her and draw attention to herself. Her mission was too important. Again, as she had so often over the past year, Kate longed for the loving presence of her father. He always had known how to stay her quick temper and guide her through danger, patiently teaching her the tricks of the dangerous trade of espionage.

But he had taught her well, and Kate vowed she would be more careful in the future. Perhaps she still could succeed if she could stay unnoticed from now on. Or, barring that, she thought ruefully, perhaps she could win Nick Fletcher's help, although she shuddered to think of what the price might be for his cooperation. After all, were they not both on the same side?

Chapter 2

The passengers—now Nick Fletcher's prisoners—were ferried to his ship from the crippled British frigate. As Fletcher had promised, the _Newgate_'s officers and crew were not slaughtered, but Kate suspected it wasn't so much out of respect for fellow seamen as it was because he had a more diabolical plan for them.

The ten crewmen who were joining Fletcher came aboard with the passengers and were led to the hold, where they could be watched for a time, until their loyalty could be tested.

The _Sea Mist_ had been badly damaged, and many of Nick's men had been wounded, with several killed. Nick knew it was unwise to take on a large number of prisoners; it made more sense to take only the most willing and valuable ones and get under way before another British ship came upon them. They would be easy prey in their condition.

Great pains were taken to confiscate or destroy the _Newgate_'s guns and ammunition. All but the smallest maneuvering sails were removed. The British ship, with officers and remaining crew, would be allowed to limp slowly to New York Harbor, if a storm didn't sink it. They might arrive in disgrace, but they would be alive. Kate knew that to John Douglass this was a fate worse than death. Yet she suspected he would survive, if for no other reason than to have his revenge on Nick Fletcher.

The prisoners were herded below to cabins, in which they were securely locked. Kate knew the others would be held for ransom, as they were all wealthy. She was neither known in America nor rich, but she could guess what her fate would be. She'd need her wits about her to make the best of this.

In the cabin, which she shared with Lady Farnsworth and her daughter, Kate had ample time to reminisce on the events that had brought her to this awful situation. Her thoughts went back four years to London and the brick townhouse her family had owned for as long as she could remember.

Kate had just returned from spending a year in Austria, where she had lived with family friends while studying music. It did not take her long to discover a difference in her father when she returned. When she'd gone to Austria, at her father's insistence, Kate left a man who was listless and bored. He still practiced the profession he'd chosen as a youth, barrister in the esteemed firm of Cantwell, Dorsett, Grindstaff, and Prescott. James Prescott was a gentleman and of an old, wealthy family. But it was a family tradition for the men not to idle away their time just tending the estates and counting their money. They should do what they could to make a contribution to the betterment of the world, and especially their homeland, Great Britain.

The family was not large. Its male Prescott heirs had been champions of causes, taking up sword and banner to support kings and principles in which they believed. As a result, many had died in battles remembered now only in family stories and historical accounts. Others had passed on, leaving no heirs or only daughters, until the family had dwindled down to James and a few distant cousins and nieces, none of whom lived in England any longer. James was the last to bear the Prescott name, and it looked as though he would not pass it on. His beloved wife, Amanda, had died giving birth to their only child, Kathleen, and he never had remarried.

Over the past few years, Kate had watched her father's zest for life turn to disinterest and complacency. He had no cause to consume him, nothing into which he could pour his thoughts and energy. She had not wanted to go to Austria, but he had insisted, telling her he would follow as soon as he had completed an urgent legal matter. But he had not joined her. Each of his letters carried one excuse or another, a mention here and there of new acquaintances and new situations that required his presence in England. He seemed to have regained some of his old zest after these new people came into his life, so Kate hadn't persisted in having him join her.

Back home again, Kate had been delighted to see her father was again the smiling, enthusiastic man she'd known as a child. The sparkle had returned to his expressive blue eyes and the bounce was back in his step. Kate was curious as to the cause of the change, and she quizzed him one evening after dinner. It was then that she learned about her father's new friends and new commitment. Now she remembered well the fire that had ignited in his eyes, the determined set of his chin when he put his mind to something. Kate didn't realize it, but she, too, had these traits, inherited from her father.

In the parlor that evening, James Prescott had told her of his disenchantment with His Majesty King George III and his lackluster politics. James Prescott was particularly concerned about the government's treatment of its American colonies. Those colonies were rich in natural resources desperately needed by Britain, but instead of allowing free enterprise to flow and benefit all, Parliament set prices, levied heavy taxes, and gave little voice in the matter to colonial representatives.

Genteel Britain society regarded colonials as lowbred riffraff, rejects of society. True, some of the original settlers in the New World were troublemakers, thieves, cutthroats, and murderers. The problem of what to do with them had been solved by shipping them to America. But most of the colonists were hardworking people from the lower classes, indebted people crushed by poverty, rejected by the wealthy, fashionable, well-educated upper classes. For them migration to the American colonies had provided an opportunity to make something of themselves outside the rigid British class system. They had used their great energy to create a civilized place out of a vast and hostile wilderness.

With determination, sweat, and toil, they had built homes, carved out farms, started businesses. These they had handed down to their sons and daughters along with a legacy of pride, honor, and freedom.

James Prescott knew this to be true, he told Kate, for he had had the privilege of meeting many of these American colonials in the year that she'd been away, and he had been quite impressed with them. Kate could see that, but she was skeptical.

One in particular, Benjamin Franklin, seemed to have had the most influence on her father. He was a respected representative of the colonies and often was in England on diplomatic duties. James had met him at a mutual friend's home, and they had instantly taken a liking to each other. Franklin had quickly become a close friend, and James had eagerly joined his circle of acquaintances and become involved in the complex issues of American-British politics.

The Americans had begun to resent England's heavy-handed rule and stern reluctance to grant the colonies the right to self-government. Men like Franklin sincerely sought to smooth out the conflicts, make reasonable compromises, bring harmony once again between the two lands. To James Prescott, this seemed completely reasonable.

Kate was at first stunned by her father's change in loyalties, for the Prescotts always had been staunch supporters of the Crown. But she recognized and respected his determination. The causes for which her family had fought in the past were not always popular ones. At any rate, she had little interest in politics and was only glad to see her father's fighting spirit alive again.

But as she met many of her father's new friends, Kate began to feel a sympathy with them, an involvement in their concerns and goals. Men like Mr. Franklin, Arthur Stillwell, Horace Wentworth, and Donald Crestmont were not the unruly, uneducated, ill-bred colonials she'd read and heard about all her life. These were men committed to their families, their homes, their businesses, the land. They sought fairness and respect in dealing with their disagreements with Parliament and the King. They wished for reasonable freedom to govern themselves while still realizing their debt and bond to the mother country. Kate began to see America as a land of promise and opportunity. She believed what she heard and encouraged her father in his pursuit of legal avenues to try to gain hearing and resolution of the American grievances. James Prescott used every resource at his command, including much of the family fortune, to defend and promote the American cause.

But Parliament turned a deaf ear to his and others' pleas for a measure of independence and more representation in Parliament. In fact, it levied even more taxes and issued more complicated regulations of freedoms and trade. James realized legal procedures were dead-ended, so he sought other means to further the American cause. That was how he came to be involved with Joshua Remfield, who headed an intelligence network working secretly for American rights, even total independence from the British Empire.

Kate had worried greatly then because her father's activities, while then not so outspoken and attention-drawing, were treasonous and might even bring him harm.

But then one evening Joshua had called her into the cloistered meeting of his associates in her father's study. Kate remembered her father had looked rather grave when she entered. Four other men, strangers to her, also were in the room. That night in late October some four years ago, Kate remembered well, for it was then they asked her to join their group. They needed her help for the cause, Joshua had said, needed her for a delicate assignment. Her father had been quick to tell her he did not approve. While what they proposed for her was not a particularly dangerous mission, there might be uneasy moments and some peril if someone should become suspicious of her true intention. James Prescott had not wanted his only daughter to become actively involved in any intrigue. But Kate's curiosity was piqued, and she asked to know the details before deciding. After she heard them, she agreed to help.

They wanted her to attend the very fashionable All

Hallow's Eve masquerade ball to be held two days later. Her identity would be kept secret because of her costume, and she could complete her assignment and be gone from the ball before the unmasking at midnight. She was to try to find out about an alleged condemnation list—a list of names and locations of American political zealots in the colonies who were considered traitors to the Crown there. The receipt of such a list into the hands of high government officials would see those named imprisoned and likely hanged for treason. Word had gotten to Remfield that a Major Stewart Hemmings was in possession of the list and would have it with him at the costume ball. He wanted to make a dramatic presentation of it to his superior officer, Colonel Jerome Wycliff, so as to influence the colonel favorably for a forthcoming promotion.

Kate was to try to verify the existence of such a list. It was too much to hope that she might obtain the list, but she should be prepared for such a possibility. She would have a partner whose identity she would know only by his blue cavalier's costume. His hat would have a large white ostrich plume in it. He would be close by all evening in the event she needed help.

Major Hemmings was in his mid-thirties, handsome, and a rather reckless sort. He also had an eye for beautiful women, so Kate had no trouble gaining his attention. Thinking back on it now, Kate smiled to herself. Her exquisite orange satin gown had been daringly low-cut and revealing and had attracted many male admirers that evening, including Major Hemmings. She had singled out Hemmings for her full attention and battery of feminine wiles as the evening progressed. She bribed a waiter to see that the major's champagne glass never was empty. The major's conceited determination to keep her attention and admiration and the effect of the large amount of champagne he'd consumed soon had him bragging about his important contributions to the military, his ambitions, and, of course, his soon-to-be-approved promotion. It was then he'd whispered rather drunkenly in Kate's ear about the list, tapping his breast pocket.

It was growing close to midnight and Major Hemmings seemed to have an uncommonly large capacity for drink. Kate couldn't wait much longer. She remembered how her heart had beat wildly as she'd deftly managed to slip a small amount of sleeping powder into his next drink when he'd turned away a moment to greet a friend. In a matter of ten minutes, the longest in Kate's life, he lost consciousness and fell to the floor. The blue-clad cavalier was quickly at her side to help in getting the major carried to an upstairs room to recover. Kate was the picture of concern and attentiveness to Hemmings as she followed him up to the room. Her cavalier quickly cleared the room of concerned guests, and they had easily retrieved the list and departed the ball as unobtrusively as they'd come.

Kate had loved it. She'd been intoxicated by the excitement, the danger. Kate's first mission had been a complete success. Her career of intrigue began as she joined her father in his secret battle to aid the American colonies. For three years they gave all they could to accomplish this end. Sometimes Kate had worked with her father on an assignment; at other times she worked alone or with another agent. Not every mission was fraught with danger or even important. But just being involved and having the respect of those men and the few other women with whom she worked was thrilling to Kate.

Until a year agò. Then everything changed. Her father was murdered in his bed in the room next to hers. As Kate stood over his body, her life came into sharp focus before her. She was repulsed by what she saw. She'd had enough. Revolutions, politics, intrigue had asked too much—her father's life and perhaps hers next. She wanted out while she still could walk away from it.

Now Kate focused on her last meeting with the man she knew only as "Blackpatch." He was her contact in London. At times Kate was amused by the complex precautions taken to disguise secret meetings, identities, confidential messages, the attempts to give a measure of safety to those doing the unsavory tasks involved in spying. Elaborate code names, passwords, and meeting schemes lent added drama to an already dangerous business. Only occasionally did you come to know the true identity of an intelligence member, usually by working on several missions with him or her. Now "Blackpatch's" last words to her echoed in her mind as she gazed unseeing through the cabin porthole.

"With your father dead, you must finish this mission alone. You know how important this is to the American cause, the cause for which your father gave his life."

"I know," Kate had replied quietly, remembering with pain her father's cold form, the assassin's dagger draining the precious life from him. The pain of her loss had lessened little in the months since he'd died. She looked at her companion levelly.

"I shall do it for him. But know this. I will do nothing more after delivering these messages. I have done enough. I grow tired of the danger, the suspicion, the fear of trusting anyone. There is no reason for me to stay here now. As I told you, I will help you in return for your finding me a way to America and getting a start there."

"Very well," he had said with a note of regret in his voice, "but we'll be sorry to lose you. Listen now, for time grows short."

With that, Blackpatch, whose identifying sign was the eye cover he always wore at their meetings, had given Kate the messages she was to relay to agents in America. So important were they that a second courier also was being given them. This was to ensure that at least one of them succeeded.

Blackpatch told Kate that a temporary position had been obtained for her as companion and secretary to Lady Farnsworth and her daughter on their journey to join Lord Farnsworth in New York. They knew nothing of the intrigue in which she was involved.

She would continue in her capacity as secretary and would stay with the Farnsworths in America as long as she, and they, wished it. It would be a chance to leave behind the dangerous life of espionage she had known for four years. She was twenty-four years old, and it was time she settled into a normal life. But first, one last mission.

Her messages were military in nature; they had to do with the British attack on New York. From a crushing attack and defeat of that important city, they planned to move on to Philadelphia, where the fledgling

United States government was headquartered. To defeat the colonials in both of these cities could mean a quick end to the fighting with Britain. She knew these were the most important messages she ever had carried.

Kate committed names and dates to memory. Nothing ever was written for fear it might fall into the wrong hands. Her contact in New York was code-named "The Hawk." As with all of her contacts, she would not know his true identity. Only the barest information was given to ensure secrecy in the event any of them were captured. He would know her as "The Blue Cameo," recognizable by the delicate ivory pin she always wore to meetings with contacts.

She was to rendezvous at the Soaring Hawk Inn and ask the innkeeper this:

"How did you come to choose the Soaring Hawk for the name of your inn?"

To which he would reply, "It is one that reaches to great heights and flies free."

Kate had smiled at the double meaning. It was the dream of many that the new nation called the United States would soar and be free from Britain's tyrannical rule.

The innkeeper would put her in touch with "The Hawk," who also wore a symbol of his code name, although Blackpatch had not known what it would be. A lapel pin, perhaps.

Kate would give her messages to The Hawk, and her job would be finished. She would be free to make a new beginning.

And so she had left London behind and sailed for America.

Chapter 3

It was two days before the prisoners were taken individually before Captain Fletcher for interrogation. Kate suspected Fletcher had purposely kept them waiting to increase their anxiety and make them more receptive to his demands. She felt her anger rising again. He was despicable!

And Kate wasn't far from the truth. Nick didn't relish his interviews with the prisoners, but he knew he had to do it sooner or later, and better later, after they'd worried a little.

At any rate, seeing to ship's business always came first and there was much to do. The dead had to be given decent burials, the wounded tended. The ship's doctor had been killed, leaving it to Nick and Bennett Higgins, the bosun's mate who had some knowledge of doctoring, to see to the dispersion of medicines and bandages.

Then Nick had spent the greater part of his day supervising the necessary repairs to the ship. He'd had little rest and was in a foul humor when he called for the prisoners to be brought before him.

Nick Fletcher smiled to himself as he thought of them. He was not above enjoying bullying them.

Two hours later Nick sat at his desk reviewing the information he'd gathered. Not bad, he thought reflectively with satisfaction. Lady Farnsworth had remained indignant and aloof, but he knew of Lord Farnsworth and felt assured of a tidy ransom from him. The daughter, Hillary, was a pretty little thing. Nick had momentarily toyed with the idea of carrying her to his bed and having his pleasure with her, until he had seen her shyness and heard her giggle like a schoolgirl. He was not reduced to bedding children, especially when there was a more promising package on board.

A devilish smile spread slowly over his lips as he thought of the defiance and rage he had seen in the blue-eyed one. A surge of anticipation swept over him as he remembered her body forced against his. He would enjoy taming that one, he reflected to himself.

The bankers' wives, Edna Bates and Myrtle Abrams, had been the sour-faced old biddies he had first thought them. Their husbands, Jon and Willard, and Evan St. Vincent, one of the King's tax representatives, were easily intimidated when Nick had drawn his sword and placed it menacingly on his desk.

They would fetch a good price. It would more than make up for the time he would have to endure them on his ship. The rebellion could well use these funds.

Nick's thoughts turned again to the spirited Kathleen Prescott. Lady Farnsworth had willingly answered his questions about her. She was new in her employ, and Lady Farnsworth felt no loyalty to protect her. Not that that would have deterred Nick anyway.

He had saved Kathleen Prescott for last. Knowing she would yield no ransom, Nick relished the thought of what she indeed would yield.

At that moment he heard her tumultuous arrival outside his cabin door.

"Unhand me, you scurvy baboons!" Kate raged. "I can walk without your inept assistance!"

That outburst was followed by a loud howl of pain from Ginty Lawson as he received a well-aimed kick to the shins. Clutching for his throbbing leg, Lawson lost his balance and toppled against the cabin door. It burst open from the force of his weight, sending him sprawling to the floor. Kate was dragged in behind him by Bennett Higgins, who was nearly doubled over with laughter.

"Ha, Cap'n, this one's a hellion! You'll be enjoyin' bringin' her to rein!"

Higgins forced Kate to a spindle-legged chair and roughly pushed her down into it. Kate's better judgment told her to stay there rather than fly at Higgins and scratch his eyes out, which was her first impulse. Still laughing, Higgins helped the suffering Ginty to his feet.

"That'll teach you to be ungentle with a lady, Ginty," Nick said, laughing heartily. "Dismissed now, lads. Leave her to me."

"Sure you won't be needin' us longer, Cap'n?" Bennett Higgins teased as he sent a lustful look toward Kate.

"If I did, it would be the first time," Nick said, laughing again. "Now get out of here, both of you."

Nick was in good spirits now as he turned to Kate. She was frowning and breathing hard. He saw no trace of fear in her large blue eyes. She looked ready to spring on him. Nick spoke to her with exaggerated politeness.

"I apologize for any mistreatment you may have received at the hands of my men. They go overboard with their enthusiasm at times."

With that, Nick walked to his desk and sat down. He wore no uniform now, but a pirate's garb. His full-sleeved, white silk shirt was unlaced and open down the front almost to his waist, revealing his muscular bare chest. His black breeches were tight-fitting and neatly tucked into knee-high, black leather boots.

Nick put his feet up on the corner of the large mahogany desk and let his gaze move slowly over every inch of Kate. She felt naked beneath his stare but refused to flinch.

Calm down, Kate told herself. Don't let anger impair your judgment again. She bit her lip to keep from asking him sarcastically if he liked what he saw. He likely would consider it an invitation. She didn't like the sly smile on his handsome, bearded face.

"Relax, Miss Prescott. Good God, if your eyes were daggers, I'd be quite dead right now." Nick saw a flicker of puzzlement pass over her face.

"Lady Farnsworth was good enough to give me your

name and certain other information about you. Shall I call you Kathleen or Kate?"

Kate hated his arrogance. She found her tongue and in a cold, steady voice answered him.

"I expect you will call me whatever you wish."

Nick laughed and rose to his feet.

"You are correct, beautiful lady. I always do exactly what pleases me." His voice became cold. "You would do well to remember that."

A long moment passed in silence. Nick's eyes held Kate's. His threatened, hers defied. Nick smiled, but not pleasantly.

"I think 'Kate' suits you. So 'Kate' it shall be."

Nick walked around to the end of the desk and sat down on the corner of it. He was directly in front of Kate. He folded his arms across his broad chest and looked at her coldly.

"And what shall I do with you, my lovely Kate? You can offer me no reward of ransom, as do the other prisoners. What do you have to offer that would please me, Kate?"

How Kate longed to slap that smirk from his mouth. Instead she held her head high and continued to meet his gaze.

"I offer you nothing," she replied icily.

Kate kept her gaze on Nick, tensely waiting for his next move. She did not let her eyes search the richly furnished cabin, for she knew there was no escape. Even if she succeeded in getting out of this room, they were at sea. There was no escaping the ship now. She would have to bide her time.

Kate did not have long to wait. Nick slowly walked around the room, rubbing his bearded chin with his thumb and finger, a fixed smile on his lips. He wanted to savor every moment. Such memories helped make long months at sea without a woman endurable.

Kate was calm now, thinking very carefully. She decided to try to take the initiative. Do the unexpected, her father always had said. Perhaps she would have an opportunity to use the small dagger strapped to the inside of her thigh. It had come in handy on other occasions. She stood up and faced Nick squarely, shoulders back and head held high.

"Captain Fletcher, I'm well aware of my position here and your plans for me. Shall I remove my clothes now, to avoid the distastefulness of having them torn from my body? Or are you the type of brute who enjoys doing that sort of thing?"

Kate enjoyed watching him stiffen suddenly, the smile vanishing from his lips. She pressed on, frowning and feigning impatience.

"Come, come, Captain. Where is your voice now? I'm fully aware that you mean to ravish me. It's part of your ridiculous pirate code or something, isn't it? You are quite predictable, really. Well, let us get on with it, shall we? The sooner started, the sooner finished." And she began to undo the buttons on the front of her dress.

Nick frowned. He felt like a schoolboy, and he didn't like it one bit. How had he lost control of the situation?

Kate stole a glance at Nick from the corner of her eye. She saw his look change to anger. Good, she thought, an angry man could be counted on to make mistakes, and she might yet have a chance to thrust her dagger home. She wouldn't allow herself to think beyond that triumphant moment.

Kate fully expected him to seize her, fling her to the bed, and tear off her clothes. Her hope was that in the ensuing moments when he was blinded by rage and lust, she could unsheath her dagger.

And, in fact, Nick did take a few steps toward her. Kate braced herself for his attack. But he halted abruptly before her. His face relaxed into a sardonic smile, and he spoke in a honeyed voice as he made her a slight bow.

"On the contrary, madame, you do me an injustice. I can see you are a woman who likes to be wooed and won in a proper fashion, thus making your final surrender all the more rewarding."

His sneering grin infuriated Kate. She could hold her temper no longer. It exploded like a thundercloud.

"You bastard!" Kate shrieked as she lashed out at his face with her nails.

Nick easily avoided her reach, threw back his head, and let out a hearty laugh. Then he swept his arm around her waist and lifted her writhing body effortlessly into his arms.

"There, there, now, Kate. Don't despair. I may be predictable, but I shall try not to act the lowbred brute you picture me. Instead, I'll be the gentle lover you desire."

Kate continued to kick and struggle and beat on his broad chest with her fists. Nick carried her easily across the spacious room and threw her unceremoniously down on the wide bed. She continued kicking and clawing as he forced her two hands down to either side of her head and straddled her body with his knees to still her.

"Ha! You fight like a tigress, Kate, as I knew you would! 'Twill be an adventure having you, I'll wager!"

Kate thrashed a moment longer, then let her body go limp as she realized the uselessness of the struggle and the pleasure she was giving him. He was far stronger than she. She could only hope he would quickly be done with her.

But Nick meant to enjoy Kate long and lingeringly, for he had been at sea for several weeks, and the sight of this lovely woman and the feel of her body moving beneath him had stirred his blood.

Kate saw the lust in his eyes. The hungry look on his face made her feel like he would devour her in his unbridled passion. Her first reaction was to renew her struggling against him, but Nick's body was like steel upon hers, making any effort useless.

Nick laughed and brought his head down to cover her mouth with his roughly. His hands seemed to be everywhere, unfastening her dress, touching her body expertly, caressing her neck, breasts, stomach. Her attempts to evade him only seemed to excite him more, and his kisses became more searching, more impassioned.

Suddenly Kate heard him laugh softly. Her eyes fluttered open to find Nick grinning down at her, holding her dagger in his hand.

"Hardly what I expected to find between your legs, my dear. Most curious," Nick said with amusement, although a slight frown creased his brow.

Kate made a futile effort to grab for it, but Nick only

laughed and tossed it away behind him. Then, he brought his mouth down over hers again, silencing her protests.

His kisses moved down her throat to her breasts, to her tightening nipples. His hands sought the most sensitive places of her body, kindling a response she resisted with all her might. She prayed he would quickly be done with her before her body betrayed her. Why did he have to be so slow, so meticulous, so expert in his assault?

Kate's heart began to pound and the blood was racing through her veins, setting her on fire. She could sense his mounting excitement as his hands and lips caressed her breasts, her stomach, her thighs.

In her frenzied mind, Kate knew she would not be able to stay Nick's ravaging of her, but she so wanted to do all in her power to lessen the pleasure of it for him. Her body's strength to resist him was waning. Now she knew she must use the strength of her mind to steel herself against his onslaught.

With a strength of will born of her stubbornness, Kate made herself go limp. She willed every muscle to relax as she focused her mind on one thought: Do not react. Yet her body would have betrayed her as she felt Nick move between her legs, for his expert touch had aroused her long-controlled senses. But her mind still was the stronger, and she closed her eyes and willed her body to total passive submission.

She felt Nick's sudden hesitation as she lay quiet beneath him. Yet, so enflamed was his desire that he could not stop what had begun, and he took Kate with an impassioned fury that forced the breath from her.

Kate heard his mumbled curse as he rolled off of her a few moments later, and she knew that she had triumphed, at least in their battle of wills.

Chapter 4

Nick lay on his back next to Kate, drained of his passion, yet filled with angry frustration, for he knew that Kate had won a victory—a small one—but a victory just the same. Her sudden change to complete and cold submission had had the effect of throwing ice water in his face, and his pleasure had been brief. Nick felt foolish and his masculine pride was more than a little wounded by this willful young woman who had resisted him so completely.

At that moment there was a pounding on the door. Nick cursed softly under his breath.

"What is it?" he barked angrily.

"It's me, Jock, Cap'n. Frenchie wants to know if you'll be wantin' your dinner yet tonight. It's gettin' late, and he says he can't keep it forever."

Nick was silent a moment before answering.

"Dinner for two, Jock. Now."

"Aye, aye, Cap'n," came the enthusiastic acknowledgment. "Two, you say? Yes, sir!"

They heard his laughter and retreating footsteps.

Nick slowly climbed out of bed, pulling on his black breeches as he got up. Tension filled the air. Kate opened her eyes to see his handsome profile reflected in the glow of the lamp he lighted on his desk. He obviously was angry as he sat down in the chair and looked toward Kate, a frown creasing his forehead.

Kate felt bruised and angry, yet she showed no outward signs of any emotion as she slowly rose and began to put on her gown. No word passed between them for some time. How she hated Nick Fletcher for his outrage against her.

"I take it this has been useful to you in the past." Nick's clear blue eyes were cold as he toyed with her dagger.

"More so than it was this evening," Kate replied matter-of-factly. She watched him closely for a few moments before posing the question that was foremost in her mind. She would not let him see the fear and humiliation she felt.

"What now, Captain? What do you plan to do with me?" she asked seriously, meeting his glance levelly.

"Now, Kate?" Nick jeered. "I'm not sure. I daresay you've lost your reputation"—he paused and, raising an eyebrow slightly, added—"if not your virtue."

Kate could feel the color rising in her face, and it was with an effort that she controlled her ire. Her tone was cold and calculated to sting when she spoke.

"I'm glad I could at least rob you of the privilege of being the first to have me. I hope it will not upset you unduly to learn that my virtue, as you call it, was freely given at the time it was lost, not forced from me by a lowbred, strutting peacock."

Kate turned to walk calmly to the porthole, letting the ensuing silence lend weight to her words. But instead of the outburst of wrath she expected to come raining down upon her, Kate heard only a hearty laugh. She whirled to face him, the anger she felt at last showing itself in her flashing blue eyes and the frown that furrowed her brow.

"*Touché,* Kate," Nick exclaimed through his laughter. "You've bested me and brought me low in this, and I'm the first to admit the victory. I must confess to envy for the man who knew you first."

"But, my sweet," he continued, his voice a little colder, "you've whet my appetite, presented a challenge to my pride, so to speak. I must know you willing in my bed before I would let you go. Therefore, your things will be moved here to my cabin."

Nick's smile was lecherous as he reached for a

stemmed goblet and the decanter of red wine on his desk.

"You wouldn't dare!" Kate shouted, her blue eyes flashing fire and glistening through threatening tears.

"I am not accustomed to being denied what I desire," Nick said levelly.

Jock Turner returned with their dinner. Silence hung heavily in the room as he set the table for them. When he left, Nick offered Kate a chair, but she refused, turning her back on him. He smiled slightly as he seated himself and began eating. Moments passed before he spoke to her again.

"I'm a reasonable man, Kate. Perhaps we could come to an agreement. Lady Farnsworth said you had no family and were hoping to start a new life in America. It's a good place to do it. I've ruined your plans to have the Farnsworths help you, but perhaps I can make amends for that when we reach New York...if you please me," he added smugly.

If Kate had had her dagger in her hand at that moment, she would have killed Nick Fletcher. But her racing thoughts told her to keep calm and play along with this man. He was dangerous, she knew, and everything was in his favor...for now. She had heard the tales of pirate captains who used their women prisoners, then gave them to their crews for their pleasure. The thought sent a terrified shudder through her. But there must come a time when he would not be in control. Then she would have her revenge on him. It was a thin thread to hold onto—that he might release her in New York. Right now it was the only hope she had. It was clear she had little choice in the matter. She would have to cater to his lecherous desires for now, even if it meant being his mistress.

Kate took a deep breath to gather her courage and turned to face Nick Fletcher.

"So be it, Captain," she said with more conviction than she felt. She was amused by his look of surprise at her sudden acquiescence. "I've always felt it best to take things as they come and make the most of them when I have no other choice. Hereupon, we strike a bargain. Until further notice, I shall rely on you to be my protector, in exchange for my cooperation in certain...activities."

Kate forced a provocative smile as she grasped the full goblet of wine that Jock had set for her and raised it toward Nick.

"A toast to our arrangement, Captain."

Chapter 5

Nick had the watch that night, so after dinner he locked the door behind him and left Kate alone in the cabin to ponder her fate.

The cabin was good-sized. Richly carved and polished oak lined the walls and beamed the ceiling. The bed was larger than usually found on a ship, even for a captain's cabin. A tribute to Fletcher's arrogance, Kate thought derisively. Scarlet velvet drapes hung from the top of the bed, held back at each of the four posts by braided gold cords. Everything was in its place, yet the room reflected the man who occupied it. At a glance, Kate could tell she was dealing with no ill-bred cutthroat. The cabin, from the impressive collection of antique pistols displayed in a barred and locked case on one wall, to the beautiful crystal wine set on the desk, gave one the feeling of quiet elegance, denoting a taste and preference for quality that would be hard found in a common pirate.

The massive mahogany desk and chair graced the far side of the cabin, situated under the horizontal row of paned windows stretching across the stern of the ship. A mahogany dining table and four matching spindle-legged captain's chairs stood in the middle of the room. Kate pushed back her chair as she sighed and rose from the table.

Her glance fell to the crumpled bed, its disorderliness

a jarring sight in the uncluttered room. It was an abrupt reminder to Kate that she was, despite her brave appearance, a prisoner, subject to the whims of a bold and dangerous man. She was sure he didn't trust her. Nor should he, Kate thought cunningly to herself. She would have to win his trust and then strike when his guard was down. You will need to tread very carefully, Kate told herself as she poured another glass of wine.

Young Jeff Blackamore, Nick's cabin boy, who looked to be about fourteen years old, brought her bags from the cabin she'd shared with the Farnsworths. As he put them down and began to clear the table, Kate couldn't resist the chance to question him.

"Did the ladies Farnsworth besiege you with questions about me, Mr. Blackamore?" she asked, trying to sound casual.

"Aye, right curious they was, miss, but I didn't tell them anything. I says for them to mind their own business," and he gave her a friendly smile.

"Thank you, Mr. Blackamore," Kate said, flashing her sweetest smile. Young Jeff was not immune to it. She knew she'd made an easy conquest, which might be useful later.

Kate's conscience was bothering her a little. Lately, everything she did seemed to be done for an ulterior motive. How ruthless you became in espionage, when your very survival might depend on the use you could make of another person. Kate didn't like what it had forced her to do, which was why she wanted to quit. She should have quit before this last mission, she realized with a sigh of regret.

But now was not the time to soften. As Jeff turned to leave, Kate saw a chance to tease him and further endear herself to him.

"Tell me, Mr. Blackamore,...ah, Jeffrey. Have you often helped a lady move into the captain's cabin?" She gave him an innocent, wide-eyed look.

"Ah...no, miss, never, miss," he stammered, shuffling his feet nervously.

Kate smiled warmly at him as she grabbed his broad shoulder and directed him toward the door.

"Liar! Now get out, my friend. I want to get some sleep."

The look of relief in his eyes told Kate he was her slave. Some men, no matter what their ages, were so easy to manipulate. Some men...Nick Fletcher? Kate wondered as she fell asleep in the large four-poster bed.

On deck, Nick strolled his quarterdeck uneasily. All was quiet on board. He usually enjoyed sharing the late watch with his men, especially on a night like this, when the wind was holding steadily and it was clear and warm. It kept him one of them, comrade as well as captain. He usually found these quiet hours calming, a good time for thinking, planning. But tonight he felt tense and ill at ease as many thoughts preyed on his mind.

They would reach Duncan's Cove north of New York Harbor in twelve days' time, if the wind held. It was a little-known inlet Nick often used when he had to be in New York. The *Sea Mist* and her crew would be safely hidden there. Once in New York, Nick would send inquiries to verify the identities of the ten men who wanted to join him. By then he'd have had ample time to observe them. That was how he chose the men who served on his ship—careful scrutiny and gut feeling. He hadn't been wrong yet, but it would be foolish not to seek verification.

He'd also dispatch the ransom messages, see to the necessary repairs, and take on supplies. All this had to be done long before Douglass' ship limped into port. What better proof of his ransom demands than the word of the defeated captain?

Nick smiled. It had been a diabolical idea, sparing Douglass and his crew. Not only did he not have to bother with them as prisoners, but it also made him look generous in the eyes of the passengers and his men. It also prolonged Douglass' defeat and disgrace. How Nick relished that. A quick death was too good for the likes of him. They'd been at odds as long as they'd known each other. Their initial dislike of one another when they'd met at the university had steadily grown into an intense hatred. It became a personal obsession between them to try to best the other in all they did. Douglass had not been above lying and cheating to get what he wanted. Still, Nick had beaten him most of the time. But he would never forget how Douglass had tricked him out of a commission he had wanted badly, under Captain Micah Torrence of the *Manchester*. It still was a bitter memory.

The sky was black and deep. Constellations dotted the darkness. Nick's thoughts turned to Kate. A frown creased his forehead as he stroked his golden beard. He usually took the moment's pleasure from a woman and so be it, with no good-byes, no regrets. How he despised the made-up women of fashion with their affected shyness and coquettishness, who were his usual bedmates. When he bent them to his will, they dissolved into whimpering children, good only for some fleeting moments of release and no deeper relationship.

He thought again of Kate, her large blue eyes, creamy smooth skin, well-rounded breasts. Her natural prettiness would have caught his eye even if he hadn't been without a woman for weeks. Nick felt his pulse quicken. Her rage had stirred him, that and the promise of a temperament he would enjoy taming. Now her ability to resist him spoke of yet another challenge.

His thoughts lingered on what they had had together that evening. He had sensed an awakening in her that she had forced herself to deny. He felt his blood stir. Next time he would not let her win the struggle within herself.

A sly smile curled his lips as he thought of Kate asleep in his bed now. He could easily slip below for a while...but the punishment for leaving post during watch was clear-cut, and the rules applied to the captain as well as the men. He would have to wait. But the anticipation heightened his desire for her.

Nick paused at the rail and watched as the *Sea Mist*'s sleek bow sliced smoothly through the water. Who had been the last woman to challenge him so? There had not been many among the scores he had known. Yet he did not have to think back very far, not even a year. Lynette had been the last. Lynette DuPree.

Nick's mouth tightened into a hard, thin line and his eyes narrowed. Unconsciously, his hands gripped the rail until his knuckles showed white against the skin.

Lynette, beautiful, raven-haired Lynette. Like Kate,

she had been strong-willed yet aloof, a challenge he could not resist. And she'd used her wealth of feminine charm and soft, enticing body to lure him into her vicious web of deceit and treachery. She caught him at a time when the lonely life of a sea captain was weighing heavily upon him, at a time when enthusiasm for the rebellion seemed to be waning, supplies were scarce or nonexistent, leaders willing to forgo personal glory and work as one of an efficient team were difficult to find. Nick's own dreams for his future and that of the country he'd grown to love seemed clouded, uncertain.

He had been easy prey for the likes of Lynette DuPree. She came into his life vibrant and alive with enthusiasm for the American cause, and she breathed new life into his own hopes and dreams, his commitment to independence and freedom. And while his instincts warned him to use caution, he chose to ignore them. He paid dearly for that. When he let himself begin to fall in love with her, when he began to depend on the warmth and passion of her beautiful body, Lynette betrayed him. She laid the trap that had come dangerously close to causing his capture at the hands of a squad of crack British dragoons. And through him, she had entrapped others as well.

By mere chance, she had escaped his enraged pursuit of her, but he had learned a hard lesson. Never feel too deeply about anyone. Vulnerability would be turned against you. He vowed he would never again let himself be trapped by a woman.

Nick's thoughts flashed quickly back to Kate. Was she cut of the same cloth as Lynette? Would they turn out to be the same in other ways? Was she something other than what she appeared? Nick brought his fist crashing down on the wooden rail. An ugly scowl settled onto his face. For her sake, he hoped she would not be too much like Lynette, for then his vengeance would be quick and complete.

Later, when his watch ended, Nick quietly entered the cabin. In the predawn light that filtered through the twin portholes, he could see Kate sleeping peacefully, her auburn hair a tousled mass around her head on the pillow. The sheet had slipped away, revealing her naked, well-shaped breasts. The sight of her spurred

Nick to hurry out of his clothes. His dangerous thoughts of Lynette DuPree had been pushed back in his mind, and now he looked hungrily at Kate. Her body was relaxed and inviting. How he would enjoy awakening her from sleep, feeling her nipples stiffening, her body aroused by his lips and hands.

Excitement surged through him as he gently pulled back the sheet and slipped into the bed. She stirred drowsily, slowly opening her eyes as she felt his hard-muscled body against hers. She started to speak, but Nick stopped her mouth with his kisses, first tenderly, then hungrily.

Kate did not resist, for she intended to keep the bargain she had struck, not for honor's sake, but for survival. She would gain nothing by resistance, for she knew how strong was his determination. And, she reminded herself grimly, if she didn't please him, he might turn her over to his crew.

So Kate let Nick's caresses awaken her body to the pleasure and excitement he well knew how to arouse. His kisses burned across her throat, her shoulders, her breasts. His hands, his lips were unrelenting as they moved over her. Yet he was gentle, taking his time with her, as if he sought to prove to her that he was more lover than ravisher. Nick teased and tormented Kate with his exploring lips until her own lips eagerly sought his and her body moved against his in writhing response. Little sounds of agony escaped Kate's lips as Nick urged her mounting desire to a heightened pitch. She began to feel the wave of agonizing pleasure move over her as he entered her. She arched her back, moving her hips to catch the pulsating rhythm of his thrusts. A long, low cry escaped her lips as she heard him gasp.

Nick had fallen into an exhausted sleep beside her, still holding her in his arms. Kate lay awake beside him for a long time, a smug feeling of satisfaction and triumph within her. It had been a long time since she had allowed herself to give in to a man's caresses, and she knew her need had been great. Nick Fletcher was an accomplished lover, used to taking what he wanted.

But a man could become a slave to his loins. He wanted her. She would use that hunger to make him need her, depend on her, trust her. Then she would strike back and have her revenge on him.

Chapter 6

Nick was up and dressed before noon to see to ship's business before returning to lunch with Kate. She was just awakening as he entered the cabin.

"Good morn, sweet captive," he said as he walked to the bed and slapped her soundly on the rump. "Would you sleep the day away? Or, mayhap you remain abed because you so hunger for my fond embrace that you stay there to lure me into joining you again."

Nick's blue eyes twinkled with delight as they dropped to the rich linen sheet molded to her breasts.

"I'm up!" Kate squealed as she hurled a pillow at Nick to detour his reaching hand and scrambled from the bed, wrapping the sheet safely around her.

Nick laughed, his mood relaxed and playful as he stood leaning against the draped bedpost, his arms crossed over his broad chest. His mouth held a mischievous grin as he watched Kate.

She made her way to the door of the wooden wardrobe against the wall near the end of the bed. Opening it, she drew out a beige damask gown trimmed in yellow velvet ribbons and a white lace petticoat to wear under it. Turning to put them on the bed, Kate was aware of Nick's penetrating gaze.

"And will you be the knave and stand there gaping while I dress, or play the gentleman and at least turn your back in order to afford me some semblance of privacy?" she asked tartly, one hand on her hip while the other clutched the sheet around her.

"Why, the knave, of course, madame," Nick answered, making her a mocking bow. "I would see in the light of day what was only felt and partly revealed by the dim light of dawn."

"Very well! Since it is obvious I am a captive first and a woman to be respected not at all, then feast your blackguard's eyes!" And with a boldness born of anger Kate released her grip on the protective sheet, allowing it to slip unhindered to the Persian rug, leaving her standing naked before him.

Kate blushed a becoming pink all over under Nick's close scrutiny. It took all her willpower to stand boldly before him, head held high, hands on hips. She was determined not to show the embarrassed modesty she felt. But some of her resolve fled as she saw desire flare into Nick's eyes as he slowly walked toward her. Taking her small chin gently in his hand, he raised her face to look into his.

"I was right, Kate, love," he murmured softly, brushing a tendril of hair away from her face. "You are even more lovely by sun's light."

He pulled her into his arms and kissed her gently, until he felt her tenseness ease. Then his kisses became more demanding, kindling a like response in Kate. She was swept away by the strength of him, his male nearness, his desire for her. In her own rising passion, Kate was only dimly aware of being lifted in his arms and carried to the bed. Nick quickly slipped out of his clothes and lay down beside her, to renew the gentle torture his lips forced upon her. Her senses reeled with the fervor of his caresses. His ardor awakened yearnings Kate long had held in check. Now at his urging, she abandoned all reserve and matched him kiss for wild kiss, caress for searching caress. While his passion flamed even higher than hers, still Nick held back, burning her with his lips and hands as they demandingly explored her body, until Kate thought she would scream from torment. And when she feared she could endure it no longer, he moved within her and mercifully brought their release in an explosive ecstasy of pulsating passion.

Nick and Kate lay in each other's arms, letting the feeling of contentment fill their minds and bodies. At length, Kate opened her eyes to see Nick watching her. He leaned over to kiss her lightly on the nose.

"I must say I prefer the impassioned woman just seen to the lifeless form that lay beneath me on that first occasion."

"As do I prefer the ardent lover to the ravishing pirate I felt upon me then," Kate replied, cocking an arched eyebrow at him pointedly.

"I shall deem it important to remember that in the future." Nick's smile held a hint of lechery as he drew Kate to him.

But Kate pushed against his broad chest, holding herself away from him to plead,

"Pray, hold, sir. Do you never feed your prisoners? Not even the ones who please you?"

She wriggled out of his grasp and jumped out of bed before he could catch her. Kate reminded herself that she didn't want to be too willing a partner. He might become suspicious. She must use him but leave him hungering for more.

Kate turned away from Nick to hide her smug smile and hastily began to dress in the beige gown she'd laid out. Nick lay back against the pillows, his arm propped behind his head. He watched her every movement. When she began to struggle with the laces that closed her dress at the back, he came to stand before her. Kate saw the sunlight playing along the muscular lines of his tanned body before he turned her away from him to fumble with the laces. As she swept her luxuriant shoulder-length hair away from her neck to allow him an easier view, Nick leaned down and kissed the exposed nape of her neck, then began nibbling teasingly at her neck and shoulder as one hand crept around to fondle the breast that lay half exposed in the low-cut neckline of her gown.

"Nick!" Kate chastised as she squirmed away and whirled to face him, her hands on her hips. A slight frown of annoyance creased her brow.

"Am I to spend all of my captivity undressed and in your bed?"

"A tantalizing idea, my sweet," Nick remarked just

as there came a knock on the door. He called a loud "Aye?" over his shoulder. From outside came young Jeff Blackamore's voice.

"Lunch, Cap'n, for two."

Nick reached for his breeches where he had discarded them on the armchair and quickly slipped them on. Kate breathed a quiet sigh of relief as she finished lacing her dress. She hoped lunch would give Nick Fletcher something else to think about for a while.

Chapter 7

Before Nick left her after their noon meal together, he told Kate that she would be joining him for dinner with his officers. While she did not relish the idea of being put on display for Nick's men, Kate did not protest; she would welcome a change of faces across the table.

Kate whiled away the afternoon exploring the cabin. She found nothing she could use to aid in her escape. The wooden barrel-topped trunk at the foot of the bed yielded only work clothes and shoes. The wardrobe closet held only dress clothes and several capes. Kate had to admire Nick Fletcher's taste in choice of colors and fabrics.

Her skillful use of a hairpin caused the lock on the gun case to release its hold, but as she had suspected, the three matching sets of antique pistols were not loaded. Neither could she find powder or shot. Nick apparently had removed every possible thing she might use for a weapon.

More use of the hairpin on the desk drawers yielded only nautical charts, ship's papers, cargo manifests, and writing materials. Not even a blunt letter opener could she find. Kate finally gave up her search and settled back in the padded leather desk chair to read Nick's log. There always was the chance of picking up valuable information reading such things.

In his log, Nick Fletcher revealed himself as master

of his men and his ship. His entries were clear and succinct, written in a precise hand. Few details were included beyond those needed to state the situation. Deaths and injuries were reported as coldly as the listing of cargo. Yet here and there a man's name was mentioned in commendation for bravery or actions beyond the call of duty. The log showed that Nick and his men had seen many battles against the British in the past year. Nick's reputation as the scourge of the North Atlantic seemed to be well founded.

Kate sighed as she closed the red leather volume and replaced it in the desk drawer. How she wished these conflicts could be resolved some other way. So many died, so many lives were ruined by war.

But perhaps the information she carried in her head would mean a quicker end to the fighting. Yet right now the chances of making contact with her counterpart in New York to pass on that information seemed rather small. She thought briefly of confiding in Nick Fletcher, seeking his help in finding The Hawk. After all, although he didn't know it, he and Kate were on the same side in this god-awful war. Only their battlegrounds differed. But she quickly dismissed the thought of enlisting his aid. Her instructions had been explicit that her information should be given to no one but The Hawk. And, most likely, Nick would not believe her to be a courier. He seemed to think so little of her except when it came to warming his bed. He might even think her to be a British double agent seeking to pass on false information. Then he probably would do even more than he was now unwittingly doing to prevent her from leaving the ship and reaching The Hawk.

No, she could not take the chance. She would have to see it through herself. As she dressed for dinner, Kate renewed her resolve to escape Nick Fletcher.

Dinner turned out to be a pleasant affair, not at all as Kate had imagined it might be. None of the other prisoners were present; they took their meals in the common galley. Nick's officers, while bold in their glances and eager in their quests for her attention, retained their manners and proved themselves to be gentlemen. Two in particular, dark-haired Nathaniel Avery and boyish-looking Anthony Hollingsworth, outdid themselves in lavishing Kate with attention and compliments.

Kate had left London with everything she owned packed in four large trunks. While her choice of ball gowns was severely limited, the three she did have were quite elegant and had been the latest in fashion a year ago. She'd worn the flattering floral silk with the tight bodice. It was low-cut in the neckline, half revealing Kate's full white breasts. She had placed a filmy pink silk scarf around her neck, letting it dip low to cover her breasts. The ends of the scarf trailed down her back. As she had planned, it did not hide her breasts, but only served to tease and torment. Kate knew every man at the captain's table longed for a breath of wind to do what they dared not.

Nick had seemed pleased with her appearance when he'd come into the cabin to dress for dinner. Kate had to admit he looked striking in his gold-trimmed uniform. She had heard the Americans scorned in London as riffraff playing at being soldiers. But Kate guessed it was more a lack of supplies than a lack of the knowledge of proper dress that kept some American soldiers from dressing with the elegance of British officers. Nick's men certainly did not seem to lack for proper dress.

The food was ample and delicious. There was fillet of haddock in a tantalizing wine sauce, spiced ham, crisp brown fried potatoes, creamed vegetables, fresh fruits, cheeses, dark bread, and several choices of wine. For dessert there was apple pie still warm from the oven. Nick explained that his cook was Pierre Drouseau, chef to royalty until Louis XVI had ascended the throne, and Drouseau had fallen out of favor. Nick had rescued him from a French debtor's prison; Pierre had been part of his crew for the past year.

"Will you join me in a stroll on deck, Kate?" Nick asked, signaling an end to dinner.

"I'd be delighted, Captain," Kate answered sweetly as two of Nick's officers tripped over themselves to help her with her chair. She laughingly thanked them as she took Nick's arm, and they left the cabin. Avery and Hollingsworth sighed as they, too, left the room. How they envied their captain.

On deck, the night was black and dotted with stars. A strong breeze kept the *Sea Mist*'s sails straining full as her sleek prow dipped and sliced through the rolling waves. Kate was glad to be out in the open air again. She paced her stride to match the roll and pitch of the ship.

At length, she removed her scarf and tied it around her loose hair to keep it from blowing in her face. Nick's eyes went boldly to her half-exposed breasts.

"I'm grateful that you didn't do that during dinner, for I might have had a mutiny on my hands. You've bewitched my officers, madame. They are your slaves."

Kate laughed as she clung to the taffrail and lifted her face to the wind. Then she looked beguilingly toward Nick.

"And have I bewitched the captain as well?" she asked innocently.

"I wonder..." Nick answered, meeting her blue eyes with his. He came to stand by her, turning her to face him. "I must admit to a certain attraction..." His finger traced a line across the mounds of her breasts.

"Attraction? You mean lust, don't you, Nick? And that is hardly a complimentary attitude to have toward a lady, sir," Kate replied sharply as she moved to turn away from him.

At that moment a crashing wave to port caused the *Sea Mist* to list over heavily, and Kate was thrown against Nick, who wrapped his arms around her. She frowned as she looked up into his smiling face, for he held her much too closely. She could feel the rapid beating of his heart against her hand as she pressed it against his broad chest in an attempt to hold him away.

"Call it what you may, sweet witch, but I want you and I shall have you." Nick stilled her protests with his lips, then lifted her in his arms and carried her to the cabin they now shared.

Chapter 8

Four days later, Kate stood next to Nick on the quarterdeck, relishing the crispness of the morning. The sun danced brightly atop the blue-green waves. The predawn slack in the wind had been replaced by a steady blow, and the *Sea Mist* again was in full sail, cutting her way smartly through the water.

Nick allowed Kate to be topside whenever he was on deck, and she was glad for the feel of the wind on her face and the open space of the deck after the confining closeness of the cabin.

Kate never saw any of the other passengers from the *Newgate*. They were allowed on deck only for a short time, just before sunset. Kate made it a point not to be there then. She had no desire to feel their condemnation or to have any distasteful confrontations. She did what she had to do to survive. She owed no one an explanation for her actions.

While on deck, she did see the men from the *Newgate* who had chosen to join the *Sea Mist*'s crew. Nick had explained to her that each was given limited duties but never left alone and always kept under the watchful eye of a regular crewman. They would have to earn the trust of their new captain and fellow sailors.

He always had to be aware of the possibility of a spy trying to infiltrate the ranks, Nick had told her, and she thought she saw suspicion in his eyes. Kate nearly had cringed at his words and quickly changed the subject.

She smiled and returned the cheerful greeting of Darby Castles, a jolly, rotund little man in his mid-forties. He'd been with John Douglass but not of his own free will. She knew that because they'd talked one morning on the *Newgate* when Kate had gone topside alone to watch the sunrise. He'd told her his story then of being waylaid by the press gang in London after he'd had a bit too much ale. She knew he welcomed this chance to sail with his fellow countrymen again, and he tried hard to please his new captain.

As Kate watched Darby move across the deck with Bennett Higgins in his wake, a strange feeling came over her—a feeling of being watched. It sent a shiver down her spine, and she drew her shawl tighter about her. She swung her head quickly around and caught the beady-eyed gaze of Hensley Forbes on her. A sardonic smile curled his thin lips. Just as on the *Newgate*, he did not attempt to hide the fact that he'd been watching her. His cold, sneering look gave Kate the impression that he knew some deep, dark secret.

Kate kept her face expressionless and turned away with an air of dismissal. She would not give him the satisfaction of knowing he had unnerved her. But she couldn't help wondering again why he seemed so interested in her. Somehow she sensed it was not a shipbound seaman's lust that prompted his attention. Perhaps Nick could tell her more about Forbes. She resolved to try to bring it up in their conversation today.

But for now, she shrugged off the uneasy feeling and watched Nick as he used a brass sextant to plot the *Sea Mist*'s position. Her mind turned back to last night and the thought of Nick's body against hers in the darkness. Her own eager response had surprised her. She was beginning to feel something for him that she didn't like. She was confused by her emotions—she responded to his lust, yet it was his gentleness that was wearing down her defenses. She could not let him arouse her body time after time and still maintain the feeling of detachment she had tried to put between them. He used her and she let him, Kate rationalized coldly, even while she knew she was not staying as uninvolved as she would have wanted. She wondered if she were becoming his captive in more ways than one, and she scorned herself and her weakness. Kate knew she had to avoid letting him make love to her if she could. But how? How, when she was forced to share the same bed with him, forced to lie near him, feel his touch, the warmth of his body?

As Kate walked away from him to stroll the deck, Nick absently gave his sextant readings to Jeff Blackamore while keeping his gaze on her. She has a provocative sway to her hips, he thought as he watched the movement of her full skirt. Several of his men put themselves in her path so they might greet her and feel the warmth of her smile. She easily had made friends with many of them.

She must indeed be a witch, Nick thought as he dismissed young Jeff with a wave of his hand. How else could she move him to want her so? Even now as he watched her, Nick felt desire rising. He had known few women like this Kathleen Prescott. She was intelligent and confident, with a strength of will that matched his own. He could talk to her about anything, from the operation of the ship to the latest London fashions. She was quick to grasp charting techniques and sailing jargon. And she was clearly unafraid of him. Nick realized he had his way with her because she chose to let him. Only in bed did he feel himself her master. Yet even then her eagerness and need enslaved him, for it made him want her all the more.

They were only about eight days from New York. He knew Kate expected to be released there with the others. But Nick doubted that he would have had his fill of her by then. He would not let her go, not yet. He relished the battle she would give him when she learned of his decision.

Nick's thoughts were interrupted by a shout of "Sail ho!" His eyes darted aloft to the high crow's nest and the man precariously perched there.

"Where about?" he shouted, shielding his eyes against the sun's glare with his hand.

"Two points starboard!" echoed the lookout's reply as Nick's gaze followed the man's outstretched arm to the horizon.

"My glass!"

"Aye, aye, sir!" The boy already was returning with the brass telescoping eyepiece.

Hands began scurrying on deck to await Nick's orders. Kate again came to stand next to Nick, straining her eyes to see the distant ship. She could make out only a small white patch on the horizon. The ship must be hours' sailing away, yet she sensed the tension in Nick and the crew.

Lieutenant Avery joined them on the quarterdeck, also raising a spyglass to seek out the ship. All was silent for a few moments before Nick lowered his glass.

"Can't be certain yet, but from her size at this distance, she'll likely be a man-o'-war. Your opinion, Mr. Avery?"

"I'd say so, too, sir," came his quick reply as he also lowered his eyepiece.

Nick walked two or three paces around the quarterdeck, absently stroking his yellow-bearded chin with his hand. A frown creased his forehead.

"Not likely to be American unless she's captured," Nick said aloud, more to himself than to anyone around him. "Could be French, but more than likely she's British. At any rate, let's not stand around waiting to find out. Get us the hell out of here, Mr. Avery. Give me ninety degrees north by northwest and every shred of cloth she'll take!"

"Aye, aye, sir!" came Avery's clipped reply as he shouted Nick's orders, sending men scurrying in every direction.

As the added canvas caught and held the steadily blowing wind, billowing out like puffy white clouds, the *Sea Mist* seemed to take wing, cutting through the blue-green ocean effortlessly.

Still on the quarterdeck, Kate grasped the side rail to steady herself against the heaving motion of the ship. The wind whipped her hair about her face. Salt spray stung her face and eyes. But she stayed where she was, exhilarated by the sleek ship's movements beneath her feet.

Her skirts whipped about her, and Kate was hard put to hold the rail with one hand and the yards of material in her skirts with the other. When she finally could look up toward where the distant ship had been approaching, she saw nothing but the infinite hazy line of the horizon.

That night as she and Nick dined alone in the cabin after his watch, Kate managed to bring the conversation around to the subject of the *Newgate* crewmen on board.

"But how do you know you can trust them, Nick?" she asked, keeping her tone casual. "After all, your life and the lives of the others on board depend on the loyalty of each man, do they not? Aren't you taking a tremendous risk having known British seamen on your ship?"

"It is a risk, of course," Nick agreed, as he reached for the bottle of deep red wine to replenish their glasses. "But one I must take at times. Unfortunately, each battle brings a loss of men, and their places must be filled as quickly as possible. I must get my men where I can find them. The ten men from Douglass' ship have documents attesting to the fact that they are Americans by birth and once were seamen aboard American vessels. The *Newgate*'s complement list showed them to be impressed volunteers. When we reach port in New York, I will have the validity of those papers checked. As I told you before, the men are carefully watched and given only routine tasks to do."

"You know ship's papers can be forged. Then you do not rely solely on legal documents to choose your men?" Kate asked persistently. She was anxious to ask about Hensley Forbes but wanted to bring him up casually so Nick would not suspect her motive.

"Of course not," Nick answered with a slight smile. "It is only a small part of what I consider. I rely very much on instinct, how the man responds when I give him orders, deal with him each day. It's a gut feeling I get, and it hasn't let me down yet. It serves me well with women also," he added as his eyes met hers. His smile widened into a grin as he saw Kate blush a becoming pink. She frowned at him and looked away.

"But why this sudden interest in the *Newgate* crew, Kate?" Nick continued to tease. "Is there someone among them who had caught your eye, perchance?"

He was baiting her, but Kate just smiled sweetly and ignored his taunt.

"Just trying to make polite conversation to make this meal bearable, Nick," she answered tartly. "I must admit I've taken a liking, though only a friendly one," she added quickly, "to Darby Castles. He's a delightful little man, and I think he wishes to remain with you and be part of the *Sea Mist*'s crew. But I can't for the life of me fathom why." She smiled again and took a bite of cobbler.

"Apparently we think alike, Kate, for that was my impression of him also," Nick agreed, overlooking her barb. "What opinion do you hold of the others? I'd be interested in knowing. You may be of help in making my decisions concerning them."

Kate could see the twinkle in his eye as he leaned back in his chair and sipped his wine. He watched her with amusement.

"I'll not continue this conversation if you're going to mock me, Nicholas Fletcher," Kate stated in somewhat of a huff as she raised her chin in the air and turned her gaze from him.

Nick chuckled softly. He loved teasing her and seeing her bristle, but he didn't want to go too far and put her off. He enjoyed their lively conversations.

"Forgive me, Kate," he said sincerely, smiling at her. "I truly am interested in your reactions in this."

"Very well, Nick," she answered, sensing his seriousness. "I think Cresswell and Bosley are like Darby. They are glad to be here and have no apparent love for His Majesty's service."

Nick nodded agreement. Now Kate had the opening for which she'd been waiting. "But Hensley Forbes is a bad one to have around, I think." Kate stopped to watch Nick's reaction. "He has a sly ruthlessness about him. I don't think he was much liked by the *Newgate* crew. I remember Captain Douglass saying once he didn't care for the likes of him either. Only a heart of stone could account for the chilling looks I've seen on his face."

"How descriptive, Kate," Nick said. For a moment Kate thought he was teasing her again, but one look at his face told her he wasn't. "I don't like him either.

Douglass and I have that in common, at least. Forbes is cunning and too much of a loner. Castles told me he is quick to use a knife. The other men keep their distance from him, and he seems to like it that way. No one seems to know much about him. I have not given him as much freedom as I have some of the others."

Kate was silent for a moment, deep in thought. So her hunch had been right about Forbes. Nick felt it, too. She was glad Forbes was well guarded.

Kate briefly discussed the other men in question with Nick before the conversation turned to the day's events. Then she saw a chance to return his earlier taunts with one of her own.

"About that ship that was sighted this morning," she began as she leaned back in her chair and looked at Nick. "Why did you decide to turn away? Was it your 'gut feeling' again, Nick, or something else?" She hid her smile behind her wineglass as she took a sip of the red liquid.

Though Nick's face retained its cool expression, Kate did not miss the slight twitching of the muscle in his jaw. "You are obviously unaware of the threat a fully armed man-of-war presents to a ship such as this," Nick retorted coolly, as if talking to a simpleton. "I am not afraid to take risks," he went on icily before Kate could reply, "but I am not a fool. A general does not take his men into battle when he is outgunned, outmanned, and certain to lose the fight. Neither does a sea captain imperil his ship and men. The *Sea Mist* and her complement would not be much good to the American cause lying at the bottom of the Atlantic. I had one advantage—speed—and I took it."

"My word, had I known you would be so touchy on the subject, I should not have broached it," Kate replied, raising her eyebrows in feigned surprise.

Nick was silent for a long moment, watching her across the candle-lighted table. Then he smiled slightly as he picked up his wineglass and leaned back in his chair.

"I think, Kate, that you knew exactly what effect your words would have on me, and I rose to the bait." His blue eyes twinkled with amusement. He drained his glass and rose to come around behind her chair.

"Since you seem to know me so well, see if you can discern what I'm thinking now." Nick traced a line along her bare forearm with his finger. He felt her tense slightly as he moved his finger up her arm to the base of her throat, then slid it over her half-exposed breast, tracing a line along the low neckline of her gown.

Kate slapped his searching hand away as she rose and moved away from him across the room. Anger sparkled in her eyes as she whirled to face him.

"Anyone could easily fathom your outrageous intentions. Is that all you can think to do with me, Nick? I am growing weary of your repeated assaults." Kate tried to keep her voice calm, her anger controlled. Her breath was coming in quick gasps, making the pink mounds of her breasts rise and fall too temptingly.

Nick moved slowly across the room to stand before her. He smiled wickedly as he spoke in a husky low voice.

"Assaults, fair Kate? Your body disclaims your words when I hold you in my arms."

"Oh, you bastard, you...!" Kate sputtered in rage as she raised her hand to hit him. He only laughed as he caught her wrist in his powerful grip and bent down to swing her off her feet and over his shoulder. Kate beat on his broad back with her fists as she furiously ordered him to put her down.

"Your wish is my command, Kate!" Nick mocked as he dumped her onto the bed. Then he threw himself down upon her, pinning her arms to either side of her head and pressing his body hard against hers to hinder her struggling.

"Come now, Kate, my sweet, admit that you enjoy our tumbles as much as I and cease wasting time."

"You lowborn beast! You..." Kate would have continued to berate him, but Nick's mouth covered hers and the protests died in her throat as his hands began their familiar arousal of her body and her passion.

Chapter 9

The next morning dawned bright and clear. Kate awakened to find Nick gone from her side. She rolled over slowly and raised up on one elbow to see him reaching for his familiar black knee breeches.

As though he had sensed that she had just awakened, Nick turned toward her. "Ah, my sleeping beauty stirs. I wanted to tell you that your presence has been requested by tonight's guest of honor at the captain's table."

"Oh?" Kate questioned, her curiosity aroused. "And whom, may I ask, is the guest of honor?"

"Jeff Blackamore. 'Tis his fourteenth birthday. When asked what special favors he would like for today, the bold rascal unhesitatingly asked to have you as his dinner partner. I'm afraid he's quite smitten with you, Kate. More of your bewitching at work here, sweet sorceress?"

Kate ignored Nick's taunt as an awful thought occurred to her. She sat up in bed, taking care to keep the sheet in place. "I trust my company will be required only for dinner and not for any other...activities."

"Have no fear, Kate. I can be generous to a boy on his birthday, but not *that* generous. I am not yet ready to share your charms with any man, young or old." And before she knew what was happening, Nick leaned down and pulled the sheet out of her grasp. His eyes swept her naked body hungrily before Kate could re-trieve the cover and scramble out of his reach.

"You have absolutely no honor at all, do you, Nick?" Kate accused, her eyes flashing fiery anger. "I have not the slightest doubt that, were you finished with me, you would not hesitate to pass me on, even to a boy of fourteen!"

Nick delighted in baiting her. He laughed heartily as he swung away from her and crossed the room to the doorway. He paused halfway through it to look back at Kate.

"Don't worry, my dear. You are safe as long as you continue to please me." He watched with satisfaction as Kate grew more red with fury.

"Wear the floral gown tonight, this time without that hindering scarf. At least we can give young Jeff some sweet dreams to occupy his thoughts, if not his bed!"

He slammed the door just before Kate's shoe struck it with a loud thud. Kate sat down hard on the bed. Tears of anger and frustration stung her eyes as she stared at the closed door. Her thoughts raced. What had she let herself in for, making such a devil's bargain with this, this pirate?

Dinner began as a formal affair, with much good food and drink and polite conversation. Young Jeff was tongue-tied most of the evening, rarely taking his eyes from Kate. She'd worn the floral gown as Nick had ordered, for she wanted to attend the dinner and feared he might not let her if she angered him. Though their relationship had moments that were almost playful, she could not allow herself to forget his reputation, nor could she forget the fact that she was his prisoner and at his mercy.

She enjoyed the shared company. The atmosphere had been a little strained until the heady wine began to soften everyone's reserve. When a few ribald quips were exchanged, the dinner took on a festive mood.

Before long, the empty platters and dishes were re-moved, several instruments of music were produced, and the singing began. Kate was amazed when Nick brought forth a beautiful six-stringed Spanish guitar, such as was the rage in fashionable London society. He proved himself a remarkable musician, playing expertly and singing in a rich baritone voice.

Kate lost count of the glasses of wine she'd had. She didn't care. She only knew she felt good and was enjoying herself. She enthusiastically joined in the festivities, adding her lilting soprano voice and vigorous handclapping to the songs she knew.

Kate did not know how or when she got to bed that night. She only knew that when she awoke the next morning, she was alone in Nick's bed. She was terribly thirsty and had a splitting headache. When she tried to stand and go for the water pitcher near Nick's desk, she found she could barely keep to her feet. Can my pain-wracked head be throwing me so off balance? she wondered through the fog in her brain. She usually could hold her wine better than this. Kate was just swearing off the evil brew forever when her glance fell on the porthole. She managed to make her way weavingly to it and learned the real reason for her exceptional unsteadiness. The sky was ominously dark, filled with churning black clouds. The sea was a surging mass of rolling, white-cresting waves. The wind was a deafening roar. The ship creaked and rolled and pitched as it tried to ride the turbulent water, its timbers straining against the force of the waves that crashed over its decks.

Chapter 10

Somehow Kate managed to get a little sleep. Her head throbbed mightily and her stomach churned. She was a good sailor when the sea was calm, but this violent dipping and rolling of the ship was more than she could take in an upright position.

After two hours of a fitful half sleep, she forced herself to dress. She had to do something. Perhaps Pierre could use some help in the galley keeping hot food and coffee ready for the rain-drenched crew, who would no doubt be catching a meal whenever they could. She knew she would see little of Nick as long as the storm prevailed, and that was fine with her. She was beginning to fear the effect he could have on her, the way her body so readily did his bidding.

In the crowded galley, Kate found herself more than welcome. Men battered by driving rain and violent wind stumbled in and out of the galley room, and Kate was kept busy bandaging cuts and bruises, serving hot, rum-laced coffee and steaming bowls of beef stew.

When she had a rare moment to rest, the plight of the other prisoners crossed her mind. But she reasoned she would do more good here, for Kate knew they would not welcome her ministrations.

Nick did not come to the galley, and by nightfall, when the storm still had not lessened in intensity and he still had not appeared, Kate wondered what superhuman strength enabled Nick to drive himself so. He would be no good to the ship or crew if he collapsed and was washed overboard, Kate reasoned with annoyance, though she told herself she cared not at all what happened to Nick Fletcher. She feared more what would happen to her if anything ill befell him. She sent steaming mugs of the rum-laced coffee to him with Bennett Higgins and Jeff Blackamore.

It was close to midnight when exhaustion finally overcame Kate, and she made her way back to Nick's cabin. The ship creaked and groaned, and Kate marveled that it still was in one piece after being battered so mercilessly for so many hours. As she fumbled to light the small lamp on Nick's desk, she was aware of the knot of fear in her stomach, fear that the ship would go down. Nature's wrath was so much mightier than this small wood and metal ship.

She sighed deeply as the lamp illuminated the room. It was then she noticed the prone figure on the bed. It was Nick, asleep where he had fallen, on his stomach across the big bed. He was drenched to the skin. His shirt and breeches were in tatters and clung to his hard-muscled body. His wavy hair was matted and tangled, hiding his face as it lay wet against his cheek.

Exhausted as she was, Kate knew she had to get him dry before he caught a chill, if he hadn't already. With her last bit of strength, she pulled off his heavy boots and then his shirt and breeches. With two large towels, Kate vigorously rubbed him dry from head to foot. She was too tired to try to wrestle his limp form into dry clothes. Instead, she turned out the light, removed her own clothes, and slid Nick's body to one side of the bed. Then she crawled into bed beside him, feeling the chill of his flesh against the warmth of hers. As she pulled the quilts over them, Kate curled her body close to Nick's. With the sea still raging violently around them, she, too, fell into a deep, exhausted sleep.

Dawn saw no letup in the storm, only a slight lessening in the ominous darkness that filled the churning sky. Kate stirred and awoke, aware of Nick's nearness. Her head rested on his shoulder, and her left arm and leg were flung across his body. As gently as possible, she lifted her limbs and started to move away from Nick, only to have him turn toward her and entrap her in his arms.

"Don't leave me yet, Kate," he whispered drowsily as he drew her closer within his arms. Kate was aware of his warm body touching the length of hers, and the feeling was unsettling.

"I feel I owe you a debt of gratitude for keeping me from catching my death last night." Nick began to nuzzle her ear as his fingers traced a path down her neck and over her tightening breast. Kate moaned, knowing what his touch would lead her to if she didn't stop him.

"Nick...please...don't," she murmured desperately, even while her body cried out for him to go on.

A pounding on the door was barely discernible over the din of the storm, yet Nick was quickly alert to it.

"Aye, enter!" he shouted to make himself heard above the howling wind.

Bennett Higgins poked his head in the door and hurriedly gave his message.

"Mr. Avery says you're to come quick, Cap'n. We've lost the aft mizzen, and the water in the hold's gettin' ahead of the bailin'."

"I'm right behind you, Bennett," Nick called as he leaped out of bed and quickly pulled on a clean shirt and breeches. Kate sighed heavily. She was again aware of the knot of fear in the pit of her stomach. Fear, or was it something else, too? She could not be sure if she was relieved or disappointed that Nick had been called from her side.

As he pulled on his high black boots, he looked at her. There was a kind of softness in his usually cold blue eyes. Or was it just a trick of the shadows in the dimly lit cabin?

"Another time, sweet Kate. That is, unless we all see a watery grave before the hour's done." And he was gone out the door.

Nick's mind raced as he sped up the narrow stairway to the upper deck. He marveled that Kate had all but made him forget this devil storm and the danger it threatened. What kind of sorceress was she?

Chapter 11

The *Sea Mist* did not sink within the hour, but she was fast losing the battle against the unrelenting tempest. Hour after hour the beautiful ship's exhausted crew struggled to keep her afloat. If she didn't go down from the weight of the water in her hold, then surely she soon would break apart from the force of the waves that crashed over her wooden decks.

In the galley, Kate busied herself with the same tasks she'd done the day before. There was little conversation. Everyone knew that each hour brought him closer either to death or to the end of the storm. No one gave up or bemoaned their plight, but it was clear that courage was waning.

More and more men were brought to Kate battered and bruised, for their fatigue was making them easy prey to the buffeting sea. Kate was glad to do what little she could for them. She desperately wished the ship's surgeon still was alive, for she knew so little about doctoring.

Young Jeff Blackamore was brought to her in the afternoon, chilled, pale, and writhing with pain. His left leg was broken, perhaps in several places, and the bone protruded nastily through the punctured skin. Kate had seen broken bones set before but never had done it herself. She gave instructions for Jeff to be carried to Nick's cabin; she followed with the surgeon's medicine bag, hoping someone on board would know how to set the leg.

In the cabin, Kate stripped off the bedclothes and ordered a man named Griffin to begin tearing the sheets into strips for bandages. She sent Ginty Lawson looking for something to use as splints. Kate found a packet of laudanum in the surgeon's bag, and mixing it with water, she held it to the feverish boy's lips. She hoped it would at least ease some of his pain. Grasping the surgical scissors she found in the bag, Kate quickly cut away the cloth of his blood-soaked breeches. Her stomach reeled as the raw and swollen flesh was uncovered. A long, ugly gash could be seen where the bone had punctured the calf of his leg. Reason told Kate that she would have to spread the cut, replace the bone, and immobilize the leg. Then it would knit together again—if he didn't die of infection. Kate knew such wounds could quickly become gangrenous. She vowed to keep young Jeff from losing that leg or his life, even while she knew her meager knowledge and the storm's hampering actions put the odds against her. Would this hellish storm never cease its raging?

Ginty Lawson returned with two sturdy wooden planks. With Griffin holding Jeff under the arms and with Lawson at his feet, Kate cleaned the wound as best she could. She was hindered by the ship's constant lurching and the flickering of the lamp as it swung wildly over their heads.

Ginty Lawson had set legs before, and he agreed with Kate on how best to get it back into place. At Kate's word he jerked hard on Jeff's leg, pulling it straight, while Kate did her best to open the gaping hole and thrust the bone back into place. Blood gushed from the cut, spilling over her hands, her dress, onto the bed and floor. Jeff screamed in agony, and Griffin and Lawson were hard put to pull and hold him steady while Kate bandaged the cut, then lashed the planks tightly to his leg to hold it straight. Only when she had finished did she allow herself to give in to the exhaustion and nausea she felt as she slowly sank to the floor in a dead faint.

When she awoke sometime later, Kate found herself lying next to the unconscious Jeff. Someone had made a quick attempt to clean up the mess made by his blood, but her hands still were pink with stains, and her gown was ruined by the bloodstains.

Jeff was thrashing and murmuring, crying out in pain whenever he moved his leg. Her hand on his forehead told Kate he was delirious with fever, a bad sign. What could she do? They were alone in the room. Apparently Lawson and Griffin had been called back on deck.

Kate glanced at the clock on the wall behind Nick's desk. Nine o'clock. The pitch darkness outside told her it was night, the night of the second day of this ferocious storm. How much more could they take?

Kate washed her hands and changed her gown. Then she set about making Jeff as comfortable as possible. She opened his gray shirt and bathed his arms, chest, and face with water, willing the fever to be washed away by the cool cloth. Jeff Blackamore was not a fully grown man yet, but he would be a strong, sturdy fellow when he gained his full maturity. His arms already bulged with muscles born of hard labor. His chest was broad, yet it tapered to a narrow waist rippled with muscle. Like Nick, Kate thought absently. Her hand stopped in midair between the bowl and Jeff's forehead as she realized with a start that Nick had come unbidden to her thoughts. His strong, sun-bronzed body whirled through her mind, and Kate was surprised to feel her pulses quicken. Was he gaining such a hold on her? Uneasiness filled her as she again took up the wet cloth to bathe Jeff's brow.

At about midnight, Kate dozed in the padded desk chair which she'd pulled up next to the bed. Jeff had quieted some, and she'd taken the opportunity to get some much-needed sleep. Now a sixth sense told her she no longer was alone with Jeff, and she opened her eyes to see Nick standing over the boy. Nick was drenched to the skin, and his shoulders drooped noticeably. Fatigue and worry lined his handsome face, ringing his eyes with dark circles. But it was the look in those eyes that held Kate silent and staring. There were pain and anguish there; she was startled.

Nick must have sensed her scrutiny of him, for at that moment he turned toward her. He had masked the look in his eyes, and his face was expressionless as he spoke to her.

"How fares the boy?"

"His leg is badly broken. The bone pierced the skin and there's a danger of infection. Already fever wracks him." Something akin to pity swept over Kate as again she thought of the pain she had seen in Nick's face.

"We did the best we could," Kate added quietly, almost apologetically. "But everything had to be so makeshift, and what with the storm and all..." She knew she was babbling. Why she wanted to try to explain things to him, she didn't know. He didn't appear to be listening to her anyway.

In the ensuing silence, Kate became aware of the wind. Could it be that it wasn't roaring as loudly as before? Or was she only imagining it in the hope of making it so? She would have questioned Nick, but he had begun to speak, more to himself than to her.

"The lad's been with me for three years. He was orphaned at age eleven and attached himself to me like a leech after I took him on as ship's boy. He's like the young brother I left at home in England. I wanted to send him away to school before this voyage, but he carried on so that I foolishly agreed to let him stay this one time more. This is my fault."

Kate was on her feet, standing next to Nick. She touched his arm.

"It was an accident, a fall. It couldn't be helped. No one is to blame." She tried to make her voice sound reassuring as she went on, touched by the distress in his eyes. "He's young and strong. He will recover."

Nick turned his eyes on Kate. His face was expressionless.

"Try to make him as comfortable as possible. The storm abates but we have heavy damage and are listing badly. It will be a struggle, but we have a chance to make our destination. A doctor will be summoned then."

He glanced once again at Jeff, then turned and left the cabin without another word. Kate was irked by his coldness, the authoritative tone in his voice. He had not even thanked her, only gave orders. But as she resumed putting the cold compresses on Jeff's brow, Kate smiled to herself. Nick Fletcher was cold, cunning, and demanding. Yet for a few fleeting moments Kate had seen him show feeling, making him as vulnerable to humanness as they all were. Yes, Kate mused, somewhere in that broad chest Nick Fletcher had a heart.

Chapter 12

Jeff's fever and delirium increased as the day went on. Kate and Bennett Higgins took turns staying with him, changing the bandage every two hours, and bathing him with cool water. Nick came often, to stand near the bed and silently watch Jeff's struggle. Nick never again let the pain show in his face, but Kate knew it remained.

The tempest had at last all but blown itself out, and everyone was kept occupied making repairs and trying to keep the *Sea Mist* afloat. Nick was everywhere, directing the pumping of the hold, instructing on repairs to the decks, masts, sails. Kate wondered when he ate or slept.

Nick entered the cabin unnoticed late that evening just as Kate knelt beside Jeff to change the discolored bandage. The odor that reached Kate's nose from the oozing pus-filled wound almost made her retch.

"He is no better?" Nick asked quietly as he came to stand beside Kate. She was startled by the sound of his deep voice so close at hand.

"His leg is worse, as is his fever," Kate stated flatly as she tried to clean the gaping, raw-edged gash with a wet cloth.

"Then the leg must be removed." Nick's voice was emotionless.

Kate looked at Nick. He was tired, bone-weary. His

usually vivid blue eyes were dull and glazed. Deep lines creased his forehead and the outer edges of his eyes.

"No, Nick, not yet." Kate's voice held a firmness she did not feel. Nick slowly turned to look at her.

"You have done all you can. The poison spreads. He will die if it is not stopped by amputation."

"There's no guarantee that his life will be saved even if you cut the leg." Kate's ire was rising as she saw the stubborn set of his jaw. He had already decided and almost challenged her to defy him. Well, challenge she would!

"And if he lives after you take the leg? What kind of life will he have?"

"He'll stay with me. I'll care for him," Nick stated quietly, looking at Jeff.

"He would not stay with you as a cripple, and you know it. But even if he would, what if something happens to you? You live a dangerous life, Nick. What would become of Jeff then? Would you condemn him to a beggar's life?"

Nick grasped Kate roughly by the arm and pulled her to her feet. His eyes now were alive with anger. He frowned menacingly. Kate had to bite her lip to keep from crying out from the pain as his grip tightened on her arm. At least he was no longer the cold, unfeeling stone of a moment ago.

"The leg must come off! There is no other way!"

"Is half a life better than no life?" Kate's words lashed out at him. Her blue eyes flashed angrily as she stood her ground before him. "If you were in Jeff's place, what would you choose, Nick? Death, or living as a one-legged cripple?"

Kate's words struck home, for Nick released his iron hold on her and whirled away to the other side of the room, muttering an oath. He angrily ran his hand through his tangled mass of sun-streaked hair. Kate knew she'd won. She already knew Nick well, knew the kind of man he was. He would not make another endure what he would not.

"Nick, listen. If we can close the cut and get his fever down soon, he'll have a good chance of surviving." Kate's tone was softer now.

"You ask for miracles," Nick retorted bitterly. "Isn't that what you've been trying to do all day?"

"Yes, but I have another idea. It's a long chance but it might work. Will you help me?" Kate's anger was passing. As Nick's eyes met hers, her look entreated him.

"Very well, a few more hours. But if this does not work, the leg comes off at dawn." The finality in his voice told Kate he meant it.

"Agreed! Now don't just stand there. Call Bennett and Jock down here. We'll need them to hold Jeff. You find a broad-bladed knife and heat it white hot in the lamp flame. We're going to cauterize this damned gaping hole right now!"

A smile of admiration twitched at the corner of Nick's mouth as he went to the door and bellowed for his men. She certainly had spunk. He hoped her idea would work; he had no stomach for crippling the boy.

Bennett was stationed at Jeff's head to hold down his arms and shoulders. Jock held his legs. Kate quickly wiped the pus from the wound and held the raw edges of it together with her hands as Nick applied the heated blade.

In his half-conscious state, Jeff screamed with pain and tried to fight his way clear of it. The smell was sickening, and Kate had to struggle to keep her senses from reeling. Nick helped her wrap clean bandages around the seared flesh. Jeff was unconscious.

"Now carry him up to the deck, where it's cooler," Kate said. "I want him stripped and wrapped in wet blankets. Use seawater, for it will be colder, and change the blankets every ten minutes. We've got to get the fever down."

Bennett and Jock looked at Nick, who nodded slightly. Then they gently lifted Jeff with a blanket and carried him topside. As Kate moved to follow them, Nick stepped between her and the doorway.

"I'll see to this, Kate. You've done enough. Rest now. You're pale as death."

"I've likely had more sleep than you have the last three days, Nick Fletcher! I've started this and will see it through. *You* get some rest before you become my next patient!" With head held high, Kate pushed her

71

way past him and sped up the stairs. Shaking his head in bewilderment, Nick followed her to the deck.

The gray light of dawn was just piercing the sky as Nick shook Kate gently to wake her. She'd slept on a pile of canvas where Nick had placed her when she collapsed with fatigue two hours before. He, too, had slept beside her, leaving the task of fever-breaking to several of his men.

"The fever has broken, Kate. Jeff's quiet now."

Kate smiled drowsily as she sat up and went to where young Jeff slept peacefully, wrapped in a dry blanket against the morning chill. Gently she unwound the bandage to see the flesh still closed. A scab was forming and no infection could be seen. Nick stood beside her as she replaced the bandage with a clean one.

"See? It begins to heal. And none too soon, I might add," she said smugly, looking from Nick to the red-edged rim of the sun on the horizon.

Nick looked down at her and brushed a stray strand of auburn hair out of her eyes.

"I have never taken orders from a woman, and I doubt that I ever will again. But this time I'm glad I did. Now go below and get some food and sleep."

As Kate moved away from him across the deck, she realized with a start that Nick had thanked her. In his own stubborn, conceited way he actually had told her he was grateful for what she'd done.

Chapter 13

Kate slept most of the day and awoke refreshed to find
Nick sleeping soundly beside her. There was something
comforting about having his warm body next to hers.
He was relaxed, handsome, vulnerable.

"My God, what am I thinking?" Kate whispered to
herself. This man is a pirate, a rebel, a ravager of
women, and who knows what else besides? She hated
him, she told herself as she slipped out of bed and
quickly dressed. How could she feel anything else for
such a man?

When she'd had a bite to eat in the galley, Kate made
her way to the small storeroom Jeff had been given. He
would not be using his hammock in the crew's quarters
for some time, but he would use it again. One look at
his injury while she was changing the bandage told
Kate it would heal. Most likely, he would not even have
a limp if he followed her orders to keep his leg still so
the bone could knit properly.

Adoration and gratitude filled Jeff's eyes as she
worked over him and told him these things. She was
moved and at the same time amused. He had so much
to learn. Jeff Blackamore had no idea that he owed his
leg and likely his life to a battle of wills between the
two people he admired most in the world. Kate now
realized what a great risk she'd taken. He might easily
have died from the infection. Kate herself may have

demanded his leg be amputated if Nick had not chosen that course and she'd taken it upon herself to defy him.

From Bennett Higgins Kate learned that her fellow prisoners had not fared too badly during the storm. Oh, they'd been plenty seasick, Bennett had related to her with a delighted wink, and there were a few bumps and bruises, but otherwise they were all right. Kate did not see them, for they were kept confined to their cabins except during an exercise hour just before the evening meal. Kate avoided going topside during those times.

In the evening, Kate and Nick dined alone in his cabin. Kate had thought much about John Douglass and how he and his men might have fared during the storm. Her mind was on him now during dinner.

"What? I'm sorry, Nick. What were you saying?" she asked absently when his voice finally penetrated her thoughts.

"I was saying," Nick answered drolly, "that I hope you know how to swim, for I'm going to throw you overboard in the morning."

"What?" Kate leveled her blue eyes on him, frowning deeply. "Whatever are you talking about?"

"Just proving to myself that you have heard not a word I've said for the past ten minutes. What in heaven's name were you thinking about?"

Kate was undaunted by his accusing tone.

"It's none of your business, but if you must know, I was thinking of John Douglass and what little chance he and his men had of weathering the tempest."

Nick's agitation deepened.

"Hopefully he is manna for the fishes by now, though in all likelihood the gale bypassed him or blew itself out before it reached him. The bastard always did have a penchant for good fortune."

"My, but you are touchy on the subject. Tell me, Nick, what did he do to earn your everlasting disdain?" Kate was enjoying his annoyance. This was obviously a sore spot with him.

"That, my dear, is none of *your* damn business, so let's change the topic of conversation, shall we?"

"Now you have whet my curiosity. Let's see now, he must have bested you at something. What could it have been?" Kate taunted, cocking her eyebrow in mock contemplation.

"We will *not* discuss it, Kate." Nick's voice was dangerously low.

"Very well, Nick. If you insist," Kate acquiesced, though she let a slight smile of amusement curl up the corners of her mouth. How she enjoyed taunting him. He annoyed her so often that she was glad for an opportunity to return it. Yet now she realized she shouldn't have baited him, for Nick's present bad mood would not make him receptive to the subject she wished to bring up next. Well, it couldn't be helped now, she thought with a sigh.

"Bennett told me today that we shall reach New York tomorrow night as planned," she stated casually between sips of wine. "Rather than delay us, the storm in fact pushed us ahead on our course."

"Bennett is getting to be like a chattering woman in his old age," Nick replied.

"Will we be near New York soon, Nick?" Kate persisted.

"Bennett told you true."

"Then I think we need to discuss the culmination of our bargain—in other words, my release." Kate looked at Nick levelly. She had rehearsed this moment in her mind over and over again, but she never knew what the outcome would be. In a few moments, she would know his decision. The look he gave her was not promising.

"There is nothing to discuss. You will not be released when the other prisoners are ransomed." Nick met her gaze steadily. He had spoken with a finality that caused a shiver to run the length of Kate's spine. But had she really expected him to say otherwise?

"Exactly when do you intend to release me, Nick? We had an agreement. I expect you to honor it." Kate tried to keep her voice controlled, but it was difficult not to show her anger.

"And I will keep my part of it, but when it damn well pleases me, madame," Nick said sternly as he rose to his feet. "Lest you forget, woman, you are my prisoner and subject to my wishes. And I do not choose to release you . . . yet."

Damn her composure, Nick cursed inwardly. Why was she not cowed by his bullying? How long could she stare at him with those accusing, anger-filled eyes?

Kate also rose to her feet but kept the table between them as she confronted him.

"In other words, Captain Fletcher, you are not a man of your word, but are truly the pompous, deceitful bastard I first thought you to be! You have no honor, no decency, no thought for anyone or anything but yourself! You have toyed with me, played your little games of lust and deception." Kate stopped to catch her breath. Her breasts rose and fell with the quick gasps she took. Her face was flushed pink and her blue eyes flashed fire. Nick thought she never looked more desirable. He could easily play the knave when there was such a delectable prize at stake. With a sardonic grin curling the corner of his mouth, Nick took a step toward Kate. But he stopped short when he saw the flash of a knife in her hand. Kate had quickly taken up the dinner knife when she'd seen the desire dawning in his eyes.

"You would be wise not to come any closer, Nick," Kate warned in a carefully controlled voice. Her anger was gone, replaced by a dangerous calm. "I assure you I would not hesitate to pierce your belly."

Nick saw the determined set of her delicate jaw, the cold glint of her eyes, and knew this was no whimpering schoolgirl but a dangerous adversary. He did not advance further.

"Know this, Nick Fletcher. From this moment on, we are enemies. I despise you with my whole being and will not hesitate to kill you if I have the chance. You may be able to use your greater strength and have your way with me, but never again will I come willingly to you. I will strike you down at the first opportunity. Never let your guard down for a moment, or you will be a dead man."

Nick stared at the beautiful, determined woman before him and knew she meant every word she'd spoken. There would be no quiet nights at sea with this fiery vixen, Nick wagered silently. But he would have to tread carefully. No woman was worth dying for.

"You indeed give me food for thought, sweet Kate,"

he replied sarcastically, keeping his eyes on both Kate and the knife.

A knock at the door shattered the tense silence.

"Beggin' your pardon, Cap'n, but Mr. Hollingsworth wants you topside," came Jock Turner's robust voice from the other side of the door.

Nick frowned and silently cursed the interruption, though he was wont to know what he had been going to do next.

"Tell him I'm on my way."

Nick backed slowly to the door, then made Kate a low, mocking bow.

"Until later, my dear," he said sweetly, then he was gone out the door, locking it securely behind him.

Once alone, Kate downed a glass of wine and sat down to gather her thoughts. She'd meant everything she'd said. How she hated Nick, hated being used, hated herself for beginning to feel something for him. He was a pirate and a scoundrel, and she'd kill him if she got the chance!

Chapter 14

Kate did not see Nick again that night nor the next day. A renewed wind had made the sea choppy, and he probably was hard put to see the still-crippled *Sea Mist* on its course, she reasoned. And he likely enjoyed leaving her alone to wonder when he would return, thinking the waiting might wear down her resolve.

"Ha! There is hardly a chance of that, Nick Fletcher!" she spouted aloud to the empty room.

Nick did indeed have his hands full controlling the ship, for his crew had been able to make only temporary repairs, and he was not certain whether she could withstand the renewed buffeting from the swelling sea. He did not release the wheel to Griffin, the helmsman, until the calm waters of sheltered Duncan's Cove lay dead ahead the next night.

The cove was located fifteen miles north of New York Harbor. From here he could conduct the ransom business, lay in supplies, and make the much-needed repairs undetected by unfriendly British ships.

Kate had watched intently from the cabin porthole as Nick and a handful of men cast off for shore in the longboat. The moon shone brightly, allowing her to watch their activities easily. She saw them mount horses that had been waiting for them on shore and thunder off into the night. The man who had brought the horses remained on shore, assumedly to take back the mounts when Nick returned.

Kate carefully laid her plan. Now was her chance. Bennett would be bringing her dinner soon, and she must escape then.

Kate dressed herself in a pair of Nick's dark breeches and a white shirt. Though too large for her, they would hamper her less than a gown. In an oilcloth sack she put a simple gray gown, shoes, what money she had, and a few small articles she wished to keep. This she tied securely to her belt. The rest of her belongings would be left behind.

Kate was poised and ready when she heard Bennett turn the key in the lock. With his usual friendly air, he strode in and placed her supper tray down on the table. Before he could look up, Kate brought the heavy brass paperweight down with all her might squarely on the back of his neck. Higgins fell heavily to the floor.

Kate ran to close the door lest someone should see what had happened, and stood with her back against it, panting for several long moments until her heart stopped beating wildly. She looked at Bennett's huge, motionless form and saw that he was breathing. Relief flooded her when she realized she hadn't killed him. He had been kind to her.

Kate took one last look around Nick's cabin. She knew she would not forget a single detail of it or the man she had grown to know so intimately here. She cringed at the thought of what a fool she'd been. She took a moment silently to curse Nick Fletcher before she turned the brass knob on the lamp to extinguish it, carefully opened the cabin door, and stole noiselessly up the stairs to the deck.

In the darkness, Kate crept to the rail where a rope ladder used earlier by Nick and his men still swung loosely against the ship's side. Crouching low, her eyes straining in the darkness to see the sailor who soon would be by on his rounds, Kate noiselessly climbed over the side, descended the ladder, and slipped unnoticed into the cold, dark water. She was glad her father had seen fit to teach her to swim, for she would need her skill to reach the distant shore. Silently she struck out for the shoreline. Her departure went unheeded on the ship.

As Kate emerged from the water, she could see the man who had brought the horses to Nick sleeping a little way down the beach. He had hidden himself and his horse haphazardly, and Kate could hear his loud snoring as she crept toward him down the deserted beach. She was glad for the moonlight and the shadows it cast from the thick shrubbery lining the beach.

As Kate gingerly sidestepped the bulk of the sleeping man, a twig snapped under her foot and she froze in midstep, only a foot away from him. She feared the wild pounding of her heart would surely wake him, but he only mumbled incoherently, turned on his side, and within a few seconds was snoring loudly again.

Relieved, Kate silently expelled the breath she'd been holding and moved toward the horse. She prayed it would not be alarmed by her sudden appearance, but she needn't have worried, for it continued chewing the grass unconcernedly as she tiptoed up and gently patted its neck.

She reached for the reins and led the horse slowly down the beach, out of earshot of the sleeping man. The sand of the beach and the roar of the surf covered any sound she made.

Then she mounted and turned the horse toward the path she'd seen Nick and his men take up the hill to the road. The mild-mannered plow horse refused to go faster than a slow trot, but Kate was unconcerned, for each step took her closer to New York and farther from the *Sea Mist*.

Kate was beginning to feel the chill of the early June night through her wet clothes when a farm loomed into sight just ahead. She decided to find the barn and stay there for the rest of the night. It would be better to be off the main road, for she feared at every turn that she would ride into Nick and his men returning to the ship.

The farmhouse was dark, and all was quiet as she walked her horse to the small barn. After unsaddling and hobbling her mount in a dark, empty corner stall, she climbed to the loft and stripped off her wet clothes. She quickly put on the gray gown she'd brought and gratefully lay down in the sweet-smelling hay, covering herself with some of it both for warmth and for concealment.

Just before dawn, Kate awoke from a restless sleep, saddled her horse, and rode out, just as she saw the farm's owner emerging from the house. He looked at her in astonishment as she headed her mount down the road, kicking her heels into his sides to spur him into his irregular jaunt.

After an hour's ride, Kate knew by the increase in the number of houses that she was approaching the city. Even at this early hour, the highway was becoming crowded with farmers, some herding livestock and others driving wagons heaped with grain to market. Peddlers bearing everything from animal furs to farm tools and household wares greeted and chatted with housewives who also were heading into the city to buy and sell goods.

Kate urged her mount on, stopping only when she came to a roadside livery stable. She left her horse there, paying the attendant for food and stall space for a day, though she had no intention of returning to claim it. In the back of her mind, she hoped he would finally get back to his owner, for she knew what the law exacted in punishment for horse theft, and the thought made her shudder. Hurriedly, she joined the bustling throng on foot and set forth for her first look at New York City.

In this spring of 1776, New York was a teeming seaport of over twenty-five thousand people. It was one of the main centers of commerce in the American colonies. The war had stopped the shipping of goods on regular merchant ships from England and hampered shipping from other nations, but pirates, smugglers, and privateers made sure the colonies still received manufactured goods and luxury products from Europe. Departing ships braved the blockades and took such American-produced items as grain, furs, and lumber to hungry markets across the ocean.

Kate had a busy morning. She had breakfast at a cozy bakery shop filled with delicious aromas, then she sought out a gunsmith and purchased a small, two-shot pistol. Kate now carried it safely hidden in the side pocket of her gown. Many rowdy seamen, waterfront laborers, and other transients roamed the streets, and Kate wanted a means of protection should some of them turn their attention to her.

New York, with its bustling people, crowded buildings, and cluttered streets, reminded Kate of London, and she felt a twinge of homesickness. She was acutely aware of her lack of friends in this strange, new place, and she had to admit to a feeling of fear and loneliness as she stood outside the Soaring Hawk Inn. The inn represented the only link with her past in London and her future in America.

Chapter 15

Kate was relieved to see that the Soaring Hawk Inn
was a respectable boardinghouse with an adjoining tavern, where a woman could enter, and while she would
draw curious glances from many eyes, she would not
likely be molested. Nevertheless, she paused for a moment to feel the cold steel of her pistol hidden in her
pocket. Her dagger was strapped to its usual place on
her thigh.

Setting a smile on her face and taking a deep breath,
Kate walked across the threshold and into the inn. Inside, the light was dim. Kate slowly made her way to
a small corner table where she could view the room and
its occupants unobserved. The room was rustic but
clean. New sawdust covered the floor, and the aroma
of bread baking filled the air.

It did not take the innkeeper long to notice Kate and
make his way over to her. His brown eyes scrutinized
her carefully. He was a large man, powerfully built,
but his face was friendly.

"Henry Jenkins at your service, miss," he introduced
himself enthusiastically. "What will be your pleasure?"

"Just some tea, if you please, sir. I am waiting for
a friend to join me," Kate said, displaying her warmest
smile.

"As you wish, miss." Henry Jenkins bowed slightly
and left.

While she waited, Kate's eyes scanned the room. As it was June, no fire burned in the wide, smoke-smudged hearth. There were three small windows that afforded little light; lanterns were lit even in the morning. There were but four or five other people present, none of them paying her any attention. Well, what did she expect? she chided herself silently—that The Hawk would wear a sign announcing himself?

The innkeeper came bustling back with a steaming teapot, cup, and saucer, which he placed before Kate.

"Can I pleasure you with anything else, miss?" he asked cordially, smiling warmly at her.

Kate took her hand away from the collar of her gown, where she had just pinned her small blue cameo. She watched his smile fade as his eyes moved to it and back to her face.

"This will be fine," Kate answered casually. Then in a conversational tone, she asked the question. "Tell me, Mr. Jenkins, how did you come to choose Soaring Hawk for the name of your inn?"

She watched him glance carefully around the room. They were still unobserved by the other guests. He leaned closer and in a low voice gave her the prearranged reply.

"It is one that reaches to great heights and flies free. I chose it carefully." Then standing straight again, he added in a normal voice, "I believe the one you wanted to see has already arrived, miss, and is at this time awaiting you. Will you follow me, please?" His alert gaze directed her to the stairway leading to the rooms above.

Nodding, Kate rose to follow him.

The stairs creaked noisily underfoot as Kate followed the burly man to the corridor of rooms above. He paused at the second door on the right. All her senses were alerted as she came to a stop behind him. She was well aware of the danger that door might conceal, for she could be walking into a trap.

She was somewhat reassured by the cold feel of the pistol in her pocket. Jenkins glanced cautiously up and down the empty hall before tapping lightly on the door. From the other side came a man's deep, rich voice.

"Come in, it's unlocked."

Jenkins glanced again down the hallway, then opened the door. As he stepped into the room, Kate followed him, being careful to stay in his shadow.

Sunlight flooded through the open window, revealing a plainly furnished room. There was only a bed, which looked as though its occupant had just vacated it, a small wooden desk and chair, a dresser, and a washstand, beside which a tall, broad-shouldered man was vigorously wiping his hair and face dry with a towel. His sun-bronzed back was to them. He wore no shirt, and Kate could see his strong muscles flexing under his skin. Something about him seemed familiar. But just then Jenkins' voice caught her attention.

"Your pardon, Cap'n. The visitor you've been awaiting is here."

Turning, the man across the room brought the towel down around his neck, revealing a tousle of sun-streaked blond hair, short golden beard, and steel-blue eyes. Kate gasped. Nick Fletcher!

She was too stunned to move. Jenkins had whirled around at the sound of her gasp, revealing her to Nick's view. He instantly hurled himself across the room, throwing himself between her and the door, which he kicked shut with his booted foot.

"You! How in blazes did you get off my ship and what are you doing here?" he shouted fiercely as his hand shot out and grasped her wrist in a paralyzing grip before she could come to her senses.

At last Kate regained the presence of mind to try to wrench free of his grasp, but it was in vain. Nick's face was dark with rage as his narrowed eyes darted from her to a very bewildered Jenkins.

"What's the meaning of this, Henry? What's she doing here?" His voice coming through gritted teeth was deadly low.

Jenkins was clearly shaken by the turn of events and Nick's menacing look. He recovered his tongue and stammered, "Sorry, Nick. I don't understand. She gave the password and wears the blue cameo!" He pointed an accusing finger at the pin at Kate's throat.

"Let me go!" Kate shouted, then winced with pain as she felt Nick's grip tighten even more. She saw a questioning look pass over his darkly scowling face as he brought his gaze to the pin at her throat. She thought he looked ready to strangle her.

"All right, Henry. I'll get to the bottom of this. Leave us," Nick ordered sternly. Jenkins mumbled assent, lunged for the door, and was gone before Kate could even call upon him for help.

Kate's thoughts raced. There must be some mistake. How could Nick Fletcher be here? Why had Jenkins brought her to him when he was to take her to The Hawk? She had no time for further questions, for suddenly she was hurled roughly to the bed, where Nick threw her on her back, pinned her arms down at either side of her head, and swung a restraining leg over her. She twisted and thrashed until the pain of his grip forced her to cry out.

"Please, Nick, you're hurting me!" she pleaded. She met his hate-filled eyes levelly and stopped struggling. Not only was it useless, but also his look warned her that he was very close to harming her. She saw that it was only with extreme effort that he didn't. She could not know that Nick was blindly seeing Lynette DuPree in Kate Prescott. His voice when he spoke was tight with anger.

"All right, Kate, I want some answers. And they'd better be to my liking, or I promise you, you shall regret it."

With that he released her arms, moved his hands roughly down her sides until he felt the bulge of the pistol, and gave a low laugh as he extracted it from her pocket. Then he stood over her pointing it menacingly at her breast and spoke through an icy sneer.

"And if you're wearing that nasty little dagger strapped to your leg, you'd best give it to me now before I'm forced to retrieve it myself."

Kate lay on her back, rubbing her reddened wrists, and fighting back tears of pain and rage. At his demand, she sat up, raised her skirt, and slowly removed the dagger from its sheath. He took it from her and threw it and the pistol down on the nearby desk. Still angry, he was at least in control of the urge to murder her. Had she played him for the fool? Lynette flashed through his mind again, and he gritted his teeth, forcing control of his rage so he could look at Kate. What game was she playing?

Kate's eyes flashed fire as she deplored her own helplessness. How she despised men who used their superior strength to hurt others. She moved off the bed and walked slowly to the window. The sunlight felt warm as it touched her, chasing away the chill that engulfed her. She basked in its warmth a few moments as she gathered her thoughts. Nick, too, was silent, assumedly for the same reason.

When Kate finally turned to face him, her face was expressionless. She spoke calmly, choosing her words carefully. She checked the anger smoldering inside her. There was more important business at hand to deal with than their feelings toward one another. Could this be a trap in which her next words would expose her as an agent? But Kate saw no other way to learn the truth about why Jenkins had brought her to Nick than to come straight to the point.

"Are you The Hawk, Nick?" Her blue eyes met his unwaveringly. Her body was rigid, alert to whatever might come next.

Nick was sitting on the edge of the small desk, one lanky leg slung carelessly over the corner of it, the other touching the floor for balance. His arms were folded over his naked chest. At her words, a slight smile curled the corners of his mouth. He was calm again as he answered her.

"That's obvious, isn't it? And you're The Blue Cameo. How the gods of coincidence must be laughing."

His apparent casualness and sarcastic tone caused Kate's fury to rise. It was with a renewed effort that she controlled it, but she could not keep the coldness out of her voice.

"You, of course, have proof of this?"

"Of course, madame." Nick was mocking her seriousness, enjoying every moment of her discomfort. How she loathed him.

With those words, Nick slowly unfolded his powerful arms, lowering the left one straight down so she could see the inside of his forearm. For the first time, Kate saw a small black image etched in his skin. She stepped closer. It was only about two inches wide and just below the point where his forearm joined his bicep—a bird in flight, wings spread to the fullest. A hawk. Kate recognized it from her memory of those she'd seen as a child roaming the forest of her grandmother's country estate.

Kate did not try to prevent the sigh of relief that escaped her lips. Her knees felt weak, and she sank into the little desk chair just before they would no longer hold her. At least it was not a trap, and Nick was the one she'd been sent to find. She knew the importance of her mission made her relatively safe from his wrath for the time being.

"Really, Kate, I'm surprised you did not notice it sooner, say, during our more...intimate... moments," Nick was saying jeeringly. "It would have saved us both a lot of trouble, you know."

Kate felt the color rise to her face. Perhaps if she moved quickly enough, she could spring on him and scratch out at least one of his taunting blue eyes. Instead, she forced herself to smile, settled back comfortably in the chair, and folded her hands demurely in her lap, matching his coolness and lack of emotion. Ignoring his last remarks, Kate cocked her eyebrow and spoke authoritatively.

"Since you are The Hawk and my assigned contact here in New York, hadn't you best be about the business of acquiring the messages I've brought rather than spending the time bullying me?"

With satisfaction she watched him frown deeply. Too late, she saw the malevolence in his narrowed blue eyes. Before Kate could evade his swift, catlike movement toward her, Nick had grasped both her wrists, pulled her roughly to her feet, and imprisoned her arms behind her, her body pressed hard against his. His voice was deadly, his face livid with fury.

"I do not need *you* to remind me of my duty. It is the very urgency of those messages that keeps me from..."

Nick did not finish his threat. Something came over him as he felt Kate wince with pain and saw her bite her lip to keep from crying out. For a brief moment he had seen a trace of fear in her large blue eyes, only to be quickly replaced by abject hatred. With an effort he regained control of his temper, abruptly released his hold, and pushed her down on the chair, cursing angrily.

"Blast you, Kate! You have a penchant for making me lose my head. You'd do well to avoid provoking me in the future."

Nick turned away from her, picked up the pistol and dagger from the desk, and stuck them in his belt. Then he walked briskly to the door, opened it, and bellowed for Jenkins.

Kate fought to control the tears that clouded her eyes. She was bruised and sore, and so angry she didn't trust herself to speak. He hardly had a right to be angry at her. After all, she was the one who'd been kidnaped and molested. *She* had the right to be outraged!

At that moment, Kate Prescott again renewed the vow she'd made to herself. Someday, somehow, she would make Nick Fletcher pay for what he'd done to her. The thought was a comforting one.

Chapter 16

Henry Jenkins must have been nearby because he appeared almost before Nick finished shouting. Nick ordered a cold luncheon set for them, instructing the stalwart innkeeper that he was expected to join them.

While they were waiting for Jenkins to return, Nick finished dressing, slipping into his familiar white linen shirt, as usual ignoring the laces that would close the front of it. He brushed his disheveled blond hair into some semblance of order, buffed the tall black boots he wore with a polishing cloth, and poured himself a large glass of whiskey from a bottle on the dresser. He neither looked at Kate nor gave any indication that he knew she still was there.

Nick's thoughts churned. So Kate was turning out to be like Lynette DuPree after all. He wondered why his usually reliable gut reaction about people hadn't warned him about Kate's deception. It warned him about Lynette, though he hadn't heeded it. He'd been too blinded by her beauty and cleverness. What a fool he'd been. He would not fall into that trap again.

His rage boiled within him as his mind whirled back in time to last summer in Boston. He'd met Lynette DuPree at a recruiting meeting. The secret government agency for which Nick worked was seeking young, influential Americans who were sufficiently discontented with British rule to be willing to keep their eyes and ears open for information useful to the rebellion. They regularly attended most of the major social events of the city, at which important British military men and leaders could always be found. This made them ideal choices for the task.

Nick wasn't in charge of the meeting, but was there on that hot midsummer night to help interview the people they needed. Most would be rejected. With just a few questions, it was easy to discern which ones would be serious in their commitment and which regarded it only as a lark. Lynette DuPree and several other women were present among the dozen men there.

Nick remembered exactly how she looked that first time he saw her. She wore a simply cut pale green gown trimmed in white lace. She stayed back in the shadows, as though trying not to appear obvious, but her beauty would not allow it. She was stunning and soon drew the attention of most of the men present. But Nick made it a point to be the one to interview her.

How well she had played her part, pretending at first to be the timid, vulnerable little French mademoiselle, ever so grateful to America for providing a refuge for her and her family. After that, as their relationship blossomed, Lynette played the zealous patriot, eager to do anything she could for the American rebellion. She claimed her family had lived in England for a number of years, but had been forced to leave because of their Catholic faith and prejudice against them by polite English society. Only in America had they found the freedom they sought. She wished to repay her adopted country.

How persuasive she was. Even now Nick cursed himself for the fool he'd been. He'd played right into her hands. Lynette had known he would value a woman in his network. There were not many women courageous enough to enter the dangerous profession of espionage. When he did find one who was as intelligent, clever, and beautiful as Lynette was, he eagerly sought to use her talents to further the cause. A woman could gain important information in a way a man never could. And Lynette had been so willing, focusing all her attention and energy first on whatever assignment he gave her, and then on him as her lover. It had been a heady experience, even for the worldly Nick Fletcher. She used her body so cleverly, bewitching him with her passion, her professed desire for him. How quick he'd been to accept the information she obtained as the truth. How trusting. How stupid!

Well, he would not be taken in again. He downed the last of the whiskey in his glass in one gulp, eyed Kate suspiciously, and went to sit on the bed. He propped the two feather pillows behind his back and leaned against them. He didn't take his eyes off Kate.

Kate sat quietly in the small desk chair, her own thoughts still in a turmoil. She forced herself to be calm, for she was determined not to let him provoke her into losing her temper again. This was a perilous and explosive situation. The tension in the room mounted. It made Kate uncomfortable and edgy, but she tried not to let it show. She wouldn't give Nick Fletcher, with his cold, penetrating gaze and vile temper, the satisfaction of knowing she was nervous. Something told her the best thing to do for now was to wait and watch.

Kate was at a loss to know why Nick was so angry with her. She couldn't know that at that moment he was thinking of another hotel room last summer, with a woman named Lynette DuPree.

Nick thought of how he had approached the Gloucester Inn with eager anticipation. He'd been separated from Lynette for over a week and the need he felt for her bordered on pure lust. She'd been sent on a particularly delicate mission seeking information on a group of loyalists who were constantly interfering with rebel plans in Boston. The identities of the members of the group were unknown. They were the proverbial thorn in the side of the intelligence network. Nick hadn't been able to figure out how they always seemed to know his plans in advance. He had checked and rechecked all of his people for a possible leak. All of them, that was, except Lynette.

Lynette had sent him word that she'd learned the identities of several key members of the Tory group, as well as some of their future plans. She would meet him at the Gloucester Inn.

It galled Nick to think that Lynette might have to gain her knowledge while in the arms of another man.

95

She always assured him that she used a potent sleeping drug which quickly rendered her informants unconscious before they could actually make love to her. Nick wanted to believe her, and he questioned her no further.

So he had hurried to the Gloucester for their rendezvous. In his haste he almost forgot his usual procedure of taking Bennett Higgins and Ginty Lawson along as lookouts when making a contact. Almost.

Nick still remembered so clearly how happy Lynette had been to see him, how eagerly she had embraced him and drawn him to the bed almost as soon as he'd arrived. But it hadn't been long before Bennett had rushed unceremoniously into the room shouting that they'd better run because the redcoats were crawling out of the woodwork from every direction. Nick grabbed his breeches and sent Bennett to check the roof. They were three stories up, but that would be their only escape now. As Nick turned to help Lynette make ready to come with them, he'd come face to face with a pistol. He still could see the evil smile on her face. He'd known then with a sickening, sinking sureness that she was that most dreaded and hated of all spies—a double agent. She was trusted by the Americans because of her connection with Nick, but she was bought and paid for by the British. The cold look in her eyes told him she'd have no qualms about killing him right then and there if he tried to escape. Only Ginty's arrival had saved them all. The heavy wooden door had swung in as Ginty pushed his weight against it. It knocked Lynette off balance, and the pistol she held flew out of her hand and clattered across the floor. Lynette lost no time in pushing a startled Ginty Lawson out of her way and running out of the room, screaming for help as she ran down the corridor. Nick and Ginty had beat a hasty retreat out the window. By perilous leaps from building to building, they had just barely managed to escape. Once safe, Nick had put out an intensive dragnet for Lynette DuPree, but she'd eluded his search. He would find her someday. She still was around, poisoning all that she touched. Her name was linked to every crucial assignment that went awry, every agent who ended up exposed or murdered. Sooner or later they would meet again, and Nick would have his revenge.

Now he focused again on Kate Prescott. Here was another clever woman spy, claiming allegiance to the colonies and saying she carried the vital information he'd waited months to receive.

Damn it, where was Henry with that food? Nick thought angrily as he rose from the bed and began to pace the room. An evil smile crossed his lips as a plan took form in his mind. He'd get the messages from Kate and check them thoroughly. He'd make certain as far as possible that she didn't carry false or planted information, as Lynette had done. Meanwhile, he'd thought of a way to keep her close at hand until he could check her out. And he could make further use of her at the same time.

Nick looked again at the beautiful and proud woman across from him. He smiled smugly to himself. And woe unto you, Kate Prescott, if you prove to be a false messenger.

Henry Jenkins' knock broke the silence. Nick opened the door, and Henry bustled in carrying dishes, utensils, and enough cold meat, cheese, bread, and wine for six men. He was followed by two stocky, towheaded boys carrying chairs and a small table.

At the sight of the food, Kate remembered she was hungry. All three dived into the food with a flourish. Nick and Henry listened silently during much of the meal as Kate related the information with which she'd been entrusted. At one point Kate noticed Nick's eyebrow raise slightly with a look of skepticism, and at that point she interrupted her narrative long enough to remind him in an icy tone of the other agent.

"A second courier also received this information and will no doubt be making contact at any time. He will verify all I've said."

"I realize that," Nick said in a low, threatening voice. "And for your sake, you'd better hope he does."

"Listen, Nick," Kate began angrily, then she stopped, knowing defiance would gain her nothing. Instead, she shook her head in disgust and continued.

With calculated calm and expertise, Kate recounted the information she had committed to memory. This was a new side to Kate that Nick was seeing for the first time. She was deadly serious and very professional.

To himself, Nick reluctantly admitted some admiration for her. There was much to be reckoned with in Miss Kathleen Prescott. Perhaps she was not like Lynette after all. He found himself hoping she was indeed the respected Blue Cameo. But his jaw clenched into a tight line as he reminded himself that that fact remained to be seen.

Kate provided the names of suspected loyalists and informants in and around the New York area, those who would help the British during the all-important attack on the city. It was Nick's job to see that they were watched carefully and "discouraged" from following such a traitorous path against the American colonies. The word "eliminate" never was used, but Kate couldn't help wondering how far Nick Fletcher would go in fulfilling his orders. She watched his brows knit together and his mouth harden into a thin line as he listened to the names she gave. A shudder went through her as she paused and saw the hardness in his narrowed blue eyes as he gazed into space, deep in thought.

Kate had one more name she wanted added to the list.

"Be sure to check carefully on Hensley Forbes, Nick," she said commandingly. "I'm suspicious of him. Call it intuition or my 'gut feeling,' as you so graphically like to put it, but I don't trust him. I'd like to know more about him."

Nick nodded agreement and told Henry to see to it personally. Then Kate continued with her report.

The British, she related, were certain that taking New York would see a quick end to the hostilities in America. The final goal of their plan was to dispatch troops to Philadelphia to stamp out the defiance that was headquartered there. The plan was typically British, unimaginative and regimented, but dangerous in its simplicity.

General Sir William Howe would command King George's soldiers. He had a reputation for being stern and exacting; he was not an opponent to take lightly.

His brother, Admiral Lord Richard Howe, was commanding His Majesty's powerful fleet. The size of that fleet was unknown when Kate had received her information, but it was expected to be large. Neither did she have the exact date set for the attack. Late in August was the projected time.

Nick's thoughts raced, formulating plans. Between now and then, a mere two months, he would have to set into motion the mechanism for helping General George Washington and his army to repel the assault. The city's defenses were weakened by division in loyalties among the people. Washington's army consisted of volunteers from a widespread area. They lacked organization and a spirit of unity, sure weaknesses in any army. Add to this the lack of adequate guns, ammunition, and other supplies, and you had a not-very-bright outlook for the Americans. Nick thought despairingly of the courageous and loyal men who made up the American army. They were businessmen, shop owners, trappers, frontiersmen, farmers, men from all walks of life, united in a cause they felt was just. He knew some had taken up the cry to arms for sheer personal profit. To be free of Britain with her crushing tariffs, taxes, regulations, and "rule from afar" would be a great boon to American enterprise. Others, like himself, joined out of a true sense of patriotism, feeling a loyalty to the land they had striven so hard to carve out of a bountiful wilderness.

But right now their main enemy was time, and they had precious little of that, Nick noted resentfully. He had much work to do.

Her report finished, Kate had risen and gone to the window. Nick and Henry Jenkins had their heads together, deep in conversation. She was for the moment forgotten. Kate smiled to herself as she sipped her wine and watched the bustling throng on the street below. The old excitement of being involved in grandiose schemes had come over her again as she'd related her information to Nick and Henry. Kate thought of her father. He always had wanted a son, but his wife had died giving life to a daughter, and James then had transferred all his love and adoration to Kate. He exposed her to a man's world of influence and decision-making and unwittingly whet her appetite for a place in a male-dominated society. But since she was a woman, Kate had been desperately frustrated when forced by that same unenlightened society to maintain her feminine and, therefore, secondary role. How many times she'd wished she'd been born a boy, even though her father often had remarked that Kate's loveliness could gain her anything she wished.

At least she had had some feeling of excitement and accomplishment when she'd joined her father in his undercover work, even continuing when he'd been murdered. Her shrewdness and courage on her assignments had gained her no little respect from her male counterparts.

But now she had to be realistic, she told herself. Her assignment was finished, and she was finished with this kind of business. There was no future in it. While she still was in sympathy with the American cause, she did not find herself so swept away with the zeal of patriotism that she wished to go on risking her life for it. Now she wanted only to find some little out-of-the-way place untouched by the dissension and fighting, where she could settle down peacefully.

A pang of bitter resentment toward Nick Fletcher flared in her as she thought of how he had caused her to lose the opportunity she'd had with the Farnsworths to make that new start. She silently cursed herself for being so drawn to him, even while she knew that there had been little she could have done to stop him from having his way with her.

Chapter 17

When Kate brought her attention back to the present, she heard Nick saying something about "Liz's summer ball." He turned to look at Kate, and a mischievous smile spread over his face. He rubbed his bearded chin between his thumb and finger, a familiar gesture to Kate. Nick cocked his eyebrow and studied her intently, his blue eyes twinkling. When he spoke, he sounded amused.

"What think you, Henry? Will she do?"

Henry laughed jovially and replied in mock seriousness:

"Well now, Nick lad, seein' as how you know the lady better'n me, I reckon you'd be the best judge of that!"

Kate felt a blush rise in her, and with it, her temper.

"Just what are you talking about? For your information, you should know that this meeting marks the end of my illustrious career of intrigue." She paused to let the calculated finality of her words sink in, and she met Nick's eyes levelly. Blue clashed with blue, but Kate would not be intimidated by the fierceness that had come into his eyes. Her words had had the intended effect. Tension loomed in the room. Then Nick's voice, cold and deadly, broke the silence.

"It's very difficult to quit our...profession, you know, especially at a time like this."

Kate was fully aware of the threat that lay behind his words. How dare he try to bully her! Her voice was vehement.

"Nevertheless, that is exactly my intention! And *you* cannot force me to do otherwise. May I remind you that I am no longer imprisoned on your ship, *Captain* Fletcher! And you would be hard put to attempt to keep me here in a public rooming house against my will, I assure you!"

Nick's first impulse was to give vent to his temper and thrash the defiance out of her. God, how she could infuriate him! Few women ever had caused such violent reactions in him. As he watched her now, seeing the open rebellion in her large blue eyes and the determined set of her chin, he knew he wouldn't win. Even if he could overpower her with his superior strength, she still would defeat him with her indomitable will. She'd certainly shown him that before. He needed her in the scheme that had taken root in his mind. Tread softly, take your time, he told himself. With an effort, Nick forced himself to be calm as he turned to Henry.

"The lady and I have some things to discuss, Henry. Leave us for now."

"Aye, Nick. I'll be downstairs when you want me."

Kate relaxed a little but she was puzzled by Nick's calm acceptance of her outburst. What was he about? She watched him closely, her senses alert.

Nick stood up and casually walked around the table, reached for the wine bottle, and refilled his glass. Minutes passed. At last he turned to Kate and when he spoke, his voice was serious but not threatening. There was a kind of gentleness in it.

"All right, Kate. I understand how you feel. God knows, there've been times when I've wanted to quit this dirty business myself." He paused to watch her reaction. A slight frown drew her brows together. Nick again cautioned himself to go slowly.

"On my ship you accused me of dishonoring our bargain. Contrary to what you may think, I am a man who keeps his word. I'll help you make a new start." Nick paused as if deep in thought. "No doubt gold coin would be the best way of settling our agreement, Kate, for it creates the most opportunities, don't you agree?"

Kate still looked puzzled, but she was listening intently. Her blue eyes followed him as he slowly paced around the room. Nick stopped and turned to face her. A slight smile tugged at the corner of his mouth as his eyes met hers.

"However, I must make one more demand on you, Kate...that you earn the coin I would give you to see you on your way."

Nick could barely suppress the mirth he felt at seeing Kate stiffen. Her eyes flashed angry fire.

"If 'earning' it means coming again to your bed, you can dismiss the thought, Nick Fletcher!" she retorted scathingly. "For that idea has no appeal to me, no matter what the payment!"

"Ah, fair Kate, you wound me deeply," Nick replied with affected hurt. "You have led me to believe that the eagerness of your lovely body against mine was due to the pleasure we both had in our lovemaking."

It took all of Kate's self-control to keep from picking up the lamp and hurling it at him. Yet, even in her fury, she knew by the sneering smile on his face that Nick was baiting her, and she was determined not to let him best her. Though her hands remained tightly clenched into fists at her sides, she willed herself to appear calm and met his look levelly.

"You are mistaken, sir. I was merely complying with the circumstances as they were dictated to me at the time," she replied icily.

Nick's soft laughter rumbled in his chest as he went to the window and propped one foot on the low sill. He leaned down to rest one elbow on his raised knee and gazed out at the lush green hills beyond the city. When he turned his face to look at Kate, his smile was warm, his tone friendly.

"Forgive me, Kate. I let you misconstrue my meaning and have deservedly received the punishment of your barbed tongue. Though the thought of bedding you is a delightful one, it is not what I had in mind."

Kate was confused but said nothing, waiting for Nick to explain.

"You could be of help in a scheme that Henry and I have contrived. You will be amply paid for your part

103

in it. There is little danger involved. In fact, you may enjoy it."

Kate eyed Nick suspiciously. She didn't trust him, but her curiosity was pricked. She would at least hear him out, if for no other reason than to have the pleasure of refusing to help him if she should so choose.

"I'm listening, Nick."

"A gala summer ball," Nick began slowly, "is being given a week from today by Liz and Charles...that is, Lord and Lady Huntington-Smythe. Elizabeth is an old...friend...of mine."

Lover, you mean, Kate thought dryly. The way he spoke her name was revealing enough.

"Liz is a patriot," Nick continued. "She will invite numerous people of influence and sympathy to our cause. It will be an ideal opportunity to catch them all together, to begin making plans of defense against the day of the British attack. However, for appearances' sake, Liz also will invite various people loyal to Britain, so my contacts must be done in secret and with the greatest of caution.

"That's where you come in, Kate. You would make a pretense of being my wife." Nick ignored the sudden raising of her eyebrow and continued. "You are unknown here. A wife will further assure the success of my disguise. Since you are knowledgeable about this mission, you also can help by making some of the contacts."

"But what of the passengers you are ransoming?" Kate interrupted, her tone practical and serious. "They could recognize both of us. Can you ensure that none of them will be present?"

"I will see to it that they're still under my influence then. At any rate, it is unlikely that their families can meet the ransom terms by that time."

Kate nodded thoughtfully, a faraway look in her large blue eyes. Nick watched her carefully.

"And what of Lord Huntington-Smythe?" Kate questioned. "What role will he play in this?"

Nick smiled. He was pleased by her astute thinking.

"Briefly, Charles is some twenty years older than his wife."

He would be, Kate thought drolly.

"Theirs is a marriage of convenience. He's wealthy and tends to lean toward Britain in his loyalties, but he is by no means a danger, merely a bothersome bore."

Kate rose and walked slowly around the room, apparently deep in thought. Actually, she had made her decision. She found the idea of the ball most appealing. She turned to Nick, and smiling coquettishly, she asked:

"And will there be at least some opportunity to dance that evening, 'husband' mine?"

Nick smiled and drew out a well-rounded purse of gold sovereigns from the desk drawer. These he handed to Kate with calculated coolness.

"I trust this will be enough to cover half of the payment for your 'services.' There will be a like amount after the ball."

"After the ball? Why, Nick, it would appear you do not trust me...your devoted helpmate in life," Kate said in mock consternation as she weighed the purse in her hand.

"I trust no one, madame," Nick replied coldly as he walked to the door and exited without a backward glance in her direction.

Chapter 18

Kate took a room at Henry Jenkins' Soaring Hawk Inn, and Nick had her belongings sent to her from his ship. On Monday they worked out the details of their cover identities and Kate's responsibilities at the ball.

Nick would be Lord Ashley Worthington, a name he had used before in New York. Lord Worthington would be newly married to Lady Kathleen Wilkeshire, played by Kate. Rumors were to be circulated that the lady was not enamored with her husband, thus giving Kate the perfect excuse for playing the coquette and keeping the young men busy paying attendance to her. It would give her opportunities to be alone with several of them, to pass on information.

"That should be a part you can readily play, Kate," Nick taunted sarcastically.

Kate gave him a cool look. "Of course I can play it...easily. And, since it will be known that we are not much taken with each other, I assume we need not spend much time in one another's company."

"As you wish, Kate," Nick stated with equal coolness. "After you make the contacts I told you about, you are to let the young dandies flock around you like bees to a blossom. They shall be so busy entertaining you that I shall then be able to make my contacts unobtrusively. I doubt that we will see any more of one another than is politely necessary."

"Fine," Kate stated flatly. Then she surprised herself by voicing the question that had sprung into her mind. "And will Lady Huntington-Smythe be among those important contacts?"

Nick cocked his eyebrow in mock surprise.

"What? So soon married and already jealous, dear wife? Have you no faith in my fidelity?"

"Oh, you're insufferable!" she exclaimed, angry at herself for asking such a question and at Nick for his flippant reply.

Kate saw little of Nick during the rest of the week, though she knew he was about. Apparently, making ransom demands and seeing to repairs to the *Sea Mist* took up much of his time, she mused, not to mention the numerous ladies of New York he was no doubt visiting. She didn't know why she felt a little annoyed, while at the same time feeling relieved that he made no further demands on her. She locked her door and barred it with a chair each night, however, to ensure that he wouldn't.

On Monday Nick sent Kate a message through Henry about Hensley Forbes. Forbes had jumped ship the day after the *Sea Mist* anchored in Duncan's Cove. A check of his credentials proved them to be false and was no doubt the reason for his hasty departure. Exactly who he was or what his purpose was remained unknown. Nick had reported the incident to his superiors in Philadelphia and had men out searching for Forbes in New York. The *Sea Mist* had been moved to another location in case Forbes was a spy. He'd inform Kate if he found out anything else. There was nothing more to do for now.

Kate got to know Henry Jenkins and his big, jolly wife, Annie. They both took it upon themselves to shower her with attention, perhaps to make up for Nick's neglect. They were very kind and interested in her, and they quickly became friends. Her first real friends in America, Kate mused, for Nick Fletcher could hardly be termed such.

Kate learned that Henry had been bosun's mate on Nick's ship before Bennett Higgins. But three years ago, during a run-in with sea pirates, Henry had taken a musket ball in the thigh, which left him with a bad limp. A man in such condition was of little use on a rolling ship's deck or making the dangerous climbs into the high rigging, so Nick had persuaded Henry to retire.

"Me, a landlubber, I says to him—never!" Henry related with a hearty chuckle during the supper they shared one night. "I'd been with Nick from the time he came over from England. We were close. I thought of him more as a son than my captain...still do..." Henry's voice had trailed off as he stared into space for a long moment. Kate and Annie exchanged glances. Annie sighed and smiled slightly as she turned her gaze lovingly to her husband.

"...Best captain I ever served under..." Henry continued. His voice was quiet and he had a faraway look in his eyes. "He was a stern one, mind ye. Wouldn't take guff or sloughin' off work from none of the men. But he never asked us to do anything he wouldn't do himself and didn't take fool risks. He treated us fair in all dealin's. A man can't ask more than that from another man."

Henry shook his head as if to clear it and brought his eyes back to Kate.

"He helped us get this place so we could make a go of it after I left the ship. Put up a good share of the money to buy the inn. We named it for him, indirect like." Henry stopped to give Kate a knowing wink. "We're payin' him back. I insisted on that. But we never would have got started without him backin' us. That's the kind of man Nick Fletcher is, Miss Kathleen...despite what you may think of him at this point!"

Henry Jenkins had a gleeful look in his eye and was delighted when Kate blushed and lowered her eyes.

"Henry, you stop your teasin', now," Annie admonished him, but not too sternly. "Miss Prescott ain't had a chance to get to know Cap'n Nick like we do." And to Kate she said, "Don't you pay Henry no mind, miss. Nick Fletcher has a hard, ruthless side to him, too, as likely you've seen, meetin' him under the circumstances you did."

Annie Jenkins agilely raised her considerable bulk and started to clear the dishes from the table.

"But we've talked your ear off enough for one supper, Miss Prescott," she said warmly. "We want you to know we're your friends, in case you ever feel you ain't got any. And you're welcome to stay here at the inn as long as you like." Her smile was friendly, and Kate felt a rush of gratitude.

"Thank you, Annie. That means a great deal right now, believe me. And my name is Kate. Please call me by it."

"Well, all right...Kate," Annie said with a broad grin. Her brown eyes sparkled as she brushed aside a strand of graying black hair that had escaped from the bun at the back of her head. Then she turned to Henry and handed him a stack of dirty dishes.

"Come on, Henry, help me here. The evening customers will be streamin' in here any minute now, and we'll be busy enough then."

Kate spent much of the week at various shops and dressmakers in an effort to bring her wardrobe up to date. She chose with extra care the gown she would wear to the ball. It had been a long time since she'd attended a ball the likes of this one, and she wanted everything to be just right. After all, there would be many eligible young men there, and Kate intended to enjoy herself, perhaps with a view toward snaring one of them along the way.

More than once as she was caught up in the delight of shopping, Kate caught herself wondering if Nick would approve of this hat or that gown. It startled her when she realized she was doing it, but she dismissed it as unimportant. What Nick Fletcher thought mattered not at all to her.

It was while Kate stood before a small millinery shop window admiring the velvet and lace-trimmed creations displayed there that she felt an uneasiness come over her. Kate seemed to have an inner sixth sense that alerted her when danger was near. She slowly turned her head from side to side to scrutinize the throngs of people who pressed in around her, but she could catch no eye observing her nor see anything amiss. More than once since arriving in New York, Kate had had the feeling of being watched by unfriendly eyes.

Nick had returned Kate's pistol and dagger to her for protection, and she began to carry the small firearm with her whenever she went out. She did not mention her uneasiness to anyone, but she was careful to go out only during the day and to stay in crowded places. At night she stayed in the inn, carefully barring her door for now a different reason.

It was during the night on Wednesday that Kate was startled from her sleep. The uneasy feeling of lurking danger made her lie perfectly still while she swept the dark room with her eyes. The cloud covering the moon drifted past, and the moonlight stole into her room through the open window. Kate's gaze moved to the door. Her hand stole to the pistol she had hidden beneath her pillow. She held her breath as she saw the doorknob being turned ever so slightly. A small creaking of the hinges told her a weight was being pressed against the door, but it held. Then all was quiet as the intruder, finding the stout door securely locked and barred, apparently gave up trying to enter.

After some moments, Kate crept quietly out of bed and tiptoed across the room, holding the small pistol cocked in her hand. She put her ear to the door but could discern no sound, not even retreating footsteps on the bare wooden floor of the hall. Perhaps the intruder still lurked outside. Kate stole to a dark corner facing the door and waited, trying to quell the trembling that made her hands unsteady. The nearby church bell began to chime the hour. Kate counted the toll. Twelve. Midnight. The room grew dark as the clouds again blotted the moon. She was glad Henry had given her a room on the second floor. No doubt that had discouraged the intruder from entering by the window.

Kate waited. The church bell tolled again. One o'clock. All was quiet. Kate was beginning to relax. Perhaps there really had been no danger at all. It might have been only Nick trying the door, thinking to come to her bed as he he had done so often when they were on his ship.

Suddenly a slight sound interrupted the quiet. Kate

pointed the pistol toward the door. She was sure she'd heard some sound, like a knock. Yes, there it was again, soft but persistent. She heard her name being called. She stole closer to the door to hear better.

"Kate. Kate, it's Nick. Unlock the door."

Kate recognized Nick's commanding tone. She removed the chair from under the doorknob and threw back the bolt that locked the door. A flood of relief swept over Kate as she saw Nick's tall profile outlined in the dim light from the hall before he quickly entered and closed the door behind him.

"Hold a moment, Nick, while I light the lamp." With trembling fingers, Kate fumbled to light it, then turned to see Nick's narrowed eyes watching her closely. His face was set in a deep scowl. She could see the tight line of his square jaw.

"What's happened, Nick? What is it?"

"You're wise to sleep with the door so carefully secured, Kate. There are bad elements about tonight."

For a moment Kate thought he was being sarcastic, but his face looked too serious. Nick caught sight of her pistol where she'd laid it, still cocked, next to the lamp on the bedstand.

"Someone tried to enter my room tonight, Nick," Kate explained as she followed his glance. The momentary look of surprise and deepening frown on Nick's face told Kate he was not the one who had tried the door earlier.

"The second courier arrived from London this evening, Kate," Nick said solemnly. "It was 'The Scorpion.'"

"Was?"

"Yes, was. He's dead. Murdered."

Kate was stunned. She felt the bed near her and sat down on it.

"Percy," she whispered. "I knew him. We've been contacts before, in London..."

"Aye, Percy Randolph. I've worked with him, too. He was a good man."

The coldness in Nick's tone made Kate look at him. His narrowed blue eyes watched her closely. She noticed for the first time that he carried a pistol stuck in the waist of his brown breeches. As her eyes again met his, Kate was struck by a dawning thought. She jumped up to face him.

"My God, Nick, you don't think I had anything to do with his death, do you?"

"The thought has crossed my mind," Nick said levelly.

Kate didn't like the deadly calm tone he used. She sensed his alertness and knew the danger she was in. He would not likely hesitate to kill her if he became convinced of her guilt. She willed herself to speak as calmly as she could, choosing her words carefully.

"Why would I want to kill him, Nick? He would have verified the information I carried."

"Or brought different facts and exposed you for a traitor."

His penetrating gaze was unnerving. Kate swallowed hard as she searched for words that would convince him of her innocence. But she could find none, no words that would convince him of the truth.

"You'll just have to trust that I'm telling the truth in this, Nick," Kate said levelly. She kept her eyes locked with his. "I cannot prove my innocence any more than you can prove my guilt. You will just have to believe that I had nothing to do with Percy's death."

Long moments passed as Kate faced him bravely.

"I tend to believe you, Kate," Nick said finally. "For I think not even you would have a taste for what I found when I returned and went to Percy's room tonight."

With that, Nick reached behind him and grasped the dagger he had placed in the waistband of his breeches. He held it in his palm so the light would catch the bloodstained blade with the gold "X" on its black hilt. He watched Kate intently.

Kate's hand flew to her mouth to stifle a scream, and she sat down hard on the bed, grasping the bedpost for support. Nick had not expected such a violent reaction from her. It was some moments before she could pull her eyes from the deadly blade to look at Nick.

"You found the dagger in Percy's heart, didn't you? I know you did," she said in a bitter voice. "It's that assassin's trademark. Quick, clean, and cowardly... while his victims sleep. I know because, you see,

Nick...he murdered my father just that way...less than a year ago."

"My God, Kate..." Nick said softly, moving toward her. But she rose and brushed past him, unseeing as she walked to the nightstand, where she reached for the small pistol she'd left there.

"He's been watching me. I've had this feeling of foreboding before. I felt it on the *Newgate* and the *Sea Mist*." Kate was silent for a moment, lost in thought. She began to pace the room. A deep frown creased her brow. "And Hensley Forbes has been the cause in both instances." Kate's voice was quiet. "He could have been here tonight. Someone was here at midnight. Someone tried to get into my room. Forbes could be the assassin."

Kate used all of her will to force down the panic she was beginning to feel. She was deadly calm as she sorted things out in her mind.

Too calm, Nick thought. She might be on the verge of breaking down. Shock could do strange things to a person. He didn't relish having an hysterical woman on his hands right now. He went to her then, but she held him away with her hands pressed against his chest.

"No, Nick. I'll be all right. I can take care of myself. The assassin will not find an easy mark should he try to test a blade on me," she told him boldly as she walked across the room. Her anger gave her courage. She still held the small pistol in her hand. She was the shrewd intelligence agent now, the same one Nick had seen when she'd given her vital information to him and Henry only four days before. Nick saw the stubborn set of her chin, the angry flash of her blue eyes, and he knew she would not need him to lean on.

Kate's voice interrupted his thoughts.

"Has Henry been able to ascertain any more information about Forbes?"

"I'll have to find out. I haven't seen Henry yet tonight. I'll rouse him now to get up a search of the grounds and then send out word again about Forbes through the network. Annie will stay with you. Will you be all right, Kate?" he asked with concern.

"Yes, yes, I'll be fine," she assured him with some annoyance as she followed him to the door. "Haste is of the utmost importance. Go now and don't worry about me."

"Bennett will stand guard at your door. Lock it behind me and don't leave this room for any reason until I return," Nick ordered. He was the captain again, confident in his actions.

Kate locked the door after he left and went to close and lock the window. Then she sank down in the armchair to wait for Annie.

Annie arrived some ten minutes later and bustled around the room, gently coaxing Kate into bed, checking the locks, and pulling the curtains tightly closed.

Kate heard Bennett's booming voice announcing his arrival on the other side of the door. Some of her professed bravado was waning. Reliving the horror of her father's death on top of the tense alertness she had maintained the past two hours had taken their toll on her energy. Having Annie there and Bennett close by was comforting, and Kate at last fell into a troubled sleep.

Chapter 19

Kate awoke late the next morning to find Nick standing next to her bed, staring down at her intently. He looked tired, and a thin coating of dust covered his dark breeches and white shirt.

"How went the search, Nick?" Kate asked impatiently as she sat up in bed, pulling the covers around her protectively. She was a little unnerved to find Nick at her bedside.

"We had no success, but our agents have been alerted that the assassin is in the area, and he may be Forbes. They have his description. He'll be found." Nick tried to sound convincing but he knew of the assassin's expertise at escape. His deadly reputation had spread to the colonies even while he still remained in England. It boded ill for all of them and the American cause to have such a man on their home ground. And if Forbes were the assassin, Nick had been instrumental in bringing him here. That fact did not set well on his conscience.

"Kate, if you wish, I can arrange for you to leave the city immediately for a place of safety I know of in New Jersey," Nick continued as he watched her closely.

Kate was silent. A frown creased her forehead as she turned her gaze from him to the sun-drenched window.

"I thank you for the offer, Nick, but I'm not leaving yet," she finally stated determinedly. Her blue eyes flashed angrily. "I won't run from him like a frightened child. I would meet him face to face if I could, but that is not the assassin's way."

Nick ran his hand through his hair to brush back a golden strand that had tumbled over his forehead.

"I rather thought you'd say something like that, Kate," he said with a weary sigh. "And I'm too tired now to argue the point with you."

As he moved to leave, a slight smile twitched at the corner of his mouth.

"At any rate, I have not the least doubt that you will do exactly what you choose in this, paying no heed to anything I might say," Nick said.

Kate returned his smile and leaned back against the pillows.

"You're learning, Nick," she said softly.

As he reached the door to leave, he paused to look back at her.

"Kate," he said seriously, "don't do anything foolish. I'll be in touch." Then he was gone.

Kate sighed. She decided that the best way to take her mind off what had happened was to keep busy. She would finish her shopping and preparations for the ball.

"I have to do something normal to keep things in perspective," she argued with a worried Henry Jenkins later that morning. "And I'll go crazy if I stay locked up in this room. Tell Nick I still intend to go to the Huntington-Smythe affair as we planned. It's unlikely the assassin is lurking anywhere about now, not with the alarm raised and so many people looking for him. He's probably miles from here."

Henry could not change her mind. So, with a disgruntled Bennett Higgins and Ginty Lawson following behind her, Kate spent all day finishing her rounds of the shops, coercing her two reluctant companions into carrying her parcels. She did not feel she needed such close protection but Bennett and Ginty had insisted they were under orders from Captain Nick to guard her, and they would rather incur her disfavor than his.

Kate received a note from Nick that business would keep him occupied until Saturday, but he would call at eight o'clock to escort her to the ball as planned. If she needed anything, Henry or Bennett would see to it. It was signed simply, "Nick." Kate had been amused—it was as impersonal as an entry in his ship's log.

She spent much of Saturday preparing for the ball. She had to admit to being excited. Finally, at almost eight o'clock, she was ready.

Her gown was the very latest creation. It was made of soft, shimmering satin in a blue the color of a summer sky. The full skirt was gathered at the tight pointed bodice and flared out at the hips. The skirt flounces were edged in delicate white lace and fell to the floor in soft pleats. The lace-trimmed neckline was squared and low-cut. Tight-fitting sleeves, also trimmed in lace, ended just above the elbow. She had decided not to wear her hair powdered, as was the customary style, but to let its natural shining color enhance the curls she had had piled high on her head with two locks left hanging loosely down the left side of her neck. Delicate blue satin ribbons intertwined the curls.

From a small gold box, Kate carefully took a long strand of creamy white pearls that her father had given her. The necklace with its matching teardrop earrings were the last remnants of the family fortune. Yes, Kate thought, smiling to herself as she put them on, they were just the right touch.

She slipped her feet into dainty blue satin shoes and surveyed herself in the long mirror. It had been so long since she had had a chance to dress like this. She felt beautiful. An excited flush rose in her as she thought of the evening ahead. Would Nick approve? For a brief moment she wondered, then briskly dismissed the thought. She didn't care. She was going to enjoy herself. Kate had forced herself to put the horror of the other night out of her mind. She wouldn't think about it, at least not tonight.

At precisely eight o'clock, Nick came to her room. Kate hardly recognized him. He wore a stylishly flared longcoat of rich brown velvet with brown silk outlining the lapels and cuffs. His waistcoat was of pale yellow silk and matched the hose that extended below his brown knee-length breeches. At his neck was a pale yellow lace jabot, which matched the delicate lace extending just below his cuffs. He wore a curled powdered wig drawn together at the back of his neck by a brown velvet ribbon. Low-cut brown suede shoes with large gold buckles adorned his feet.

To enhance his disguise, he had shaved his beard, and for the first time Kate saw all of his face. His strong, chiseled features made him indeed very handsome, she had to admit to herself. For a few moments they stared at each other in silent appraisal.

"You'll do, Kate," Nick spoke at last, affecting a bored tone. "What a pair we shall make tonight. Are you ready, 'wife'?"

Was that all he had to say? Kate felt the anger exploding in her as she bit her lip to hold back the compliment she had been about to pay him on his appearance. After all the hours she'd spent in shopping and getting ready, Kate was furious. In a huff, she swept up her long blue satin cloak from the bed, whirled it around her shoulders, and strode briskly to the door. She paused in front of Nick long enough to call him a pompous baboon, then walked quickly down the hall to the stairs, leaving an amused Nick following close behind her.

Good God, but she is beautiful, Nick mused as he followed Kate down the stairs. She seemed to be recovered from the events of Wednesday night. He delighted in her fury. Her large blue eyes flashed such fire and her face flushed so becomingly when she was angry. Nick found himself half wishing that he could have known her under different circumstances, when so many critical matters weren't plaguing his mind.

Chapter 20

The carriage ride to the Huntington-Smythe town house was accomplished in virtual silence. Kate had angrily decided not to speak to Nick, so she sat on the opposite side of the coach and looked out the window, pretending to be totally absorbed in the passing street scenes.

Nick smiled to himself as he watched her. He could read Kate so well when it came to her feelings about him; her reactions were totally predictable. This was no calculating and murderous Lynette DuPree, as once he had suspected. He felt sure now that Kate was indeed The Blue Cameo, as she claimed. The way she'd acted when he confronted her after Percy Randolph's murder had convinced him. Yet it wouldn't hurt to have Kent Treville lend credence to what his instincts told him was true.

Kent was under his command now, but he had worked with The Blue Cameo in London and could identify her. Kent would be at the ball tonight. Once Kate's identity was verified, Nick knew he had to accept the information she'd brought as the truth, too. He had no choice. No other messenger was forthcoming, and he didn't have time to delay any longer. He'd see Kent first tonight, dispel the uncertainty, then make his secret contacts to pass on the information.

Kate felt her spirits lift as the carriage pulled up in

front of a majestic three-story building fronted by five huge white pillars. Maroon-liveried servants bustled everywhere, waiting on guests who seemed to be arriving in droves. The house was ablaze with light. Music, laughter, and the calling of friendly greetings could be heard everywhere. Kate was filled with excitement as Nick helped her down from the carriage. He smiled at the expression on her face. She looked ravishing. Her blue eyes sparkled, the pink flush of exhilaration filled her cheeks. For a brief moment Nick felt the temptation to kiss her, but Kate whirled past him and up the white stone steps before he could act.

They had just entered the outer hall when a lovely young woman broke away from a small group at the archway to the ballroom. It was obvious that she'd been watching for them. She virtually ignored Kate as she extended her outstretched hands to Nick. His face lighted up as he saw her, and his grin was almost boyish as the beautiful young woman stood before him, elegant in sparkling white silk and diamonds.

Nick grasped both her hands in his and drew them to his lips, kissing them feelingly. The look that passed between them spoke volumes. Kate felt like a dowdy intruder next to this golden-haired goddess.

"Ashley, darling! I'm so delighted you could come!" the woman proclaimed radiantly, still holding Nick's hands locked in hers.

"Nothing could have kept me away, Elizabeth. You're looking exquisitely beautiful tonight."

Of course, this had to be Lady Elizabeth Huntington-Smythe, Kate admitted to herself angrily as she felt a pang of envy rise in her. Even if Kate were not really Nick's wife, others thought she was, and she was for some unknown reason feeling a wife's outrage at the scandalous frankness of the glances Nick and Lady Elizabeth exchanged. Others noticed, too.

Kate was certain that it was convention only that caused Elizabeth to pull her luxuriant brown eyes away from Nick and focus her attention on Kate. The look in those eyes, so warm only seconds before for Nick, would have struck fear in any other woman, so cold were they.

"And *this* must be your blushing bride. I'm delighted

to meet you, my dear." Her smile was sweet, but her voice was venomous.

Others in the room had turned to watch them. Conversations died away. Kate didn't like being ignored and then being made to feel like an afterthought. She fought for control of her temper, and when she spoke, it was with calculated condescension and utter boredom.

"And you must be Lady Elizabeth, of whom I've heard so many, ah...interesting...things." Kate's smile matched Elizabeth's in mock sweetness.

A slight ripple of laughter was heard around them. Kate watched Lady Elizabeth flush deeply, the smile vanishing from her lips. She pressed her advantage by going on quickly.

"My husband and I do hope to enjoy your ball." Her bored tone left not the slightest doubt that she expected to do nothing of the sort.

Nick was furious at the turn of events. He knew he had to act quickly to divert the explosion that was coming. A quick glance around revealed his good friend Guy Chadwick just emerging from the ballroom. Stepping between Kate and the glowering Elizabeth, Nick gripped Kate's elbow and forced her to turn toward the ballroom.

"But we take you from your other guests, Elizabeth. We'll have more time for conversation later. Right now I see another old friend we should greet. Excuse us, please."

Elizabeth smiled warmly at Nick and turned away to a couple just coming in. She ignored Kate completely. Through gritted teeth, Nick spoke to Kate in a low tone that left no doubt that he meant her to obey.

"Come, my dear, there's someone I want you to meet." And he fairly pushed her ahead of him toward Guy.

As they crossed the hall, Nick unleashed his wrath on her.

"Do you want to ruin everything? It's idiocy to make an enemy of Liz. She can be deadly. And she's very important to the success of our venture tonight. I only hope I can smooth over the damage you've done. I'm beginning to wonder about your ability to accomplish this charade."

Kate was feeling some guilt at having let Lady Elizabeth's baiting unnerve her. But she would by no means admit it to Nick. Still forcing herself to smile and nod to people as they passed, Kate lashed out at him.

"Your precious Lady Elizabeth could take a lesson in courtesy to guests, as could *you* in husbandly behavior!" She shook her arm free from his grasp.

Nick's scowl deepened as she turned her most charming smile on Guy Chadwick, giving him her hand and dropping her long, dark eyelashes demurely.

"I'm Kathleen Worthington. Ashley has been most eager for us to meet."

At the risk of losing his temper completely, Nick deemed it best to drop the subject for now. Grudgingly, he had to admit that Liz had behaved badly, too. She was such a jealous wench. He remembered how she had raved when he'd told her that Kate would be impersonating his genuine wife.

His genuine gladness at seeing Guy was evident in his tone as he made the formal introductions.

"Kathleen, Guy Chadwick. Guy, my wife."

Guy Chadwick bowed and smiled charmingly. Kate liked him immediately. Upon hearing his name, she realized he was one of the five men she was to contact tonight. He knew of their charade.

He was tall and devilishly handsome. His deep brown eyes reflected amusement as he lingered over Kate's hand and spoke in a low tone to avoid being overheard.

"What was that little skirmish with Liz about, old man?"

Nick shook his head in a gesture of bewilderment.

"A clash of wills between two fire-breathing she-dragons!" he replied in the same low voice, his anger still evident.

Guy raised a black eyebrow and gazed at Kate in affected shock.

"What? Has our dear Liz finally met her match? My congratulations, Lady Kathleen. Not only are you beautiful, but you also have your wits about you. My admiration for you grows with each passing moment."

Kate laughed, her own anger gone. Yes, indeed, she was going to like the dashing Guy Chadwick.

Chapter 21

As the evening wore on, Kate's head began to swim in the confusion of meeting so many people. Her smile seemed to be frozen in place as she was introduced and congratulated on her marriage again and again. Apparently "Ashley Worthington" was well known among those present, although it became clear from several comments she heard that he had been absent from the social scene for some time, supposedly traveling abroad. Kate couldn't help wondering with some vindictiveness how they would react to knowing the pretentious Lord Ashley Worthington's true identity and the activities that had been occupying his time so completely of late.

More than three hundred people were crowded into the brilliantly lighted ballroom. The light from hundreds of candles was reflected in the huge crystal chandeliers which hung sparkling over the dancers. Thousands of pinpoints of light from their dangling prisms touched everything, lending a fairylike atmosphere to the elegant room.

The orchestra was excellent and played a great variety of music. Kate danced almost all of them, hardly seeming to have the same partner twice. She was the object of much attention. Accounts of her confrontation with Lady Elizabeth had spread through the crowd like wildfire. This along with the fact that she was new to their midst and Ashley's beautiful unknown bride combined to make her the center of attention, especially among the men.

Kate mostly ignored the women and their critical stares and aloofness, as they vainly tried to cover their envy of her with disapproval.

With the men she chatted, laughed, and made promises with her large blue eyes, playing the coquette with just the right touch of innocence, which was just what she was supposed to do. So much attention was drawn to her that no one paid much heed to Nick as he moved unobtrusively around the room, whispering in low tones to this man and that, quietly leaving the dance floor from time to time, only to return a short while later to seek out yet another confidant.

Earlier in the evening, Kent Treville had met with Nick and identified Kate as The Blue Cameo. He also corroborated her story about her father's murder and her desire to be finished with espionage. Then he'd had to leave to follow up a lead he was working on for an assignment.

Nick felt relieved after their clandestine conversation, but he couldn't take the time to examine why he felt that way.

Occasionally Kate caught a glimpse of Nick as she was whirled around the dance floor. While he took the opportunity to dance with Lady Elizabeth several times, he almost completely ignored Kate, except to stand by her from time to time to make an introduction. Kate couldn't help feeling more than a little annoyed by Nick's lack of attention. Yet she knew they must keep their distance if they were to play out the rumors so graciously circulated by Elizabeth that theirs was a marriage of convenience. Nor did Kate truly wish his attention, she told herself adamantly as she conveyed a warm smile on yet another partner.

But later Kate again felt a twinge of irritation when once, as she was swung around near to where Nick and Lady Elizabeth were dancing, she heard the laughter in his voice and saw the unconcealed warmth of his gaze.

Sometime near midnight, Nick did claim her hand for the next dance. Kate was so surprised that she let him lead her onto the dance floor without protest. The music was slow and mesmerizing. So smooth and expert a dancer was Nick that Kate found herself fairly floating across the floor, totally caught up in the rhythm of the music and moving in one motion with him. They didn't speak, but their eyes met and held and Kate felt a surge of excitement run through her. She didn't understand how he could affect her so. She must have a weakness for handsome, arrogant men, she told herself dryly. Kate was puzzled by his sudden attention, since he had all but ignored her for most of the evening. She suspected he had an ulterior motive.

At length the music ended and Nick led her out onto the veranda. A slight breeze filled the air, bringing with it the delicious fragrance of countless early-summer flowers. Kate turned her face into the breeze and welcomed its coolness.

"I must admit you dance very well," Kate commented sarcastically, adding under her breath so that only Nick would hear, "for an oaf of a pirate!"

She looked away and reached up to pick a fragrant white blossom from an overhanging branch. As she brought her hand down, Nick caught it in his and drew her closer to him. She started to resist, but when she saw the amusement in his eyes and the sardonic smile on his face, she decided to yield and see what game he played.

"Now that you seem to be in a somewhat more receptive mood," he began teasingly, his blue eyes twinkling, "I have to talk with you." Before she could frame a retort, he continued in a low voice, "I've managed to contact almost everyone I need to tonight. They seem to realize that this time the British mean business, and they have pledged their full support. Sir Robert Krenshaw, whom you were to see tonight, will not be coming. I'll arrange for him to be contacted by someone else."

Kate pulled away from him, anger flooding through her. She kept her voice low but did not try to hide her irritation.

"You could have told me that inside, without subjecting me to the chore of dancing with you. Why did you, Nick? Just doing your husbandly duty?"

Nick was laughing at her. How he enjoyed taunting

her and watching her temper rise. Yet he could be very charming when he chose to be.

"All right, Kate," he teased, his handsome profile etched in moonlight. "In truth I wanted to see what I was missing. You are so popular with the gentlemen here tonight that I had to claim my husbandly privilege for at least one dance. I found it most enjoyable and not a chore at all."

"Well, kindly spare me your attentions from now on!" Kate muttered angrily as she turned and started to walk briskly away from him.

Nick caught her hand once more and pulled her around to face him, catching her small chin in his hand. He slipped his other arm around her waist and drew her to him.

"Ah, Kate, sweet vixen, how I love to see the fire dance in your eyes," he said softly as he leaned down and touched his lips to hers.

The music, the moonlight, Nick's nearness made Kate's senses reel. Her arms stole up around his neck as her lips answered his. His arms encircled her possessively.

But the moment soon was shattered by a loud female voice behind Kate.

"Ashley, darling! But there you are. I've been searching everywhere for you. Have you forgotten you promised me this reel?"

It was the ever-present Lady Elizabeth descending upon them. Nick quickly stepped away from Kate, cursing under his breath. Kate sighed deeply, knowing the moment was forever lost.

"Of course I didn't," Nick called congenially. "I was just now coming to find you."

As he moved past Kate, he leaned over and, smiling devilishly, whispered so only she would hear.

"Alas, duty calls, my love." And he walked away from her.

"Oh, I hate you, Nick Fletcher!" Kate seethed as her clenched fist crushed the fragrant blossom she still held.

Chapter 22

Kate was sulkily sipping a glass of champagne after a particularly breathtaking Irish jig when Guy Chadwick came to claim her hand. She followed him gratefully when he suggested they take a turn about the east terrace. The room suddenly had gotten suffocatingly warm, and Kate's head was beginning to swim. She held tightly to his arm as they emerged out into the cool night air. Guy led her to a stone bench a small distance away from the other couples who had sought the privacy of the shrub-bordered terrace.

"Well, Lady Kathleen, you are cutting quite a pretty figure in there tonight," Guy said, his warm brown eyes dancing with mischief as he sat down beside her. "I venture you have given the wagging tongues a month's worth of gossip!"

Kate laughed. Her head was beginning to clear and she felt exhilarated.

"Please, Guy, call me Kate," she pleaded merrily. "Thank you for coming to my rescue. I couldn't have stayed standing for another dance."

"So many were your admirers that I fairly had to fight my way to you." Guy smiled charmingly down at her and didn't try to hide the admiration in his eyes. "You are exceedingly beautiful, Kate." He was serious now as he leaned closer to her. Kate felt a strange attraction to him. Or was it just the champagne blurring her senses, making her remember Nick's similar closeness?

Guy stood up, breaking the spell. Once again his voice was light as he spoke.

"But I think we should now take a little stroll through the garden. It's beautiful by moonlight." In a lower tone he added, as he reached to help her up, "And we have some things to discuss."

Kate knew what he meant, and she flushed guiltily at having neglected to seek out Guy sooner. She had made her other contacts, surreptitiously passing on the information she had first given Nick. Only Guy remained to be told. They strolled silently along the carefully manicured garden path, amid the leaf-laden oaks and maples until they were well away from the house.

Cautiously, Kate revealed the details of the impending British invasion of New York and Nick's instructions for Guy. They paused under a low-hanging oak. Guy was silent as he contemplated the implications of her words. Kate leaned her back against the tree's wide trunk, raising her head to gaze at the star-crowded sky. There was much to be done, Guy knew, but nothing more could be done tonight. And here was a beautiful woman, face upturned, blue eyes sparkling in the moonlight, ripe for kissing. He saw the tops of her lovely breasts showing rounded above the low-cut neckline of her gown. No man would be strong enough to resist such temptation, he thought, smiling to himself.

Guy Chadwick moved closer to Kate, slipping his arm around her waist and drawing her to him. She didn't resist as he pressed his lips to hers and crushed her body against his. The warmth of her response somewhat startled him. He hadn't expected her to be such an easy conquest. With conceited satisfaction and mounting desire, Guy continued his heated embrace, moving his hand up to caress the soft flesh of her breast.

What Guy did not know was that it was not his face that flashed through Kate's mind nor his fervent kisses that she felt on her lips. It was Nick she saw, his hands, his lips upon hers. Her mind, blurred by champagne, whirled in torment as Guy's lips became more demanding.

Abruptly the moment was ruined by a deep voice, heavy with sarcasm.

"What a tender little scene I've happened upon."

Instantly Kate jumped away from Guy, alarmed and confused. Guy hurled around, his face an angry scowl. They both stared in the direction from which the voice had come.

Nick Fletcher was leaning casually against a nearby tree, his arms crossed in front of him, a sneering smile on his face. Kate was speechless. Her mind was a jumble of thoughts and feelings that had possessed her only moments before. It was Guy who recovered his senses first and finally broke the tense silence.

"Why, who goes there? A jealous 'husband'? Good grief, my dear, we are discovered!" And he laughed heartily as he slipped his arm around Kate's waist and drew her to him.

Nick walked toward them, still smiling menacingly. His voice was deceptively quiet.

"You can thank heaven that she *isn't* my wife, Guy, for I'd hate to have to kill an old friend like you in defense of my honor."

Guy threw back his head and laughed again.

"But Nick, old man, haven't we always shared everything along the way?"

Kate pushed herself out of Guy's reach. She'd sort out her confused thoughts later. Right now she only knew that she was furious—with Nick for spying on her, with Guy for assuming too much, and with herself for letting her control slip.

"Stop it, both of you!" Kate shouted as she turned her blazing blue eyes on Nick. "What are you doing here, Nick? Spying on me?"

"Hardly, Kate," Nick remarked drolly, his blue eyes cold as ice. "I was searching for you when I saw you slip away so cozily with Guy. Word's about that Captain John Douglass has arrived in the harbor. It would be better if we left this gathering now...together."

Guy was momentarily forgotten as Kate grasped the significance of Nick's words. Douglass would be shouting for Nick's head at the first opportunity. She was glad Douglass had made it safely but knew that having Nick and Douglass in the same city was bound to lead to their paths crossing eventually. Kate might then be implicated, especially after appearing here at the ball. Better to put as much distance between them as possible.

"Yes, I understand. Of course, we'll leave at once," Kate agreed, temporarily setting aside her anger at Nick, replacing it with level-headed reasoning.

Guy offered no protest as Nick took Kate's arm, and they began to walk down the path back to the house. To anyone watching, they appeared to be three old acquaintances having a friendly stroll in the garden.

Guy turned to leave them at the door to the glittering ballroom. Kate bade him a speedy good-bye, smiling at him. His eyes lingered hungrily on her as he watched Nick and Kate make their way across the ballroom to Lady Elizabeth and her husband. He would see Kate again and possess her. Guy Chadwick promised himself that.

Kate and Elizabeth were obligingly sweet to one another during the farewells. They were both good actresses, and anyone watching would have thought they were fast friends. Elizabeth insisted on seeing them to the hall, but Kate discovered this was not so much out of courtesy as it was to have a few moments to talk with Nick. Kate could not discern what they whispered between them, but she did catch Elizabeth's last words before they reached the door.

"...alone later," she said. Kate frowned as she saw the answering look in Nick's eyes, but she didn't understand why she felt so annoyed.

Chapter 23

Kate did not feel much like talking during the ride back to the Soaring Hawk Inn. She was suddenly very weary and her head throbbed from all the champagne she'd had. She could not see Nick's face clearly in the dark carriage, but knew by the frown she glimpsed marring his forehead that he was displeased about something. In the back of her mind, Kate sensed he was more than a little agitated, but the fog clouding her brain kept her from thinking it through to a cause.

In fact, Nick himself could not quite understand the anger he felt. He dismissed it as caused by John Douglass' untimely arrival, yet as he felt Kate lean sleepily against him now in the carriage, he realized that he had felt more than a little annoyed at the sight of her in Guy's arms. She looked so fetchingly beautiful in the moonlight. He certainly couldn't blame Guy for wanting to make love to her.

He thought of the first time he'd had Kate and how she'd fought him and steeled herself against him, yet tonight she seemed anything but unwilling in Guy's arms. In disgust, he confessed he was unable to understand women.

Kate's head nodded, coming to rest lightly on his shoulder. Her hair brushed his cheek, and her hair's faint sweet scent and softness caused his blood to stir.

Damn her, Nick cursed inwardly. Why did she affect him so?

He steeled himself against the rising torment he felt and made his tone cool and detached.

"I'll be staying out of sight for a while until things with Douglass die down. Boston should be safe. I need to go there anyway to round up men and supplies for General Washington. Henry Jenkins will look after you if need be. You'll be paid the agreed-upon sum and are free to go where you wish. However, I suggest you leave New York, not only because of your involvement in this night's activities, but also because of the impending siege with the British."

Kate murmured agreement to all he said. She was only half listening, for she was too sleepy to focus her mind. How cold and unfeeling Nick sounded. A stranger. Well, fine, she thought drowsily. She would be just as happy to be rid of him as he would to be rid of her.

But Kate didn't want to think anymore. How she longed to slip between the cool, crisp sheets of her bed and lose her weariness in sleep. She must have dozed because the next thing she knew she was being gently lifted in Nick's strong arms and carried effortlessly up the inn stairs to her room. Henry Jenkins bustled ahead to light the way and unlock the door. Realizing she would soon be in the big, soft, bed about which she'd been dreaming, Kate gratefully submitted to being carried. She rested her head against Nick's broad shoulder. The warmth and smell of him so close sent her half-conscious mind into a strange turmoil.

In her room, Nick gently laid Kate on her bed. From a foggy distance, she heard Nick talking softly to Henry.

"Thanks for waiting up, Henry. Leave us now and have one of your lads pack my things. Douglass has arrived and I'll need to be leaving for the *Sea Mist* tonight."

"Aye, Nick," came Henry's quiet reply, "I'll see to it myself and to your mount, too."

"Here, pack these, too, Henry. I won't be traveling in them." And Nick removed all of his dress clothes except his ruffled shirt and breeches.

Henry closed the door softly behind him. All was still

except for the creak of the window as Nick opened it to let the cool night air into the stuffy room. The moonlight flooded the room, touching everything with a silvery glow. It spread over Kate. For a moment Nick watched her, seeing the gentle rise and fall of her rounded breasts where they showed above her gown. She stirred in her sleep. A smile swiftly crossed her lips and disappeared. The moonlight played softly over the contours of her lovely face. Nick thought of another time when he'd seen Kate like this, in his bed on the *Sea Mist*. He again felt the stirring within him. Reluctantly he shrugged off the thought of her soft yielding body beneath him. He must leave her, for there was no time to lose. Danger stalked him in the person of British dragoons, no doubt already aware of his presence in the area. The longer he delayed here, the greater the chance of discovery and disaster to them all.

As he turned to leave, he heard Kate stir again. This time she moved uncomfortably, a slight frown furrowing her brow. Her cumbersome gown hindered her movements. Nick walked to the bed and turned her gently on her side. As he fumbled with the laces at the back of her satin gown, Kate awoke with a start and moved swiftly away from him. She turned on him angrily, her large blue eyes flashing in the moonlight.

"Nick! What are you doing?" she demanded.

"Easy, Kate," Nick said tiredly. "I was only trying to make you more comfortable before I left."

Fully awake now, Kate watched Nick warily as he reached to light the lamp at the side of the bed, then stood smiling at her, his arms folded across his chest.

"Believe me, Kate, you can rest assured your virtue was not endangered."

"Your actions in the past would prove that extremely doubtful!" she countered tartly. "Now will you please leave?"

She stood up and walked quickly to the wooden cupboard near the door. Opening it, she hung up her cape, kicked off her shoes, and began trying to unfasten the laces at her back.

"Here, let me help you or you'll never get to sleep at this rate," Nick spoke with some annoyance.

Kate clearly was agitated, but she submitted to his awkward attempt to loosen the bindings.

"Damn!" Nick cursed as he tugged on an unyielding lace. Kate heard a loud tearing noise as the gown's eyelets surrendered to Nick's rough treatment.

"Now you've done it!" Kate cried angrily as the suddenly loosened gown slipped off her shoulders. She moved to catch it, lost her balance, and fell against Nick. He caught her in his arms. The gown slipped to the floor, leaving Kate clad only in her thin silk petticoat.

The faint fragrance of her perfume reached Nick, and the stirring he'd felt before renewed as he felt the warmth of her body against him. Kate struggled to be free of his arms.

"Let me go, Nick!"

She continued to fight as he swept her up into his arms and carried her to the bed. She saw the dawning desire in his eyes, the determined set of his jaw.

"No, Nick! Let me go!"

Nick smiled wickedly and dropped her down on the bed. Kate tried to scramble away from him, but he caught her by the front of her petticoat and tore it down its full length, leaving her lying naked before him. Then he pulled himself down over her, pinning her helplessly under the weight of his body. Kate beat on his chest with her fists, twisting and fighting to free herself, but the effort was in vain. Nick's mouth covered hers, stopping her protests. His hands were hot on her flesh and seemed to touch her everywhere, awakening wild sensations. Her body writhed and twisted, betraying her with its response. The unleashed demon in Nick made him oblivious to all but the mounting fervor in his blood and Kate's undulating form beneath him. His lips found her full, rounded breasts and the nipples hard with impassioned desire. His breath was coming in quick gasps as he moved between her thighs. Kate's hips rose up to meet him. Nick felt the tremor of ecstasy convulse through her body. A breathless cry escaped her lips as she clung desperately to him. Her body writhed. Nick's own fulfillment quickly followed as he felt the throbbing pulsations within her.

After the torrid eruption of their all-consuming passion was spent, there was left only the need to hold each other. Each basked in the nearness and warmth of the other. Then came the gentle teasing with touch and caress, the slow ecstasy of renewed arousal, and again the wonderful, impassioned climax.

Kate lay in Nick's arms, tired, but feeling peacefully content. She nestled close against him and was quickly overcome by dreamless sleep.

Nick, too, felt a strange contentment he had not known before. It was exciting making love to this woman. She was all fire and eruption, consuming him in her need, giving him measure for measure all of herself in return for all he gave.

Yet now, after, it was almost as pleasurable just to lie with her in quietness, holding her in his arms. More than just two bodies had been joined this night, Nick knew. She has more than that of me, he thought. His brow furrowed into a troubled frown. His head told him he could not allow this. Even now he should be gone from her. Danger stalked him, and each moment he delayed brought the danger nearer. Yet he could not bring himself to stir from Kate's side. Too much he relished having her sleeping peacefully in his arms.

It was only when he thought that he might bring her into the danger by staying that he gently laid her away from him and left the bed. In his mind he knew that there were responsibilities to be met, people awaiting his commands and directions, history to be written in the days and months ahead. One man's personal need for a woman could not be considered, could not be allowed to jeopardize the more important plans and commitments that had been made for the whole cause.

Nick knew he must leave her, yet he tarried a moment longer to gaze at Kate's moonlit form, burning the sight of her into his memory. He must put her aside. He could not allow himself to become entangled in the web of her beauty and passion. He had to leave her in such a way that he would not be able to return. Burn his bridges behind him.

He was thoughtful for a moment before he lit the lamp on the desk, using his body to shield its light from Kate. In the drawer he found paper, quill, ink. He quickly scribbled a few lines, paused to reread them, then put the paper under the small pouch of coins he'd left there earlier. Kate would hate him after reading this. Little chance would remain that she ever would open her arms to him again. And so it must be. There was no place in his life now for the ties of a woman.

He took out another sheet of paper and hastily filled the page. This note he would leave with Henry to give to Robert Krenshaw. Robert would see to Kate.

Then, with only a quick last glance at Kate, Nick extinguished the lamp and walked from the room, out of Kate's life.

The warm morning sunlight was streaming into the room when Kate stirred from her sleep. She stretched leisurely, still filled wtih relaxed contentment. She slowly turned her head to look for Nick beside her, but no one was there. Kate sat up with a start and looked quickly around the room. She was alone. Nick was gone.

Her thoughts raced. Where could he have gone? Perhaps he had only gone back to his room. Her conscious mind swept back to the night before. She vaguely remembered hearing Nick tell Henry he was leaving on the *Sea Mist* as soon as possible. Of course, she thought, he can't stay in New York with John Douglass right at hand. Neither, for that matter, should I, she said to herself. Now she remembered Nick's telling her all this in the carriage coming back from the ball.

The ball. Kate frowned, and her delicate mouth thinned to a hard line. She suddenly remembered Lady Elizabeth's whispered promise of a rendezvous. Kate's anger flared. Of course Nick had left—to go to her!

Kate's fury mounted as she kicked off the covers and jumped out of bed, all the while cursing Nick Fletcher and wishing catastrophe upon his head. As she washed, Kate's thoughts took a more lenient turn. Perhaps Nick hadn't gone to Elizabeth after all, but had gone straight to his ship. A wicked smile spread over her face as she thought of Elizabeth anxiously awaiting Nick all night. She would forgive Nick his abrupt departure if he had stayed with her rather than Elizabeth.

As Kate walked to the wooden cupboard to get her clothes, her glance fell across the desk, where she saw a small brown leather bag. She walked over and picked it up. Coins jingled inside. A moneybag. A sheet of paper had been left folded underneath it. She opened it and recognized Nick's bold hand. It read:

Miss Kathleen Prescott,
Herein find the agreed-upon sum for services rendered last evening. My fellow patriots and I appreciate your cooperation even though it had to be purchased. From here we part company, so I bid you farewell.
Capt. Nicholas Fletcher

Kate felt her face grow hot as her blood began to boil. The audacity, the arrogance, the utter contempt-ibility of him! Services rendered, cooperation, indeed! Nick had no doubt chosen his words carefully so that she could not miss their double meaning. Obviously nothing that had passed between them during the night meant anything to him other than the selfish satisfac-tion of his lust. She had been a convenient outlet for him. How could she have let herself begin to trust him, begin to feel something for him?

"Nick Fletcher, I hate you!" she shouted, flinging the leather moneybag against the wall with such force that it burst open, scattering gold coins everywhere. Then Kate flung herself across the bed and released her anger and frustration in a flood of tears.

Chapter 24

That afternoon Kate spoke to Henry in the crowded dining room. Everyone was talking about Nick Fletcher, his defeat of John Douglass, and the ransoming of the passengers, who had just been set free. Patriots extolled Nick's virtues while loyalists cursed him. Kate learned that Nick had just barely escaped the city the night before. He had delayed leaving almost too long, Henry had told her with a twinkle in his eye, giving her a knowing wink. Kate had blushed deeply in embarrassment and anger. So even Henry knew how Nick had used her.

"British patrols have roadblocks everywhere, and search parties comb the streets for him," Henry continued conversationally in the event anyone overheard. "Why, it is even rumored that the rascal attended the Huntington-Smythe ball with a beautiful unknown woman, although that could not be substantiated."

Then, in a lower voice, Henry grew serious.

"It is not safe for you to stay in New York, lass."

"I know, Henry, but I've hardly had time to think of what I shall do next. Everything has been happening so fast," Kate said, a worried expression marring her pretty face.

"I know," Henry agreed, shaking his head. "But I've an idea, if you're game to hear it." He didn't mention that it really was Nick's plan, that he had delivered

143

Nick's message to Sir Robert this morning and had his cooperation. Nick, knowing how any suggestion from him would meet with outraged rebellion from Kate, had told Henry to make it seem as if it were his own idea.

"At this point, I'm open for any suggestions," Kate assured him with a relieved smile. Henry nodded assent and went on speaking in a low voice.

"Sir Robert Krenshaw is what we call a gentleman farmer. He has an estate over New Jersey way, called High Creek Farm. You could spend some time safely there, if you've a mind to, until you decide what you want to do."

"But Sir Robert doesn't even know me," Kate interrupted. "I didn't get the opportunity to meet him last night. Why would he help me?"

"Nevertheless, he knows about you and is agreeable to helping you," Henry explained, ignoring her direct question.

Before Kate could query him further as to how Sir Robert Krenshaw happened to be called to her rescue, Henry was summoned to help with a boisterous group of young men on the other side of the room. As he rose to leave, he whispered,

"Stay out of sight. Sir Robert will be here tonight. Be ready to leave at a moment's notice." He smiled and turned away.

Dusk had just fallen when a light tap came at Kate's door.

"Who is it?" she inquired softly, her ear to the door.

"Henry, lass," came a familiar voice.

Kate opened the door to reveal Henry and a stranger. The two men stepped into the room, and Henry craned his neck to cast a sweeping glance down the hallway before closing the door behind him.

"I can't be away from downstairs too long at this time of evening, lass," Henry explained. "This be Sir Robert Krenshaw. Sir Robert, Miss Kathleen Prescott."

The introductions made, Henry turned to go, and Kate scrutinized the man who stood before her. Offering her hand, she gave him a warm smile.

"Sir Robert, it's good of you to come. I do appreciate your taking time for me. I assume Henry has told you of my plight. I confess to being at wit's end as to what should be done."

The tall, distinguished-looking man before her bowed slightly and raised her fingers to his lips. His hair was jet black except for some graying at the temples. His eyes, under thick, arched brows, were as dark as his hair, and they surveyed her openly. A thin, well-trimmed moustache gave his face a sinister appearance until he smiled at her. His voice was deep and rich when he spoke.

"On the contrary, the pleasure is all mine, Miss Prescott. I hope I may be of assistance." His warm smile was a welcome sight to Kate.

He appeared to be about forty years old, but he had not allowed himself to go to paunch as so many men did. He was impeccably dressed in a dark brown riding suit; only the dust on his tall brown leather boots betrayed the fact that he had traveled recently.

The polite amenities completed, Kate motioned him to the desk chair and seated herself on the edge of the bed. Deciding to put her trust in this man, Kate came straight to the point.

"Please call me Kate, Sir Robert, and let us not lose time on pleasantries."

He nodded his agreement, an amused smile drawing up the corners of his mouth.

Kate continued seriously, "You know, I assume, of the part I played last night with Nick Fletcher." Kate felt her face grow warm as a blush tinged her cheeks pink. She turned her face away so he would not see it and walked nervously to the window. In her mind she wondered exactly how much he did know. Well, no matter, she dismissed the thought angrily. What was done was done.

"Yes, Kate, I know," Sir Robert answered, "and I sincerely regretted being unable to attend the ball and not seeing you. You made quite an impression."

He followed her with his dark, penetrating eyes, the friendly smile still on his handsome face. He had not missed her blush, and knowing Nick Fletcher, he could easily guess the reason for it. To himself he admitted admiration for Nick's taste in women. This auburn-haired beauty with her well-shaped figure and large blue eyes was enough to turn any man's head. He was still somewhat puzzled by Nick's hastily written note, briefly explaining Kate's situation and Nick's part in it. He had ended the message by saying only that he would consider it a great favor to have Robert see Kate safely settled somewhere into a new life. His words had left no doubt that Nick was washing his hands of Kate. Well, he owed Nick many a favor and, while this was quite a responsibility, Robert Krenshaw had the feeling that meeting this woman was going to change his life. He was rather excited by the prospect.

He rose and strode slowly about the room, speaking with polite ease.

"I also know of your activities and intentions prior to coming to America. I would deem it a privilege to try in a small way to repay my nation's debt to you."

Kate was surprised at the extent of his knowledge, and her face must have reflected this, because Sir Robert laughed softly and went on to explain.

"Of course, I did not know of you by name. Few of us know personal identities, as you know. But I have heard of your exploits as The Blue Cameo in England and since your arrival here."

Kate was beginning to like this handsome gentleman, whose manner and speech reflected dignity and good breeding.

"Thank you for being so gallant, Sir Robert," Kate said, smiling at him warmly. "You are very flattering. "As a result of my...activities...with Nick Fletcher, I find myself at open ends as to the course I now should take. Quite frankly, can you offer me some arrangement that will ensure my safety for the time being?"

Kate turned her black-lashed blue eyes fully upon him and, for just a moment, Sir Robert Krenshaw surprised himself by the thought of the intimate arrangement he would have liked to have made with her. But he pushed that thought to the back of his mind.

"Exactly why I'm here, Kate, to offer you refuge at my farm." An amused smile spread over his face as he saw her eyebrow raise slightly in question. He went on to explain.

"Actually, you'd be doing me a tremendous favor as well. You see, I am a widower with a blossoming and very inquisitive fifteen-year-old daughter, Laura." Sir Robert seemed a bit embarrassed as he continued. "Laura has had the best of tutors to see to her education. In addition, we always have been very close. But of late she has reached the point where she needs a woman to talk with, if you know what I mean."

He glanced at Kate, who smiled knowingly.

"She will be having her coming-out ball this summer and she needs instruction, finishing touches on her manners, proper behavior around young men. A good young ladies' finishing school, like the one you no doubt attended, would be in order, but with the war between America and Britain, I hesitate to send her away. If you would agree to come with me to my home as, say, a distant cousin of mine, and take on the role of instructor, confidante, friend to Laura, I would be most grateful. You would be free to stay as long as you wished in that capacity, until such time as you set yourself another course."

Looking at her levelly, he questioned, "Is this proposition to your liking?"

In reply, Kate smiled and motioned to her packed luggage. "Would immediately be too soon to leave?"

Chapter 25

When Nick left Kate just before dawn, he headed
straight for the *Sea Mist*. As he gave the order to hoist
sails, he couldn't help but be amused when he thought
of Lady Elizabeth waiting in vain for him all night.
How she would rant and rave at him when next they
met. It would do her good to be disappointed, for she
had become entirely too demanding. But still she had
her good qualities, Nick thought as he let his mind's
eye see her creamy white skin, her golden hair, her
supple body so eager for his embrace. Liz never would
refuse him, like that blue-eyed vixen whose vision interrupted his thoughts even now.

"Women!" he murmured crossly under his breath as
he gave Griffin the compass directions to lay in a course
for Boston Harbor. Then Nick made his way to his
cabin, bellowing for Pierre to get him some breakfast.

The cabin seemed to be missing something. Nick had
not been back aboard the *Sea Mist* since before Kate's
escape, and he now realized with a start that what was
absent was her presence. For two weeks he had shared
his private world with her, talking with her, teaching
her about the sea, partaking of the delicious fruits of
her passion...

The pink rays of dawn flooded through the porthole
and fell across the big four-poster bed, revealing its

stark emptiness. No warm, willing woman awaited him now.

As Nick poured himself a glass of whiskey from the crystal decanter on the sideboard, a deep frown lined his brow.

"I can easily replace you, Kate Prescott," he said aloud, shattering the stillness of the room. "You mean nothing to me." He downed the strong amber liquid in one swallow and poured himself another.

Nick sat on the bed and pulled off his tall black boots. The whiskey in his empty stomach was having its usual mellowing effect. He needed sleep. As he put his boots down beside the bed, a flash of color caught his eye. Bending down, he grasped the end and pulled it out from under the bed. It was a length of filmy pink silk, and the delicate fragrance that reached him made him think immediately of Kate. He recognized it as the scarf she'd worn over her low-cut gown the first night she'd dined with him and his officers. It must have been overlooked when he'd had her things sent to her at Henry's.

Nick held it close to his nose and let the perfume fill his head. It held the fragrance of fragile spring flowers and filled his mind with tormenting thoughts of other times he'd been aware of it, when he held Kate in his arms. He looked at the empty bed. How strange that she keeps haunting me, he thought wearily before he sank against the pillows and closed his eyes in sleep, still holding the pink scarf in his fingers.

Boston Harbor was its usual hub of activity when Nick ordered the *Sea Mist* anchored safely among a dozen American merchant vessels. The few British patrol ships that regularly prowled the waters at the mouth of the harbor never would expect to find Nick Fletcher's ship in so obvious a place. It was a risk, but Nick knew he could depend on his fellow American captains to come to his defense should a British ship chance to sight him. Ever since the Boston Tea Party back in '73, this city had been a hotbed of rebellion. British captains avoided possible conflicts whenever they could, which was why Nick was here. He would have a good chance of gathering support, financial and otherwise, for the defense of New York in this high-spirited city.

Nick's mind already was savoring the meeting of old friends as he made his way along the crowded wharf to the Rum and Tankard Tavern. He no more than stepped through the doorway of the familiar tavern when a shriek of pleasure rose above the din of the crowd, and the voluptuous Meg MacGregor came running to him, throwing herself in his arms. Nick was laughing heartily as he swept Meg off her feet and whirled her around until they were both dizzy.

"Nick, love, it's gladdened to the quick I am to see you!" Meg greeted him when she could again breathe and the room had stopped its wild spinning. "You've been too long away."

"Ah, that I have, me fiery lass," Nick said, imitating her thick Scottish brogue. "But I'm here now and anxious to pick up where we left off when last we were together, Meg, darlin'."

Meg MacGregor blushed a becoming pink from the roots of her flaming red hair to the tips of her gold-buckled shoes. The memory of the last night she'd spent with Nick Fletcher two months before flashed vividly through her mind. In fact, the many delightful nights she'd passed with this passionate man tumbled through her mind in glorious recollection.

Laughing, Meg led Nick to one of the few empty tables. Shouts of greeting marked their progression across the room as Nick's friends recognized him.

"A tankard of your best ale, MacGregor!" Nick shouted to the tall, bewhiskered man behind the plank counter. "And none of that watered-down sea brine you try to pass off on your unsuspecting patrons!"

Duffy MacGregor roared with laughter at Nick's insult, as did everyone within earshot. Meg's father knew, as did everyone else who frequented his establishment, that his ales, as well as his tavern, always were at their best.

That night found Meg where she had dreamed of being every night for the past two months, in Nick's arms. He seemed hungrier than usual for her tonight. Could it be that he at last sought none but her favors?

That was her one constant wish, that Nick Fletcher would belong solely to her. She would give her soul to be his wife, to have him near whenever she needed him.

Meg and Nick had had an intimate dinner together in his room, during which Nick marveled at his good fortune in having Meg. Not only was she pretty and possessed of a soft, well-rounded figure that sparked many a man's desire, but she also was cheerful and witty and had a contagious zest for life. Meg usually was balm for what ailed him, but tonight Nick found her less appealing than usual. Yet he could see nothing changed in Meg. Could it be him then? He dismissed the thought. He was just tired, weary from months at sea, fighting battering winds and equally destructive man-made conflicts. He knew the pressures of a leader in a little-organized, ill-equipped rebellion. Meg would work her magic on him and charge him with her vitality. With these comforting thoughts, Nick had carried her to bed.

Meg was warm and unresisting, allowing her body to be awakened by his searching touch. How she longed for him. She ran her hands over every inch of his hard-muscled body, memorizing the feel of him, his tantalizing male smell, for she knew this might be all she would have of him for long weeks to come. Passion exploded in Nick as he was awakened by Meg's expert exploring and equally ardent response. His lips hungrily sought hers, then traced a burning path down her throat to her hardened nipples and beyond.

Meg writhed and strained beneath him, meeting the demands of his caresses. Through the daze of her desire she heard him murmuring softly against her ear, her throat.

Nick was oblivious to all but the rising frenzy within him and the impassioned woman beneath him. In his whirling mind he saw her. The shining mass of auburn hair framing the delicate lines of her lovely face, large, black-lashed blue eyes beckoning him closer, deeper.

"Kate, Kate," he murmured huskily, his voice barely a whisper.

But it was loud enough for Meg to hear, and she instantly stiffened at the sound of another woman's name on her lover's lips. At the tensing of her body,

Nick's eyes flew open, seeking the piercing blue eyes that tormented him. Alas, in the dim light he found only flashing green ones, narrowed to dangerous slits by the deep frown furrowing her forehead.

With an agonizing groan, Nick rolled off Meg to sit on the edge of the bed. Even here Kate haunted him. What power did she have over him?

"Meg, I..." he began haltingly.

"Who is she, Nick?" Meg shouted. "Who is this woman who commands your thoughts and passions even while you lie with me?" Meg's eyes blazed with fury as she accused him. Tears of anger and hurt made them liquid green pools.

"A witch, a damned sorceress, she is!" Nick answered angrily as he pulled on his black breeches and turned to face her. "She haunts me and gives me no peace!"

He snatched up his shirt and boots and strode to the door, almost ripping it from its hinges in his haste to be gone from the room. As the door banged shut behind him, Meg began to weep bitterly.

"Nick, Nick!" she cried desperately, her anger gone. But it was in vain. He did not come back, and Meg knew he never would.

Chapter 26

Kate had bid Henry and Annie Jenkins a fond farewell as her luggage was being loaded on Sir Robert's carriage. She and the Jenkins had become fast friends in the time she'd spent at the Soaring Hawk Inn, and it was with regret that she said good-bye.

The night enveloped them as the horses sped full gallop away from New York. Kate and Sir Robert, separated by the darkness within the carriage, spoke little. After three hours they stopped at a comfortable-looking roadside inn for a late supper and lodgings. Kate was grateful for Sir Robert's quiet, reassuring presence during supper, for she was feeling displaced and lonely. Loneliness had a habit of stealing its way into her consciousness ever since her father died.

Sir Robert reminded her in some ways of James Prescott. Dignified, confident, yet warm and friendly, Sir Robert Krenshaw was indeed like her father. However, Kate was aware that Sir Robert did not see her in a fatherly way. While he made no advances, she felt his appraising eyes upon her more than once during the leisurely supper they shared in an intimate private dining room.

Later, in her own comfortable room, Kate lay awake for a long time, watching the flickering flame of the candle, her thoughts miles away. Unbidden, Nick Fletcher came to her mind. Was it only last night that he had held her in his arms so possessively? Was he lying with someone else tonight? Had he forgotten her already?

"Very likely!" Kate retorted aloud to the empty room. "And I am about to forget *him* forever!" And with an angry huff, she blew out the candle and settled down into the thick feather mattress. She forced herself to think of the future and various things she might do, until exhaustion overtook her and she fell into a restless sleep.

In the morning, Kate awakened early. She felt refreshed and ready to face the new day, in spite of the fact that she'd slept fitfully. The weight of uncertainty which had bothered her so last night had lessened with the daylight. She flung open the window, basking in the warm June sunlight as she dressed in a pale yellow linen gown trimmed with delicate yellow velvet ribbons. A ruffled matching bonnet and yellow kid gloves and shoes completed her ensemble. She was pleased with her appearance as she glanced in the mirror on her way out the doorway.

After a pleasant breakfast, Sir Robert and Kate were on their way again. This time the driver kept the four matched grays at an easy canter. Kate enthusiastically watched the passing landscape from the window. This was the first real opportunity she'd had to see the open countryside of her newly adopted land and she didn't want to miss anything.

Sir Robert was amused by her childlike excitement and indulgently answered her many questions. He relished seeing her vivid blue eyes bright with delight. Kate was amazed by the vast extent of the lush green forests and rolling mountain foothills. Having lived most of her life in bustling, overly crowded London, Kate was in awe of the beauty of the wilderness. Suddenly they would leave the wilderness as a town would spring up before them. Even some good-sized cities dotted their route as they traveled farther and farther into what was known as the New Jersey colony. For a short time they would touch civilization, only to leave it far behind and plunge again into the wilderness lurking just around a bend.

By the time the carriage turned into the winding,

tree-lined lane of High Creek Farm, Kate and Robert had developed an easy friendship. He was a gentleman, distinguished and scholarly. Yet he had just enough humor about him to keep him from being stuffy, Kate thought. Like Nick, he was deeply involved in the war against Britain, though on the political level. He was one of New Jersey's senators to the Second Continental Congress, which acted as the colonies' voice to King George—at this time a very angry voice. Robert preferred to battle with words rather than guns, at least for now, he had told Kate.

As the carriage rounded the final turn of the lane and High Creek Farm suddenly came into view, Kate knew instantly that she would love it here. As the carriage slowed in its approach to the rambling gray stone house, Kate looked in admiration at the picturesque setting in which it lay. High, rolling hills lined with trees walled in the valley in which the house had been built. High Creek could be seen majestically cutting its way through the hills, carving out the bed of the beautiful valley as it went.

"High Creek is far enough away to be safe during flooding time," Robert had explained to Kate in a tone that told of his love for his home, "but close enough to hear its rushing force as the water cascades over hidden rocks."

The horses had hardly stopped when the front door of the house was thrown open and a lovely girl of about fifteen with flowing red hair came bounding toward them, her full green skirt held high so as not to hamper her running. She reached them just as Robert opened the carriage door, and she threw her arms around him before he had an opportunity to descend the first step.

"Papa! Papa!" she cried joyfully. "You're home at last!"

By half carrying the excited girl, Robert succeeded in exiting the carriage. He set his daughter at arm's length before him.

"Now, now, Laurie girl," he chastized her with mock sternness, the loving twinkle in his black eyes betraying him. "Where are your manners? You would think I'd been away on business for a year instead of only two weeks!"

The girl, Laurie, clutched at his hand and looked up at him adoringly.

"But I've missed you so," she pouted. Then her attention quickly turned to Kate, who now had become visible in the carriage doorway.

"I've brought someone with me, Laurie," Robert explained as he moved to help Kate down to the ground.

Laurie came to stand beside her father, her eyes widely curious as she stared openly at Kate.

"Miss Kathleen Prescott," Robert introduced, "my daughter, Laura."

Laurie's penetrating green eyes never left Kate's face as Laurie curtsied automatically.

"Hello, Laurie," Kate greeted, extending her gloved hand to the lovely young girl. "I hope we shall be friends."

Laurie ignored Kate's outstretched hand and, turning her gaze on her father, questioned in an accusing tone, "You're not going to *marry* her, are you, Father?"

Kate laughed softly as Robert blushed to the tips of his ears. She rescued him by putting her arm gently around Laurie's small waist and turning her toward the house.

"Good heavens, no, Laurie! I am a distant cousin to him, an old family friend." The lie rolled easily off her tongue. "Your father has simply offered me the hospitality of his home for a while. You see, I'm new to America, and I don't know too many people."

A noticeable look of relief showed on Laurie's pretty face as she walked with Kate up to the house.

"In that case," Laurie said, suddenly remembering her manners and making her tone friendly again, "welcome to High Creek Farm. I hope you'll like it here."

Chapter 27

The household staff accepted Kate as readily as Laurie had. They were pleasant and helpful, and it was not many days before Kate had settled comfortably into the routine of everyday living at High Creek Farm. Laurie was her constant companion. She had her father's engaging manner and a youthful exuberance that made her irresistible. Kate felt like a schoolgirl again and spent the ensuing days riding horseback through the lush forest paths, going on picnics in the rolling green meadows, and swimming uninhibited in the quieter waters of High Creek.

During the first few days, Kate saw little of Robert. Messengers and serious-looking businessmen arrived at all hours of the day and sometimes at night. Robert was closeted in his study with them most of the time. The situation in Philadelphia, where Congress was based, changed by the hour it seemed, and Robert needed to keep abreast of it. But on two or three occasions he managed to get away from his desk in the evening to take a stroll with Kate.

During these times, as they walked along the flower-lined paths of the various gardens surrounding the house, Kate and Robert talked of many things. Invariably their talk turned to politics, to which Kate listened eagerly. She asked many questions.

While she wanted nothing more to do with actively

participating in the revolution, she enjoyed the politics of it. She relished the lively discussions with Robert Krenshaw. Sometimes she would take the British side of an issue just to tease him. Then how his patriotism would glow! Through Robert, Kate again saw the unfolding of a new nation, one striving to be free of the shackles of the past. Men sought in America a place where the kind of man you were mattered more than what the names of your ancestors had been. She learned more about men like General George Washington, Thomas Jefferson, Benjamin Franklin, men who were striving with their very lives to create the new nation. Kate found herself tempted to be drawn again into the excitement of the history-making events. Robert was a very persuasive spokesman.

Kate was confused. She even found herself feeling some admiration for that scoundrel Nick Fletcher's daring exploits for the new country that were so glowingly recounted by Robert Krenshaw. But, she told herself, she certainly did not admire Nick Fletcher himself, not after what he had done to her. He had turned her life upside down, then discarded her. Well, she was finally rid of him now, and that was just the way she wanted it. She'd make out all right on her own somehow. She forced herself not to think about him.

Yet he always was to haunt her, it seemed. Robert spoke often of him. Even Laurie Krenshaw brought Nick into the conversation one warm, sunny day as she and Kate picnicked in a small grove of trees. Nearby, High Creek gurgled its way along the outline of the grassy bank. Bees hummed in the air. Kate basked in the peacefulness of the scene.

"Papa says you know Captain Nick Fletcher," Laurie said, trying to bring up the subject casually. "Do you really, Kate?" Her tone became eager.

Caught off guard, Kate frowned slightly at the mention of Nick's name. She didn't like the unpleasant reminder of him marring her contentment. But she tried to appear nonchalant as she answered Laurie.

"Why, yes, I know him, Laurie, but our acquaintance only lasted a short time. I would hardly call us fast friends." She tried to keep the sarcasm out of her voice as she watched Laurie's green eyes light up with excitement.

"Oh, but don't you think he's just simply divine? I mean, he's so tall and handsome!" Laurie ran on, closing her eyes dreamily and clutching her hands to her breast.

With an effort, Kate suppressed the smile that tugged at her lips. "Divine" was not how she would describe Nick Fletcher. Avoiding Laurie's question, Kate continued the conversation, mindful of Laurie's obvious feelings for Nick.

"Are you well acquainted with Captain Fletcher, then?"

"Oh, yes. Nick has been here often to see Papa on business. They're good friends," Laurie answered, trying to sound matter-of-fact. "Papa says he's a very important person in the rebellion, that he is very much admired and respected."

And feared, Kate thought dryly.

"I've danced with him several times," Laurie was saying dreamily. "Papa gave a gala party just last Christmas, and Nick came. He was dressed so elegantly. It was so exciting. He is such a wonderful dancer. I felt like a feather in his arms." Laurie sighed deeply and closed her eyes, obviously remembering their dance together.

Kate unwillingly felt herself transferred to a similar scene, when Nick had held her in his arms and guided her effortlessly around the dance floor. He could be charming when he wanted to be. Unfortunately, he seldom chose to be that way, Kate thought angrily, barely concealing the frown that had creased her brow before Laurie opened her eyes.

"Tell me more about him, Kate," Laurie begged, her heart showing in her eager eyes.

"Oh, some other time, Laurie," Kate entreated with some annoyance, uneasiness pulling at her mind. "It's getting late, and we should be getting back."

She hastily started to gather up the remnants of the picnic, avoiding Laurie's eyes. As they were mounting their horses, Kate's eyes caught the disappointment in Laurie's. Kate relented her harshness. She put her hand over Laurie's and, softening her tone, spoke honestly.

"Laurie, your Nick Fletcher and I didn't part on the best of terms, so anything I might say would be colored by that. Learn about him for yourself whenever you see him again. Firsthand knowledge is always best."

Laurie smiled, her eyes adoringly fixed on Kate.

"All right, Kate. In a way, I'm glad. I was half afraid you might be in love with him yourself, and I wouldn't have a chance against you."

"You need have no fear of that!" Kate said emphatically. Then, with a laugh, she reined her mount toward home and forced herself not to think of the stirring she'd felt in her blood when Nick's name had come into the conversation.

Chapter 28

Laurie Krenshaw's sixteenth-birthday ball was set for the Saturday of June 22, and the two weeks preceding the gala event saw High Creek Farm and all of its inhabitants in a flurry of activity. It was to be Laurie's coming-out party, as much of a debutante ball as could be fashioned in the wilds of the New Jersey colony. There were invitations to be sent, new gowns to be ordered and fitted, and dozens of decisions on food and beverages to be made. The house itself was turned almost upside down in the servants' efforts to clean it thoroughly, giving a hard-rubbed sheen to all that could be polished. Excitement rose to an intense pitch as the day grew nearer.

Robert had returned from Philadelphia one afternoon, looking tired, his handsome face lined with worry. Kate was anxious to hear of the latest turn of events, so she sought out Robert after dinner on the night of his return. Besides, she told herself, she'd missed him, missed his quiet manner, his gentle humor. She knocked softly on the door of his study, a room she had not entered before.

Kate heard him say to come in, and she entered to find him standing by a large stone fireplace. This room clearly was a man's haven. Books of many sizes, colors, and shapes lined three walls. Red leather chairs with ornately carved wooden arms and legs dotted the room.

A large walnut desk stood off to the side. A few papers were neatly arranged on it. Luxuriant Persian rugs muffled the sound of Kate's steps as she entered.

Robert had been looking at a portrait of a beautiful young woman which hung above the mantel. She looked very much like an older version of Laura Krenshaw. The smile was vibrant. The green eyes sparkled with mischief.

A warm smile spread over Robert's face as he turned and saw Kate. He walked to her, his hands outstretched.

"Robert, it's so good to have you back," Kate said sincerely as she put her hands in his and let him lead her to the comfortable leather sofa to one side of the fireplace. "We missed you at dinner."

"I fear I slept through it," Robert explained. "I was dead tired. Believe me, there's been little sleeping by anyone even remotely connected with Congress this past week."

"I take it that means things are reaching a climax?" Kate asked.

"I'm afraid so. Great Britain's continued indifference and deaf ear regarding our demands have pushed even the most conservative Tories to the brink of voting for independence. Where before a compromise may have been possible, now a complete break is imminent. Even as we sit here, a committee including John Adams, Ben Franklin, and Tom Jefferson are drafting the document that will change the history of America and Great Britain forever. It's a formal declaration of independence."

They were both quiet for a few moments.

"There will be more fighting, then...much more," Kate stated. She looked at Robert Krenshaw. His face was somber; a frown furrowed his brow.

"There can be nothing else. Many are swaying toward total independence from Great Britain. I was not in favor of a complete break at first. I'd hoped, as did so many others, that a compromise could be reached. After all, that country is our heritage, our motherland. Many of us can trace our ancestry back centuries in England, Scotland, or Wales. We are their children. Yet instead of treating us fairly and giving us some intelligent measure of independence, Britain views us with hostility and disdain, treats us as errant nuisances, to be put down with an iron hand. I fear total independence is the only recourse now. But Britain needs our natural resources and markets for her manufactured goods. She'll fight, all right, and she's a great military nation. Her soldiers are expertly trained, well equipped."

Robert stopped, deep in thought.

"It doesn't sound very promising," Kate said, sighing deeply. "We can't possibly be prepared to meet such a force. We'll be crushed. What freedoms and privileges we have gained could be lost."

Robert smiled wearily.

"So some think, but now the majority feels that is a risk that must be taken if we're ever to have the freedom we want, the freedom of which we've dreamed."

Kate glanced at the portrait above the fireplace. The woman painted there seemed to exude hope, a zest for life. They could use some of that spirit now, Kate thought.

Robert's gaze followed Kate's.

"That is Juliette." His voice broke the silence. "She was my wife."

"She was very lovely. I was just thinking how vibrant and full of life she looks. So like Laura."

"Yes, she was just that way. Always laughing, always seeking some new adventure. Laura is very much like her."

The quietness, a sadness in Robert's voice made Kate glance sideways at him. He was looking at the painting, lost in thought, consumed by memories. After a few moments, he spoke. His eyes still were on the woman captured on the gilt-framed canvas.

"She was twenty-eight when the portrait was completed. The artist, a close friend of ours, captured Juliette perfectly. How she would rant at him to hurry and finish. She hated the hours of sitting for him. She only did it to please me. I insisted she see it through and always have been grateful that I did. A month after this portrait was finished, she died in my arms. She'd been out riding and was caught in a drenching rainstorm. It was autumn and she caught a chill. She was quickly down with a fever, then a congestion of the lungs set in. I was away on business and arrived home only in time to watch each strangling cough drain the life out of her during those last hours."

"Robert, I'm so sorry," Kate whispered, touching his arm gently. The pain in his handsome face moved her.

Kate's touch seemed to remind Robert of the present. He passed a hand over his eyes as though to wipe away the painful thoughts and then looked at Kate, the gentle smile on his lips again.

"Forgive me, Kathleen. I did not mean to go on so. All of this happened seven years ago. I have accepted her death and, I think, recovered from my grief. Yet"— he looked again at Juliette's portrait—"sometimes it seems like only yesterday she filled this house with her joy, her love. The pain returns then, for a while."

"You loved her very much," Kate said softly.

"More than anything. She was my life. I don't know what I would have done if I hadn't had Laura to care for and raise. I'm afraid I've indulged her greatly."

"It must be very difficult for you to watch her grow so like Juliette."

"Painful, but a blessing, too, for I know that through Laura, some part of Juliette lives."

As does your love for her, also, dear Robert, Kate wanted to say. But she did not speak her thought.

"But come, enough of this sad reminiscence," Robert continued, his tone somewhat lighter. "I have no wish to burden you with what is past. Laura tells me you have been an immense help in organizing this birthday gathering of hers that's fast approaching. I am grateful, Kathleen. I've not seen her so excited and happy in a long while. So tell me what I can do to help. I left a troubled Congress to be part of this celebration. What yet needs to be done?"

Kate laughed as she rose from the sofa. Robert stood also.

"You can do nothing. Your being here is the most important thing to Laura. Only woman's work remains, last-minute details, some of which I must tend to now. So I will bid you good night, Robert."

It was the evening of the day before the ball and Kate, Robert, and Laurie had just begun to have dinner when there was a commotion in the hall outside the dining room. A moment later, Nick Fletcher sauntered in, a devilish grin perched on his handsome face.

"Nick!" Laurie shouted with glee as she jumped to her feet and ran to fling herself into his outstretched arms. "You're here! You're here!" she cried happily as Nick grabbed her around her tiny waist and lifted her in the air. He was laughing.

"Of course, little one! Did you doubt I would be? I promised to be here, didn't I?" He swung Laurie in a circle off the floor, finally bringing her back to her feet at his side, where he looped his arm around her waist and led her back toward the table. Robert seemed just as pleased to see Nick as he, too, rose from his place at the head of the table to clasp Nick's hand in greeting and pound him enthusiastically on the back.

"Good to see you, Nick, you rascal! We'd about given up on you, seeing how we had no word you were planning to come. But that's just like you. I should expect it by now. Come, join us for dinner. Your arrival is timely."

As Nick saw Laurie to her chair, Robert motioned toward Kate, who until now had sat in annoyed silence. Nick Fletcher was the last person she wanted to see. The memory of his abrupt departure and sarcastic note at Henry's inn still was all too fresh in her mind.

"You know Kathleen, of course. She has been our guest for a few weeks now and is a delightful addition to our little family." Robert smiled affectionately at Kate, who sat at the opposite end of the table from him. She returned his smile, but only nodded stiffly toward Nick. He smiled slightly at Robert's message, that he had not told Kate about Nick's arranging for her to come to High Creek Farm. That was just the way Nick wanted it.

"Ah, yes, Kate!" Nick replied with enthusiasm. "This is an unexpected pleasure." He made her a mocking half bow, never taking his flashing blue eyes from her face.

"You're entitled to your opinion, Nick," Kate remarked drolly as she reached for her wineglass and daintily lifted it to her lips.

Nick was undaunted. He seemed to be in an excellent

humor and only laughed merrily at her retort as he took his place across from Laurie at the table. Servants arrived to set a place for Nick and bring him the first course. Conversation focused on trivia until the servants again had exited. Kate spoke only when she was addressed. Then Nick and Robert fell into deep conversation concerning the rebellion in Boston, and Kate had some moments to reflect on the scene as she absently nibbled at her food.

Laurie fairly bubbled with excitement. She wiggled impatiently in her chair and never took her green eyes from Nick. How she longed to have their conversation ended so she could tell him more of the plans for tomorrow. She'd gotten to tell him some things about her ball gown, but she was all but bursting to tell him more, to feel his full attention on her again. She couldn't eat her dinner but only toyed with it as she followed Nick's every movement.

Kate smiled as she watched Robert's young daughter. Laurie truly was smitten with Nick. She wore her heart on her sleeve and drank in every word, every gesture of Nick's. Poor darling, Kate thought to herself sadly, she'll only get a broken heart out of this. Nick Fletcher is for no woman very long. Besides, she doubted that even Nick would stoop to robbing the cradle and taking one so young as Laurie. However, one never could be sure where he was concerned, she added with annoyance.

Kate turned her gaze to Nick. His face still was clean-shaven, as it had been the last time Kate had seen him, and his rugged good looks stood out boldly. His white-streaked golden hair caught the sunlight as the last rays of dusk flooded through the long windows behind him. He wore his usual buccaneer's garb of tight black breeches, black knee-length leather boots, and white full-sleeved silk shirt. The front laces of his shirt were invariably untied, revealing his smooth, bronze-tanned chest in a deep vee.

Nick's clear blue eyes met Kate's, and she quickly averted hers, but not before she saw the amused grin steal onto Nick's face at having caught her scrutiny of him.

At last a delicious-looking dessert of fresh strawberries, cake, and cream was served, but Kate had no appetite even for that. She just wanted to escape the room and Nick's frankly assessing eyes. But she forced herself to eat some of the dessert, savoring the sweetness of the sliced berries before she made an effort to excuse herself. After all, she didn't want to be rude to Robert and Laurie.

"If you will forgive me, gentlemen, and Laurie," Kate said as she slowly rose from her chair, "I beg you to excuse me. I have several things that yet need to be done before I retire." She smiled warmly at Robert, barely flicked her eyes over Nick, who still smiled mockingly, and nodded to Laurie.

"You won't forget you promised to help me dress tomorrow, will you, Kate?" Laurie asked as she reluctantly pulled her eyes away from Nick to look at Kate.

"Of course not, Laurie. I'm looking forward to it. Good evening, everyone."

Robert and Nick politely stood to bid her good night. Robert looked disappointed at her leaving. Nick seemed vastly amused by some secret jest only he understood. Once out of their sight, Kate bustled angrily up the carved mahogany staircase to her room.

"The nerve of him!" she muttered as she entered her room and closed the door rather noisily behind her. "Acting just as polite and proper as any English lord, as though nothing had occurred between us—as though he has not molested, used, abused, insulted, and deserted me! He's insufferable! 'Tis a good thing, Nick Fletcher, that I was not serving the dessert tonight, for you may well have found yourself wearing it on your head!"

Kate sank angrily down on the luxurious blue brocade divan but could not suppress a slight giggle at the thought of how Nick would look with strawberries and cream dripping down his face.

"It's the least he deserves!" she said, laughing as she began to untie the laces binding her coral taffeta gown.

As she hung it in the tall walnut wardrobe closet and slipped into her white lace dressing gown, Kate's thoughts seemed to linger on Nick and the details she had noticed about him as she'd watched him through dinner. The strange uneasiness she'd felt at Laurie's mentioning of Nick the day they'd last picnicked to-gether returned to disturb Kate. She should be absolutely enraged with him, yet she realized she wasn't. In fact, she was rather glad to have him here. His presence promised to enliven what she'd feared would be a rather dull party. How she would enjoy baiting him, teasing him.

As she put the finishing touches on the wrappings around the white Spanish lace mantilla and delicately carved ivory hair combs she was giving Laurie for her birthday, Kate mused on her plan. She would ply Nick with compliments and smiles and breast-heaving sighs before she would lay him low with an aloof rebuttal when his interest was aroused. While dutifully brushing her shoulder-length hair its nightly one hundred strokes, Kate pictured her cream-colored ball gown, glad now for having chosen the more daring one. It would suit her purposes perfectly. She laughed a bit wickedly at her reflection in the mirror. Yes, she was going to enjoy tomorrow's ball immensely!

Chapter 29

Saturday dawned sunny and warm. The household was in its last-minute preparations for the evening's festivities, and people bustled in and out, to and fro throughout the day. Kate spent the greater part of it with Laurie, supervising the hairdresser's activities, seeing to a light application of makeup, and finally helping her dress.

Laurie was a vision of loveliness in her emerald-green silk gown with its white eyelet lace overskirt. Her green eyes blended vividly with the hue. The tops of her small, round breasts showed ever so slightly above the gentle scoop of the neckline. Above-the-elbow gloves almost touched the gathered cap sleeves. Her hair had been piled high and powdered white in the latest of styles, with matching green silk ribbons intertwining the coils of curls. A green velvet ribbon set with an ivory cameo encircled her slender white throat. Laurie Krenshaw would turn many dashing young men's heads this evening, Kate had thought as she'd left Laurie for her own room to finish dressing.

Now, as she stood ready before her own full-length mirror, Kate was pleased. As she whirled around to imagined music, her cream-colored silk chiffon gown, trimmed in delicate yellow velvet ribbons, lent a feathery lightness to her shapely figure. The neckline was scandalously low-cut, revealing the abundant roundness of the tops of her breasts. The gown was sleeveless, but Kate wore no gloves, preferring instead to leave her richly tanned arms bare. It was fashionable in this day and age for a woman to keep her skin covered from the sun's darkening rays and thus keep her complexion as pale as possible. But Kate was not one to be enslaved by convention. Her gown's creamy color enhanced her bronzed skin. Even her breasts were tanned, a fact Kate was sure would set many a man to wondering how they happened to be so. She smiled, remembering she'd gotten so tanned from the many uninhibited swims she'd enjoyed in the secluded reaches of Crystal Rock Pool on the far side of the farm.

A light touch of kohl to enhance her blue eyes, a dab of powder to take the shine from her nose, and a bit of red to enliven her lips were the extent of Kate's need for makeup. Like Laurie's, Kate's hair had been powdered white and piled high in curls on her head. Her pearl necklace and earrings were matched by a string of smaller pearls intertwining her hair.

Robert had told them all to be ready an hour in advance of the arrival of the first guests so Laurie could receive her birthday presents beforehand from him, Kate, and Nick. As Kate slipped into her dainty yellow silk dancing slippers and took one last scrutinizing look in the mirror, she smiled. She always enjoyed balls and she was determined that tonight would be no exception.

When Kate entered the parlor a few minutes later, she saw that the others had arrived before her. Robert was resplendent in a fashionably cut brown silk long-coat and breeches with yellow waistcoat, lace-trimmed shirt, and jabot. He came quickly forward to greet her, smiling warmly as he reached to take Laurie's birthday gift from Kate. She returned his smile, seeing in his eyes the approval and honest appreciation for her appearance that she'd hoped to see.

Laurie looked lovely and fairly sparkled with excitement as she took Kate's gift from her father's hand and began to open it eagerly. In the ensuing moments, Kate glanced at Nick, who stood by the marble fireplace with one arm propped on the mantel, an amused smile still on his lips. He wore an outfit of deep blue velvet with a blue and white brocade waistcoat, white lace-trimmed shirt, and blue jabot. The utter simplicity of the lines of the suit told of the tailor's expertise, for the longcoat fit perfectly to the shape of his body, flaring at the broad shoulders, tapering at the narrow hips. The breeches clung closely to his muscular thighs. Unlike Robert, he had not had his golden hair powdered. It was neatly brushed and pulled back and held with a black cord at the back of his neck. The whole effect was that of a dashing rogue, and it was obvious by the mischievous look in his eyes and the twitching smile on his lips that Nick intended to play the part to the hilt.

Their eyes met, and Kate smiled enticingly before turning her head toward the sound of Laurie's loud exclamation of joy. Laurie lifted out the beautiful lace mantilla and ran her fingers over the smooth ivory combs.

"Oh, Kate, it's elegant! And the combs are so splendid! Thank you so much!" Laurie gave Kate a quick hug before she ran to open the next present, from Nick.

The box was rather large and gaily wrapped in yellow paper, which Laurie wasted little time in removing. Lifting off the box lid revealed only another box inside. This one was wrapped in bright red paper. Laurie laughed merrily as she removed this box and proceeded to unwrap it also. What she found inside made her gasp with delight.

"It's beautiful! Oh, Nick, you remembered! And it's just like yours!"

"Made by the same Spanish craftsman," Nick said as Laurie carefully lifted a beautiful guitar from the box. As she slowly swept her thumb across the six strings, the rich timbre of the sound filled the room. Kate recognized it as indeed being just like Nick's, the one she'd heard him play on the *Sea Mist* those days before they reached New York. She glanced at Nick, but he was watching Laurie, who continued to strum the strings.

"When will you teach me to play, Nick?" she asked eagerly. "You promised that, too, don't forget!"

"Oh, impatient little wench!" Nick exclaimed with a laugh. "One step at a time. Your lessons will have to wait a while, for I must return to Philadelphia tomorrow. And at any rate, first you must practice the things I already have taught you on mine."

"Oh, I will, I will, every day, for hours!" Laurie promised earnestly, trying to hide her disappointment that he would be leaving so soon. Then she dropped her eyes shyly. "Thank you, Nick. 'Tis indeed an exquisite gift. I shall cherish it always."

When Laurie raised her green eyes to Nick, they were brimming with tears and held so much warmth for him that Kate's heart went out to her. She wanted to tell her not to love Nick, to warn her of the hurt that was certain to be coming, but she said nothing, for she knew the head wouldn't listen when the heart was afire.

Robert stepped forward then, holding a flat, narrow, black velvet box. His face was full of love and pride for his daughter as he handed it to her.

"It was your mother's wish that you be given these on your sixteenth birthday, Laura. They were her favorite pieces. She wore them often..."

His voice caught and broke off as he watched his daughter slowly open the velvet case. Her eyes widened in surprise.

"Oh, Papa..." was all Laurie could whisper as she gazed at the exquisite gems that lay encased in white satin at her fingertips. The necklace had a square-cut emerald surrounded by tiny diamonds in its center. Two smaller emeralds, also diamond-studded, embraced the larger one on either side. A single strand of diamonds ran from the emeralds to the silver clasp. Earrings and a bracelet with diamonds and a single emerald in each made up the remainder of the set. How they sparkled in the candlelight. Kate recognized them from the portrait of Juliette in Robert's study.

"Will you wear them tonight, Laura?" Robert asked quietly. Laurie pulled her eyes away from the hypnotizing jewels. With a leap, she flew into her father's arms, weeping softly.

"Yes, Papa, oh, yes..."

Gently, Robert helped her untie the ribboned cameo she wore and replace it with the stunning emerald necklace. It was perfect. The tears in Laurie's vivid green eyes were reflected in the brilliance of the shining stones. As she put on the earrings and bracelet and

174

placed her hand on her father's outstretched arm, a change could be seen taking place. The excited little girl of only moments before fell away, replaced by a lovely young woman. Laura Krenshaw had come of age.

"May I escort you, Miss Prescott?" Nick inquired in not too mocking a tone. He, too, had been touched by the moment, realizing with some regret that he as yet had no daughter to see grow up as fine and lovely as Laurie.

"I'd be honored, Captain Fletcher," Kate answered, smiling at him as she placed her hand delicately on his arm, and they followed Robert and Laurie out of the room.

Chapter 30

The numerous guests, many of whom would be staying overnight or longer, soon began to arrive. Guy Chadwick was among the first, and he wasted no time seeking out Kate. He was handsome and elegantly arrayed in a dark green velvet longcoat and breeches with matching green silk waistcoat and white ruffled shirt.

"Ah, Kathleen, your loveliness is breathtaking," he murmured as he drew her hand into his and brought it to his lips to kiss it lingeringly. His penetrating brown eyes appraised her boldly, and the look and smile he gave her were nothing less than lecherous.

"You will, of course, promise every dance to me, will you not, sweet beauty?" he coaxed.

Kate withdrew her hand from his possessive grasp and eyed him in mock wonder.

"Why, Guy Chadwick, you are entirely too assuming. I am acting as Sir Robert's hostess, and as such I am required to offer my attention to all the guests here this evening." Kate spoke with seriousness, her blue eyes wide with innocence, but they both knew the double connotations of her words. Guy's eyes twinkled with mischief. His smile was warm.

"In that case, lovely lady, I can only look forward to receiving my small portion of your favors, and I do so with excited anticipation."

He bowed deeply and kissed her hand again as Kate

laughingly turned away to greet some other guests. Good, Kate thought to herself. He will play along. She glanced around quickly, meeting Nick's eyes when she found him watching her. A slight frown wrinkled his brow, but a knowing smile curled on his lips. The game had begun.

Scores of guests filled the magnificent ballroom. Soon nearly a hundred people were milling around talking and calling greetings to their friends. The atmosphere was charged with excitement and gaiety. Robert Krenshaw led his daughter to the middle of the ballroom floor amid cheers of happy birthday and best wishes. Their dance marked the start of the festivities, and after they had taken two graceful turns around the perimeter of the dance floor, other couples began to fall into the rhythm of the music. Soon the white-and-gold-ornamented ballroom was alive with whirling, elegantly dressed dancers.

Kate never wanted for a partner, and in fact always had several eager squires, young and old, vying for her hand at the start of each number. She was enjoying herself immensely, teasing and flirting with this young dandy, making promises with her large blue eyes to that middle-aged squire, and engaging in deep conversation with yet another man who took her fancy. Men followed her wherever she went, enchanted by her loveliness, her wit, her low-cut gown, until Kate thought she would smother from the press of them and sought relief by choosing one of them and leading him a merry step around the marble dance floor.

The women for the most part met her with snobbish disdain, which delighted Kate tremendously, for she knew their behavior stemmed from jealousy and fear of losing their husbands' attentions and perhaps more to her. Yet some of them and those Kate had met during her stay at High Creek Farm greeted her warmly and chatted and gossiped with her.

Guy and Robert were constantly in attendance to her, and Kate enjoyed playing one against the other with her coquettish taunts. They willingly played the game with her.

As the evening sped by, Kate saw little of Nick and danced with him not at all. He made no attempt to approach her, preferring, it seemed, to dance and keep company with any one of a dozen of the prettiest and most available young women present. Once Kate caught the sound of his deep, rich laughter and turned to find him bent ever so closely to a beautiful olive-skinned young woman. Kate was a bit piqued by his lack of attention, for she had a score to settle with Nick Fletcher and had hoped to see some gain in her revenge tonight.

Yet it was with real gratefulness that Kate greeted Nick when finally he chose to honor her with his presence. Guy had gone off to fetch her champagne, Robert had been descended upon by a bosomy matron for a dance, and short, plump Squire Devon was making his way determinedly toward her. Kate couldn't bear to dance with him again, for he trod mercilessly on her toes the one time she had consented. So she smiled gratefully at Nick as he led her out through the sidelines crowd, past the disappointed Squire, and onto the dance floor.

"I daresay you have rescued me, kind sir," she teased as they moved in perfect step to a minuet.

"Oh, say you so, madame?" Nick questioned, cocking an eyebrow in mock surprise. "Was Squire Devon such a threat, then?"

Kate laughed.

"Threat, no, but a near-crippler, yes! He has little sense of rhythm and no sense of left or right. I feel certain neither my toes nor my slippers could have survived another onslaught such as he calls dancing."

"Then I am glad I was able to effect your rescue before such a disaster could take place, sweet Kate," Nick stated with affected gallantry, "for I would despair to see you incapacitated and unable to grace the dance floor."

"Ha, you are gallantry itself, Nick," Kate replied laughingly when next they met in the circling and were drawn together by the step for a brief moment. She dropped her long lashes coyly. "Such unselfishness is indeed noteworthy, sir...yet so seldom seen in you!" And she whirled away from him, smiling, to meet her next partner in the progression of the dance.

When they came together at the end of the dance,

Nick was smiling with amusement but his blue eyes held little warmth as they met Kate's.

"I see your tongue has lost none of its poisonous sting from the first time we met, Kate. 'Tis a pity."

They had reached the outer edges of the ballroom. Kate turned to Nick and continued to smile graciously as she aimed the tirade of insults she'd been planning for him.

"Its sting measurably increases when you are around, Nick," she retorted sarcastically. "It must be something about you.... Let's see... could it be your outrageous conceit, or your supreme audacity? Do you think I enjoy being treated the way you treat me? You are insensitive, cruel, lecherous, and selfish. And those are some of the better things I can think of to call you!"

With that, Kate turned on her heel and, catching sight of Guy Chadwick awaiting her near the terrace doors, made her way toward him, head held high.

"Damn, but she's a feisty wench!" Nick muttered under his breath. As he watched the graceful sway of her skirt as she walked away from him, Nick wondered why he found himself more than a little perturbed by Miss Kathleen Prescott. True, he had seen through her game of coquette and entered into it with amused willingness. So why was he so annoyed by her sharp words, by the warm smile she now bestowed on Guy? She meant nothing to him. He had deliberately rebuffed her. Shaking his head in bemusement, Nick turned and made his way toward the dining room, where an impressive display of delicious food had been laid for the guests' enjoyment.

Chapter 31

At about one o'clock, the orchestra took a well-deserved intermission, and people wandered in and out of the house and gardens, enjoying the warm summer night. Not a platter was emptied on the buffet table that wasn't immediately replaced by another heaping mass of tantalizing delicacies. Fine wines and champagnes flowed like water. Lighthearted laughter and conversation could be heard everywhere. It was indeed a successful party, and Kate fancied it would be well talked of in the weeks to come.

She was having a wonderful time. Only one incident marred the delight of the evening—her encounter with Nick. While she'd accomplished what she'd planned, somehow she did not take much pleasure in the bitter words they'd exchanged. She didn't see Nick again during the ensuing two hours, nor did she wish to, for she knew if she did, her temper would flare again. She could not forget his ill treatment of her, including his harsh farewell the morning after Lady Elizabeth's ball.

Kate was walking alone in the east rose garden. She had made a hasty exit from the ballroom when she'd seen Lord Henry Hayden making his way toward her through the crowd. Unlike most of the men she'd encountered and toyed with this evening, he refused to play the games of flirtation. He was in his mid-thirties, darkly handsome, and fancied himself quite the ladies' man. During their dance he'd asked Kate point-blank to leave with him for his room for a midnight tryst which he assured her she would not regret. It had taken a good deal of control on Kate's part to refuse him demurely rather than laugh in his arrogant face and label him a pompous ass.

Now he followed her out into the rose garden. Kate had no desire to be caught alone with him here, so she quickly made her way to where some score of people were gathering on the marble benches at the opposite end of the garden. She could not see who was the center of attraction, but she heard the gentle plucking of a stringed instrument being tuned and knew that someone was no doubt going to provide a musical interlude while the orchestra was out. Kate walked toward the group, hoping Lord Hayden wouldn't have the audacity to make his suggestions in a close crowd. A quick glance over her shoulder revealed that he still followed her. She worked her way through some of the men and women and found a seat on the end of a stone bench. An elderly matron sat next to her, eyeing her suspiciously. That ought to keep Hayden at bay, Kate thought amusedly.

The handful of people crowding around the seated musician began to disperse in search of seats of their own, and for the first time Kate could see who it was. She groaned inwardly as she glimpsed his head of wavy blond hair bent low over the instrument, listening with a practiced ear to the tuning his fingers performed. Nick! She should have known, should have recognized the mellow tones of the superbly made guitar.

Nick raised his head then and caught her annoyed look upon him. A devilish smile touched his lips, and Kate knew from his look that he, too, was thinking of the last time he'd played in her presence and how that night had culminated.

Kate's frown deepened. She was glad for the darkness, for she knew her cheeks would be pink from the flush that had swept through her. How she wished she could leave, walk away from those steel-blue eyes and their knowing look. But she knew her departure now would be all too noticeable. Besides, she probably would only run headlong into the presumptuous Lord Hayden, and she didn't relish that. So Kate settled against the back of the stone bench to relax and enjoy the songs while she waited for an opportunity to slip away unobtrusively.

Nick gently strummed the metal strings of the guitar for a few more moments, then broke into a lusty sea chanty. By the time he'd reached the fourth verse of the slightly bawdy song, which depicted the misadventures of a lovesick sailor, he had captured his audience's complete attention. Even Kate found herself caught up in the fun of the lyrics, clapping in time to the music and joining in the merry refrain with the others.

Nick indeed could weave a spell with his fine voice and expert playing. It was no wonder she'd been so affected by him that night on the *Sea Mist*. Most of the women now listening so intently would be easy prey to his charm and roguish manner, if they weren't prior to this.

Kate noticed Guy Chadwick watching her intently from across the garden. He smiled warmly as their glances met, and Kate knew she soon would be sharing the marble bench with a different seat partner if he could maneuver it. She didn't mind, for she liked Guy and enjoyed his quick wit and extravagant compliments.

Enthusiastic applause followed each of Nick's songs. Kate noticed that more people had crowded around the garden and terrace behind Nick to enjoy the music. Laurie and Robert joined them, and a place was made for them on a bench near Nick.

"Thank you, ladies and gentlemen," Nick said, pausing at the end of a popular folk song to snatch a glass of champagne from the tray of a passing servant. "But if you persist in this enthusiasm for my poor entertainment, I shall feel coerced into going on for hours!"

Loud shouts of approval resounded from the audience until Nick laughed and raised his hand in pretended surrender to their wishes.

"This next is a merry ditty taught to me by an Irish chap who's been a shipmate for a goodly time now. It's a lively thing but cannot be enjoyed fully unless it has two dancers to show its rhythmical quality." Nick was silent a moment as he glanced around the crowd. He looked knowingly at Kate, who dropped her eyes in embarrassed refusal.

"Guy, old man. You're just the one for it. You know 'The Lass and Lad of Kilkenny' as well as I. Choose one of these lovely ladies as partner and accompany me in this."

Guy flashed his most charming smile.

"All right, Nick. But how shall I choose from such a vast array of beauty?" He swept his hand in a circle that took in all in the garden. Many excited giggles and whispers could be heard as Guy walked toward Nick, scrutinizing the crowd. He paused only a moment before stepping over to Kate.

"Ah, fair Kathleen. Will you honor me in this dance?"

Kate knew the complicated steps to the jig and would enjoy doing it with an experienced partner. But still she hesitated, wondering at the propriety of doing such a bold and energetic dance at this affair. But the crowd was not to be cheated. Exuberant words of encouragement and applause came from all, making Kate cast caution to the wind and jump up to sweep Guy a deep curtsy, joining him in the open space that was made in front of Nick. She glanced at Nick, who smiled mischievously at her. Kate tossed her head defiantly, and holding her chin high, took her position on Guy's right, bestowing a fetching smile on him. Nick struck several dissonant chords to simulate the whine of a bagpipe, and the dance began. It started slowly, with both partners stepping close, then parting in teasing gestures, the innuendoes of which were lost on none of those who watched. As the music quickened in pace, hands picked up the beat and clapped the rhythm. Kate and Guy whirled and kicked, bowed and turned. At last the song ended with a flourish of racing steps and Kate and Guy stopped in perfect time, collapsing in each other's arms, laughing and breathless.

Thunderous cheers and applause echoed through the garden as people rushed to compliment them. Men pounded Guy enthusiastically on the back, and women surrounded Kate, begging to be taught the steps. She only escaped when Guy mercifully led her away in search of a thirst-quenching beverage.

When they returned to the garden, glasses in hand, it was to find Laurie and Nick singing a lilting duet. Laurie's voice was delicate and high, but it blended well with Nick's when hers carried the melody and his the harmony. Laurie blushed with delight and embarrassment when their song ended and a rousing round of applause sounded from the audience. She looked adoringly at Nick, who continued to strum the guitar as he thought of yet another tune to sing. He warmed quickly to his assumed role of troubadour and easily could render hours of songs, which the crowd here gathered seemed determined to have.

He paused, motioning a servant to refill his glass. He downed the bubbly liquid in a single gulp, savoring the relaxed, mellow feeling it caused within him. His eye caught sight of Kate chatting amiably with Guy Chadwick, and he knew what his next song must be.

"Ladies and gentlemen, next I would sing you a ballad of love and passion which may be unbeknownst to most of you, but which I am certain you will enjoy. It is called 'The Pirate and the Princess.'"

Nick seemed to be enjoying himself immensely, singing the lusty parts with gusto. He looked only at Kate, sang directly to her. His blue eyes flashed with mischief. Kate knew he was trying to embarrass her, and she refused to shrink from his steady gaze. It was some moments after the song ended with a movingly sad refrain that Kate realized a hush had fallen over the garden as everyone watched them enthralled. At length, it was Robert who broke the spell by announcing somewhat nervously that it was time to cut the birthday cake, and he bade Laurie come inside to do the honors.

Voices and laughter sounded again as men and women moved to go inside. Kate forced herself to look nonchalantly away from Nick's penetrating blue eyes as she rose to go into the house with the others. She was angry with him for putting her on display so. She could just imagine the gossip that would start. She heard Nick laugh softly as she brushed briskly past him. She would have given him a good tongue-lashing, but handsome Sir Frederick Redford came up just then to request Kate's hand for a dance, and she decided to save her wrath for later. She did not look back at Nick, but smiling warmly, linked her arm through Sir Frederick's and accompanied him inside.

Chapter 32

The early-morning hours sped quickly by, and for Kate the ball seemed to dissolve into a series of whirling, faceless men who held her too closely and acted too boldly. Kate was tiring of playing her coquettish games. Too much champagne was causing the lightheaded dizziness she was feeling now. Pleading a headache that was no exaggeration, Kate excused herself from her last partner and slipped out onto the terrace to let the soft summer breeze cool her. She found a cushioned wooden chair near one of the tall, narrow windows of the ballroom and sank gratefully down into it. She closed her eyes and tried to relax, hoping to ease the throbbing inside her head. It was some moments before she realized she could distinctly hear a conversation between two women through the open window and that they were talking about her.

"Do you see her? Who's she dancing with now, the hussy? I don't think she's had the same partner twice all night."

"You'd think these men would see through the likes of her and not act so blatantly attentive."

"Did you see how wantonly she did that new dance with Guy? And that song Captain Fletcher sang to her. Scandalous!"

They must be standing just on the other side of the window from Kate. She recognized their voices. The high, whiny one belonged to Medrith Biddington, the other to Abigail Leathers. Even in the short time she'd been at High Creek Farm, Kate had learned of their wagging tongues.

Kate leaned her head against the high back of the chair and again closed her eyes. She was tired. It had been a long, exciting day, and the hour was growing late. Already those guests who would not be staying overnight were beginning to leave.

Medrith and Abigail were talking again. They kept their voices low, but Kate was so near to them by the window that she could hear them clearly.

"Don't you think it unusual that she's staying so long with Sir Robert?" Medrith asked slyly.

"It does seem strange since she's not even a close relative or anything." Abigail was beginning to follow the gist of her friend's words.

"Don't say who told you, but I've heard that she's Sir Robert's mistress," Medrith stated with malicious satisfaction.

"No! You don't say it?"

Kate's eyes flew open, and she sat upright in the chair, fully alert. This was getting out of hand. She certainly didn't want the likes of these two spreading such a lie.

Abigail still was talking. Her voice was high-pitched with excitement.

"But are you certain? Sir Robert always has been such an honorable man."

"But a man nonetheless. He is still fairly young, and although I hate to admit it, she *is* rather pretty and very clever. Sir Robert would be a fine catch for any woman and an easy one for the likes of her. Besides, I heard it from Captain Fletcher's own lips when I spoke to him about it this evening." Medrith's squeaky voice had a definite note of triumph in it.

"Captain Fletcher told you? How delectable! Won't we have a tidbit to tell the others at afternoon tea on Tuesday!"

Kate could feel her anger growing. This was too much. Nick a party to such malicious slander against her and Robert? She found it a little hard to believe

188

even of him, but then she would put nothing past him. At times he could be very cruel.

Kate stood up and composed herself, brushing the wrinkles from her cream-colored gown. She walked to the open double doors and back into the ballroom, making her way straight for the two whispering women. So intent were they in their conversation that they didn't notice Kate's approach until she stood directly in front of them. Keeping her voice low and her smile sweet, Kate spoke with complete composure, yet the threat in her words could not be missed.

"You should take care where you concoct the nasty rumors you're so well known for spreading, lest an involved party overhear you and take offense at your lies. Guard your tongues, ladies, for I assure you, two frumpy spinsters are no match for me."

Kate stayed only long enough to see the mistresses Biddington's and Leathers' mouths drop open in astonishment before she turned on her heel and walked away from them. She was glad no one else had been standing within earshot. The nerve of them! Now to find Nick. She'd have his head for this if it were true.

She found him with a small group of men, who politely parted to let her through when she approached. With her most provocative smile she nodded her thanks to them, then turned her dazzling blue gaze upon Nick.

"May I have a few words with you, Captain Fletcher?" Her voice was sweet and endearing.

"Why, of course, Miss Prescott." Surprise showed in Nick's eyes for just a moment before his familiar mocking smile came to his lips. "You'll excuse us, gentlemen?"

Kate led Nick onto the terrace and to a secluded spot away from the ballroom before she turned and unleashed her fury on him.

"I have just overheard an interesting conversation concerning Robert and myself which seems to have been instigated by you! What do you have to say for yourself, Nick Fletcher?" Kate stood with feet apart, arms akimbo, and looked Nick straight in the eye.

"Whoa, my enraged tigress. Before you scratch my eyes out, pray explain what in heaven's name you are talking about." He seemed completely amused by her anger as he sat on the terrace railing, one lanky leg on it while the other touched the stone floor for balance. He crossed his arms at his chest and waited.

"You deny that you had a conversation this evening with Medrith Biddington and that the subject of my being Robert's mistress came up?" Kate's blue eyes flashed angrily but she kept her voice low on the chance of being overheard.

"Oh, that," Nick said simply, his mocking smile widening into a grin. "Yes, I spoke to her earlier and she did mention something to that effect. But I neither confirmed nor denied anything she said."

"Oh!" Kate threw up her hands in exasperation. "You might as well have shouted it to the rooftops, for she took your noncommittance as affirmation of the lie. And you knew she would!" Kate angrily pointed an accusing finger at Nick.

"But fair Kate, how could I have said otherwise?" Nick asked with affected innocence. "For in truth, I do not know the answer myself."

"Oh!" was all Kate could declare as she stamped her foot in fury and clenched her fists at her sides. "I swear, Nick Fletcher, you have a penchant for exasperating me mightily! I suppose I should have expected such wicked assumptions from the likes of Medrith Biddington and Abigail Leathers, but from you I might have hoped for a better attitude. If you think so little of me, at least you could have given your friend Robert more credit for decent behavior, for he is a man of honor and principle! But, of course, *you* would know little of such virtues, finding them hard to see in others since they are so lacking in yourself!"

Kate dared not say more, for angry tears blurred her eyes and caught in her throat. She turned away from Nick and leaned wearily against the nearest white column. Neither one spoke for some moments. The music from the ballroom floated to them. Kate was startled by the nearness of Nick's voice when at last he spoke. He must be standing right behind her.

"Nay, sweet Kate, you do me an injustice," he said, his voice quiet. "I would only think well of Robert were he to take you to his bed, for you are a beautiful and desirable woman."

Kate was surprised by Nick's words, for she had expected his usual snide retort and was hard put to understand the sudden gentleness in his voice. She slowly turned until she faced Nick, leaning back against the wide column with her hands tucked behind her. She looked up at him for a long moment. Her anger subsided, to be replaced by uncertainty. She was suddenly tired of the constant conflict between them. Nick was standing very near her. She could see the oval of the moon reflected in his eyes. He had a slight smile on his lips, not his usual mocking sneer, but an expression of ease and gentleness.

"You are truly an enigma, Nick Fletcher," she said finally, sighing.

He laughed a little.

"I've been called many things, my lovely Kate, but never that."

She ignored his amusement and went on as if completing a thought.

"I am indeed at a loss to understand you.... You are a daring and ruthless rebel, at home with rough sailors and noblemen alike. I know you could kill without a qualm anyone who dared to stand in the way of anything you desired. You can be very cruel.

"And yet I have seen you to be gentle and caring, as with Jeff on your ship and Laura today. And passionate, vulnerable... You are a complicated man, Nick. I think you frighten me a little, for I do not know what to expect from you from one time to the other."

"I could say many of the same things about you, Kate. So I frighten you, do I? You have given me the distinct impression that you are not frightened by anything." Nick's tone was light but held a tenderness he seldom showed. He had moved very close. It seemed just the right thing for him to bend his head to meet Kate's lips. She did not resist, but put her arms around his neck and met his kiss with equal feeling. It was not a passionate, seeking embrace, only a sharing of nearness on a warm moonlit summer's night.

A strange feeling stirred in Kate, a pleasure, an excitement at being so near to Nick, feeling the strength of him. They only parted when a laughing young couple stumbled out of the double doors from the ballroom and stopped to put their heads together for a brief whispered exchange, only to break again into laughter before they moved down the steps to the garden.

Kate moved quickly away from Nick and made to smooth an imaginary wrinkle from her gown. She felt unnerved. She had to think, but to do so, she had to get away from Nick, from his warmth, his maleness.

"Nick, I...I must be getting back. It grows late, and I'm very tired." She made to move away, but Nick encircled her small waist with his arm and drew her again to him. He kissed her long and tenderly before letting her go.

"Good night, sweet Kate. Pleasant dreams."

Kate dreamily opened her eyes to see him smiling mischievously down at her. His look told her he was well aware of the effect he was having on her. Kate suddenly felt foolish. She should never have been so frank with him. He would only use it to hurt her. With a slight shove, she pushed past Nick and hurried back into the ballroom, with Nick's soft laughter echoing behind her. She sought out Robert and Laurie to bid them a hasty good night, then made her way to her room with as much composure as she could manage.

What she did not know was that Nick also had been unnerved by Kate's response, her nearness, her softness as he'd held her in his arms. Not even five more glasses of champagne in quick succession removed the stirring that had ignited within him on the moonlit terrace. He thought he'd been playing a game, the same game Kate had started, but now he wasn't sure. His champagne-muddled mind whirled with memories of Kate in his arms as he made his unsteady way to his own room not long after Kate's departure.

As he undressed, he felt his anger building. He desired Kate. She held a strange attraction for him. There was some crazy chemistry between them. Probably more than he'd ever wanted a woman, he wanted her. Her body at least, he told himself. God, she was beautiful, passionate. The blood began pounding in his temples. He grabbed the bottle of brandy on the small table next to his bed and poured a large amount of it into a glass, then downed it quickly. It burned his throat and further clouded his brain. He lay down on the bed with his breeches still on. Suddenly he was bone weary and not thinking straight. He had to get the wench out of his mind, out of his blood, or he'd know no peace. Damn her! He would not let her enslave him. He had vowed to be finished with her. But he wanted her. Why not have Kate for his man's needs, then leave her when he tired of her, as he did with all the others? She would be just another warm, surrendering body in the night. That's all he would allow.

Nick's senses whirled. He should seek her out now and relieve the desire building in his loins. She would fight him. How she would fight before finally meeting his passion with her own. The thought was almost more than his blurred mind could bear. He started to get up, but weariness and the liquor took their toll, and Nick fell back against the pillows to let sleep overcome him and stop his tormenting thoughts.

Chapter 33

In her room, Kate undressed slowly, lost in thought.
She didn't understand the strange disturbance she felt
at being with Nick again. That his kisses upset her was
all too clear.

Kate's thoughts wandered as she slipped into her
silk nightgown. The moonlight streamed through the
double doors standing open to the small balcony outside, lending a soft serenity to the pale blue velvet of
the draperies and plush woven carpeting. Kate loved
this room and its peaceful elegance. A light blue brocade divan and two matching sitting chairs graced one
wall, while the large walnut four-poster bed, hung with
a pale blue velvet flounced canopy, claimed the central
focus of the room. She could enjoy staying here for a
long time.

Yet a strange discontentedness had tugged at her,
even before tonight's unsettling episodes with Nick. For
what was she still searching?

Kate strode slowly across the room and out onto the
balcony. The night was clear and warm. Stars dotted
the deep blackness. Kate stood for some moments lost
in the feeling of awesomeness that the vastness of the
universe always gave her.

Suddenly an uneasiness returned to her. She glanced
down at the shrub-lined courtyard below, but saw it
was empty now. She shuddered, but whether it was

from the cool breeze that lightly swept the trees or from her own nervousness, she didn't know. Turning, she entered her room. She thought to close the double doors behind her but changed her mind, as the room still held much of the heat that had rendered the day uncomfortably warm.

She drew back the fine linen coverings from the bed and lay down on the cool sheet. She felt tired. Her eyes closed easily, and soon she was asleep.

The inner sixth sense that had alerted her to danger in the past suddenly went off in her mind, bringing her instantly awake yet unmoving in the dark. She knew she was not alone in the room. A slight movement near the balcony caught her eye. The moon had dropped in the sky, but a last shred of light still edged through the open doorway, revealing a dark form silhouetted there. The arm was raised, and Kate saw the glint of moonlight reflected on a steel blade.

Panic gripped her. A piercing scream escaped her lips as she threw herself across to the floor on the other side of her bed. It was only a split second before the dark form lunged across the room and brought the death-wielding blade down on the bed where Kate had just been.

Kate was on her feet in an instant. She seized the heavy porcelain lamp from the nightstand near her and threw it across the bed with all her might. The lamp fell to the floor with a splintering crash, only inches from the now-retreating shadow. In the flash of a second, he was gone through the double doors. Kate heard the thud of his feet touching the ground after he jumped from the balcony.

Kate stood frozen, unable to move. It was only after her bedroom door crashed open and Nick ran in and drew her into his arms that Kate realized she was trembling uncontrollably. Robert followed close on Nick's heels and lighted the bed lamp near the door. The lamp's warm glow flooded the room, to reveal Kate slumped and weeping in Nick's arms and the porcelain lamp lying in a heap of shattered pieces on the floor near the balcony doors.

But it was Robert's murmured oath as he stood by the bed that brought Nick and Kate's attention to him.

They followed his gaze to the dagger plunged to its hilt in the bed's mattress, in the spot where Kate had lain. When she saw its long black hilt with the ominous gold "X" etched into it, Kate felt her mind explode. She heard herself scream, then darkness mercifully engulfed her.

Nick swept her limp form into his arms and left the room. As he entered the hall, he passed Laurie, who stood in shocked silence next to Kate's bedroom door. His shout brought her green eyes questioningly to him.

"Laurie! Fetch brandy and smelling salts to my room at once!"

After only a moment's hesitation, Laurie turned and fled down the stairs to do Nick's bidding. Robert could be heard shouting for his men at the top of his voice, directing those who staggered sleepily from their rooms to arm themselves and search the grounds for an intruder.

Nick carried Kate to his room down the hall and placed her gently on the bed. Her breathing was shallow, and she was deathly pale. "Damn!" Nick swore under his breath. Where is Laurie with that brandy? He felt shaken himself by the closeness of Kate's escape from death. God, that assassin was a brazen and determined bastard to follow Kate from London even to here.

Laurie finally arrived, and Nick quickly snatched the small container of smelling salts from her hand and held it for Kate to inhale.

"Pour some brandy, Laurie," Nick ordered quietly.

In a few moments, Kate tossed her head away from the pungent odor and opened her eyes. A momentary feeling of panic swept over her as her memory returned.

"Nick?" Her voice was but a whisper.

"I'm here, Kate," Nick murmured softly as he took her hand in his and leaned close to her. "It's all right. You're safe now."

"Nick, the assassin . . . he was here for me, tonight. . . ." Her voice trailed off as she lay back on the pillows, closing her eyes to shut out the terrible memory.

"Hush now, Kate," Nick soothed. "I know what happened. Robert's having the grounds searched. The assassin will be found. Here, have some of this." He took the glass of brandy from Laurie's outstretched hand and held it to Kate's lips. When she had swallowed half of it, the color began to return to her face. Kate looked at Nick gratefully.

Laurie stood off to the side of the room, a look of confusion and pain distorting her pretty face. She had gathered only bits and pieces of what had happened tonight and could only surmise that Nick Fletcher, the love of her life, apparently had saved Kate from something terrible. Yet she could not hold back a twinge of jealousy at seeing Nick with Kate now. There was an intimacy in the way he looked at her that belied Kate's claim that they were just acquaintances.

Kate had just fallen into a troubled doze when Robert entered and told Laurie to seek out Mrs. Jeffries, the housekeeper, and send her here, then get back to bed herself. All would be explained in the morning. Reluctantly, Laurie cast a last longing glance at Nick and left. In a few moments, Mrs. Jeffries came in and Robert told her to sit with Kate the rest of the night. Then he drew Nick down the stairs and into his study, drawing the door closed behind him.

"I fear the sneaking bastard has made good his escape, Nick," he stated angrily as he drew the dagger from the pocket of his coat. "We'll take up the search at dawn, but I hold no high hopes of uncovering anything. The man's a damned phantom!" Robert paused a moment, turning the dagger carefully in his hand. "Good God, that assassin here, in my house. The utter audacity of it!"

Robert's glance fell on Nick, who stood before the dying embers of the fire, one foot resting on the raised stone base of the fireplace. Nick's voice was deceptively calm when he spoke.

"You've posted guards?"

"Yes, and they're well armed."

Nick accepted Robert's answer with silence. Long moments elapsed, with each man deep in his own thoughts. Then Nick's voice coming deep and low broke the stillness.

"Kate will need close watching for a while after this. Her spirit is strong, but the past will return to haunt her. This assassin murdered her father and has tried before to get to Kate."

"My God," was all Robert could reply.

"I'll stay another day and join you on the search at dawn."

Robert nodded in agreement as Nick turned and strode from the room.

The search party returned in late afternoon the next day without having found even a glimpse of a trail and little hope of finding one. The assassin had covered his tracks well. After dinner, Nick strode into his room to find Kate asleep in his bed.

"She rests quietly?" he asked Mrs. Jeffries in a low voice.

"Aye, sir, 'tis a fairly quiet day she's spent. Sir Robert gave her some laudanum to calm her. She slept mostly, only to be tormented by evil dreams, poor dear. Touched not a bite of food all the day, did she."

"Thank you, Mrs. Jeffries. I'll stay awhile if you'd like to take your supper."

"Aye, thank ye, sir. I'll return shortly."

Nick stood over Kate for a long moment. Her face was pale and somewhat drawn, but still lovely as she lay relaxed in slumber. He walked out on the balcony and looked down. A broad-shouldered groom with two pistols stuck in his belt strode a small circle under him. The groom nodded in recognition when he saw Nick. Turning back into the room, Nick found Kate awake and watching him.

"If I didn't think it would bode you ill, Kate, I would crawl in beside you and make a concentrated effort to take your mind off what's happened." Nick smiled at Kate as he spoke.

She smiled a little at his jest, but turned her face away from him to glance toward the balcony doors.

"I gather you again had no success in...your search," she said flatly.

"None. His escape was complete," Nick answered, watching her intently.

"So it was before," Kate continued in a tone devoid of emotion. "He seems to vanish into thin air. Almost like a phantom, a devil, that the earth swallows for a time, until he seeks a new victim..."

Kate was silent then, but Nick saw a tear begin a path down her cheek. He knew she would not be able to take much more of this. Damn, he cursed inwardly. If only he could find the bastard.

At length he came to sit on the edge of the bed, taking her face in his hand and turning it toward him, where he met her far-off gaze.

"Listen to me, Kate. He's a man, no phantom. A man we both know—Forbes. I'm sure of it now. I've just learned he was seen in Trenton two days ago. That's only two hours' ride from here. He must have traced you here. Or perhaps he was after me. Only he knows." He paused for a moment. "No, Forbes is not a phantom. He's ruthless and cunning, but he'll meet his end like any other of us, only more quickly. His kind always does."

Kate watched Nick. He looked so tired.

"Thank you, Nick," she whispered. "I appreciate all you've tried to do."

Nick felt a strange urge to take her in his arms and press his lips to hers, blocking out the world around them. But Kate turned her head once again toward the balcony.

"You have to leave, I know, Nick." Her words were hushed. "You're needed in Philadelphia. These are crucial times. There is nothing more you can do here. I'm certain Robert will see to everything."

Kate turned liquid blue eyes to him. A part of her hoped he would not go, but she did not say it. As Nick rose to leave, his eyes held hers in silent understanding. Personal needs could not be considered. Yet Nick felt a strange reluctance to leave Kate, a reluctance he didn't want to admit. He wanted to stay and protect her, give her some of his strength.

A movement at the door caught his eye, and he turned to find Laurie watching him. When his gaze met her green eyes, she dropped them in embarrassment and hurried to explain her presence.

"Forgive me. I...I didn't mean to interrupt. Papa sent me to stay with Kate for a while."

"It's all right, Laurie. Come in," Nick said, grateful for the intrusion. "I was just taking my leave."

He strode to the door and, turning, looked a last time at Kate. The pink glow of dusk filtered into the room, lending a softness to all it touched. Kate met his glance. A slight smile showed on her delicate lips. Nick looked at Kate, marking her loveliness in his memory, then walked from the room.

Chapter 34

For several days after the attempt on her life, Kate was nervous and uneasy. She had stayed in Nick's room, not wanting to return to her own room, where the near-fatal event had occurred. Though no sign of Nick remained, his room still seemed to hold his strength, his protection.

Robert was with her constantly. He was kind and gentle, understanding her fear and mental anguish. She and Robert were very close, but not lovers. Kate would not allow it. She first had to straighten out many things which tormented her thoughts, not the least of which were her feelings about Nick Fletcher. There was something between them that had drawn them together from the start. It made their relationship explosive, exciting. Kate was all too aware that that attraction was not present with Robert Krenshaw.

Perhaps it still would happen between them, she sighed hopefully. Robert was such a good man. There was much to be said for gentleness, caring, sharing, being comfortable with each other. Kate welcomed the security of it, and Robert seemed content with things as they were.

A knock at the door interrupted her troubled thoughts. Robert entered the large, sun-drenched bedroom when he heard Kate's soft call to come in.

Kate was dressed in a yellow linen morning gown.

Her face still was pale, her smile wan as she greeted him. Robert's determination deepened.

"Good morning, Robert." Kate held her hands out to him. He took them and guided her to the brocade divan, where they sat down.

"Good morning, Kathleen. How are you feeling today?" Concern marked his face as he watched her. Kate smiled again.

"With such attentive solicitations from you and your household, how can I be anything but improved?"

"Good. I am glad to hear that. Perhaps, then, you are ready for an outing." He held up his hand to stop her protests. "Nay, hear me out, Kathleen, before you decline.

"I have to be back in Philadelphia tomorrow. Congressional meetings are heating up. The Whigs are calling for ratification of a declaration of independence. Things are coming to a head, and I must be there. Why don't you come with me and see the city, take in some social events? It would do you good, I think."

His look showed great concern, and Kate couldn't disappoint him. Perhaps it would be good for her to have a change of scene for a while.

Laura was not to be left behind when she heard about the proposed trip. She begged and pleaded, with Kate on her side, until Robert threw up his hands in surrender and agreed to have her along.

Laura was so excited that she forgot her hurt at seeing Kate and Nick together the day of the assassination attempt. Kate had helped her gain her father's permission to go to Philadelphia. They were friends again.

They arrived in the city in the late afternoon. Philadelphia, Pennsylvania, had been planned and established by William Penn on the west bank of the Delaware River in 1682. It reminded Kate very much of New York City, but with its teeming population of forty thousand people, Philadelphia had the distinction of being the largest and richest city in the colonies, leading all others in commercial and cultural opportunities. And even while the guns of war exploded in neighboring colonies, business in Philadelphia went on nearly as usual. The city was alive with people—merchants, peddlers, housewives, sailors, aristocrats, and workingmen. Only the topics of conversation had changed to include the latest congressional action or movement of troops by General Washington.

Most of the shops were closing by the time Kate, Robert, and Laura passed in the carriage. Customers laden with purchases could be seen walking everywhere. Peddlers sought to tempt them with yet one more item to purchase as they scurried by. Housewives carrying the day's shopping set their sights on home and preparing the evening meal.

As the carriage passed down one of the main streets, Kate and Laura caught sight of women as they stopped for a moment on a street corner, their baskets laden with fresh fruit, vegetables, meat, and baked goods. But it was the many shops filled with goods of every description, and partially revealed by colorful window displays, that brought squeals of delight from Laura and a touch of excitement to Kate.

She remembered how she had enjoyed her shopping trips when she was in New York with Nick getting ready for Lady Elizabeth's summer ball. The evening of the ball and the night after with Nick sped quickly through Kate's mind. A slight frown crossed her brow as she pushed the unpleasant thoughts from her mind. She would not let the past mar this adventure. She was determined to enjoy herself. But in the back of her mind, she unwittingly wondered if she might see Nick here in Philadelphia.

She glanced at Robert Krenshaw seated across from her in the carriage and realized he had been watching her. She smiled warmly at him.

"Oh, Robert, this is going to be fun. Thank you for bringing us," she said enthusiastically.

"Oh, yes, Papa, thank you," Laurie chimed in. "But I fear I will fairly burst until tomorrow morning, when we can begin to explore these glorious shops!"

Robert smiled indulgently at both women—the bubbling, blossoming one who was his beloved daughter, and the beautiful, mysterious one to whom he'd grown so close. He felt pride and passion stir within him. They would make a handsome family. Watching Kate as she turned laughing back to the window, Robert Krenshaw became determined to make Kathleen Prescott his own. He had thought much about it. He hoped the time they would spend together here would convince her to accept his proposal of marriage later on. He was going to do all in his power to overwhelm her with attention and concern for her happiness and well-being. He was a little unpracticed in the art of courtship, but he felt it would all come back to him when needed. He was exhilarated by the prospect.

So it was with heightened spirits that they all arrived at the Krenshaw home in Philadelphia. It was a large red-brick, two-story house. The familiar five white pillars, so popular in colonial architecture, spanned both stories across the front. Kate marveled at its beauty as the carriage followed the driveway into a flower-lined inner courtyard.

Robert helped Laura and Kate down from the carriage. Kate brushed at the journey's dust that clung to her traveling gown. She would be glad for the chance to freshen up after the long hours of traveling.

The large double white doors at the top of the stone steps had been flung open, and an immaculately dressed butler hurried to assist them.

"Sir Robert, it is good to have you back and with Miss Laura, too," he welcomed enthusiastically.

He nodded cordially to Kate as he stepped back. He was an older man, in his late fifties, with graying hair and a warm smile. Kate was glad Robert didn't demand formal comportment from his house employees. Again she was reminded of how like her father Robert Krenshaw was. James Prescott always had regarded the people in his home as part of his family, perhaps because he had so little actual family to regard as such. Their problems had been his, their joys a pleasure to him. It had hurt him deeply when he'd had to let them go because there was just no money left to support them all.

Robert treated his people in the same way, and she admired him for it, Kate thought as she walked beside Robert to be presented to the staff assembled in the hall. The thought flashed through her mind that in

Robert Krenshaw she perhaps sought a substitute for her dead father. Kate pushed that revelation aside as she stepped forward to greet Madison, the butler; Mrs. Peacham, the housekeeper; Mrs. Peabody, the cook; and Daisy, the parlor maid. As Robert saw Kate to her room, he explained there was no need to have a larger staff, as this house was kept only for himself for his frequent trips to the city.

"Changes could, of course, be made in the future, Kathleen," he said as they stopped in front of the door to the room that had been designated hers. His dark eyes twinkled mischievously as he looked at Kate.

Kate looked questioningly at Robert, but he did not elaborate. They were standing alone in the hall. Laurie had bustled past them to her own room, calling for Daisy to come and help her unpack. Robert and Kate were very close to each other.

"Ah, dear Kathleen," Robert said somewhat wistfully, "having you so near is becoming a very difficult situation for me to endure. You are a very desirable woman."

Then he leaned down and kissed her gently. Kate didn't resist. She had been expecting him to do this and was somewhat surprised that he had waited so long. But then, Robert Krenshaw was a gentleman.

He stepped away from her and seemed a bit flustered by the situation in which he found himself.

"Forgive me, Kathleen," he said. "I do not mean to be so impulsive. It's just that you looked so lovely standing there."

Kate laughed softly.

"Oh, Robert, don't apologize. You flatter me with your attention."

He seemed vastly relieved that she had not taken offense.

"Dinner will be in two hours," he said, changing the subject. "Rest now and refresh yourself from the journey. I will see you then."

His smile was warm as he left her.

In her room, Kate removed her dress and washed away the grime of the trip, hardly noticing the beauty and richness of her room. As she lay down on the large comfortable bed to rest, she could not stop her troubled thoughts.

"Oh, Robert," she said in a whisper, "this is so unfair to you. How I wish I could care for you, want you, as you do me."

She sighed.

"Perhaps I can make myself love you. It could happen between us," she said with determination. "I would be a fool not to. It would solve so many problems."

What a mercenary way to consider a relationship, she thought sadly as she fell into a light sleep.

Chapter 35

At breakfast the next morning, Laura Krenshaw was fairly bursting to be on with their shopping excursion.

"Oh, Kathleen, can't you hurry, please?" she pleaded as Kate poured a second cup of tea.

"Yes, Laurie," Kate said, laughing, "I'll hurry. I'm anxious to get going, too." Then to Robert she said, "I am sorry you can't come with us this morning as we'd planned."

"So am I, Kathleen," Robert answered, his face serious. "But last night's messenger brought rather alarming news and I must leave."

He brushed his napkin across his lips and rose to leave. A smile now showed on his face as he looked from Laurie to Kate.

"And since I know you two cannot wait much longer to attack our good Philadelphia merchants, I shall leave you in Ivan's able hands. He knows the city well and will be a capable guide and escort for you."

He removed a folded sheet of paper from his vest pocket and handed it to Kate.

"I have made a list of the best shops which you may be interested in visiting. I am known to each proprietor, and you may charge any purchases to my account."

As Kate made to protest, Robert continued,

"No, please, Kathleen, I insist. Let me do this for

you. Buy what you wish for yourself and Laura. It would please me greatly."

"Very well, Robert," Kate agreed with a warm smile. "If that is your wish. Thank you."

"I shall try to meet you both for luncheon at the Harrington Hotel. Ivan knows where it is. Shall we say about one o'clock?"

"Yes, that will be fine, Robert," Kate agreed.

Then she, too, rose to her feet and motioned for Laurie to follow her.

"Oh, and Laura," Robert called to them as they reached the archway to the hall, "you are to do as Kathleen says in all things, do you understand? I insist upon this."

"Yes, Papa," Laurie agreed impatiently, "I shall listen to Kathleen most carefully. Now can we *please* go?"

Kate and Robert both smiled at her youthful exuberance as she grabbed Kate's hand and fairly dragged her from the room.

Ivan Townsend, Robert Krenshaw's burly coachman, did indeed know Philadelphia. He took them down crowded main streets and narrow, winding back avenues with the skill of an experienced driver. Townsend was a large man with muscles that bulged from handling the spirited Krenshaw teams of Thoroughbreds. He waited patiently just outside the door of each shop Kate and Laurie visited; Kate was glad to have him along. She did not like the looks some of the more unseemly citizens of the city cast toward Laurie and herself as they walked from shop to shop. Kate was relieved to see them turn away when Ivan would appear behind them.

Laurie was unaware of any lurking danger, however. While she tried very hard to conduct herself with the dignity and propriety she felt befitted her age and position, she many times forgot herself and would squeal with the delight of an excited child over a lovely bonnet or a glittering trinket.

Just before one o'clock, they arrived at the Harrington Hotel. From the look of it, it was a very exclusive hotel and restaurant. As Kate and Laurie entered the lobby, they were both impressed by the elegance of their surroundings. A huge leaded glass window over the entrance doors allowed sunlight to blaze its way into the hundreds of cut-glass droplets of a magnificent crystal chandelier that hung from the high-ceilinged lobby. Thousands of rainbows from the prismatic glass flashed around the room. Dark, rich wood paneled the walls, on which hung portraits and paintings in ornate gold frames. Blue velvet draperies and plush deep blue carpet accentuated the room's elegance. It was indeed an establishment frequented by only the most well-to-do.

"My, this is something, isn't it, Laurie?" Kate whispered to her young companion as they made their way toward the main desk on the other side of the lobby.

"Oh, yes, Kathleen," Laurie answered, awestruck. "Please tell me if I do anything wrong. I don't want to make any mistakes in etiquette *here*."

They were directed to the main dining room, where a serious-faced, black-suited maître d'hôtel approached them austerely. Upon learning who they were, he led them to a table set for three. It was by an outreaching bay window and looked out toward a flowered courtyard. It was an inconspicuous table but a good one, affording them the view of the dining room at one angle and the courtyard at another, yet lending them some privacy from the busy main dining area.

"Sir Robert reserved his favorite table this morning, Miss Prescott," the waiter explained, his face ever serious.

"It will do nicely, thank you. What is your name?" she asked.

"Morgan, miss, at your service this afternoon," he answered with a slight bow. He was about forty years old and of slight build. He rather reminded Kate of a strutting peacock. She could not resist playing him along.

"Yes, well, Morgan, this is my first visit to Philadelphia and your Harrington," Kate stated aloofly, stifling an affected yawn with her gloved hand. "And whether or not I ever wish to return here will depend in large part on you and the service you render this afternoon."

"I understand perfectly, Miss Prescott. Have no fear, your every wish is my command," he answered sternly.

"Very well, then, Morgan, please see to something

cold for us to drink while we wait for Sir Robert. Lemonade would be nice, don't you think, Laura?"

Kate turned to Laurie and was hard put to stifle the smile that threatened to escape her lips.

"Yes, that will be fine," Laurie answered.

They both giggled mischievously when Morgan had gone.

"Oh, Kathleen, isn't this grand?" Laurie gushed, though in a subdued tone.

"Yes, Laurie, it's very beautiful." Kate sat with her back to the window so she could survey the luxuriant surroundings.

Highly polished dark-wood paneling and gold brocade hangings and carpet decorated the room. Elegant crystal, silverware engraved with an elaborate "H," and delicate, flower-patterned china were on each gold linen tablecloth.

"I'm so glad you came to High Creek, Kathleen," Laurie said suddenly, dropping her eyes in embarrassment. "I have so needed someone—another woman— to talk to, be friends with. And I love being here in Philadelphia. Papa never would have let me come except for you. Thank you."

"Oh, Laurie," Kate said quietly, patting the young girl's hand, "it has been wonderful for me, too."

Chapter 36

Kate and Laurie's beverages had just been served when Robert Krenshaw arrived. They chatted quietly for some time about the morning's activities before lunch was served.

"Your father's friend, Mr. Franklin, was much the topic of our session this morning, Kathleen," Robert interjected as they began to eat.

"Oh, is he in the city?" Kate questioned with interest.

"Yes, but for how long, I don't know. He wants to go to France to marshal more support for our cause. Some do not want outside interference, preferring to settle our differences with Britain ourselves. And so the arguing went, and it will continue this afternoon. We had to break for luncheon to allow tempers to cool. There is a dinner reception being given in Franklin's honor tomorrow night. We could attend if you so desire."

"Yes, Robert, I would like that very much," Kate agreed eagerly.

"All right, then, we will go. All of us," Robert said, smiling at an ecstatic Laurie.

"I am sorry your morning was not as enjoyable as ours," Kate said, smiling sympathetically at him across the table. Then her breath caught in her throat as she glanced over Robert's shoulder to see a man and a woman making their way to a table in a small alcove near the entrance door. She had only caught a glimpse of the man, but there was no mistaking that giant frame topped by fiery red hair. But it couldn't be, Kate thought as she shook her head.

"Kathleen, my dear, what is it?" Robert asked as he leaned closer, alarmed by her expression.

The sound of his voice drew Kate's attention back to their table.

"Oh, Robert," she assured, smiling and waving her hand to make light of the situation. "It's nothing. I just happened to see someone I thought I knew—an old friend from London. But it couldn't be."

"Oh? But perhaps it is your friend, Kathleen. Philadelphia draws people from all over the world," Robert said as he turned to follow Kate's glance. "Which person is it? Perhaps we can..."

Then it was Robert's turn to be stunned into silence.

"My God, it can't be," was all he managed to gasp as his gaze reached the alcove where a tall, well-dressed man and strikingly beautiful young woman were being seated.

"Do you know Gentleman Jack Donovan, too, Robert?" Kate asked incredulously.

"Who? You mean that large man in the corner?" Robert asked, a deep frown creasing his brow.

At Kate's nod he shook his head.

"No, no, I don't know him. It's the woman with him I'm surprised to see."

"Who, Papa? Who do you mean?" Laurie asked with excitement, straining to see the people Kate and her father were discussing so intently.

"Ssh, Laura, don't make a scene," Robert said sternly as he turned to face Kate, his back again to the room. It was obvious he didn't want to be seen by the one he'd recognized.

Properly chastised by the tone of her father's voice, Laura fell silent and was forgotten in the ensuing conversation.

"We're obviously talking about the same pair, but not the same person," Kate said, keeping her voice low and stealing surreptitious glances in their direction across the room. "I'm sure now that's Jack Donovan. There can be no two like him in the world. I was stunned before because I thought he'd been killed—in an accident, a boating accident," she added quickly when she heard Laurie's sharp intake of breath.

"We did some...work...together back in London," Kate continued, looking meaningfully at Robert. "But that was well over a year ago, when he vanished. He was presumed dead."

Kate glanced again in the direction of the alcove table, where the diminutive, black-haired beauty was leaning very near to her companion. In the next moment his bellowing laugh filled the room, drawing stares of disapproval from nearby diners. The man paid them no heed. That was Jack Donovan, all right.

Robert watched them also. When he spoke, his voice was grave.

"Your friend is keeping dangerous company."

"Who is she, Robert?" Kate asked levelly. Kate was calm and controlled, but her senses were tingling.

"Her name is Lynette DuPree. I haven't time to explain," Robert said evenly. "There are some people who must be notified."

His eyes met Kate's. She nodded knowingly. He could say no more in front of his daughter.

"I must go. Laura, don't look so stricken," he said gently as he glimpsed the look of fear on her face. He tried to lighten his tone. "I promise to explain more later. But for now, I must forgo our luncheon and see some people about this matter. Kate, Ivan will see you both safely back to the house. I'll see you there later."

Kate nodded agreement and watched him move slowly toward the back exit. En route he encountered Morgan. He stopped for a moment to whisper something to the waiter, then left by the back door. Kate watched Jack's table. The woman still gave him her rapt attention and had not seemed to notice Robert's departure.

For Laurie's sake, Kate knew she should stay and go through the motions of finishing lunch, if only to calm the worried girl. Besides, Kate thought, no doubt Jack had the situation well in hand. He could be very cunning and dangerous, and he was highly regarded in the intelligence network. He was unswerving in his loyalty to America, the country that gave the illegitimate son of a nobleman and an Irish serving maid the chance to find respect and make his fortune.

Yet, he was a man and a lover of women, Kate knew. His head could be turned by a beautiful face, a swaying skirt. If he was on a mission now and involved with this DuPree woman, he might be in grave danger. Kate would stay, and she and Laurie would quietly finish their luncheon. And watch the alcove table.

Kate had to think. She probably should keep out of this as much as possible. She was finished with such things, she reminded herself. Yet it would seem there always was something occurring to pull her back to this dangerous business. Robert would take care of this, she was sure. Yet it would not hurt to have lunch and keep her eyes open. There was little chance of Jack's seeing her. His back was to her, and Kate was partially hidden by the shadowy corner should he turn in her direction.

Jack Donovan had meant a great deal to her at one time. She did not want to think of his being in danger, possibly at the hands of the lovely woman with whom he seemed so captivated.

"Laurie, please don't look so upset," Kate said, noticing the deep frown on her young companion's face. "Let us enjoy this delicious luncheon before it gets cold. I'm afraid Morgan will be devastated if we do not take to our food with proper relish. And, besides, I'm hungry from all our shopping this morning. Aren't you?" she asked, attempting to change the subject and direct Laurie's attention to anything but the couple across the room.

"Are you certain everything's all right, Kathleen?" Laurie asked uneasily. "Father seemed rather upset."

"He was just surprised to see someone he hadn't expected to see in Philadelphia," Kate assured her, patting her hand. She tried to make her tone light. "So come now, finish your food, and we'll order something wickedly delicious for dessert."

Laurie smiled and seemed to be relieved by Kate's words. She turned her attention to the food at hand. They spoke of their shopping and purchases, the delicious food. Kate kept the conversation flowing, all the while stealing surreptitious glances at Jack Donovan and his lovely companion. The couple seemed to be enjoying their lunch very much, judging by the laughter that filtered across the room at regular intervals.

When it came time to leave, Kate suggested they leave by the back door so as to go through the lovely flower-filled garden they had seen through the window at their table. Laurie readily agreed, not suspecting Kate's true motive for leaving by that way.

Once back on the street, Kate and Laurie found Ivan Townsend waiting at the carriage. It was on the side street next to the hotel. As Ivan assisted Laurie up into the carriage, Kate made as though to search through her handbag.

"Oh, dear," she said, "I believe I've left my gloves at the table. I must have Morgan fetch them for me. I'll only be a few moments. Laurie, you wait here."

Kate smiled at Laurie, then turned and walked back around the corner to the lobby entrance of the Harrington Hotel. Her gloves were in her handbag, as she well knew.

Chapter 37

Kate had decided to leave a note for Jack Donovan. She had to talk to him. She had to find out what had happened to him when he had disappeared a year ago. And her sixth sense was overpowering her. Jack was in danger; she just knew it.

As Kate entered through the street doorway to the lobby, she saw reason to duck behind the first high-backed blue brocade chair she came to. Jack Donovan stood laughing at the front desk. He could not take his eyes from Lynette DuPree, whose face wore an expression of enticement and promise. Kate watched as Donovan took the room key the desk clerk handed him and then pointed the way to the carpeted stairway. Lynette DuPree smiled enchantingly, hooked her hand through his arm, and went up the stairs with him.

Kate was uncertain what to do; then she noticed three men converging at the bottom of the stairs. Kate's experienced eye told her they had been lurking in different places in the spacious lobby, waiting. Their backs were to her until one of the men, the smallest of the three, half turned to say something to his companions. Kate's hand flew to her lips to stifle the gasp that would have escaped them. Her heart beat wildly and a knot of fear tightened in her stomach as she recognized him. Forbes! She was certain of it. There was no mistaking his round-shouldered stance, even in the elegant clothes he now wore. The other two men were large and stocky, waterfront types hired for brute strength rather than intelligence. They looked uncomfortable and unaccustomed to the fine clothes they had on.

Forbes motioned to them to follow him up the stairs. Kate was certain they were after Jack. The situation was obviously a trap designed by Lynette DuPree. What should Kate do? Summon help? She didn't want to cause a commotion now and let Forbes know she was there. Besides, the lobby was nearly empty. Even the desk clerk had stepped away to a back room, leaving the area unattended.

Keep your head, Kate told herself. And follow them. She couldn't think of anything else to do at the moment. The men had disappeared up the enclosed stairwell. As inconspicuously as possible, Kate made her way across the lobby. At the registration desk, she paused only a moment to glance at the row of slots where the desk clerk had gotten Jack's room key. The only one empty toward the end of the row was No. 208. That must be Jack's room.

Kate hurried up the two flights of stairs and cautiously glanced around the corner and down the hallway leading to rooms 200 through 210. The hall was empty. Kate studied the corridor carefully. Where were those three men? She had to warn Jack. Were they in his room already, or lurking somewhere else?

Kate noticed a door without a number across from room 206. It might be a broom closet, she thought. A place to hide if she needed it—if Forbes and his cutthroats weren't already concealed there. She regretted being unarmed.

Kate started casually down the hallway as though she were a guest returning to her room. She pretended to be searching her small handbag for her key.

As she came nearer to Jack's room, she could hear voices—men's voices and a woman's higher-pitched tone. So the men are in there, Kate thought with alarm. They were arguing, their voices growing louder and louder. As she came abreast of the door of room 208, Kate could hear scuffling. She heard the crash of breaking glass. A lamp must have been knocked to the floor in the fighting.

She was about to run back down the corridor for help when she was stunned to a standstill by the sound of two shots from inside the room. Obeying her first impulse, Kate dashed for the broom-closet door across the hall. By a miracle, it wasn't locked. She barely had time to duck inside and pull the door closed behind her before she heard the door to Jack's room being jerked open. Through the keyhole, Kate could see Lynette DuPree and Hensley Forbes come running out.

"You stupid fool!" Lynette DuPree shouted as she glanced up and down the corridor. "Why did you have to shoot him? Now we'll never find it." Her face was livid.

Forbes was replacing a small pistol in his coat breast pocket.

"The bastard would have killed us all. He was like a rampaging bull. Come on, let's get out of here."

"This way," Lynette DuPree ordered as she led the way down an adjacent hallway. "I know a back way out of here."

They disappeared past Kate's range of view from the keyhole. The other two men Kate had seen in the lobby did not come out. All was quiet from Jack Donovan's room.

Kate waited another few moments, then opened the door and stepped out. She rushed across the hall, and with her back against the wall beside the open door to Jack's room, carefully looked around the doorframe and into the room. Nothing stirred.

"Jack?" Kate called. "Jack Donovan, can you hear me?"

There was no sound except for a low moan. Kate threw caution to the winds and entered the room. It was then she heard a commotion on the roof outside the open window. Shouts came from the street below. Kate rushed to the window and looked out in time to see a man jumping off the narrow edge of the roof. He landed with a thud almost at Ivan Townsend's feet. It was one of the men Kate had followed from the lobby. He lay moaning on the pavement, clutching his leg.

"Hold him, Ivan! Don't let him get away!" Kate shouted.

A startled Ivan Townsend glanced up at the window.

His jaw dropped open as he recognized Kate, then he came to his senses, nodded to her, and knelt to get a firm grip on the moaning man at his feet.

Kate whirled around from the window and rushed to the figure on the floor.

"Jack! Jack!" she cried as she knelt down and carefully turned him on his back. Blood flowed from two gaping holes in his chest near his heart. Kate frantically pulled at her petticoat to rip away large pieces of the delicate, cream-colored cloth. These she wadded and pushed into his wounds to try to stop the bleeding. Blood seemed to be everywhere. She heard footsteps and voices in the hall.

"Here!" she cried. "We're in here!"

Two men dressed in fashionable clothes ran into the room, followed by several others.

"Please, please help us. This man's been shot," Kate pleaded. "Someone get a doctor."

The first man nodded and rushed from the room.

"You there, please get a constable up here at once," Kate ordered the second man. "And you, send a messenger to Sir Robert Krenshaw's house on Sycamore Street. Tell them there to find him and have him come here immediately. The rest of you move back and give this man room to breathe."

A third man turned from the room. The others stepped back a few paces. No one seemed to question this beautiful woman's right to issue orders.

"God, Kate, where did you come from, lass?" It was Donovan speaking, his voice barely above a whisper as he looked up at her through clouded eyes.

"Shh, Jack, don't talk now. Be still. Save your strength. You're badly hurt."

"Have to talk, or pass out," Jack whispered, ignoring her pleas. "So glad you're here."

His voice was so soft Kate had to bend over to make out his words.

"Jack, please, be still," Kate pleaded. Tears rolled down her face. His face was ashen. "Please hang on. A doctor is coming." Where is that damned doctor?

A slight smile crossed Jack Donovan's lips briefly.

"Don't worry your pretty head, darlin'." A fit of coughing silenced him for a moment. The blood trickled

222

through Kate's makeshift bandages. She pressed her hands over them to try to stop the flow.

"...take more than two little bullets to bring down Jack Donovan," Jack was saying again before another coughing spell racked his huge frame, pulling the slight smile from his lips.

"Listen, Kate, lass," he whispered to her. She bent down so her ear nearly brushed his colorless lips. No one else in the room could hear him.

"They're after the book." Donovan paused for breath. This effort was costing him dearly.

"You've got to take it, keep it safe. Very important."

He choked again. The bullet must have punctured a lung, Kate thought with despair. Blood could be filling his lungs right now, drowning him, and there was nothing she could do. She felt so helpless.

"Jack! Jack!" was all she could cry through her tears.

"Shh, little one," Jack whispered. "Listen now, very important. Suppose to meet The Hawk tomorrow morning, Tap and Nog Tavern. Give him book. It's under the desk drawer there." He feebly lifted his hand to point to a small rolltop desk across the room.

"You must get it to him. You must..."

His voice trailed off. Kate looked into his brown eyes. They were dull and half closed. The sparkle Kate had known so well in the past was gone from them.

"Yes, Jack, yes, I'll do it for you. I promise. Don't worry, dear Jack," she whispered, the tightness in her throat almost choking her. Tears made her vision swim, and she brushed her hand across her eyes in an attempt to clear them. She cradled Jack's head against her breast. His skin felt cold against her hand.

"That's a good lass, Kate..." Jack murmured. "Always were a good team, you and I..."

He smiled at her. His brown eyes opened wide and for a moment the life, the old sparkle, was there. Then it was gone forever.

Gentleman Jack Donovan died in Kate's arms.

The doctor and the constable arrived, as well as the hotel's manager. It took a great deal of control for Kate to hold herself together. She wanted to scream in rage and grief at the tragedy that had taken place here. Jack was dead. Murdered.

The constable asked her several questions. He was a big man with a full, bushy moustache. His face wore a very serious expression, but his eyes were kind and his voice had been gentle as he coaxed Kate away from the dead man and led her to the straight-backed chair in the corner. At the moment, she seemed to be fairly calm under the circumstances, but the constable knew she was close to hysteria. So he asked his questions quietly and waited patiently for her to answer.

Kate tried to keep her wits about her, tried to blot out the thought of Jack's lifeless body. She must be very careful about what she said. She could not deny knowing Jack. Too many witnesses in the room had heard her call him by name. So she answered as vaguely as possible, telling the constable that Mr. Donovan was an old friend of her family whom she'd just happened to see in the hotel dining room earlier. When she'd sought him out to renew old acquaintances, she'd found him shot.

The hotel manager paced the room, nervously wiping his brow with a handkerchief. Such things just did not happen in *his* hotel. He almost collided head-on with Robert Krenshaw when Robert rushed into the room.

"Kathleen, Kathleen, darling. My God, are you all right?" Robert's handsome face went pale as he saw the blood on her dress and hands.

"Oh, Robert, thank God you're here," Kate said, sobbing, as she ran to the comforting circle of his arms. Tears streamed down her face.

"He's dead. Jack's dead," was all she could say as she buried her face in Robert's shoulder.

Robert held her closely for a few moments until he felt her rigid body relaxing somewhat.

"Here, darling, come over here," Robert coaxed gently as he led her to the bed. "Lie down here. It's all right. I'm here. I'll take care of everything."

Kate nodded gratefully. She was so glad he was here. She wouldn't have to think anymore. Robert would take care of everything. He'd said so. Kate closed her eyes and tried to shut out the room and all it held. In the back of her mind she heard the murmur of voices, then, a bit later, a little commotion as people began coming and going from the room.

Kate didn't want to think. Just lie here, she told herself. Don't think about Jack's murder at the hands of that woman. Don't think of Jack's last words, his last smile. Oh, Jack.

Last words. Unbidden, Jack's last whispered words flashed through Kate's mind. A book. A hidden book. The desk. The Hawk. Nick. She tried to sort out the words. Jack must have been on an assignment, delivering some sort of book to The Hawk. It must be important. Jack had given his life for it. And Kate had promised something. What? She forced her mind to focus on the words. She had promised Jack to get the book to Nick.

Kate's mind began to work again. She had to get the book without anyone's seeing her. Not even Robert must know. It would put him in too much danger.

The constable was dispersing the crowd and trying to calm the nervous manager. The undertaker arrived and began talking in low tones to Robert Krenshaw. Their backs were to Kate. Slowly, Kate rose from the bed and walked to the small desk. A large, white china pitcher and bowl were on one side of the open desk area. She poured water from the pitcher into the bowl and washed Jack Donovan's blood from her hands. She was standing in front of the little desk's one long drawer, her back to the rest of the room. As she rubbed her dress with the towel as if to remove the bloodstains, Kate carefully pulled open the drawer with her hidden hand. She slid her hand along the underside of the drawer. It touched something soft. Leather. A small leather book was wedged into the crack where the left side and bottom of the drawer came together. She removed the book and closed the drawer noiselessly. Turning so that her right side was hidden from view, she tucked the small volume into her pocket.

Such a small book, she thought as she continued to rub at the bloodstains on her bodice. Such a small thing to cost a man his life.

Robert came over to Kate then and put his arm around her shoulders.

"Come, Kathleen. Come with me. There's nothing

more we can do," Robert said as he gently guided her toward the door.

Kate opened her eyes. For a moment she didn't know where she was. But then the pale yellows and golds of the richly furnished room brought back memory. She wished it hadn't. With it came the sadness, the heavy, deep sadness.

She was at Robert Krenshaw's home in Philadelphia. And Jack Donovan was dead. And buried.

Kate rose, pulled on a silk robe, walked over to the window, and pulled back the heavy gold velvet drapes. The long window opened onto a shrub-lined courtyard below. The sun still shone brightly from its late-afternoon place in the blue sky. Kate relished its warmth for several minutes, willing it to chase away the chill that surrounded her heart.

Jack had been buried this morning, in a small cemetery on the outskirts of the city. She and Robert thought they would be the only ones attending. No one had known if Jack had any next of kin. Robert had promised to make inquiries of those who might know.

Robert had been so good to her, so kind and understanding. Kate was glad to draw on his strength, let him put all in order. She had explained all to him up to the part about the hidden book. She still didn't want to involve him. She would take care of it herself somehow.

And so they had seen to Jack's funeral this morning. His final resting place was at the top of a small rise overlooking Philadelphia, in the land Jack had made his own, sought to build into a free country, the land for which he had given his life.

Word evidently had spread about his death, for more than two dozen people came to pay their last respects to Gentleman Jack Donovan. It had been a touching scene.

Kate turned from the window. She thought of the small, brown leather-bound book carefully hidden away under the drawer of her nightstand. She had examined it thoroughly earlier that morning. It was a code book of some sort, filled with numbers and strange letter combinations. She could make no sense of it, but apparently Nick could. And she would see him tonight. They still were going to the dinner reception for Benjamin Franklin in the evening. Robert had protested, certain it would be too much for her in her state of mind. But Kate had insisted when he'd mentioned that Nick was likely to be there. She wanted to be rid of this costly little volume as quickly as possible. Be done with all of this murderous intrigue. The price was too high. First her father, then Jack, and how many others dead or about to die for "the cause"? Her own life had been shattered, her future uncertain. And for what? Kate had thought she knew at one time where her loyalties, her convictions lay. But death had a way of blurring principles.

Chapter 38

Sir Robert Krenshaw and Miss Kathleen Prescott were being announced in the spacious reception hall. Many people stopped their conversations to watch them as they descended the steps to the main level. They made a striking pair.

They were followed by Laura Krenshaw and her escort for the evening, Brent Jarvis. Young Brent was the son of an old family friend. Robert had arranged for Brent to escort Laura because Robert was sure he could trust the level-headed youth. Brent and Laura had been childhood playmates and still were good friends.

Robert Krenshaw was well known to all present in the reception hall. He was an elegant figure in dark green silk coat and breeches, with a ruffled white silk shirt, cuffs, and hose. His white powdered wig was of the latest design and fashion. A twitter of admiration rippled through the crowd of ladies present.

Many an expert male eye turned to examine the beautiful woman on his arm. Her hair was powdered and piled high on her head. She wore a gown of shimmering gold taffeta with a delicate white lace overlaid skirt. The edge of the lace on the low-cut bodice just barely concealed her well-rounded breasts. The lovely smile she bestowed on Robert Krenshaw as he led her into the hall made him the envy of many a man there.

Robert and Kate quickly were surrounded by groups

of people greeting them, making introductions. From what Kate could gather, most of the Continental Congress was present in the large, brightly lighted room. Together with their fashionable wives, they made an impressive assembly. Some of the greatest minds of the age were present. Kate felt honored to be among them.

Kate was listening intently to a discussion Robert was having with Richard Henry Lee of Virginia. On June 7, Robert explained to her, Lee had introduced the resolution for independence to Congress.

"It hasn't passed yet, you understand," Lee said. "But it will, just as soon as the committee finishes adding suitable justification wording to it. The Congress feels the declaration should list our grievances, why we feel driven to break with Britain. A fellow Virginian, Tom Jefferson, is drafting it," he added proudly.

"Mr. Franklin and Mr. Adams, who also are on the committee, have added a few amendments, but I understand the document is nearly ready. We should be voting on it within a day or two. It will change the world, you know, Krenshaw, change the world."

Richard Lee beamed with pride. Kate couldn't help wondering if the declaration would indeed pass as easily as Lee seemed to think. Even though the general tide of feeling had turned to total independence, the Tories loyal to Britain still were a force with which to reckon.

Kate and Robert moved on to a group of three men, interrupting what sounded like a lively discussion of birds.

"I still say the falcon is the best predator to use," Roger Sherman was saying emphatically.

"Nonsense," Robert Livingston interrupted. "An eagle is far more fierce and regal. The black one, the one with the white head feathers, would be the best choice."

"You mean the *bald* eagle, Robert?" Sherman asked jokingly. A chuckle rumbled from the group as they turned to look at Kate and Robert.

"Whatever are you discussing, gentlemen?" Robert asked after the introductions.

"The bird of prey that would best represent our new nation," Livingston offered.

"I understand Mr. Franklin favors the wild turkey," the third man, John Adams, interjected.

"A turkey!" Livingston stated in disbelief. Even Kate had to smile at this suggestion for a national symbol.

"On the contrary, gentlemen...and lady," Adams said, nodding to Kate, "I tend to favor his choice. The wild turkey has played a necessary part in the development of this country. Since the days of the first colonists' arrival, it has been an important food source. And there is no fiercer fighter than an enraged wild turkey."

Kate could not be certain whether he was serious or not. At any rate, the others were not convinced, and the discussion continued at a lively rate as she and Robert excused themselves.

"Speaking of Mr. Franklin," Robert said, leaning down slightly so Kate could hear him above the din of voices, "that's our guest of honor right over there."

With a slight nod of his head, Robert indicated a group of six young men and an older man off to one corner of the room. The older man must be Benjamin Franklin, Kate thought. A book she had recently read about him had placed his age at seventy. It was hard to imagine that this stout, balding man in wire-rimmed spectacles could be the great writer, philosopher, scientist, inventor, and statesman who had become a legend. He was an outspoken champion of freedom, dedicated to reason and the natural rights of man. Here was the tenth son of a Boston soap boiler and tallow chandler. Had he been raised in class-conscious Britain, it was unlikely he would have had the chances America had offered him to better his lot in life. He was the epitome of the American ideal of individual opportunity and achievement. America had given him much, and he gave much in return. His ideas, words, and actions were helping shape a land of separate colonies into a united democratic nation.

"Oh, but I must meet him, Robert," Kate said eagerly. "Do you think he would mind the interruption? He seems seriously engaged."

Kate watched the animated gestures of the men surrounding Benjamin Franklin. He seemed to be amused by their talk. His lined face wore an indulgent smile as he nodded and spoke a word or two to each of them.

Robert Krenshaw chuckled softly.

"Ben Franklin mind an interruption by a beautiful woman?" he asked. "Not likely. Come along."

Still smiling broadly, Robert took Kate's elbow and guided her across the room.

Franklin saw them approaching. His face broke into a wide smile as he reached for Robert's outstretched hand.

"Robert, so good to see you at something besides stuffy congressional meetings," he said warmly. "It's been too long since we've had a chance to have a friendly chat."

"Thank you, Mr. Franklin," Robert replied. "I would welcome any discussion with you at any time, sir. But allow me to introduce my guest for the evening. Miss Kathleen Prescott, may I present Mr. Benjamin Franklin."

Benjamin Franklin took Kate's outstretched hand in both of his. His smile was warm and friendly.

"I am delighted to make your acquaintance, Miss Prescott, and honored that you have chosen to bestow your beauty upon this humble gathering this evening."

Kate adored him at once. "On the contrary, Mr. Franklin," she contradicted. "It is I who am honored by this meeting, for I have indeed heard of you and have long wanted to meet you."

Franklin bowed slightly at her compliment as Kate continued.

"I believe you knew my father, James, some years ago. You had a great influence on his life and mine, too, as a matter of fact." If you only knew how much, sir, Kate added in her thoughts.

A look of surprise crossed the elderly statesman's face.

"You are James' daughter? But of course, I see the resemblance now."

Then Franklin turned to the young men with whom he'd been talking.

"Excuse me, gentlemen," he said, "but we will have to continue our discussion later—after dinner, perhaps.

I would like to talk to this young lady privately. Her father and I were close friends."

They could do nothing but agree with the elderly man, for while his tone was conversational and he still smiled, there was left no doubt that the matter was closed. Franklin pointed the way to a small alcove, and Robert and Kate followed him. While Kate seated herself on the small brocade sofa, she heard Franklin speaking to Robert.

"Indulge an old man, Robert, will you, and fetch us some champagne. I promise not to steal away with your lovely lady while you are gone."

"Of course, Mr. Franklin," Robert replied, looking askance at Kate. She nodded her head in approval. "I think I shall check on Laura and Brent, too. I'll return shortly."

"Forgive my boldness, Miss Prescott, but I feel the need to discuss something with you," Franklin explained as Robert disappeared in the crowd.

"Do not apologize, sir. I am honored."

Benjamin Franklin's bushy gray eyebrows knit in a slight frown.

"I but recently learned of your father's tragic death. News travels slowly in times of war. Please allow me to offer my sincerest condolences. Your father was a treasured friend, a great believer in freedom and democracy. These things always are gained at a dear price. Your father made the ultimate sacrifice. I am deeply sorry."

Kate knew Benjamin Franklin meant every word he spoke. She felt tears filling her own eyes.

"Thank you, Mr. Franklin. My father valued your friendship as well," Kate said in a hushed voice.

"Kathleen. May I call you Kathleen?" the older man asked, then continued at Kate's nod.

"Kathleen, I feel personally responsible in some ways for your father's death. Had I not met him and involved him in America's affairs, he might still be alive."

"Oh, no, Mr. Franklin, do not think that way," Kate hurried to tell him. "You gave my father a reason to live again. My mother died when I was born. He never remarried. Then I was grown and gone from him. He was very lonely and discontent. Your cause gave his life new meaning. He plunged into it with relish. He knew the chances he was taking, but he was willing to take them for that in which he believed."

"You are very kind, my dear," Franklin said, patting Kate's hand. "I know I cannot change what is done. Regrets do not change history. But I can see to the future a little—your future, Kathleen."

Kate looked at him in surprise.

"Again, forgive my boldness, my dear, but at my age circumlocution does not pay." A slight twinkle appeared in Franklin's eyes for a moment.

"I am concerned for your welfare. Are you well provided for? May I be of assistance in any way?" he asked seriously.

Kate had been right in her impression of this man. He was indeed concerned for all, a true humanitarian. Here was an offer Kate was only too glad to hear. It was just what she needed now.

"My father was not always practical in money matters," Kate began to explain to this man who was a relative stranger. But she found his sincerity real and worthy of her trust.

"He spent a great deal of money in his efforts for America. When he was killed, most of what he had remaining went to pay his debts. I have a small trust fund from my mother which I will receive when I reach age thirty, and I can draw upon that if necessary. But it is in England, and I want to be here, must be here. The only thing I know for certain about my future is that I want to start a new life here in America. I have had difficulty, however, in doing that up to now."

The small leather volume tucked safely away in the side pocket of her gown flashed through Kate's mind. After tonight she would be free—free of the past, free to start anew.

"And Robert Krenshaw," Franklin was asking, "does he play a part in your future plans?"

"You do come to the point, sir," Kate stated with a smile. "I'm not certain. He has been very kind to me. He is a wonderful man. I think perhaps we could have a life together, if I read our relationship truly. It would be the solution to many difficulties for me."

Kate's voice trailed off, and she could not meet Franklin's kind eyes.

"You speak of kindness and solutions, but not love," he chided gently. "While I realize many people begin their lives together without love and love does come later, I think one is much happier and more likely to remain so when love is there at the start."

He paused for a few moments, then went on.

"Do not rush into something you may both regret later just because it is convenient for the moment. If I may continue to speak honestly, let me say that a woman of your background and beauty would find many doors open to her in Philadelphia and other cities...." Franklin paused and smiled as Kate's eyebrow raised in question.

"Honorable doors, Kathleen, although I'm sure the other kind would be just as readily opened to you." The twinkle was back in his eyes.

"Opportunities such as those you might be seeking are available, and I will gladly help you in finding them if I can. You have only to call on me." He paused for a moment as his eyes searched the crowd. "I see your Mr. Krenshaw returning," he said as he caught a glimpse of Robert making his way toward them, "so I'll say only this more, Kathleen. You must decide your future, your own destiny. But I would deem it an honor and a privilege to help you if you should so desire it. It would be a small measure of payment to the debt of friendship I owe your dear father."

"Thank you, Mr. Franklin. Thank you so much," Kate said gratefully. "I may indeed do just that."

"Good. I shall hope to hear from you. Robert always will know how to get in touch with me." Then a thought struck him and he added, "And if you happen to be in Albany, you might call on Lady Victoria Remington." At Kate's questioning look, he would say only, "She is an old friend of your parents. I know she would want to help you. Trust me in this."

They both stood as Robert Krenshaw reached the alcove, bearing glasses of champagne for each of them.

"Again, my sincerest thanks, Mr. Franklin," Kate said as she raised the delicate glass goblet to her lips, "for this little conversation. I will give your words careful thought."

If Robert Krenshaw hoped to learn what had transpired between Kate and the elderly statesman, his hope was not realized. At that moment they were surrounded by three bustling matrons seeking Mr. Franklin for his valued opinion on something or other. Franklin excused himself and allowed them to lead him away with only a shrug of his shoulders and a backward friendly smile to Kate and Robert.

"So did you enjoy your talk with our illustrious Mr. Franklin?" Robert asked, trying to conceal his curiosity with little success.

"Yes, very much so. He is a remarkable man, Robert. Quite remarkable," was all Kate would say as she sipped her champagne and followed the departing Franklin with her eyes. Her mind raced. Her curiosity was piqued by the mention of someone in New York who had known her parents. And having Benjamin Franklin as her mentor in Philadelphia certainly would be a great advantage to her. At least now the horizon of her future looked much brighter, or it would be after she completed the unfinished business she had come here to do, Kate told herself determinedly.

She turned her prettiest smile on Robert Krenshaw and linked her arm in his.

"I will tell you all about it later, Robert. For now, didn't you say there were some other people here you wished me to meet?"

Robert could refuse Kate nothing when confronted with that devastating smile.

"And I say we need to develop our own monetary system if we are truly to be an independent nation," a stocky, white-haired gentleman was saying heatedly, pounding his fist into his palm as Kate and Robert approached the small group.

"That is a monumental undertaking, Hensford, and very unnecessary," retorted the bearded man next to him, shaking his head.

When Robert and Kate walked up, the topic was suspended while the polite amenities were observed. The men's wives, who had been standing with their husbands and looking quite bored by the conversation, suddenly perked up with interest as Kate joined the group.

"What do you think, Krenshaw?" the man introduced as Everett Davenport asked, bringing up the subject again. "I say we should stick with English currency. Everyone knows it and has it, and the British pound is known and respected around the world."

"My personal opinion is that we should compromise, gentlemen," Robert answered. "Use British currency now and perhaps later develop our own monetary system. Right now we have enough to do just trying to win this cursed war and getting this government established, without adding more controversy to it."

The men nodded agreement and continued talking, but Kate no longer was listening. She had heard a robust laugh from a nearby group, and her attention was drawn to it. She knew that laugh—Nick's laugh.

She followed the sound and saw him. He was surrounded by several beautiful young women. He seemed to be ignoring them as he continued speaking to two well-dressed young men. Had he felt her gaze upon him, or was it by chance that he looked up just then, his steel-blue eyes meeting Kate's? She smiled and tipped her head toward him in acknowledgment. He returned her nod, with the slight sardonic smile Kate knew so well. He looked very handsome, dressed in a dark blue velvet coat and tight-fitting breeches. The cloth seemed molded to him, outlining every muscular curve of his well-proportioned body.

Kate felt excitement stir in her. He does indeed have a magnetism about him, she thought to herself.

Nick disengaged himself from the group and, much to the visible disappointment of the other ladies, walked toward Kate's group.

"Worthington, old boy, join us here. We could use your opinion," Everett Davenport summoned as he saw Nick heading their way. He stepped aside slightly to allow room for Nick to join their small circle.

"Krenshaw, you know Ashley Worthington, I believe," Davenport said.

Robert and Nick exchanged polite nods of greeting. Nick's face wore a slightly bored expression.

"...And this lovely creature is Miss Kathleen Prescott. This lucky devil Krenshaw has had the good fortune of finding her first."

Well, not quite first, was the simultaneous thought that passed among Kate, Nick, and Robert.

"Why, Mr. Worthington, I believe we met recently in New York at Lord and Lady Huntington-Smythe's summer gathering. You were there with your lovely bride, were you not?" Kate asked innocently, her blue eyes sparkling with devilment.

God, she's beautiful, Nick thought as he took her outstretched hand in his and raised it to his lips. He could not keep the corner of his mouth from twitching into a smile. He knew it was a rather bold gesture to kiss her hand. Polite English society tended to frown on this French custom. Of course, Kate remained undaunted.

"You are quite right, Miss Prescott. Our first meeting is one I long will remember. How good to see you again."

Nick was delighted to see Kate blush, though her expression did not otherwise change.

"And is your lovely wife with you this evening, Mr. Worthington?" Kate asked. Her voice was just a trifle chilly. "I should enjoy meeting her again."

"Alas, no, Miss Prescott. I regret to say she is not. She is in France staying with relatives. I felt it best that she be there, far away from this terrible war." Nick's tone remained bored and belied the concern his words should have expressed. It was obvious to all that he said the words because it was expected of him.

He is quite an accomplished actor, Kate thought. She wondered why she was becoming annoyed with this game they were playing.

Nick's attention was drawn to the lively discussion of the monetary issue. A plan was forming in Kate's mind. She began to fan herself with her white lace handkerchief and pretended to grow disinterested with the conversation. After a few minutes, she touched Robert's arm.

"Robert," she said, as he turned his attention to her, "I think the champagne has gone to my head. I believe I'll take a little walk in the garden to cool off and clear it. No, please don't leave your friends," she added quickly as he made to turn away to join her. "I'll only be a few moments, and I'll be quite all right, really."

Then, before he could say or do anything more, Kate turned and walked across the room. At the double glass doors leading out to the patio and garden, Kate paused and looked back toward the group she'd just left. As she'd hoped, Nick Fletcher was watching her. Their eyes met, and Kate inclined her head slightly toward the door. Then she turned and entered the garden.

For some minutes, Kate admired the beautiful roses drenched in moonlight, most of their delicate petals closed to the night air. She enjoyed their fragrance and picked a few of the smaller white blossoms to entwine in her hair. She knew it would take Nick a little time to get away from the discussion inconspicuously and make his way to the garden. She had no doubt he would come. Even so, his deep voice coming very close behind her made her jump in surprise.

"What a romantic setting for our rendezvous, lovely lady," he said in a hushed voice.

Kate swung around to face him, annoyed by the lecherous tone in his voice.

"Do not flatter yourself, Nick," she said coolly, growing angrier by the moment as his amused smile widened into a grin.

"I need to talk to you, and we haven't much time. Robert could come out here at any moment, and I do not want him to know of this."

Nick knew Kate well enough by now to recognize this was no flirtatious game. He took her elbow and led her behind a large blue spruce pine nearby. It would hide them to anyone's view from the patio doors.

"All right, Kate, what is it?" he asked, serious now, too.

Kate wasted no time getting to the point.

"You were to have a meeting with Jack Donovan this morning, were you not?" she asked.

Nick's eyebrow raised in surprise. He watched her steadily as he nodded his head. Kate reached into the side pocket of her gown and withdrew the small, brown leather-covered book. It was barely three by three inches. Glancing around the garden to make certain they weren't being observed, she handed it to Nick, who quickly tucked it into the breast pocket of his coat.

"He was to give you this," Kate explained in a hushed tone, "but he was murdered before he could get it to you. By sheer chance I was there when he died. No one else knows I have it, not even Robert."

"It's the code book, then?" Nick asked, keeping his voice low, also. "I know about the trap. We thought they'd gotten the book, too. How did you get into this, Kate?"

"There's not much time to explain now," Kate said, again glancing around the garden to be sure no one was watching them.

"It was Hensley Forbes, Nick. I saw him myself with Lynette DuPree at the Harrington Hotel when..."

The look on Nick's face made Kate stop.

"Lynette DuPree?" he asked through clenched teeth. He grasped Kate by the shoulders. His eyes had a cruel glint beneath deeply furrowed brows. "Lynette DuPree is in Philadelphia and with Forbes?"

"Yes, yes," Kate answered quickly, trying to pull away from his tightening hold. "I'd have thought you'd have that information by now, from Robert or the man who was captured at the hotel."

Nick seemed to come to his senses, and he released her shoulders.

"I just arrived in the city this evening. I haven't had a chance to talk to Robert yet. And the cutthroat who was caught was murdered in his jail cell this afternoon before he could reveal anything."

Now it was Kate who was stunned by Nick's words. Dead? The man was dead? The only link to finding Jack's murderers was dead? Kate's mind reeled. But Nick had continued talking, taking no notice of the shocked expression on her face.

"I once was drawn into Lynette DuPree's treacherous circle of deception and murder. It nearly cost me my life. She works secretly for the British and is exceedingly adept at what she does. I know how she got to Donovan. You took a great risk, Kate, keeping this book and getting it to me with Lynette and Forbes on the scene."

240

Nick looked at her. She seemed to be very pale. Her shoulders sagged in despair.

"I promised Jack I'd do it," was all she would say.

"You and Donovan were...close?" he asked gently, sensing the change in her.

"Yes, at one time. It seems a very long time ago."

Kate was silent. Something inside her seemed to snap. This was all too much. Angry tears escaped her eyes. Her fists clenched. Her voice was tight and low.

"How I hate this business. It's ugly and dirty and cruel. Jack died for nothing, nothing."

Nick drew closer to her. He took hold of her shoulders again, more gently this time, and looked into her eyes.

"Now listen, Kate. I'm sorry Donovan's dead. He had a reputation as a good man and a good agent. It's hell to lose someone you care about. But he knew the risks. That's something you learn fast in this business. You know that. Donovan lost his life, but he'll save many because of this book. This is war, Kate. Lives are sacrificed. It's not pleasant, but that's the way it is."

Kate wrenched her shoulders free from his grasp. Her eyes were aflame with anger.

"You know, it's funny, Nick, but our dear Mr. Franklin said words very similar to those to me not thirty minutes ago. Only when he spoke them, they sounded good and honorable. Now I see that they are not. Murder never is honorable. Death always is the end, no matter how it comes. Even though the person you love died for some so-called glorious cause, he still is gone forever. I've learned those cruel lessons and many more besides. And I've had enough. Enough to last a lifetime! I will do no more. I am determined to make a new life for myself, Nick. I want to forget my father, Jack, deceit, murder, all of it. And that includes you, too. Have your dreams, fight your wars. Kill yourself and anyone else who gets in your way. I don't care. I want no more of it. No more."

Kate brushed at the angry tears on her cheek. Then, without looking at Nick Fletcher again, she turned on her heel and hurried back to the reception hall.

Chapter 39

Two days after the reception for Benjamin Franklin, Kate and Laurie left Philadelphia to return to High Creek Farm. Kate did not see Nick again after the reception and she told herself she was glad of that. Now she could concentrate on making her new life.

Robert Krenshaw did not return with them; he could not leave Philadelphia. Each day brought new reports of the arrival and movement of shiploads of British troops in strategic areas.

Then, on July 4, the Continental Congress formally declared the United States of America a nation independent of England. Everyone knew that such independence would not be won easily from the British, but there could be no compromise. Total conquest would be needed for Britain to regain its power over the colonies. The explosions of the guns of war grew louder as brother fought brother and battles were born from the need to defend loyalties to two nations.

High Creek Farm seemed to follow its normal routine, but armed guards regularly patrolled the grounds. Kate began to feel a contentment, a belonging at High Creek that she had not felt in a long time.

Guy Chadwick called on her several times and Kate enjoyed flirting with him, seeing his brooding brown eyes follow her hungrily, betraying his thoughts.

Strange that I've never felt like playing the coquette

with Robert, Kate thought to herself. With him she did not have to play romantic games. They were friends and, as such, could be themselves. They rode and picnicked and held deep conversations long into the night. They spent as much time together as Robert's frequent trips to Philadelphia would allow. He was a kind and understanding companion. Kate found herself drawn more and more to his quiet strength and gentle manner. While he was always the perfect gentleman and never did more than kiss her good night, Kate sensed that their relationship was deepening.

July faded into August. An exhausted Robert returned from a two-week stay in Philadelphia. He brought news that the war was moving closer to New York and Philadelphia. Reports of new outbreaks of fighting came almost daily to the farm. Kate was concerned, but for the most part she wanted to forget the rebellion and her past participation in it. She wanted to make definite plans for the future.

As much as she loved High Creek Farm and the wonderful people there, Kate knew she would soon have to come to a decision. She could not stay there indefinitely, in a state of limbo. Things were changing. Robert's manner was different, less formal, more intimate. She knew he wanted her, but he did not pressure her; he allowed her to grow to need him in her own good time. Kate knew that she was beginning to depend on his companionship and security. Sooner or later she would have to make a commitment or leave the farm. She just wasn't certain of her feelings for Robert.

Kate was puzzling over these things as she and Robert took their evening walk in the shrub-lined flower garden.

"Is something troubling you, Kathleen?" Robert asked with concern. "You've been rather quiet."

"How perceptive you are, Robert," Kate answered him as they paused to sit on a stone bench. The evening was clear and warm, and Kate was silent for a few moments, listening to the insects chirping their songs to the night.

"It's so peaceful here," she began, looking up at the stars dotting the sky. "It's easy to forget that there is a war being fought." Kate looked up at Robert. She had to speak what was on her mind. He watched her intently.

"Robert, I've very much appreciated your friendship and generous hospitality, but I cannot continue in this state of uncertainty. I must think of my future."

"I knew you would be reaching this point, Kathleen," Robert said quietly as he reached out to pluck a rose from a nearby bush. It was pink, the color of a maiden's blush. He placed it in Kate's lap. "Have you come to any decisions?"

Kate shook her head. She knew she was forcing an unspoken issue between them—her place here in Robert's home, his life. She wasn't sure what she wanted him to do. She wasn't sure what she wanted to do.

"I was hoping you would help me reason out some things."

"Do you wish to leave High Creek Farm, Kathleen?" he asked quietly. "Laura has become very fond of you...as have I."

"Yes, I think so, Robert. I think I must," Kate answered. "I cannot stay here with you like this."

She paused and looked at Robert. He took hold of her shoulders and looked at her levelly.

"But I am asking you to stay, Kathleen...stay as my wife."

Of course, Kate thought, Sir Robert Krenshaw would offer me nothing less than an honorable place. "You honor me greatly," she said, tilting her head to rest her cheek against his hand on her shoulder. She kissed his hand gently. "You are a dear man, Robert Krenshaw. I know my presence here has been awkward for you."

"I do not care what others say, Kathleen. I want you for my wife." He let his hand slip down to hers, and they began to walk the path again. "My motives are purely selfish. I want to make it right between us. I have fallen in love with you, Kathleen. I want you, and I want you to continue to share my home, my life." He stopped to look at her.

"What can I say, Robert?" she asked quietly. "You've been so kind and open with me. I owe you so much?..."

Kate's voice trailed off. She was so unsure of what to do. Were gentle companionship and security enough reasons to pledge the rest of one's life to another? she wondered.

"I'm sorry, Kathleen. I don't mean to make things complicated for you. I certainly wouldn't want you to accept my proposal out of gratitude. I have been so glad for the unique gift of your friendship. You have brought excitement and meaning back into my life. Whatever I did for you was done with as much benefit to me as to you. I didn't plan to fall in love with you, but I have, and I offer that love to you as honorably and sincerely as I can."

"Robert, I care for you deeply," Kate explained. "But to be your wife...I'm not certain it's the forever kind of love that I feel."

"Perhaps you could learn to love me in the way I love you," Robert murmured, his lips pressing into her soft hair. "I'm willing to take that chance."

"You deserve better than that, Robert. You're a wonderful man." Kate's voice was whispery with emotion. Her vivid blue eyes were bright with tears. "You should have a woman who will love you deeply and cherish you always...as Juliette did. How I wish I could be like her for you, but I'm not sure I can. Are you certain I can take her place in your heart?"

A pained look crossed Robert's face, and Kate knew she had touched a still-tender part of him.

"I'm sorry, Robert," she continued gently, "to speak this way. But, if we are to consider spending the rest of our lives together, we must be honest. I know you loved Juliette very much and that you have mourned her deeply all these years."

Robert's eyes took on the faraway look Kate had seen before, whenever he spoke of his dead wife.

"Juliette was the love of my life, my soul. The time we had together was wonderful. I was devastated when she died. I realize now, though, my long mourning of her was wrong. It did not bring her back to me...."

There was a catch in his voice that caused a tightness to rise in Kate's throat. Her heart went out to him. Oh, to be loved like that, she thought longingly.

"...And it kept me from going on with my life as I should have. Juliette would not have wanted me to mourn her so, I know. She was too full of life and joy.

But I would not allow myself to get close to another woman...until now, with you, Kathleen."

His eyes cleared, and he looked directly at Kate. She glanced away from his penetrating gaze.

"All right, Robert, let us say you have resolved your feelings of loss for Juliette. I am glad I have helped you in that. But, in truth, Robert, you know little about me...of my life before we met."

Kate could not bring herself to look at him. She walked a little distance away from him.

"I have learned all I need to know about you these past weeks you have been here, Kathleen," Robert assured her.

"No," Kate continued sternly, turning to face him. Her eyes sparkled in the moonlight. "There is much you do not know. And when a man proposes marriage to a woman, he has the right to know about her past."

Kate stilled his attempted protest with a raised hand. She looked away again as she spoke.

"I have never been ashamed of what I've done in my life. Perhaps I would change some things if I could. But at the time they happened, what I did seemed the right thing to do. I have lived a somewhat...unrestrained...life. Some might even call it wild. I have done some things that would hardly be deemed proper. You are familiar with espionage work, Robert, the acting, the treachery required. I loved the danger, the excitement. It was an enormous adventure for my father and me. But when it cost him his life, it suddenly came into vivid focus for me. That price was too high to pay."

"Kathleen," Robert interrupted, sensing her pain, "you do not have to tell me anything of this."

But Kate shook her head.

"It is your right, Robert, and I will not hold you to your proposal after I have had my say.

"I have been in love with several men, or at least I thought I was in love with each at the time. And, being young and in love, I was not discreet with my...favors, shall we say?" Kate smiled, slightly amused at the difficulty she was having in saying these things.

"One thing or another prevented my marrying any

247

of them. So, you see, I do not come to you...pure. I would not deceive you in that."

Before Robert could say anything, Kate quickly continued.

"Your friend Nick Fletcher was the most recent man, Robert, though I came not willingly to his bed. I was his prisoner and bargained for my life in that way. So my life was saved, but I found out Nick Fletcher uses people to his own selfish ends, then ruthlessly discards them. I suppose I shouldn't have been surprised to discover that. Perhaps a better woman would have chosen death rather than the course I took....But I have a strong instinct for survival, Robert, and it often makes decisions for me."

There was an uncomfortable silence and Kate feared she had shocked Robert. But she wanted to be honest with him. Perhaps, by being so, she was hoping Robert no longer would want her. He would make the decision for her.

"Dear Kathleen," Robert began, smiling at her. "You did not have to tell me these things. What happened before we met is not my concern. Your past has molded you into the woman I love. You are an intelligent, vibrant, and exciting woman, one who has seen much of life. You don't acquire such attributes in a convent. And now you add frankness to the qualities I have come to admire. What I care most about is how you feel about me, about us, and the life we might have together. Do you accept my proposal?"

Kate laughed softly, releasing the tension that had grown within her.

"Oh, Robert, you are exceptional. I think I should marry you quickly before another woman has a chance to snatch you away! How grateful I am to Henry Jenkins for bringing you to my rescue."

They began walking hand in hand back toward the house. Robert decided it would do no good to tell her it was Nick who'd brought them together. Now he wondered what really had transpired between Nick and Kathleen. For, while Kathleen claimed to hate Nick and his use of her, she had continued to work with him, even after she'd escaped his ship. And she had been civil, if somewhat cool, to him whenever they had met.

This was a strange relationship, Robert thought. Nick's puzzling message asking Robert to take Kathleen under his wing was very unlike him. Perhaps there was more between Nick and Kathleen than either one of them would admit. Robert didn't want to think about that possibility.

He was brought out of his troubled thoughts by Kate's voice.

"Robert, I do not think I will accept your proposal, at least for now. I must give it more careful thought, and I think you should, too. Thank you for not withdrawing it. You are a true gentleman, too much so perhaps..."

They had reached the house.

"Let's allow things to stand for a while, shall we? Until we get to know one another better." Her smile was warm as she looked at him.

"All right, Kathleen, if that is your wish," Robert reluctantly agreed.

At the door, Kate turned and kissed him gently before bidding him good night and going inside.

She is so lovely, Robert thought. He felt a stirring in his blood that he hadn't had in a long time. He had almost told her Nick was the one responsible for her being with him—that he had not abandoned her as heartlessly as she believed. But he held his tongue, selfishly perhaps. To tell her would not help his cause. And besides, it had been Nick's express wish that she not know. So be it, then, Robert resolved as he, too, entered the house.

Chapter 40

In the morning some two weeks later Kate heard men's voices as she approached Robert's study in search of him. He had left for Philadelphia two days after their talk in the garden and had returned only late the previous night—too late for Kate to speak to him. She had been doing much serious thinking about his proposal. Still undecided, she was now tending toward it. But something held her back. Perhaps talking with him would help her decide.

She knocked on the study door, waited for Robert's call to come in, then strode into the sun-drenched room. The conversation stopped when she entered.

"Good morning, Robert. It's so good to have you back." Kate smiled warmly and walked toward him. But as soon as Kate glimpsed the man with Robert, she stopped.

"Nick. So you are back again," Kate stated flatly.

She felt confusion sweep through her. She had thought long and hard about her feelings for Robert and had decided she wanted him, wanted what he could give her—love, companionship, security. So why this sudden fluttering in her stomach at seeing Nick? She hated him; he represented everything she wanted to forget. And she could not forgive his abuse of her. But try as she might, neither could she forget the passion they'd had together.

Nick's penetrating eyes boldly swept her from head to toe, lingering at the low-cut neckline of her gown. Kate felt herself blush, yet she could not take her eyes from his face.

"Such a warm welcome leaves me speechless, Kate," Nick said mockingly, a rakish grin spreading over his face.

He had let his golden beard and moustache grow back, but even these did not hide the gauntness of his features, the deep lines and dark circles of fatigue around his eyes.

"You've never been speechless in your life, Nick," Kate replied, trying to make her tone light. His appearance shocked her.

She heard him chuckle in amusement as she turned and, putting on her warmest smile, continued her greeting to Robert.

"We've missed you here, Robert," she said. "I hope you are home to stay for a while."

"Kathleen, you're looking lovely, as usual. I'm afraid I don't know how long I'll be here," Robert said, taking her outstretched hands in his. "Come, sit down and tell me what's been happening these past two weeks. Where is Laura? I haven't seen her this morning."

He led her to a nearby chair.

"I looked in on Laurie this morning," Kate explained. "She seems to be a bit under the weather."

"Oh? Shall I have the doctor summoned?" Robert asked, a look of concern touching his face.

"No, no," Kate assured. "It's nothing that serious. A quiet rest in bed today should be enough."

Robert smiled warmly at Kate. "I'll look in on her later."

At that moment the butler knocked, entered, and announced the arrival of Alex Jamison, a neighboring squire. The look on Robert's face told Kate he'd been expecting him.

"I do not wish to interrupt you further, Robert. We can continue our conversation later," Kate said as she rose to leave. "Since it promises to be dreadfully hot again today, don't stay shut up in here too long, gentlemen. I think I'll take a ride to Crystal Pool. Perhaps you could join me there later, Robert?"

She looked up at him hopefully, her wide-eyed expression giving her face a childlike loveliness.

Robert looked at her longingly, then shook his head.

"As much as I'd like to, Kathleen, I'm afraid I can't. Nick has brought word that the British attack on New York could occur any day. We've much to discuss. I am sorry."

"So am I, Robert," Kate said as she walked toward the door.

Alex Jamison was just entering. She nodded a greeting to the tall, stocky man.

"Good day, gentlemen," Kate bid them as she left the room, closing the door behind her.

Nick smiled to himself. Poor Robert. She was bewitching him, too. He knew he'd left Kate in good hands. Robert had mourned Juliette long enough. Nick was pleased with himself for playing Cupid. At least he thought he was pleased.

Kate headed her horse carefully down the narrow, winding path to Crystal Pool, a large pocket of sparkling clear water that had filled an eroded section in the soft sandstone. The day was unbearably hot, and Kate looked longingly at the quiet pool. She and Laurie had refreshed themselves often at this secluded spot, laughing and splashing like children. Now Kate could not resist shedding her clothing and easing herself into the cool water. She swam contentedly for a while, diving and floating. The water was tinglingly cold on her naked body.

Kate had just broken the water from a deep dive when she had the feeling she was no longer alone. She brushed dripping hair from her eyes and surveyed the bank where the path led by the pool. Kate felt anger moving through her as she recognized the intruder sitting on the grassy bank watching her intently, a sly smile on his bearded face.

"Nick!" she shouted. "What are you doing here?"

With an effort, Kate continued treading water, careful to keep all but her head under water.

Nick's smile spread into a mischievous grin.

"Ah, another warm welcome from our dear Kate," he replied casually, addressing his horse. "Such a display of affection might be construed as an invitation to join the lady, wouldn't you say, boy?"

"What do you want, Nick?" Kate asked scathingly, growing angrier by the moment as she watched him begin to unbutton his white linen shirt.

"Why, merely to avail myself of the refreshing coolness that you are so selfishly enjoying, my dear."

"A gentleman wouldn't *begin* to consider coming in here!" Kate shouted, feeling a little panicky as she watched Nick pull off his black riding boots. She was tiring from her swim and treading water, and longed to get out and rest.

"Now, when have you ever known me to be a gentleman?" Nick asked, his blue eyes flashing devilishly as he threw his shirt over his saddle horn.

"Don't you *dare* come closer, Nick Fletcher!" Kate ordered.

But Nick only laughed as he stripped off his black breeches and plunged into the water. His naked, hard-muscled body hardly disturbed the surface of the water as he entered it.

Before Kate could swim away from him, she felt his hands grasp her waist as his golden head emerged before her. He held onto her as he shook his head free of water.

"What have we here?" he asked in mock surprise. "A mermaid, and a damned pretty one at that!"

His blue eyes surveyed her openly, lingering on her full, round breasts revealed in the clear water.

"Let me go, Nick!" Kate shouted, embarrassment and rage giving her the strength to struggle against him.

"Oh, no, you don't!" Nick warned as he grabbed her upswinging arm and then pushed her head underwater.

Kate came up sputtering and furious, hitting out in every direction with clenched fists, but making contact with only air and water. Nick had easily dived out of reach. She heard his taunting laugh as he broke the water a little distance away. Then she saw him dive again. Kate searched the surface of the water watching for him, but Nick came up behind her, took hold of her shoulders, and forced her underwater again. When she was able to break the surface, he was gone.

"Damn you, Nick Fletcher!" Kate muttered vehemently as she spun around in the water to try to locate him before he could surprise her again. She dived underwater, opened her eyes, and searched for him in the pool's depths. She spotted him about thirty feet away, just propelling himself toward the surface. My turn, Nick, Kate told herself smugly. Swimming below the surface, she closed the gap between them. She could tell by Nick's twisting and turning that he now was searching for her and soon would submerge as she had done.

With a strong kick, Kate propelled herself up out of the water just behind him, clasped his shoulders, and brought her weight down hard upon them, forcing Nick underwater. Then she shot away from the spot with smooth, skilled strokes, laughing merrily.

Nick surfaced quickly, and the pursuit was on. Kate was a strong swimmer and, forgetting her tiredness, she led him a merry chase around the pool, diving and changing direction often to throw him off. But still Nick managed to overtake her and half drown her two more times. He gave her no opportunity for retaliation but stayed aggravatingly just out of reach.

At last Kate could feel her muscles beginning to tighten from fatigue. She struck for the grassy bank, with Nick in hot pursuit. She had just reached it and was stepping out when Nick grabbed her ankle, making her lose her balance and fall back into the water. They were both laughing as he caught her in his arms.

"Caught you at last, you little minx! Or I should say mermaid, for you swim like one," he said, amusement brightening his tired eyes as he looked at her.

"Let me go, Nick, please," Kate begged breathlessly through her laughter. "I'm exhausted. I can't swim another stroke."

Nick swept her up in his arms, rose out of the shallow water, and carried her to the bank. He gently put her down on the long, soft grass and lay down next to her. For long moments they lay silently together, letting the warm summer sun burn the wetness from their bodies. Kate was very much aware of Nick's naked form beside her.

"It's nice to hear your laughter again, Kate," Nick

said drowsily, raising up on one elbow to look at her. "I think I've actually missed it...and you. Though I can't for the life of me fathom why, since you vex me sorely whenever we're together. You must have cast a spell on me, sweet witch."

Nick had been glad to see Kate this morning, and there seemed to be something right about being with her like this now.

Kate was confused by the gentleness in his tone. The intense blueness of his eyes held her locked in his gaze.

"These past weeks have weighed heavily on you," Kate said in a hushed tone as she saw again the dark circles under his eyes, the lines of fatigue in his face. "I noticed it when I saw you this morning with Robert."

She raised her hand to brush a strand of dripping golden hair out of his eyes. Nick caught her hand in his and raised it to his lips, kissing her fingertips softly. Kate felt something stir within her.

"I didn't think you could see anything about me when all your attention seemed to be for him," Nick teased as he leaned down to kiss her moist lips.

When his kiss grew more fervent and his hand began to move over her body, Kate pushed against Nick's naked chest and murmured a weak protest. Something in the sound of it made Nick pause. He raised his head a little away to look at Kate and saw her deep blue eyes growing liquid with tears.

"Why do you torment me so, Nick?" Kate whispered, turning her face away from him to hide her tears. "I want to make a new life for myself, burying the past. Yet it seems whenever I try to go about doing that, you reappear and ruin everything. Why, Nick? Why can't you leave me alone?"

She turned her eyes beseechingly on Nick. He would not meet her gaze but looked instead out at the pool of shimmering water.

"I confess I do not know the answer to that myself, Kate." His mind was in an odd turmoil. He was uncomfortable with what he was feeling. Hadn't he wanted Robert to have her? Hadn't he wanted to be done with her?

Nick was quiet a few more moments before he pushed these disturbing thoughts from his mind and spoke. His tone was lighter now. "After today you can rest easier, Kate, for I vow to be gone from your life, to disrupt your future no more."

A devilish smile turned up the corners of his mouth as he leaned closer to Kate. "But now, sweet witch, I would have you one last time, so I will have pleasant memories to warm me on next cold winter's night!"

Kate tried to protest, but Nick stopped her mouth with his, seeking her hungrily. Yet even as Kate struggled against Nick, she felt the blood rush through her veins, bringing with it the eager response she wished she could have held back. Nick's mouth moved searingly down her slim, smooth neck, to her tightening nipples. His hand moved over her wet, naked flesh, teasing and tormenting her passion to wakefulness.

Suddenly Nick rolled away from her and brought himself to a crouching position, all his senses alert. Kate was too surprised to speak as her eyes fluttered open and she looked at Nick. Then she gasped as she followed his gaze and saw Robert Krenshaw guiding his horse down the path toward them. It was obvious from the look on his face that he had been watching them.

"Robert!" Kate gasped in a shocked whisper. Then, suddenly remembering her nakedness, she snatched up the blanket she'd laid nearby for the picnic lunch and threw it around her.

Upon recognizing Robert, Nick visibly relaxed and reached for his breeches. Unlike Kate, he showed no signs of embarrassment but casually pulled on his black, tight-fitting trousers, an amused smile curling one corner of his mouth.

Robert looked directly at Kate. His voice, when he spoke, was cold and accusing.

"I see you found someone else to join you on your...outing."

"Robert..." Kate began pleadingly, but he turned away from her with an air of dismissal and addressed Nick in the same icy tone, as though Kate were no longer present.

"Guy has arrived with news from New York. He says it's urgent. You'd better come with me."

A frown flickered over Nick's face at the mention of

Guy's name. His presence could mean only one thing: The threatened invasion was under way or almost so.

"I'm right behind you, Robert," Nick said, his voice serious as he pulled on his black-leather jackboots. As he quickly pulled on his shirt and swung up on his horse, he looked at Kate as if he suddenly remembered she was there.

"Coming, Kate?" he asked, his offhanded tone revealing that his thoughts were elsewhere.

"Go on ahead!" Kate replied sharply, clutching the blanket around her.

As the two men disappeared from view, Kate sank down on the soft grass, tears stinging her eyes. She felt angry and frustrated. She cursed Nick Fletcher for coming here and being so disarming. She cursed Robert for coming to find them himself when he could have sent a lackey. And she cursed herself for being so weak when it came to Nick Fletcher. Now he'd done it to her again, played havoc with her life, her plans. How could Robert ever want her now?

"Damn you, Nick Fletcher!" she cursed aloud as she gathered up her clothes and hurriedly put them on.

The household was in a flurry of activity when Kate entered the house and went straight to her room. What it was all about, she wasn't sure. She only knew she had to figure out what to do when she had to face Robert again. And Laurie. How would she ever explain to Laurie what had happened? Laurie knew about her father's proposal to Kate and was eager to have Kate for her stepmother.

Kate lay on her bed, tired and miserable. The sounds of the activity in the house filtered up faintly as sleep tugged at her eyelids. She dropped off into a restless sleep, tormented by what she would say to Robert when next she saw him.

But she would not have a chance to say anything to him, for when she awoke two hours later and went downstairs, it was to find that Robert, Nick, and Guy Chadwick all had left for New York. The British fleet was only a day away from New York Harbor. All the efforts these past months to gather and organize the army to defend the city would be put to the test soon. The battle was at hand.

Chapter 41

Almost a week passed. Alarming reports reached High Creek Farm as battered and defeated men straggled back to their farms and homes. The British fleet, commanded by Admiral Howe, had entered New York Harbor at dawn two days after Robert, Nick, and Guy had so speedily departed High Creek Farm. Thirty heavily armed ships of war had spewed volley after volley of murderous cannon fire against the city's defense batteries, crumbling the stone walls and destroying most of the city's weaponry. Then the well-disciplined, scarlet-coated infantry troops had landed. Some thirty thousand crack British soldiers had swarmed ashore, cutting a wide, bloody path through the American lines.

The Americans, quickly recruited and even more quickly trained, did not fight as a disciplined unit. Their strength lay in the courage and skill of individual men, but organization and strong leadership were needed to repel the waves of advancing professional soldiers. The patriots fought bravely, but time after time they were driven back. Finally their leaders, men like Nick Fletcher, Robert Krenshaw, and Guy Chadwick, who valued life more than a questionable victory, ordered retreat. They realized that dead men could not fight another day.

The actual fighting had lingered on for four days before the British Union Jack had been raised and the city declared taken. After that, the number of retreating American soldiers increased greatly, and everyone at High Creek Farm was kept busy seeing to their needs and helping them on their way. Kate and the others would fall exhausted into bed each night, going instantly into dreamless sleep.

At dawn of the seventh day, Kate was aroused from a deep sleep by Laurie's hysterical crying, as she shook Kate to waken her.

"Kate, Kate, oh, please wake up!"

Kate sat bolt upright, instantly awake. She grasped the weeping girl by the shoulders and shook her gently.

"Laurie, what is it? Calm down and tell me!"

"Oh, Kate, it's Papa," Laurie sobbed through gasping breaths. "Uncle Guy brought him home. He's been shot! Oh, it's terrible!" Laurie hid her face in her hands and wept loudly.

Kate threw off the sheet and jumped out of bed. She swept up her thin cotton dressing gown, pulling it on as she dashed out of the room and down the stairs.

Two husky grooms were just carrying Robert into the house. Kate suppressed a cry as she saw him. He seemed to be covered with blood. His dirt-caked face was contorted in pain even though he was unconscious. Kate ran to him. Guy Chadwick entered behind him, looking little better than Robert. Guy's face was gaunt, his dark brown eyes sunken within the dark circles surrounding them. Several days' growth of beard showed around a deep, blood-caked gash in his cheek. His filthy, makeshift uniform was in tatters.

Kate looked from Robert to Guy, fear reflected in her wide-eyed stare.

"Is he alive, Guy?" she asked, holding her breath.

"Yes, but his leg is bad. He's lost a lot of blood," came Guy's half-whispered reply as he swayed dangerously on his feet. Kate ran to catch his arm around her shoulders to support him.

"Take Sir Robert up to his room!" Kate ordered sharply to the two hesitating grooms. "And be careful of his leg!"

"Jerome!" she shouted at the astonished butler who had just entered the hall. "Send for the doctor and have water boiled! Bring it to me with plenty of bandages! Move, man!"

Her authoritative tone spurred him to action, and Kate heard him bellowing her orders.

"Easy, Guy," Kate cautioned as she helped him mount the staircase, just behind the grooms. She led him to an empty guest room next to hers, and he collapsed gratefully on the bed.

"Are you hurt anywhere besides your face, Guy?" Kate asked as she unbuttoned his coat and bent to pull off his heavy boots.

"Don't think so," he muttered hoarsely. "Just hellish tired. Haven't slept in three days...." His voice trailed off as he closed his eyes. Guy would be all right until after she had seen to Robert.

Kate spent most of the morning with Robert. She feared the doctor would not come, for she knew there were many injured men requiring his attention. So she took matters into her own hands. Robert Krenshaw had taken a musket ball in the thigh. The ball had traveled straight through, leaving a clean wound, but he had bled profusely. Kate cleaned the wound thoroughly and bandaged it. The biggest danger was infection. She ordered the wound cleaned and rebandaged every two hours. She was frightened by the ashen tinge around his mouth. The small amount of brandy she had been able to force between his lips had brought some color back into his cheeks. His breathing was shallow but steady.

Laurie stood off in a corner of her father's room, whimpering softly as she watched Kate. Laurie seemed grateful to be able to do something when Kate asked her to sit with her father while she looked in on Guy.

That evening, Kate walked in the garden, her thoughts in turmoil. Robert still had not regained consciousness, although he seemed to be resting easier. Kate found herself wondering about Nick Fletcher and what had happened to him in the battle.

She turned at the sound of a footfall on the stone path and saw Guy walking toward her. He had bathed and shaved, very carefully, Kate reflected to herself as she glimpsed the clean white bandage down the length of his left cheek. He was wearing one of Robert's shirts and blue breeches, above black leather boots. Kate noticed again his rugged good looks.

"How's Robert?" he asked, falling into step next to Kate as they turned and continued walking.

"Rallying, I hope," she answered, glancing sideways at Guy, "but still unconscious."

Guy nodded and, tapping his bandaged cheek gingerly, smiled down at Kate. "My thanks for this. You seem to be quite an accomplished nurse."

"I've picked up a bit of knowledge here and there. It comes in handy."

Kate smiled back at him, feeling some of her tension drain away. They walked a little way in silence, then Kate stopped, catching Guy's arm to stop him. He turned to look at her.

"It was very bad, wasn't it, Guy? The battle, I mean."

"It was hell!" he answered vehemently. He looked out over the tree-lined hills surrounding the valley. A look of pure hatred darkened his narrowed brown eyes. "We were outnumbered three to one in most of the assaults," he went on, his voice low and tight. "But still our lads fought bravely, taking two of those bloody, scarlet-coated bastards to every one of our men who fell. General Washington was forced to call our retreat. We withdrew to Manhattan Island. Howe was slow in pressing his advantage for some reason. Fortunately, unfavorable winds then kept his ships from entering the East River and coming after us, or I fear I wouldn't be here to tell about it. That would have been the end of General Washington's army, I'm certain."

A silence fell between them.

"Guy?" Kate ventured after a few minutes. She had to ask the question that had been haunting her thoughts. "What of Nick?"

Guy Chadwick's frown deepened as he brought his eyes to meet hers. His mouth was pulled into a tight, grim line as he answered.

"We're not certain, Kate. I saw him take a musket ball and go down two days ago. He'd been in the front lines, fighting like a madman. He knew the *Sea Mist* was no match for the fleet, so he and his men elected to fight with the infantry. They fought like they were possessed, but they didn't have a chance!"

Guy's voice had risen as his rage mounted. "When Nick was hit, redcoats swarmed over him before anyone had a chance to get to him. But word has it that he wasn't killed, only took a nasty wound in the side. One man said he saw Nick being carried to the temporary stockade set up in one of the barricades that wasn't completely destroyed."

Relief showed on Kate's face.

"But that's not all, Kate," Guy went on grimly. "John Douglass is in charge of prisoners. If Nick is a prisoner, it's almost a certainty that bastard will exact a painful revenge. They have been enemies for a long time."

Kate had a sickening feeling in the pit of her stomach. Nick. Nick hurt, perhaps dead. Kate's mind reeled. She told herself she hated him, hated his arrogance, his ill use of her. Yet she knew that she admired him also, admired his courage, his convictions, his strength. The memory of his arms around her, his lips warm and searching on hers, swept into Kate's thoughts unbidden. She sighed deeply and shook her head to dispel the disturbing picture her mind held. That was all in the past now. She looked at Guy.

"What now, Guy?" she asked in a hushed voice. "All those lives lost. All those men wounded and killed. And for what? A cause we can't hope to win? Britain is too great a power to fight."

Kate saw determination blaze in Guy's eyes, heard the steel in his voice as he answered her. "We *can* win! Plans already are being made to retake New York. Many of our men had never fought the British before. We were no disciplined, experienced fighting machine. Some of our lads fled in the face of that, and I can't blame them. The redcoats were well equipped, well trained, everything we still are becoming. But we're learning. The British often are ill led. Their generals are hesitant. Every battle sees new gains in strategy and strength for our army. We can't fight them face to face, man on man, in straight, disciplined columns, which is the way of fighting those blasted redcoats know so well. Next time we'll fight like the woodsmen and hunters we are, using the ways of the Indians. Lightning strikes and quick retreats. Sabotage. The British may control New York now, but they are overconfident. Keeping the city won't be an easy task."

Guy was silent for a while as they started to walk back toward the house.

"Damn, but we could use Nick badly!" Guy swore, his tone heated. "He has a way about him that can rally even the most dispirited men. I've seen him do it countless times."

Kate nodded agreement. She found herself wanting to know what had happened to Nick. Her thoughts raced. Her determination to be finished with treachery and intrigue suddenly fell away. She felt excited, alive, more so than she'd felt in months. As they reached the house, Kate turned to Guy.

"Perhaps there's something I could do besides just bandaging the wounded. I have an idea."

Chapter 42

Kate fidgeted with the ribbons of her pale blue ruffled bonnet. It matched her low-cut, lace-trimmed silk gown perfectly. She was sitting nervously in Robert Krenshaw's elegant gold and red carriage, awaiting permission to enter past the forbidding iron gate of the makeshift stockade for an audience with John Douglass.

With wide-eyed innocence, she had presented herself to the young corporal on duty, bending forward to talk to him so that her full, rounded breasts were revealed to his gawking eyes. She had purposely called him "lieutenant" and dropped her lashes demurely. He had puffed out his chest and saluted smartly as he hurried off to relay her request.

As Kate waited, her nervousness mounted. She let her thoughts drift back to the night before, when she had presented her plan to Guy and Robert, who had regained consciousness that evening.

"There's a chance," she'd explained, her eyes bright with excitement, "that I could get in to see Nick, or at least find out if he's alive."

"Short of having a well-armed regiment to storm the walls, how do you propose doing such a thing?" Robert Krenshaw had asked dubiously, grimacing with pain.

There had been no time for Robert and Kate to talk. Inwardly they both knew they had no future together.

But they would have to say those words at another time, after wounds to heart and limb mended and the uncertainties of war were ended.

Kate began to explain, trying to keep the eagerness out of her voice. "You both know that I was a passenger on John Douglass' ship, the *Newgate*, last June. We'd struck up a fairly close friendship, and I know he would have liked to have carried it farther."

A wicked smile curled her lips. Robert scowled, but Guy continued to watch her intently, the gist of her plan beginning to dawn on him. "However, Nick interrupted that by besting him in battle and taking his passengers prisoner. Still, there is a good chance that John Douglass doesn't know of my subsequent ...association...with Nick, other than that I was his reluctant prisoner. And, of course, he never knew I was a courier."

"On the other hand," Guy interjected seriously, "there's just as great a likelihood that he knows everything. He's not stupid. He came very close to catching Nick the night of Liz's ball. And if he were as taken with you as you imply, he very likely made inquiries. Though you've kept out of sight," he went on, holding up his hand to stop her protests, "your beauty hardly promotes anonymity, Kate. Someone is bound to have recognized you at the ball...."

"That's a chance I'm willing to take!" Kate retorted. "This will be my approach: I will go to Douglass as an old friend, yet a woman ruined by Nick Fletcher." She ignored Robert's derisive half laugh. "I'll let it be known that I would like to have my own revenge on Nick and also would like to renew my friendship with Douglass. With luck, his ego will goad him into trying to impress me, I hope by exhibiting Nick to me as his prisoner. I may even be able to get information about future British movements."

Kate paused, looking from Guy to Robert for approval.

"You treat this like a game, a preposterous game!" Robert cried incredulously. He had not seen *this* Kate before.

"Espionage *is* a game, Robert, a very dangerous game, and one I have played many times."

She looked to Guy for support. He was silent, absorbed in thought.

"It never will work!" Robert denounced hotly. "It's too tenuous to hold any chance of success!"

Guy looked from Robert to Kate, a sardonic smile dawning on his face.

"Which is, my good Robert, precisely why it *can* succeed!" Guy stated emphatically. Rising, he motioned for Kate to follow him.

"Come along, Kate, we've much work to do and little time."

As they reached the door of Robert Krenshaw's room, Guy turned back. "We'll be borrowing your carriage and four of your best bays. Frightfully sorry you can't join us," he said teasingly, laughing as he saw Robert's angry scowl. "It'll be like old times. Nick's ship is anchored at Duncan's Cove; I'll send there for some of his lads to help," Guy continued. "We'll meet them at the Soaring Hawk. Wish us luck now, what say, Robert?"

"You'll need more than luck, you bloody rascal," Robert hurled at him. A smile curled the corner of his mouth as he looked at Kate. "But I hope you succeed. Things would be too damned dull for my taste without Nick around here. Take care."

Kate's thoughts came back to the present as she rested her head against the plush red cushion of the carriage seat. The next few hours would be dangerous ones. She felt somewhat relieved to know that Guy was masquerading as the driver in the box overhead. He had a hat pulled down over his eyes and to one side to hide his bandaged face. Higgins and Lawson, two of Nick's crew from the *Sea Mist,* also were there, as groom and footman. Kate had been glad to see them again. They all carried concealed weapons in the event a speedy escape had to be made. Kate had her pistol in her small drawstring purse.

In her trepidation, Kate imagined a score of redcoated dragoons swarming down upon them because John Douglass had seen through her deception. For the hundredth time, Kate asked herself what she was doing there, risking her life for someone she didn't even like!

But she knew part of the answer: excitement. She loved the danger. It was at that moment that Kate knew she never would have been happy with Robert Krenshaw and his quiet life at High Creek Farm.

At length the young corporal returned, saying Captain Douglass considered her visit an honor and would see her at once. He directed them to the headquarters building.

Bennett helped Kate out of the coach. She glanced up at Guy, whose face was carefully blank. She walked toward the office door. They all knew this could easily be a trap, with John Douglass lurking inside, ready to order his men to arrest them.

Kate swallowed hard as she put out her hand to open the door. She put on her most seductive smile and stepped daintily over the threshold into what might easily be a lion's den.

Chapter 43

Kate stood still for a moment to let her eyes adjust to the dimness of the office after the bright sunlight outside. No one pounced on her as she stepped forward. She smiled provocatively at the sergeant at the desk. He jumped to his feet when he saw her.

"Good day, Sergeant," Kate greeted. "I'm Kathleen Prescott. Captain Douglass is expecting me."

Kate was amused at his lecherous look. Yes, she thought to herself smugly, she had chosen her gown well.

"Yes, ma'am, he is, ma'am. Just a minute, please," the sergeant stammered, saluting smartly. He turned to the door just behind him, and knocking, hesitated only a moment before opening it.

"Miss Prescott is here, Captain," Kate heard him say. She resisted the urge to look into the room beyond. She'd know soon enough if her plan would work. Things were going well so far. Too well?

"Good!" came John Douglass' enthusiastic reply. "Send her in, Sergeant."

Kate walked into the office, exaggerating the sway of her hips. She continued to smile beguilingly, trying to hide her nervousness. She watched John Douglass carefully as he came to grasp her outstretched hand.

"Kathleen, how good it is to see you. You look lovely."

His tone was warm as his eyes moved over her appreciatively.

Kate dropped her eyes, pretending shyness at his compliment. She was wary of his friendly tone. She looked at him again. His welcoming smile seemed to be genuine. Kate breathed an inward sigh of relief. Douglass held out a chair for her, which she accepted. Then he sat down at his desk.

"Oh, John, it is so good to see you," Kate began in a honeyed tone. "You're looking well. I was so worried about you...." She lowered her eyes in apparent embarrassment. "After that horrible episode with that monstrous pirate Fletcher, I was afraid I'd never see you again."

Kate let her shoulders droop as she sighed deeply. She appeared to be in great distress. Douglass jumped up from his chair and walked quickly over to her, concern showing on his handsome, dark features.

"Try not to think of it, my dear," he coaxed, taking her hand and holding it tenderly.

"Oh, John, it was a nightmare!" Kate cried, throwing herself into his arms and sobbing, as though unable to be brave any longer.

"I know, Kathleen, I know," he soothed, stroking her hair where it fell in luxuriant curls from under her bonnet.

With a visible effort, Kate brought her tears under control, daintily dabbing at her blue eyes with a lace handkerchief.

"When I learned, just recently, that you had survived and were the commander here, I was so happy." Kate looked into his sympathetic eyes, a wide-eyed look of innocence on her face. "I've hoped against hope that you still would be my friend, even after...after ...what happened," she said falteringly. Two large tears overflowed her eyes.

"Of course I am, Kathleen. Of course I am," Douglass assured her. Then anger punctuated his tone. "It must have been terrible for you being in the hands of that blackguard Fletcher!"

For a brief moment the anger in Douglass' voice and genuine concern on his face made Kate regret her deception. He did seem to be a decent man. But as she quickly reminded herself, he was the enemy. And appearances could be deceiving. She was a perfect example of that.

Kate let a frown crease her brow, and she made her tone cold.

"I hate him! I wish I could kill him for the use he made of me! It was so humiliating! And had it not been for the generosity of some old family friends I chanced to find here in New York, I don't know what I might have done after that evil Fletcher had his way with me and then cast me aside."

"Believe me, Kathleen, I know the hatred you feel, for mine is as great," Douglass comforted as his arm encircled her shoulders in a gesture of sympathy. He paused, looking at her closely, uncertain whether to reveal to her his triumph over Fletcher. But as Kate had hoped, his vanity triumphed.

"But we shall have our revenge, Kathleen dearest," he said quietly, his mouth a tight line and his gray eyes cold with a wicked glint.

Kate suppressed a shudder as she saw the hatred on his face. She was glad his wrath was not directed at her. She would not allow herself to think that after today it might be focused on her.

"But what do you mean, John?" Kate asked innocently.

His eyes narrowed as he leaned closer and spoke in a low voice. "What would you say if I told you I have Captain Nicholas Fletcher imprisoned in this stockade at this very moment?"

Kate felt her pulse quicken at his words as she feigned the shocked expression she knew he expected.

"But surely you jest, John. How can that be? It is too good to be true!" she cried excitedly, putting out her hand and grasping his, a genuine smile of triumph lighting her face.

Douglass put his other hand possessively over hers, basking in her reaction. "Believe me, my dear, it's true," he boasted. "And also know that he is at this moment suffering painfully for his outrageous insults against us!"

"Do not torment me, John," Kate chided with pretended annoyance. "What *are* you talking about?"

"Fletcher was wounded and captured during the last day of this skirmish with these riffraff colonists," Douglass explained contemptuously. "As a rebel traitor, he is incarcerated in the cells below this building."

"A pity he was not killed!" Kate spoke hotly, turning her eyes away so he wouldn't see the relief in them at learning that Nick was at least still alive.

"But Kathleen," Douglass placated, a malicious gleam in his eyes, "that would have been too easy. He will die soon enough, either from his wounds or by the hangman, have no fear of that. But we want him to suffer a bit first, don't we, my dear?"

Kate had to work hard to keep the disgust out of her voice as she looked at him and forced a look of admiration onto her face.

"Oh, John, you are brilliant!" Then dropping her voice, as if revealing some long-awaited pleasure, Kate said, "How I've hoped and prayed to see him dangling someday from a yardarm! And if he happens to meet with rough handling on the way to the gallows, well, so much the better!" Kate smiled at him, all the while thinking that what she had just said was not so far from the truth.

John Douglass returned her smile. He raised her hand to his lips and kissed it lingeringly. He looked into her eyes, making no attempt to hide his desire. Experience told him that a woman who exhibited such a degree of hatred would be just as intense in her passion.

Kate pretended shyness at his bold appraisal, pulling her hand away and strolling to the window. She stood there looking out, as if deep in thought. Then she turned to Douglass again.

"John," she entreated, "may I ask a favor of you?"

Seeing his puzzled look, Kate continued. "I'd deem it a great favor," she said quietly, letting her eyes make promises she never intended to keep, "if you would allow me to see Fletcher. It would give me so much pleasure to see him suffering and let him know how I'm enjoying the fate that has befallen him."

Remarkable, Douglass thought. "Of course, my dear.

I understand," he replied indulgently. "But I must warn you, it is not a pretty sight."

"All the better! Will you lead the way?" she asked, linking her arm through his.

Chapter 44

They walked gingerly down the long, winding stone stairway, being careful not to slip on the wet slime that clung there. The smell of mold was heavy in the air, and Kate felt a shiver run up her spine, both from the increasing chill in the air as they descended deeper into the earth and from the oppressive atmosphere. She thought with horror of what it would be like to be imprisoned in such a place. Involuntarily she clung a little tighter to John Douglass' arm.

At length the stairway opened into a large room, off of which Kate saw six barred doors. She could hear cries of pain and had to take a deep breath to fortify herself.

Two red-coated soldiers who had been playing cards at a small table came smartly to attention when they recognized their captain.

"Open the door to Fletcher's cell," Douglass ordered after returning their salute.

Kate watched one of the soldiers turn a key in the lock of the first door on the right.

"This way, my dear," Douglass directed, taking a glowing kerosene lantern from a hook on the wall and keeping a careful watch on her face for any sign of reluctance.

Kate walked forward boldly, lowering her head to enter through the cell doorway. She stopped just inside to let her eyes become accustomed to the dim light. The stench of mold and human wastes was overwhelming, and she felt a wave of nausea pass over her. She coughed delicately, raising her scented handkerchief to blot out the smell.

"Are you certain you wish to go on, Kathleen?" Douglass asked earnestly.

"Yes, yes, I'm all right," Kate declared. "But I can't see a thing."

Douglass descended three steps and placed the lantern on a small table. Kate shuddered as she heard the scurry of fleeing rats.

As the lantern illuminated the room, Kate had her first glimpse of Nick. It took all of her will to keep from crying out, for she knew John Douglass watched her closely. With a supreme effort she forced a diabolical smile to form on her lips. Lifting her skirts, she swept down the steps and walked directly in front of Nick.

He was chained hand and foot to the cell wall, his arms outstretched to either side of him. He hung forward against the chains, his golden head, matted and filthy, resting on his chest. Kate feared he might be dead. Beneath his tattered shirt, his body showed red and bloody where the lash had raised wide welts across his chest. From the way his shirt hung down behind him, Kate guessed his back had felt the whip as well. A filthy, makeshift bandage, stiff with blood, covered the side wound he must have received during the fighting.

But it was as Nick slowly raised his head to look at her that Kate had to draw again on all her fortitude to keep from uttering a cry of horror. As it was, she could not stop a sharp intake of breath as she saw his bruised and battered face.

His lips were cracked and swollen. Blood had dripped out of the corners of his mouth and was caked in his golden beard. His left eye was blackened and almost swollen shut. More blood, oozing its way down his face from an ugly gash above his right eyebrow, left his face streaked red. His eyes were glazed and unseeing.

Kate's anger and disgust flared. No human being ever should be treated like this, she thought. He must be in excruciating pain, yet not a sound emerged from his lips.

Kate knew she dare not show the feelings smoldering within her. Swallowing hard, she directed her anger to the purpose at hand. Taking Nick's chin roughly in her left hand, she forced him to look at her. Her voice was hard and unfeeling as she taunted him, even while her stomach churned sickeningly because of what she had to do.

"Well, well. How does it feel to be on the receiving end of ill treatment, Captain Nick Fletcher? Finally you are getting your just reward for all the evil you've caused, including your disgusting treatment of me, you filthy swine!"

With that Kate brought her right hand down hard across his face. She felt her heart wrench within her as she saw him grimace in pain. With an effort he brought his head back to face her, his blue eyes glinting with fury. His mind was clouded with the confusion born of half consciousness, but he knew the force of a blow and saw it only for what it appeared to be through his dulled senses—an attack.

"Bitch! I'll see you dead!" he spewed at her in a hoarse whisper.

Thank God there's still some life left in him, Kate thought with relief. She let a sinister laugh escape her lips as she turned away.

"Ha, you are hardly in a position to make good your threats, Captain Fletcher, so I suggest you save your strength for the further punishments you can expect from my dear friend Captain Douglass."

She walked over to the amused Douglass and slipped her arm possessively through his, a look of triumph on her face.

As they walked back up the three steps and through the doorway, Kate dared not venture a look back, for she knew she could not endure seeing his tortured, hate-filled face again.

She was grateful for the long walk back up the stairs to Douglass' office, for it gave her time to recover. Her determination to best him enabled Kate to face Douglass with gratitude on her face as she took a glass of wine from his outstretched hand.

"Thank you, John, for letting me do that. You can never know what it meant to me," she said truthfully.

"But I do know, Kathleen, for I have felt the same satisfaction over these past few days of dealing with him," Douglass agreed conceitedly.

"John," Kate asked, "when will you be...ah, interrogating Fletcher again? I should greatly desire to be there."

"My word, you are a bloodthirsty one, aren't you," Douglass commented laughingly. "But I understand how you feel. As a matter of fact, it will likely be tomorrow. He has needed some time to recover. We'll make it tomorrow afternoon, after we've lunched together," Douglass continued assumingly, with a self-satisfied smile that Kate wished she could have wiped off his face with a pistol butt.

"I would like that very much, John," Kate said in a honeyed voice. "But now I must go. I feel rather drained by all this excitement, and I've taken enough of your time."

"Of course, my dear," Douglass agreed. "Until tomorrow, at noon. I'll send my coach for you."

"You're too kind, thank you. I'm staying at the Soaring Hawk Inn," Kate replied, allowing him to kiss her hand lingeringly.

"Back to the inn, driver," Kate ordered the disguised Guy Chadwick as Douglass helped her into the waiting carriage.

"Until tomorrow, John..." Kate whispered to John Douglass, smiling beguilingly, a look of promise on her face.

Chapter 45

"My God, that doesn't give us much time!" Guy Chadwick cursed as he ran his hand worriedly through his black, curly hair and paced around the room.

Back at the inn, he, Higgins, Lawson, and Henry Jenkins had listened intently to Kate's recounting of her visit.

"But it's all the time we have," Kate said urgently. "I doubt Nick can last through one more session with that maniac."

"We realize that, Kate," Guy said with exasperation. "But this is so damned risky, and you'll be in constant danger. I don't know if I can allow it. *Nick* never would allow it! He would never put you in such a position."

Kate rose from her chair, an angry frown marring her forehead.

"Then I'll make the decision for you, Guy. We have to do it. Nick is your friend, isn't he? You can't leave him to die when there's a chance to save him. We need him to help retake New York. We need him to help win the war. Isn't that worth the risk? We've got to try!"

Kate thought the luncheon with Douglass never would end. She had forced herself to eat some of the delicacies placed before her, so as not to arouse his suspicions. But she was beginning to feel the strain of willing herself to smile and be pleasant and chat amiably about any subject Douglass happened to raise.

Kate glanced surreptitiously at the maple wall clock in Douglass' office where they were having lunch. Two o'clock. Thirty minutes until Lawson and Jenkins created the diversionary explosion in the arms storehouse. She thought of Guy and Higgins dressed as farmers, making their way by wagon to the supply depot directly behind this building. The two real farmers who delivered food supplies daily to the garrison lay trussed up in their own barn.

"That was a most delicious luncheon, John," Kate complimented as she put down her napkin. Raising her wineglass, she took a sip and looked at Douglass, arching her left eyebrow and letting smugness sound in her voice. "I hope the rest of the afternoon's activities will be equally as enjoyable."

Douglass laughed, raising his glass to her.

"So you still want to go through with this?" he asked, thinking how beautiful she was and how he would enjoy watching her during Fletcher's interrogation. Then there was the thought of the evening together to occupy his mind, too, for he had further plans for the lovely Kathleen Prescott.

"Of course!" Kate replied curtly. Then, in a softer tone, blue eyes wide, her lower lip pouting, she added, "You won't disappoint me, will you, John?"

"I never could deny you anything, my dear. I am your slave," he said charmingly. It was all Kate could do not to jerk her hand away when he raised it to his lips. She saw the lust in his cold gray eyes, and she shuddered with dread as he turned and went to the door.

"Sergeant Mackey! Tell Sykes to bring the prisoner Fletcher to the interrogation room at once!"

"Yes, sir!" came the quick reply.

"This way, my dear." Douglass motioned her to follow him to a door leading to a room off to the left of his office.

Kate felt a wave of revulsion pass through her as she entered the room and saw the implements of torture displayed around the room. She guessed they were exhibited as much to intimidate their victims as to be handy for their evil tasks.

"I think you will admire Sykes," Douglass was saying. "He is a civilian and has a rare talent for... persuading...prisoners to loosen their tongues. Fletcher has proved to be a rare challenge for him, but I trust we will see him break today."

Kate walked slowly around the room, examining various instruments. Here and there she stopped to pose a question, the answer to which Douglass was more than happy to supply. He watched her closely, all the time reveling in the thoughts of having her in his bed. She did not seem to be at all squeamish in the presence of such sadistic instruments nor reluctant to see a man tortured, albeit a man who had used her badly. Perhaps bedding her would be more of an adventure than he had dared to hope.

A window and a door were on the opposite side of the room, and Kate made her way toward them. She stopped to glance out the window, casually looking up at the sky as though to study the weather, then continued to stroll the room nonchalantly. Kate wasn't sure she could go through with this. But she had no choice, she told herself. Her thoughts raced. It was a stroke of luck that the door next to the window led out to a deserted alley, for across that alley was the supply depot where Guy and Bennett were waiting. The captured British corporal who had willingly traded his freedom for details of the layout of the stockade had told them true.

Just keep your nerve a little longer, Kate told herself.

A full twenty minutes passed before the door opened, and Nick was half carried, half dragged into the room by a giant of a man. Kate never had seen anyone so huge nor so evil-looking. He had a long, jagged scar from his temple to the corner of his mouth on the left side of his face, so that his mouth was permanently curled in a demonic sneer. A black patch covered his left eye.

Effortlessly he thrust Nick's battered body against the wall and chained his arms to two widely set iron rings cemented there. Kate saw the look of pain on

Nick's face as he slowly lifted his head to look at them. Hatred blazed in his blue eyes as he recognized Douglass and Kate standing together before him.

"I see you brought your whore to the spectacle today," Nick muttered fiercely through cracked and swollen lips.

Kate gasped, stunned by the viciousness of his words. Her heart twisted with pain to think he could hate her so. He must truly think she betrayed him now. But that would help him through what lay ahead. Stay in a rage, Kate prayed. It will give you the strength you'll need.

"Shut up, swine!" came Syke's low, hoarse voice as he brought his huge fist down on the right side of Nick's face.

"I'm sorry, Kathleen. I never should have agreed to let you be here," Douglass confessed uncomfortably, coming to where she stood pale and trembling.

With an effort, Kate straightened, thrusting out her chin defiantly.

"On the contrary, John, I am determined to stay."

Inwardly, she willed Henry's explosion to come soon, before she and Nick had to endure much more of this.

Sykes' blow had knocked Nick senseless, and it was some minutes before he was revived by a bucket of water. Suddenly the quiet was shattered by a deafening explosion, which was followed almost instantly by another explosion, then another, as powder kegs burst from the impact of the first blast.

"What the devil...?" Douglass shouted just as Sergeant Mackey burst into the room from the outer office.

"It's the arms storehouse, I think, Captain Douglass!" he yelled above the noise of the explosions. "Looks like it's going up!"

"My God!" Douglass cried. "All right. I'm coming!" Then, as he dashed for the door Sergeant Mackey had disappeared through, he remembered Kate.

"Stay here with Sykes! You'll be far enough away to be safe!" And he disappeared from sight.

Well done, Henry, Kate thought to herself as she moved to close the door that Douglass had gone through. Sykes had gone to the window at the opposite end of the small room, his back to her, curious to see what was causing all the commotion outside.

Kate looked at Nick. He was conscious again, shaking his head as if to clear his senses. She lowered her right hand and found the pocket hidden in the folds of her green damask gown. Her pistol felt cold to the touch as her hand closed around it. She made herself stop and think carefully. She was a good shot, but she never had aimed at a man before. Her stomach turned over with dread, but she ignored it, knowing what she had to do. Don't think of him as a person, for he is hardly human. The head or the heart, Kate thought to herself. Either one would ensure instant death.

The noise from new explosions was deafening as Kate slowly moved across the room. Carefully, she withdrew her small pistol. Holding it with two hands, she pointed at her target. She saw Nick's blue eyes widen in surprise as he looked up at her. She clenched her teeth and slowly eased back the trigger.

The sound of the shot was drowned out by the commotion outside, just as Guy had said it would be. Only when she saw Sykes pitch forward in death, the back of his head blown away, did Kate know that her bullet had hit home. Numb with shock, she stood motionless, the smoking pistol still held out in front of her. She had killed a man. True, a man like Sykes was deserving of it, but still . . .

"Kate!" Nick shouted hoarsely at her. "Kate!"

Tears streamed down her face, and she began to tremble uncontrollably as she turned to look at Nick, confusion showing in her face.

"The keys, get the keys, Kate!" Nick ordered, feeling a sudden surge of energy. Damn, he cursed under his breath. If only his head would clear. For an instant he'd thought she was going to shoot *him*.

Pale as death, Kate shook off her dazed state, dropped her pistol, and ran to Sykes' body, where she ripped off the ring of keys at the side of his belt. She was careful to keep her eyes focused on the task at hand and not on the bloody mass so near her. In a moment Nick was free, his wrists and ankles showing raw and bloody from the manacles.

"Quickly, out this way!" Kate shouted as she motioned Nick to the back door of the room leading to the alley.

Nick stumbled as he attempted to follow her. Kate ran back to him, throwing his arm around her shoulder and taking on as much of his weight as she could. She heard Nick's heavy breathing as he fought to stay conscious. They crossed the narrow, deserted alley and entered the supply depot, where Guy Chadwick and Bennett Higgins rushed to them, each taking one of Nick's arms around his neck and half carrying him to a far door leading to the wagon outside.

No one noticed them as they gently laid Nick in the straw-covered bed of the wagon. His face was ashen, his teeth clenched against the pain. Kate followed Nick into the wagon and lay down next to him. She was vaguely aware of the continued sound of explosions and the strong, acrid smell of smoke in the air. Guy and Bennett quickly covered them with an old canvas, then jumped up into the seat and whipped the team of nervous horses to life. Guy headed them through the now-unguarded main gate and gave them their heads, letting them plunge full gallop down the road, leaving the smoking garrison behind them.

Kate took Nick's head in her arms and moved her body closer to his in an attempt to keep him from being jostled by the pitching wagon.

"Hang on, Nick, hang on," she whispered, seeing his eyes closed tightly and his mouth twisting in a grimace of anguish. Fresh blood flowed from the gash in his eyebrow. Kate could feel the warmth of it on her skin as she cradled his head. His back and chest showing under his tattered shirt also were bleeding. Thoughts of Jack Donovan dying in her arms rushed through Kate's mind. No, not Nick, too.

"After all we've been through to free you, Nick Fletcher, you'd better not die!" she murmured angrily, more to herself than to him.

It was suffocatingly hot under the heavy canvas. Kate was struggling to push it off of them when they rounded a turn so sharply that she was certain they would overturn. She was pitched over on top of Nick, and when she finally was able to regain her place next to him, she realized with horror that his body had gone limp beside her.

"My God!" she cried as she heaved the canvas aside

and quickly felt for a pulse at his neck. Relief flooded her body as she felt blood throbbing in the vein against her fingers. Nick still was alive.

After what seemed an endless time, the wagon roared to a stop, the horses rearing and snorting and sending up clouds of dust as they felt the sharp pull of the bit in their mouths.

"We're here!" Kate heard Guy shout as the wagon lurched to a stop and a number of hands sought to help her out.

As prearranged, they had come to Huntington House, Lady Elizabeth's luxurious country home. Hers was the closest, Guy had argued when Kate had protested, and since the taking of New York, Lord Huntington-Smythe had been detained in Boston, so he would not be around to interfere. The staff was loyal to Lady Elizabeth, so Nick could recuperate in relative safety. There hadn't been enough time to arrange anything else, so Kate had grudgingly agreed, not relishing the idea of having to spend any amount of time under the roof of Lady Huntington-Smythe.

Gentle hands carried Nick's unconscious form quickly into the house. The horses and wagon disappeared from sight. In a matter of moments, no evidence of their arrival remained.

Lady Elizabeth, looking devastatingly beautiful in a white silk gown, her golden hair piled high on her head, quickly took control of the situation, sending servants scurrying in every direction to fulfill her orders. A doctor already was waiting to tend to Nick as he was carried into Lady Elizabeth's own bedroom.

Kate did not follow, but instead turned tiredly to follow the young parlor maid who had been assigned to show her to her room. The superhuman courage and strength she had needed that afternoon finally were taking their toll. Her bedroom was spacious and bright, but Kate hardly noticed the elegant white velvet draperies and gold-trimmed furnishings as she poured water from a china pitcher into a bowl. She washed away the dirt and perspiration and Nick's blood from her breasts, arms, hands, and face. Another man's blood on her. Just like Jack's. Only Nick was not dead. At least, not yet.

Slipping out of her ruined gown, she fell exhausted across the wide four-poster bed.

Kate dosed fitfully. A half-formed thought tugged at her consciousness, troubling her sleep. She kept remembering Nick's limp form beside her in the wagon. At that moment, she had willed him to live. The thought of his dying, or being gone forever, brought her a feeling of terrible emptiness.

Kate sat up in bed and stared unseeingly at the dusk-shadowed room about her, her mind in a turmoil. In the wagon she had desperately wanted Nick to live, so that all their efforts to free him wouldn't have been in vain. At least that was what she told herself. Or perhaps it was pity she felt for his tortured body. Surely it was patriotism, or her love of adventure and danger that she never could seem to overcome, that had made her risk her life to save him.

But as Kate sank back into the deep feather pillows, she knew that none of these things were true. With a sigh, Kate let herself admit what it was she did feel for Nick Fletcher. Here was a man like no other she had ever known, a man who moved her to depths of feeling she could not explain. Kate groaned and buried her face in the fluffy white pillow.

"My God, you've done it this time, haven't you, Kathleen?" she mumbled into the pillow, rebuking herself contemptuously. "You've finally really fallen in love. And with whom? Nick Fletcher! A man who cares nothing for you! What irony!"

Kate laughed scornfully as she closed her eyes, finally to sleep, tormented by Nick's face coming into and out of her dreams.

Chapter 46

Hours later, Kate was awakened by a soft knock at her door. Through sleepy eyes she saw Lady Elizabeth enter and come toward her. Kate raised up on one elbow, feeling stiff and sore from the bumps she'd gotten during the wild wagon ride.

"What do you want?" Kate asked with irritation. Lady Elizabeth was lighting the small lamp at the side of her bed. Kate never had liked this lovely creature who now stood before her, and now she knew why. They were rivals...rivals for the same man. Nick.

Nick! Memory came rushing back to her, and she sat up in alarm.

"How's Nick?" she asked urgently. "He's not...?"

She could not bring herself to say it and was relieved to see Elizabeth shake her head as she answered.

"He's still unconscious, but resting easier. The doctor has seen to his injuries. He'll have great pain and make everyone's life miserable for a while, but he'll recover."

Kate turned away from the look in Elizabeth's eyes. It was so full of love.

"Thank you for telling me," Kate murmured automatically, still looking away.

"Kathleen," Elizabeth said softly, "I've come to thank you."

Kate swung her head around in surprise.

"What? Thank me?"

"Yes, to thank you, for Nick's life. Guy told me what you did. You are very brave. I'm eternally grateful."

Large tears showed in Elizabeth's soft brown eyes as she sat down on the edge of the bed and looked intently at Kate. Here was the woman Nick loved. How could Kate hope to compete with anyone so lovely, so elegant?

Before Kate could recover from her surprise, a young girl dressed in a maid's uniform came to stand in the doorway.

"Yes, Dora?" Elizabeth asked as she noticed the girl.

"Madame wished me to let her know when Captain Fletcher was awake."

A cry of joy escaped Elizabeth's lips as she jumped up and dashed to the door. Kate, too, scrambled off the bed, hastily pulled on a white silk wrapper that had been laid out for her, and followed Elizabeth to Nick's room. When Kate entered, Elizabeth already was rushing to Nick's side. Kate stopped just inside the door, suddenly aware of her disheveled appearance.

"Nicholas, my love, you are awake," Elizabeth sighed breathlessly, grasping his hand.

Kate could not see Nick's face from her place by the door, but she heard the warmth in his voice as he murmured Elizabeth's name. A sinking feeling swept through Kate, and tears stung her eyes. If she'd had any thoughts of trying to wrest Nick from Elizabeth, they were quelled now. Turning quickly to leave, Kate saw Guy Chadwick leaning nonchalantly against the fireplace mantel, watching her. Their eyes met, but Kate quickly dropped hers to hide her tears as she turned and ran down the hall to her room.

"Damn!" she cursed aloud, throwing herself down on the cushioned window seat. "Why did I have to fall in love with you, Nick Fletcher?"

Angry tears trickled down her cheeks as she gazed out the window at the moonlit night. A soft tap sounded at the door, but she ignored it. At length the door opened a little.

"Kate?" she heard Guy ask.

The room was dark, but Guy saw her profile in the moonlight-drenched window.

"May I come in?" he asked tentatively. Then, receiving no answer, he decided to come in anyway. "Are you all right, Kate?" he asked softly, concern telling in his voice.

"Yes," Kate heard herself whisper, though she didn't look at him.

"I know this has been a harrowing two days for you. We've all felt the pressure. We couldn't have done it without you," Guy stated gently as he came to stand by her and put his hand reassuringly on her shoulder.

"Thank you, Guy," Kate said, looking at him. "I guess I am drained. It was worse than I'd thought it would be. I went into it as somewhat of a lark, you know. I guess I didn't realize what might happen. Nick was hurt so badly...and I've never killed a man before, Guy, not even a man like Sykes, who deserved to die."

"I know, Kate," Guy sympathized. "It was a hard thing to do. But we're all grateful to you, Nick most of all."

"I don't want his gratitude! I don't want anything from him!" Kate lashed out, jumping to her feet and pacing the room.

She was silent for a few minutes. Guy said nothing but watched Kate closely. He had seen the look of love on her face in Nick's room.

As she lighted the lamp on the bedstand, Kate spoke, her voice solemn and purposeful.

"Guy, what are the rest of you going to do now? I mean, when are you leaving here?"

"Now? Bennett, Ginty, and I plan to leave at midnight," Guy explained, not surprised by her sudden change of subject. "They'll rejoin the *Sea Mist* crew. The ship is anchored in Duncan's Cove. It should be safe there, until Nick's ready to go aboard again. Henry insists on going back to the inn, although I think it's dangerous. I'm going back to Chadwick Manor. The less time spent around here, the better, is my feeling."

"Yes, I agree," Kate replied, staring into space. Then she turned, looking at him intently, her decision made. "Guy, I want to go with you to Chadwick Manor."

Guy was quiet for a moment.

"Are you sure, Kate? You'd be running away, you know."

"We all need to get away after this day's work," Kate

291

retorted, purposely misconstruing his meaning. "Didn't you say there was a hospital set up on your estate?" Kate went on.

"Yes."

"I could help with that, Guy. I need something to keep me busy, to keep my mind off what's happened." There was a note of urgency in her voice.

"All right, Kate," Guy acquiesced. "If that's what you want. It sounds as though you need some time to sort things out. You're more than welcome."

Guy walked slowly to the door, his expression contemplative. If Kate wished to deny what she obviously felt for Nick, Guy thought to himself smugly, then let her. What a turn of luck for him. The very opportunity he had hoped for, and she herself had suggested it. At Chadwick Manor he could pursue her at his leisure. Unrequited love made a woman vulnerable. She would fall easy prey to his charms. The gentle, understanding approach would be the one to use. He would have Kate. Guy was determined to possess her. He smiled to himself as he paused at the door and turned back to Kate.

"Be ready to leave at midnight, Kate."

Kate borrowed a black riding habit and a few other things from Lady Elizabeth, who made only a weak protest when Kate told her she was leaving. Most of Kate's things still were at High Creek Farm. She'd send for them later. At midnight, without seeing Nick again, Kate mounted the horse Guy held for her and departed Huntington House.

Chapter 47

Kate stared unseeingly into the flickering flames of the fireplace in Guy Chadwick's study. She had been trying to read, but her mind wandered, as it did so often of late, and she found herself thinking of Nick again. It was impossible to get him out of her mind.

Kate had cared deeply for a few other men in the past. There had been Tom Driscoll, whom she'd thought she loved. She thought of Tom now. She had been only a girl of sixteen when they'd met—so young, so naïve. Her father had wholeheartedly sanctioned the idea of their marriage when Tom had proposed it. Gentle, steady Tom, builder of ships. They were to have been married in the autumn after that one last voyage to test his latest designs on his brigantine *Celeste*. The summer months had sped away for Kate as she planned the wedding. She'd been so excited; the future had looked so wonderful.

But then, at the end of August, word had come that the *Celeste* had barely limped back to port, most of her crew dead from the terrible fever that had come from the drinking water. Tom was dead.

Kate had been devastated. How she had mourned Tom. After almost a year in this low state of mind, her father, in desperation, finally had convinced her to travel to Paris to attend a finishing school and have a change of scene. He had not accompanied her, for he was committed to several important legal matters, and he could not bear to continue to watch his beloved daughter so distraught with grief.

Kate realized now that she had not really loved Tom. Hers had been a schoolgirl's infatuation. He was handsome, charming, and very rich. She saw now that much of her mourning had been for herself—self-pity for all she had lost.

She'd been careful about men the past few years, wanting to avoid hurt. Jack had been the last man in her life, over a year and a half ago. Gentleman Jack Donovan. The big, red-headed Irishman. They'd been on assignment together—the three of them, her father, Jack, and Kate. Their work had stretched into several weeks. Jack had taught her many things, including how to feel again. He was big and bold and full of life. The world was his oyster. His personality drew people to him like a magnet. Yet he could be gentle and understanding. He had been so patient and tender with her, nurturing her passion as a gardener nurtures a delicate flower. Kate had felt a great tenderness for him. He was a good man. She loved him, but it had been the love one feels for a cherished friend. When Jack had disappeared from the riverboat on which they'd been traveling, Kate had been frantic with worry. But there had been nothing they could do. Her father feared he may have been murdered, his body thrown overboard. For their own safety, they had fled the ship at its next stop. They never were able to find out what had happened to Jack, until Kate had seen him at the Harrington Hotel that terrible day when Fate had dealt him her last hand. What a shame it was, Jack's death. Such a waste. The world needed men like Jack Donovan.

A half-burned log shifted in the grate, and the noise of its movement brought Kate's thoughts back to Guy's study. The world needs men like Nick Fletcher, too, she thought, to fight its battles, win its causes, build its nations. Daring, courageous men who fight for their beliefs.

But then there was Nicholas Fletcher, pirate, seducer of women. How had she ever let herself fall in love with him? Kate asked herself scornfully. She felt like a moonstruck schoolgirl and cursed herself for her weakness. Letting her feelings run so rampant could only lead to hurt, she knew. But try as she might, she couldn't keep thoughts of him from pervading her mind. There was a dull ache in her stomach. When her thoughts lingered on their shared moments of love-making, Kate knew a longing for Nick that left her feeling weak and empty. She cursed herself and shook her head, trying to force thoughts of Nick from her consciousness. She would overcome this, she tried to convince herself. No man would claim her, use her! She needed no one!

Yet the thought of Nick's handsome face, his piercing blue eyes, continued to torment her. She longed to feel his hard-muscled body against her, his lips and hands touching her tenderly, passionately. Oh, why did her mind torture her with its memories?

Kate knew it was more than just a woman's longing for a man that she felt. She had grown to respect and admire Nick. He was strong of will, daring of spirit, and intensely loyal to people and causes he felt were just.

"Oh, if only he weren't so damned handsome and yet so damned arrogant, too!" Kate whispered vehemently, angry at Nick and herself again. Then the tears began to flow, for Kate felt the hopeless frustration of one who knows no hope of fulfilling the love she has come to feel.

She toyed with the idea of going after Nick, of using every wile and trick she could think of to win him away from Lady Elizabeth. Kate was accustomed to going after what she wanted. Yet her pride held her back. She wasn't sure that having Nick would bring her anything but more pain, for he did not seem to be the kind of man who could be tied to one woman. And she never could share a man. Besides, Nick didn't love her. He only used her and cast her aside. How she hated him! And loved him. And wished she were dead to end this torment.

So the days passed, with Kate's feelings leaving her unpredictably moody. One moment she would be happy and laughing; the next, quiet and sad.

Chapter 48

At first Guy Chadwick had stayed well away from the makeshift hospital located about a half mile from the main house of his family estate. A large barn had been quickly but adequately refurbished with cots, divider screens, and operating and dispensary facilities. A large shed attached to the barn had been converted to a kitchen, where meals were prepared for the battle-worn soldiers. There was an abundance of bed linen, bandages, instruments, and medicines, all provided by the wealthy Guy Chadwick.

But Guy had kept his distance from the place, having no desire to see or be among the maimed and broken men and boys who passed endlessly through its wards. He was more inclined to the life of wealth and ease he had known since birth. What few social gatherings there were in this time of national strife he attended with a flourish, dressing with the utmost care, with an eye to the latest European fashions. He had a devilish wit and charm, which made him a favorite with the ladies.

Kate attended several affairs with him, amid many whispers and much speculation, which delighted her no end. But much of the time she was too exhausted from her long hours at the hospital to want to do anything but fall into bed at night. She would sleep deeply. No steel-blue eyes or handsome, smirking face invaded her dreamless sleep, and that was the way she wanted it. Nick Fletcher haunted her thoughts enough during her waking hours, whenever she had a few moments to herself for reflection.

Therefore, much to Guy's chagrin, he had not much opportunity to ply his case and woo the fair damsel, as was his plan in bringing Kate to Chadwick Manor. It did not take Guy long to discern that if he wanted to spend more time with Kate, he had to be where she was, and that was the hospital. His intentions were to see Kate as often as her self-appointed duties would allow and to lure her away from the wearying, unending tasks.

Hour after hour, Kate helped the doctor stitch cuts and bandage gaping holes in every limb, on every part of men's bodies. She fed men too tired, weak, or maimed to do it themselves. She wrote joyous letters to worried loved ones for soldiers who would eventually return home, ravaged by war, but alive. And she labored by lamplight long into the warm late-summer nights trying to find the words to write to families who would not see their men again.

So Guy found himself thrust more and more into the activities of the hospital. Even the rakish and carefree Guy Chadwick could not long be around these brave but anguished men without being affected. He began to help whenever he could with the patients, moving them, talking with them, using his wit to bring laughter where there was much pain. But his real contribution came in freeing Kate and Dr. Weatherby from the administrative requirements; he was constantly seen inventorying food, supplies, medicines. His efficiency kept their supplies at an ample level, at considerable expense to his estate, Kate knew.

Kate began to see Guy Chadwick in a new light. There was a seriousness, a purposefulness about him that she felt was long needed and very appealing. This newfound dimension of the man had more influence on Kate than any of his well-practiced courting techniques.

Kate was in her bedroom. The hour was late. She was weary but determined to finish the sad task before her. It was the last letter she could write tonight. Kate was tired, tired of men moaning in pain, boys dying; tired of broken bones, blood; tired of war; tired of being the one to write these awful letters. She turned down the wick of the lamp and walked to the open doors of the balcony off her room. The night was warm but pleasant. Moonlight touched the lawn and the coarse, gray stone of the manor house.

The tears would not stop. Kate thought of the inadequate words she had just written. She felt herself giving in to hysteria. You have done what you can do, she told herself. You cannot save them all.

On the balcony Kate stretched and breathed deeply of the fragrant air. She thought of young Jeff, Nick's cabin boy. She was glad she'd been able to help him. At least he was safe now on the *Sea Mist,* anchored safely in Duncan's Cove, awaiting Nick's return. Perhaps Nick already was away on his ship. His wounds had been bad, though, and he probably would still be mending at Lady Elizabeth's. Besides, she thought coldly, he would likely not be too anxious to leave that attentive lady.

"This isn't like you, Kate Prescott," Kate chided herself aloud as she went back into the bedroom and undressed for bed. "If you want Nick, go after him, as you do anything you want. Don't let a little thing like a beautiful, wealthy woman who has his love stand in your way!" she said sarcastically as she slipped on her thin lace nightgown and lay down on the cool white sheets. Even Nick had told her one day on his ship when they'd spotted the British man-of-war that it was foolish to stay and fight when you had no chance of winning. And her chances of winning him away from Lady Elizabeth were slim at best. But even if Kate succeeded in getting him, what then? She doubted Nick would be a good husband, and that was what she needed and wanted now. God knew, Nick was short on patience, tolerance, and compassion when it came to her.

"I would be so much better off just to forget him. That's what I must do," Kate tried to convince herself as she tossed and turned, pounding her fist into her pillow, taking out her frustration on it. Exhaustion finally took its toll, and she was released for a while from the longing that haunted her.

In the morning, as Kate lounged in her large, four-poster bed before rising, she came to a decision. She had to get away, even if only for a little while. The hospital and haunting thoughts of Nick were getting down her usually buoyant spirit. A couple of days' holiday would do wonders for her, she decided. Perhaps she should act on Mr. Franklin's suggestion that she see Lady Victoria Remington in Albany. Kate's curiosity again was piqued by his evasiveness, his unwillingness to give her more information.

She would go at once. She thought to invite Guy to go with her, but then she remembered that he'd told her he was leaving early this morning for Hillsboro to buy more supplies for the hospital. Perhaps it was better that he was not here. He might try to dissuade her from going. After all, there was a war on. But there was no fighting reported in the vicinity to which she would be traveling.

Kate looked at the ornately carved clock on the marble mantel—eight o'clock. She threw back the sheet. She dressed quickly in a pale yellow cotton gown with matching bonnet. Her steps were light as she went downstairs to the kitchen to get a quick bite to eat and leave a message for Guy. The hospital would survive without her for a couple of days. Casualties had not been heavy the past few days, so the doctor would get by for a while. Kate wrote a quick message to him also, as she waited for Guy's carriage.

So, one hour after awaking, Kate was on the road for Albany. As Fenton, the driver, skillfully held the horses to an even canter, Kate settled back to plan her holiday. It took most of the day to travel from Chadwick Manor to Albany. Established in 1614, this small city located on the Hudson River had the distinction of being the second-oldest permanent settlement in the original thirteen colonies.

It was getting dark when Fenton finally stopped the carriage before a suitable-looking inn on the outskirts of the city. He told Kate that this was a favorite lodging place of Mr. Chadwick's. Kate was tired from the journey and glad to stop for the night.

After a restful night's sleep and a hearty breakfast the next morning, they were again on their way. The innkeeper had given Fenton directions to Remington House. It was only a half-hour's drive from the inn.

As the carriage wound its way slowly through the crowded streets to a well-to-do section of the city, the houses became large and elegant. They turned down several streets lined with huge trees and carefully manicured shrubbery.

Soon they came to a stop in the circular courtyard drive of a large brownstone house. White wrought-iron shutters covered the many long windows along the first and second stories. The elegance of design showed the skill of a fine architect.

Carlton, the footman, opened the door for Kate.

"Remington House, miss," he said, offering his hand to help her down.

Kate was feeling some trepidation as she stepped down to the flagstone pavement. She really had no business being here. She was not expected, and there was a good chance Lady Remington would not even see her. Yet Mr. Franklin had been so insistent.

Well, I've come this far, I might as well go the rest of the way, Kate thought as she straightened her back, took a deep breath, and climbed the ten stone steps to the door.

Her knock was answered by a stout, middle-aged butler. He looked down his nose at her in obvious disdain at seeing an unexpected, unescorted young woman on his doorstep.

"Yes, miss?" he asked coolly, his eyes glancing quickly from Kate to the liveried driver and two footmen, and the Chadwick crest emblazoned on the side of the carriage. His disapproval had visibly lessened when his eyes returned to survey Kate.

"Miss Kathleen Prescott to see Lady Remington," she answered, suppressing a smile.

"This way, please, miss," he directed without changing his expression.

"Wait for me, Fenton," Kate turned and called to the waiting driver.

After showing her to the parlor and bidding her wait, the butler closed the sliding doors behind him. Kate was left to survey her luxurious surroundings and wait to see if Lady Victoria Remington was receiving total strangers today.

Kate smiled to herself a little at the thought as she glanced around the beautiful room. Well, she decided, if Lady Remington wouldn't see her, she would spend the day shopping. It felt good to be away from the hospital for a while.

The room was done in powder-blue and cream hues. A brocade sofa faced across from the cream-colored marble fireplace. No fire had been set in the grate, as the day promised to be pleasantly warm. There were two long, glassed-in doors that led to a small rose garden. The first killing frost of the autumn season had not yet arrived. Roses of many hues drenched the garden in color.

Kate had turned away from the outside scene and was admiring some delicate white porcelain statues enclosed in a glass cabinet when the double doors to the hallway slid open and a middle-aged woman entered. At the sound, Kate turned to see a thin woman of medium height elegantly attired in a pale blue linen gown. Kate's first thought was that the woman matched the room perfectly; then she noticed that the woman seemed startled.

After a moment of mutual observation, the older woman recovered herself. She smiled warmly, and her soft brown eyes shone as she came forward into the room, holding out her hands to Kate.

"You are Kathleen, of course," she said happily. "I would have known you anywhere. I'm so glad you're here. Come, sit here, and we will talk. I'm Victoria Remington."

She led the bewildered Kate to the sofa, never releasing her hand.

"Lady Remington, I wasn't certain you would see me, or even recognize my name..." Kate began awkwardly.

Lady Remington patted her hand gently.

"Of course I know of you, my dear, and I have longed for this meeting for a great while. In fact, I have been trying to find you for months. Imagine my surprise and delight when Jerome told me you were here, that you had found me. However did you find your way to me, Kathleen?"

Kate stared at the lovely woman before her. Her shining brown hair, though flecked with gray, still was thick and done up in the latest fashion. Her face had few lines. Her bright and lively brown eyes met Kate's with warmth and friendliness.

"Forgive me, Lady Remington, I don't mean to stare. It's just that I'm somewhat at a loss in this situation. I am sorry to come uninvited, for as far as I know, we are unacquainted. But for Mr. Franklin's insistence, I would not be here."

"Ah, Benjamin, of course," Lady Remington said with understanding. "He is a dear friend, and I shall be forever grateful to him for directing you here. How much did he tell you of me and my family, my dear?"

"Very little," Kate answered. "To be honest, he told me only enough to whet my curiosity. He said that since I seemed to have no immediate family still living, and few friends here in America, perhaps I could find a friend and mentor in you. He said you were an old friend of my family."

"Yes, so like Benjamin," Lady Remington said and laughed. "Yet in those few words, my dear, he has done us both a great service."

At seeing Kate's confused look, Lady Remington laughed again.

"Have patience, Kathleen. All will be explained to you shortly. Will you have some tea?"

Kate longed to continue this strange conversation but knew she dare not further tread on the social proprieties by refusing the customary tea. So she had to wait and bide her impatience while Lady Remington called for tea. It arrived promptly, and Lady Remington served the steaming liquid in delicate translucent china cups, with a variety of pastries.

"Forgive me for being frank," Kate began as soon as a proper interval had elapsed, "but Mr. Franklin said you were an old friend, yet I do not recall ever meeting you before nor even hearing your name spoken in my youth. I confess to wondering, then, how you can be a close friend of my family." Kate watched the older woman carefully.

"Yes, let us speak frankly, my dear," Lady Remington said with a smile. "I admire that. It doesn't surprise me that you have not heard of me before. I knew your parents long ago, before they were married. I have not seen or spoken with your father since before your mother's death. Your father and I wrote to each other for a year or two after that, but I lived in Paris and then here, and finally we lost touch."

She paused, lost in thought. When her gaze again focused on Kate, her voice was soft and low.

"You have your father's eyes, you know—so blue, so expressive. When he smiled, his eyes seemed to smile, too..."

Kate shifted uncomfortably under Lady Remington's gaze. That was exactly the way she remembered her father's eyes. And this woman had remembered this about him for almost twenty-five years. It was both comforting and disturbing to speak of her father like this. Kate had longed to do so, but there had been no one to share her memories.

"Do you know of his death?" Kate asked quietly, feeling long-suppressed tears pushing against her eyes.

Lady Remington touched her hand and spoke gently. "Yes, my dear. I had asked Benjamin to get in touch with your father for me when I learned he and James were friends. It was shortly thereafter that he learned of your father's death. He said the circumstances surrounding his death were questionable, that he did not die of natural causes. Beyond that, I know no details."

Kate sensed a feeling of great loss and pain from the older woman as she spoke. Kate felt a closeness to Lady Remington. Here was a woman she could trust. Lady Remington seemed to be waiting for Kate to speak, allowing her to continue the story if she chose. Kate knew that the matter would be closed if she decided not to elaborate.

"My father was murdered as he slept." Kate's voice broke as she spoke. She rose from the sofa and slowly paced the room. "I don't think he suffered."

A look of anguish crossed Lady Remington's face briefly, but she said nothing. Kate could feel the sympathy emanating from the older woman.

"During the last few years of his life," Kate went on

to explain, her voice controlled but strained, "my father was deeply involved in furthering the American cause. He firmly believed America should be a free and independent nation. When his public outcry gained him little except influential enemies, he chose to work quietly. He worked closely with Mr. Franklin. When I finally learned of his deep involvement and commitment to the revolution, I decided to join him in it. His patriotism for America was infectious. But I think now I joined the intrigue more for the adventure of it than from dedication to a cause.

"But murder gives an ugly taint to adventure. Father was killed because of his vast influence. That is when I decided to get out. Start a new life. It has not been easy." A sob escaped Kate. She could no longer hold back her feelings.

"Oh, my dear. I am so sorry," Lady Remington said as she came to Kate and gathered her in her arms. "Come sit with me and we shall mourn together. You, for the dear father you lost, and I, for the man I loved but could not have. His murderer robbed us both."

Chapter 49

The two women wept together.

"You are no doubt surprised to learn that I loved your father," Lady Remington began softly. Her red-rimmed eyes took on a faraway look. "It was a long time ago, but still I remember it well. We were very young, your mother and father and I. Amanda and I were close friends, like sisters. We spent much of our youth together, as our mothers were good friends.

"I remember when we first saw your father. It was at a coming-out ball. Your mother and I had just had our own several months earlier and were greatly enjoying the lively social life of young debutantes. James was one of the many young blades that season, yet he stood out in the crowd because of his looks, his charm, and his humor."

There was a long silence as Lady Remington went back in her mind to that evening so many years ago. She began to speak again.

A bewildered but enthralled Kate listened as Lady Remington continued her story of her friendship with Amanda and their competition for the attention of James Prescott. He courted them both, but she began to realize that it was Amanda he preferred.

"One night he came to call," Lady Remington continued. "I never shall forget it. He told me that he was in love with Amanda, your mother. I was amazed that

I stayed so calm. I suppose it was because I was not completely surprised.

"Still, I loved him. I was determined to try to win him. It almost destroyed my friendship with your mother forever. This may seem shocking, but I set about to seduce James, thinking he would then do the honorable thing and marry me. I knew I would be able to make him learn to love me.

"I planned things very carefully. It was at another party. It was very late. We had all had too much to drink. Many of us were staying the night, because it was a good distance from London.

"When the party finally ended, we found our way to our rooms. I remember James needed to be helped by a servant to find his room. I waited until the house was quiet. Then I slipped into his room." Here Lady Remington paused in her story to look at Kate. "You will think me a terrible woman upon hearing this, but I was desperately in love."

Kate nodded but still said nothing; she was spellbound.

"James was in a deep sleep, brought on by the liquor he'd had.

"I was able to wake him enough to arouse him to make love to me. At the climax of his passion, he called Amanda's name. I was devastated, heartbroken. I realized then I never could make him love me. I slipped out of his room, determined to put him out of my mind, out of my life. But it was not to be."

Lady Remington paused, deep in thought, and Kate had a moment of her own to reflect on trying to get a man out of your heart, your life. Her heart went out to the woman beside her.

"Kathleen, for what I am about to reveal, I must ask your vow of silence. You must promise that you never will speak of this unless I personally release you from your vow. Will you so promise?"

Lady Remington looked anxiously at Kate, trying to read her thoughts. Kate was at a loss for words, but she knew she must give her promise, for she felt certain she would learn nothing more if she did not.

"Yes, of course, I pledge you my word, Your Ladyship."

"Then come, Kathleen," Lady Remington said as she rose and turned toward the door. "I wish to show you something."

Kate followed her down a long hallway into a book-lined study.

Lady Remington sat down in a chair and gestured to Kate to sit in one beside it. Lady Remington's hand directed Kate's attention to a picture over the mantel. Kate did not recognize the man in the portrait.

"My late husband, Charles," Lady Remington explained. "He was a fine man. He died two years ago. I miss him very much."

Lady Remington raised her hand to stop Kate's words of sympathy.

"Let me continue my story, Kathleen, for it is this next part that was the reason for my search for you.

"Charles was the son and heir of a thriving shipping company owner in Boston. He was handsome and polite, gentle and caring. We had met through family friends, but I had not taken much interest because of my love for your father. After that disastrous night, I was determined to forget James. I then turned my attention to Charles. He was an easy conquest, for he truly was in love with me. He was leaving within two months for a position in his father's company office in Paris. He asked me to marry him, and I accepted. We had a hasty but beautiful wedding and a wonderful twenty-three years together. I grew to love and cherish him and will forever hold precious the memory of those years with Charles."

Lady Remington rose and crossed the room to another portrait hung above the row of book-filled shelves.

"These are our children. Sara Jane, the youngest," she pointed to a smiling, auburn-haired young woman of about nineteen. "She is just recently married and living in Boston." She pointed to the other woman in the portrait, a lovely, blue-eyed replica of herself. "My daughter Margaret Renee. And my son."

Here Lady Remington paused to watch Kate's face as her eyes came to rest on the tall, handsome young man in the painting.

"Peter James Remington."

Kate was stunned. She opened her mouth to speak,

then closed it. The blue eyes that looked back at her were so familiar. The straight nose, the curly brown hair. Only the mouth and slight smile she could not place, until she realized they matched Lady Remington's.

"Peter James?" Kate questioned as she pulled her gaze away to look at the woman next to her.

"Your half brother, Kathleen."

"But how? Did my father ever know? Where is he now? Is he here?" Kate's questions tumbled out in a rush. Lady Remington smiled understandingly and raised her hand to stop the flow of questions.

"Be patient, my dear. I will answer all your questions. You have a right to know."

She glanced back at the portrait of her children and continued.

"Your father never knew it was I in his arms that night. Alas, I am certain he remembered nothing of the event. He would have approached me had he suspected. He was that kind of man.

"In the weeks that followed, I tried not to see James, for I was certain I somehow would reveal the guilty secret of that night. I concentrated on winning Charles. But soon I discovered I had another secret to hide. You see, I was both cursed and blessed the night I lay with your father. Cursed because I knew I never would have his love, even though I carried his child. But I was blessed also because by having that child, I always would have a part of James with me.

"I planned to tell him but not marry him. I knew he never would love me the way he loved your mother. I felt he had the right to know about his child, yet I knew it would only bring unhappiness to all of us. Disgrace to me and my family. Shame to James. Heartbreak to Amanda. Charles posed the perfect solution by asking me to marry him. We were quickly wed and left the country for Paris. My son was born eight months afterward. He was thought to be premature. He had blue eyes like Charles. Only I knew whose blue eyes they really were. Charles loved Peter with all his heart. He was so proud of him. I could not bear to tell him the truth. Perhaps you will think me selfish and cowardly, but, believe me, I have paid dearly over all these years by having to bear this secret."

Lady Remington was silent for a moment.

"Your mother and I kept in touch by letter. She was so happy to be pregnant with you. She was kind and sweet and had no malice in her for anyone. I loved her dearly. I think she would have forgiven me for what I did, but I could not bear to bring her pain.

"After she died in childbirth, your father and I corresponded for a few years, then we lost touch. You were his life and joy, Kathleen. He loved you more than anything in the world."

"I know," was all Kate could whisper.

"I thought often of telling James about Peter after your mother died, but I couldn't do it. By then I was in love with Charles and so content with our life together. I was afraid Charles would not look on us with the same love and devotion if he knew. Then I became pregnant with Margaret and knew the secret must remain within me for the sake of holding my family together.

"We lived in Paris for ten years, then came here to America. Peter's resemblance to James did not become so apparent until he was older. By then we lived here, and anyone who might have remembered my association with James Prescott still was in England. Charles never had met him. My secret was safe, but a terrible weight to bear. One night of youthful impulsiveness has caused a lifetime of pain. Oh, do not misunderstand. I have never regreted having Peter. I love all my children dearly, but Peter holds a special place in my heart. He is a fine son, one any man would be proud to call his own.

"When Charles died, I sought out Benjamin Franklin. He is an old friend and often travels to England. I asked him to contact your father for me. I decided to tell James he had a son. Charles no longer could be hurt by the truth. But it was too late. Your father was killed before Benjamin could find him. He was terribly elusive those last months. You have explained that in telling me of his secret work. You were still alive but not to be found. And then today you appear, like a ghost from the past, looking so much like the blending of

James and Amanda that I would have known you anywhere.

"So that is the tale. I feel greatly relieved at finally having told it. Benjamin suspected some of my secret, but you are the first to know all the truth. I hope you can forgive me, Kathleen."

Lady Remington laid her hand on Kate's arm and looked at her beseechingly. Kate was silent for a long while, deep in thought. She was shocked, overwhelmed by what she had heard. She needed time to absorb all this. When she finally spoke, she chose her words carefully.

"It would have brought the greatest of joy to my father to know he had a son, for I feel each man always hopes for a son to carry on his life and name. But my father gave me his total love, and I doubt he would have cared for a son any more than he did for me. However, that is in the past now and cannot be changed. In my heart, I feel he knows about Peter. God is just in that.

"I know what a heavy burden you have had to bear withholding this secret. You did it out of love, and I suppose you did the right thing. We all do things we wish we could change afterward. I am grateful you have confided in me, for you have given me what I thought I did not have—blood family, a brother. I cannot tell you what that means to me."

Kate was weeping as she leaned forward and embraced Victoria Remington. She felt the older woman sigh deeply. She wept with Kate, her joy and relief flooding forth. When finally she could speak, she said, "Kathleen, now you see why I must have your silence. Peter knows nothing of this. He loved Charles as his father and holds dear his memory. They were very close, and Charles' death affected Peter greatly."

"Yes, I understand," Kate continued for her. "To learn now that Lord Remington was not his natural father could be devastating."

"Peter is strong," Lady Remington said proudly. "I do not think such knowledge would destroy him. If I thought as much, I never would have told you all of this.

"And yet no man could help but be affected in some

ways by learning such a truth. And what purpose would it serve now? It only would bring him pain. I cannot decide whether I ever will tell him. And until I do, I must have your silence."

"Yes, I understand. But may I at least meet Peter? Oh, I do so want that. To know my brother...True, he is only my half brother, but family still. You could introduce me as I truly am—the daughter of two old friends of yours," Kate said eagerly.

"Of course you shall meet him, my dear," Lady Remington assured her. "In fact, I insist that you stay here with me until he returns from Canada where he is seeking support and supplies for His Majesty. From what you have told me, I fear James would have been greatly distressed to learn his son is a loyal British subject. As for me, I leave politics to others. I am first an Englishwoman, yet I feel the American cause is in many ways just also. So I try not to take sides and strive to keep my children out of the dangers of war. At any rate, Peter is due to return the middle of October. I would so love to have you stay here with me, if you have no other commitments. Please consider this your home."

"Oh, Lady Remington, you are too kind," Kate admonished. "You make such a generous offer, and you hardly know me."

"Nonsense, Kathleen," Lady Remington said gently. "You are James' daughter. Had events chanced to be different, you may have been my daughter as well. You always will be welcome in my family. After Peter returns, we will be making preparations to leave for France at the end of November. We are going for an extended visit with my daughter Margaret and her family. My husband's brother is an official high in His Majesty's court. At my asking, he has arranged a diplomatic post for Peter in France. Peter does not know of my influence in this. He would not accept the position if he did. I know I should not interfere in my son's life so. But I will not have him maimed or killed in battle. He wants to join the army. So far I have managed to dissuade him. I think he will accept the diplomatic post if he believes he is doing something important for Britain. I shall strive to convince him of that. I want my son alive. Surely, you can understand that, Kathleen. War is such a senseless waste."

"Yes, I agree with you, Your Ladyship," Kate replied. "I have seen first hand the destruction to life and limb that war brings."

"You could come with us, Kathleen. Let me offer you the refuge of my family. It cannot be easy for a beautiful young woman alone. Come, you must tell me how it is with you," Lady Remington coaxed.

"I fear you may find some of it not to your liking," Kate admitted, her eyes downcast. "You are right. The last year or two have been very difficult. Father, in his zealousness, spent much of our family wealth for America. There is little left. I must admit to you that, at the moment, my future is most uncertain."

Lady Remington's smile was gentle as she lifted Kate's chin with her finger until their eyes met.

"Please call me Victoria, Kathleen, and tell me. Unburden yourself. I will not be shocked. I will not judge you, I promise. I opened my soul to you; now you must trust me to care about you as your own mother would have done."

"I would so love to talk to someone," Kate said gratefully.

"Then I am here to listen," Lady Remington assured her.

Without going into great detail but still relating the important events, Kate told Victoria Remington about her life, ending with her espionage work with her father and her encounters with Nick Fletcher. Although she did not admit to loving him, Kate sensed that Lady Remington knew the true inclination of her heart, for she smiled knowingly as Kate related more and more about him and the part he was playing in her life.

Lady Remington was adamant about Kate's staying with her and accepting the refuge and protection she and Peter could offer her. She was greatly alarmed by the stories of the attempts on Kate's life.

Kate was amazed that she felt so open and comfortable with someone she had just met. She had only felt so with her father. It was such a relief to share her thoughts, fears, and feelings with someone as caring and understanding as Victoria Remington. Yet, Kate sensed also that here was a woman of strong will and capability. She felt she could be a pillar of strength, and Kate needed that now, to raise her own flagging spirit.

Kate agreed to spend that one night with Lady Remington, but she had an obligation to Guy and the hospital. She could not just pick up and leave. And she had much to sort out in her mind. She needed time to think and decide. Lady Remington understood and reluctantly agreed. They spent their remaining time together talking of the past. Kate felt a great reluctance to leave when the time for it came the next morning. She promised to return as soon as possible. She could not leave the hospital until she was sure Guy had found a replacement for her. The need was so great there. Yet she was almost certain she wanted to go to France with her half brother and Victoria. In the space of a day, Kate had grown very close to this proud and elegant woman who, but for a chance of Fate, might have been her mother.

And here indeed was the answer to the question of her future. After all, how many choices did a twenty-four-year-old unmarried woman of limited reputation and financial means have in these times? Her chance with Robert Krenshaw was gone, Kate knew. Nick had made no offers and wasn't likely to. He only ruined all the plans she made. Guy Chadwick was a possibility, but, while she liked him very much, she did not love him. With the Remingtons, she would be among friends, family. She could put the horror, the uncertainty of the past year, the past few months, behind her. Perhaps in Paris she would then have the chance to find someone to love, someone who would love her in return. She would have time and not have to decide things while under the pressure of immediate need.

As she waved good-bye from the window of the carriage the next morning, Kate couldn't help but feel happy, and very grateful to Mr. Benjamin Franklin, that dear man of Philadelphia. He had wrought a miracle in her life.

Chapter 50

Guy Chadwick was outraged with Kate when she arrived back at the manor that night. He ranted and raved for a full twenty minutes on what a foolish idea it had been for her to go to Albany alone in such dangerous times. He paced angrily about the room, shaking his finger at Kate menacingly. She knew she should be sorry for worrying him so, but she could only try to hold in her laughter and look at the floor in pretended remorse.

"How could you do such a thing, Kate, especially without first consulting me?" Guy finally ended his shouting, coming to a halt directly in front of her.

Kate slowly raised her eyes, blinking her long, dark lashes beguilingly, as she looked at him.

"Oh, Guy, I am sorry for not telling you I was going," she said sincerely. "But I really didn't plan it. It was just an impulse. I realize now it might have been dangerous, but I was only in Albany two days, and I was very careful. I had to get away for a while. You can understand that, can't you?"

Kate had risen and was intentionally standing very close to Guy. She heard his breath quicken and was well aware of the effect she was having on him. He took a deep breath and forced himself to step back from her.

"Of course I can understand how things were getting to you here, Kate. But you took a foolish risk. I never would have forgiven myself if something had happened to you."

"You're right, Guy, it *was* foolhardy, but nothing happened. I won't do it again. Next time I need a holiday, I'll spend every minute with you."

Kate moved toward him coquettishly, placing her hands on his shoulders. Guy removed her hands and smiled at her.

"No need to work your ways on me, vixen. I am putty in the hands of a beautiful woman, as you know. You are forgiven—this time. So come, let me hear all about your trip."

Kate laughed. She could barely contain her excitement. How she wished she could tell him everything. But she told him only about Benjamin Franklin's suggestion that she visit Lady Remington, an old friend of her parents. She did not mention that she might join the Remingtons in November; she wanted to give more thought to that decision.

"I have heard of the Remington Shipping Company. It has a notable reputation," Guy said after Kate had related her story. "Charles Remington was a fine man, but a staunch supporter of the Crown. Does his son take that position, too?"

"I believe Lady Remington mentioned they were Tory in inclination, Guy, but we really didn't get into politics. I did not get to meet Peter; he was away on business. And what difference would it make? I'm through with political intrigue. I want only to make a new life. Perhaps the Remingtons can assist me in that.

"But now, dear Guy, I am going to bed. I've had a long journey, and I'm dead tired. If you wish, we can continue this conversation tomorrow."

She smiled charmingly and blew him a good-night kiss as she left the sitting room.

Later, Guy lay on the large bed in his darkened room, smoking a thin cheroot. He was deep in thought. Moonlight flooded the room, making the smoke he blew dance and swirl. Where, he wondered, would he find the three wagons he needed to transport the dead tomorrow? Where was the new supply of laudanum to ease the anguish of amputation? He would have to travel to

Scarsdale tomorrow to find these and so many other necessities.

Guy was dead tired, but he had a feeling of contentedness, accomplishment he had not known before. It felt good to be helping these men who passed through his hospital, to be thinking of others instead of just himself. He believed in the revolution. America was a new nation, linked to England but not enslaved by it. This vast land could not be ruled from across the sea by laws and leaders steeped in archaic traditions and class systems. It had to be designed, shaped, ruled by the men who invested their lifesblood in the new land. He was sorry it had taken war to bring this about. The fighting in New York had sickened him. He wasn't like Nick Fletcher, a leader. He was a follower, and followers seldom were important, seldom made a difference in the outcome of events. But, at the manor, at the hospital, he was important. What he accomplished made a difference in men's lives, and he liked the feeling of it.

Only one thought marred his contentedness—Kate. His thoughts drifted to the room across the hall where she was asleep. In the weeks she'd been at the manor, he'd had little chance to pursue her. He thought he sensed a new attitude toward him when they were together. Her impulsive excursion to Albany, with all its possible dangers, had unnerved him. It made him realize that he cared for her, really cared. He still longed to have Kate, to feel her warm against him, to release the passion he had felt for her from the first time he'd seen her.

Yet now there was something more—a friendship had grown between them, a closeness. Guy was beginning to be in love with Kate.

He snubbed out the small cigar in the ashtray on the bedstand. He had an urge to see Kate, to watch her sleeping peacefully. It had become his habit of late, though Kate did not know it. Her door never was locked, and Guy enjoyed spending a few quiet moments in her room before returning to his own for the night. Many times he had longed to join her, to hold her closely, make love to her.

Guy marveled at his ability to withstand the temp-

319

tation of the beautiful Kathleen as she lay in slumber. She needed her rest. He could wait. Besides, his sixteen-hour days working for the hospital were taking their toll on him. He slept soundly each night, only occasionally having tempting dreams of the lovely woman who shared his home but not his bed.

Guy's hand had just touched the doorknob of Kate's room when a bloodcurdling scream came from within. Guy twisted the doorknob and pushed open the door with a mighty shove. Inside he found Kate sitting up in bed, holding her head in her hands. She was sobbing violently. He rushed to the bed and gathered her into his arms.

"Kate, Kate, darling, what is it? What's wrong?" he asked softly.

"The dream...a nightmare..." Kate sobbed in a hoarse whisper. Her sobs wracked her slim frame as she clung to him. Guy held her closely, stroking her hair and murmuring soothing words. At the door his housekeeper appeared with a lamp. A worried frown creased her forehead beneath her ruffled nightcap.

"Is Miss Prescott all right, sir?" she asked with concern.

"Yes, she'll be fine, Mrs. Rand. It was only a bad dream. Leave the lamp and go back to bed. I'll see to her," Guy answered.

"Very well, sir," she replied, much relieved. "Just call if you need me."

Guy heard her shuffling steps go down the hallway. He tightened his arms around Kate. He could feel her tears on his chest as she softly cried out her anguish. Finally the tears subsided and only Kate's jagged breathing broke the stillness of the night.

"Can you tell me about it?" he asked gently, still holding her and stroking her hair. "Would it help?"

Kate pulled away from him a little and reached for her lace handkerchief on the bedstand. She wiped her tear-stained eyes and cheeks before answering.

"It's the same nightmare I've had before, of finding my father murdered. The knife glistens with his blood as I pull it from his chest...." Kate's voice was barely a whisper. An anguished cry escaped her lips as she again pressed against Guy.

"There now, darling, you're safe here," he said softly. "Hold tight. I'm here. You're all right. You're safe, Kate."

Kate clung to Guy. She was so grateful to have him near. She thought of the times Nick had held her like this when the assassin's vicious attempts on her life had been so close at hand. She had gotten strength from him then, too, known his protection.

But he had left her each time, and she'd had to rely on her own strength. She didn't have much of that now. The hard work, the misery and anguish at the hospital had taken their toll of both physical strength and mental fortitude. She felt so lost and alone just then, and frightened. She needed Guy.

"Hold me, Guy, please hold me," she pleaded.

The softness of her lips against his bare chest was torture to Guy. He tightened his arms around Kate.

"Don't be frightened, darling," he soothed. "I'm here."

After a while, Kate quieted and relaxed against him. He thought she might be asleep. He gently laid her back against the pillows. But as he turned to move away, she caught his hand and drew him back.

"Don't go, Guy. Please don't go," she pleaded. "I feel so alone. I need you. Please stay with me...."

In the flickering lamplight, Kate's eyes were wide and shining from her tears. A saint could not have refused her—and Guy Chadwick was no saint. But something held him back. He sighed deeply and sat down next to Kate on the edge of the bed. He took her hand as he looked long and deeply at her. She was so beautiful and he wanted her so much, loved her so much. The smile that finally touched his lips was tender.

"You know, sweet Kate, since the first time I saw you months ago," he began softly, "I've wanted to hear you say those words to me. That you needed me, wanted me. In the past weeks we've been together here I've longed for it more than you know. But now that you have said them, now that all I desire is within my grasp, I cannot accept what you offer, Kate."

Kate sat up and started to protest, but he stopped her words with a finger pressed gently against her lips.

"No, hear me out, my Kate, for by saying these things, perhaps I can make my heart accept what my reason knows is true.

"You're tired, frightened, and so vulnerable now. You've been through so much. It would be easy to press my advantage..." Guy paused. His eyes went to the lamp's flickering flame, and he watched it unblinkingly for a few moments. Then he brought his gaze back to meet Kate's eyes. She watched him intently.

"But that would not be very fair of me, now would it, my love?" He smiled again and tried to lighten his tone. "I may be a rogue, but still I believe in fair play. And I don't consider it fair to either of us to take advantage of your weakness now. I also refuse to make love to a woman who is in love with another man."

Kate had to speak now.

"Guy, no. You're wrong. There is no one else," she said firmly.

"I wish I could believe you, Kate, but we both know that's not true," Guy said. He brought her hand to his lips and kissed it gently.

"It's taking all the strength I possess to resist you, believe me. But my pride is strong. I will not play second to Nick or any other man. I couldn't bear to know you were thinking of him when I held you in my arms."

"No!" Kate protested. Her eyebrows knit into a frown as she spoke. "I do *not* love Nick Fletcher. I want to forget him. How could I love a man who cares nothing for me? But I could love you, Guy. Truly I could. I think I am a little in love with you already. We could try. We could grow to love each other in the way you want."

Kate was unmindful of the lure of her beauty as she pleaded with Guy. Her shining hair was curled around her shoulders. Her body strained against the lace of her low-cut nightgown. It was almost more than Guy Chadwick could bear. The sight of her quickened his pulse and threatened his reason. He released her hand and rose to pace the room, which seemed suddenly hot and stuffy. He walked to the partially opened window and raised it its full length. The night breeze felt cool on his perspiring face and chest.

Neither Kate nor Guy spoke for a while. Kate watched him closely. She was so confused. The nightmare of her father's death was so vivid in her mind; it pressed aside all other thoughts. She didn't know how she felt about Guy, or even Nick, for that matter. She slumped against the pillows and sighed deeply. She felt so tired.

Guy came to sit by her on the bed again.

"Nick always would keep coming between us, Kate," he told her with quiet conviction. "I think I've known that since the day we took Nick to Liz after the escape from Douglass. The look on your face in the bedroom when he said Liz's name devastated me, for I knew then you loved Nick, but I overlooked it because I wanted you. I thought I could make you love me. I still want you. I do love you. But I can't bring myself to betray you or Nick. He's like a brother to me. You say he cares nothing for you, but I know you are wrong. Perhaps Nick doesn't realize it himself, but there is magnetism between the two of you; it will keep drawing you together until you finally stop fighting each other and give in to the voice of your hearts."

He looked suddenly uncomfortable. "My word! I must be getting old, taking on this role of father-advisor," he joked nervously as he stood and looked down at Kate.

"I don't know what to say, Guy," Kate said softly. She couldn't meet his gaze. She lowered her eyes to her hands, which were absently smoothing a wrinkled handkerchief.

"Say good night, love, and go to sleep," he stated flatly as he bent over to kiss her forehead. "I'll sit up here in the chair and watch over you. Should the nightmare return, I'll be close by."

As he reached over to turn down the lamp, Kate reached out and took his hand. She raised it to her lips and kissed it gently. Guy looked at her. Her blue eyes shone brightly with tears, but she was smiling as she whispered, "Thank you, Guy. Dear Guy..."

As Guy Chadwick settled into the cushioned armchair and sat watching Kate's moonlit form, he thought of Nick. He felt mad as hell at his friend. He'd just given up Kate, the woman he could have loved and cherished for the rest of his life, to Nick, and the bastard didn't even know it! Nick always was so involved running around the countryside rousing rebels and fighting wars that he'd let Kate slip through his fingers. Damn him for his blindness! He deserved to lose her!

But Guy knew he couldn't let that happen, not to Nick, not to Kate. If he couldn't have Kate, then he'd give her up only to Nick Fletcher. The task was to get the two of them together. And it would be no easy task. But he would do his best. In the morning he would go to see Nick and somehow bring him to his senses.

Chapter 51

After an early breakfast, Guy Chadwick left word for Kate that he had pressing business to attend to. Then he rode straight for Huntington House.

When Guy arrived, he was shown into the parlor, where Nick and Elizabeth were having a heated discussion. Upon seeing him, their voices stopped. Nick clearly was agitated, but he appeared relieved to see Guy. Elizabeth was irritated by the interruption, for she tapped her foot impatiently and scowled at Guy.

"Hello, you two," Guy greeted exuberantly. "How nice to see you both looking so well."

He kissed Elizabeth's trembling hand, trying hard to hide his amusement. He shook hands with Nick, who looked almost totally recovered. The gash he'd taken over his right eyebrow would leave a scar, but it was mending well. Guy could see a slight bulge under Nick's white shirt where the bandaged bullet wound still was healing. In the deep vee of Nick's unlaced shirt, he could see some pinkish welts. The wounds from the whip were healing, too.

"Liz, my dear," Guy addressed Lady Elizabeth sweetly, "would you mind if I spoke to Nick alone? It concerns a mutual acquaintance who is in need of help. But I don't want to bore you with the trying details. It will take only a short time."

Guy turned back to Nick with an air of dismissal.

Elizabeth could not see the broad grin on his face, but she sensed that she was being laughed at. She was too enraged to speak, but she had too much pride to make a scene. She knew from experience that they would side against her.

"We'll continue this later, Nick," she said icily.

"That one is a bit trying at times, isn't she, old boy?" Guy questioned, letting the merriment continue to show on his face.

"They all are, sooner or later," Nick replied in a chilly tone. "Being at such close quarters with Liz these past weeks is beginning to wear very thin. Actually, I'm sick to death of it!"

Guy laughed. He walked to the sideboard against one wall and poured himself a cup of coffee.

"I'm glad to see you looking so well, Nick," Guy said. "Apparently Liz has been diligent in her ministrations to you."

"'Diligent' is not the word I'd use," Nick replied. He smiled slightly and shook his head. "Actually, I'm being damned hard on her. She's been good to me. I'm hardly an ideal patient. This forced idleness is driving me crazy. But enough of this. It's good to see you, Guy. Where in the hell have you been keeping yourself? And who needs help?"

"The answer to both of those questions is the same," Guy answered. Nick noticed a change in his friend's tone.

"A certain auburn-haired, blue-eyed beauty, whose providential appearance on the scene has changed both our lives, is the one I mean," Guy continued.

Nick's face registered understanding. "Kate, of course," he said dryly. "How is our reckless little spitfire these days?" he asked with an air of indifference which belied the turmoil rising in him at the mention of her name. "I trust she's been bringing much pleasure into your life these past weeks." Nick's eyes had a cold glint, and his voice held a smugness that infuriated Guy.

"Only if you measure pleasure by sixteen- and eighteen-hour days working in a hospital full of bleeding, crippled, and dying men. It is not a pretty sight, as you well know," Guy retorted. His face was dark with anger. His brown eyes flashed.

"Damn it, Guy, come to the point!" Nick demanded. "What the hell are you talking about?"

"What I'm talking about is what the past four weeks have been like with Kate. She's been working herself to the point of exhaustion every day in the hospital at the manor, and she's got me doing it, too! Pleasure, he says. Ha! She spends all her time keeping busy so she can forget you, Nick. She's in love with you."

"You've lost your senses!" Nick countered incredulously.

"No. No, I haven't, my friend. Believe me," Guy continued with mounting anger. "Nick, I've held Kate in my arms, wanted her with every fiber of my being. But I let her go because I knew it was you she wanted. You. Not me. I tell you, Nick, Kate's in love with you."

Nick was frowning as he strode to the sideboard and poured himself a brandy. He downed the amber liquid in one gulp. Knowing Nick like a brother, Guy knew that it was better to keep silent when confronted by that explosive look.

Nick walked to the open French doors. He was silent for a long while, looking out at the luxuriant garden, wrestling with himself. At length he turned back to Guy, who saw that the grim tightness around Nick's mouth had lessened some.

"I'm sorry, Guy," he said. "I know what it cost you to admit that to me."

Guy chose his next words carefully. "I'd like to know your intentions, Nick. Are you going to let her pine away with a broken heart? Or are you going to tell the wench you love her?"

Nick's laugh was quick and cruel. "What makes you think I'm in love with Kate? I'm grateful to her, of course, for saving my life. But gratitude isn't love, for God's sake."

"I certainly know *that*," Guy replied sharply, annoyed at his friend's coldness. He was silent for a moment as he thought of Kate's feeling toward him—only gratitude. He tried to push aside the hurt he felt.

"But I know you, Nick. I've seen how you look at her, how your face changes when you speak of her," Guy said intently. "Why can't you see the obvious?"

Nick turned back to the doors, feeling the sunlight

warm on his face. A strange feeling settled over him. Love? Did Guy have to put into words what he refused to admit to himself? In the back of his mind, perhaps he felt he was falling in love with Kate. But he had fought to keep it from happening. True, Kate haunted his thoughts. She moved him as no other woman had. After Kate, he had no longer found pleasure with Meg or Liz or any other woman. Yet how could her oft-declared hatred for him have turned to love? he puzzled. Perhaps she had not let herself admit the feelings within her. Was there an unconscious joining of their kindred spirits, a binding of their souls before their minds realized it, admitted it? He wondered when Kate finally had come to the realization that she loved him. Then he thought of another woman.

"I thought I loved Lynette, Guy. Remember?" he spoke quietly. A frown showed on his brow. "And that turned out to be a dangerous business."

"Lynette wasn't half the woman Kate is," Guy answered hotly. "She was selfish and conniving. You were blinded by her beauty. We all saw that."

Still frowning, Nick turned back to Guy.

"You're in love with Kate," Nick stated, watching his friend's face intently.

Guy walked slowly over to Nick.

"We know each other too well, Nick," he said. "We might have known it would come to this someday— both of us wanting the same woman. Yes, I love her. And because I love her, I want her happiness above all things. Her happiness is loving you."

"I still say you're out of your mind," Nick said tersely. "She wants me out of her life. She's made that perfectly clear many times."

Guy shook his head in wonderment. He forced his tone to be patient. "You thickheaded fool, can't you see it?" he almost shouted at Nick. "Ever since you first took Kate to your bed on the *Sea Mist* months ago, your lives, your very destinies have been intertwined. My God, Nick, admit your responsibility for making her life a shambles!" Guy threw up his hands in exasperation.

Nick was feeling uncomfortable under his friend's angry assault. He hated to admit it, but what Guy said was true. He had used Kate badly. She'd had her life planned out, and he had ruined things for her on more than one occasion when he'd used her for his own ends. His guilt made him defensive and angry at Guy in return. But before he could frame a retort, Guy continued his barrage of accusations.

"And how has she repaid you? Did she call out the dragoons, as Lynette did? No. She's helped you and the cause. And she saved your blasted life, at considerable risk to her own, I might add. I very much doubt that we could have freed you without her. She could have left you to Douglass. But no, she fell in love with you and had to see you free."

Guy stopped to catch his breath and let his anger cool. But Nick's ire had been building until he could hold his tongue no longer.

"Now you listen to me, Guy. Don't make Kate Prescott sound so saintly. She used me to her selfish ends, too. She withheld things, schemed, and bargained to gain her way. I didn't throw her to the wolves, you know. I put her in Robert's care, and she could have had a good life with him if she'd chosen it. But her own desires and ambitions ruined that. The lady is quite capable of taking care of herself, believe me. And she'd be the first to tell you so!"

With that Nick turned and walked briskly to the sideboard and poured himself another brandy, confident that he had somewhat redeemed himself. But Guy was not cowed.

"Not this time, Nick," was his simple statement. "I see through this show of temper. It's not like you to deny the truth. If you don't believe me, ask Kate herself. You owe her that much. There's nothing to stop you, unless you're frightened by her power over you."

Nick's head shot up in anger. "Tread carefully, Guy," he warned through clenched teeth.

"Oh, cool down, Nick," Guy said in exasperation. "You know I'm right. She's gotten into your blood and you don't like the vulnerability it gives you. Kate's in the same position. She's used to taking care of herself, being independent, in control, but loving you has opened her to hurt. She's alone and confused."

Nick ran his hand through his blond hair and sighed

wearily. For the first time in a long time, Nick Fletcher was uncertain of what to do next.

Guy sensed his hesitancy and softened his tone. "Look, Nick, all I'm saying is that if you'll let yourself feel what's in your gut, you'll see that you love Kate. Stop denying it. If you care anything about Kate, go to her, help her, love her. Don't wait too long, Nick. You could lose her."

Nick remained silent a few moments longer, his mind racing. At last he drained his glass and faced Guy. "There are few men who would stand up to me and say the things you've just said. Few men I'd *allow* to say them. But I guess these things had to be said. I'm not sure what I feel for Kate. She haunts me when we are apart, drives me to distraction and passion when we're together. I do want to see her again. The thought of her eats at me constantly. I never seem to have enough of her. Is that love, Guy?"

Guy came to stand by Nick, putting his hand on his shoulder. He laughed softly and shook his head. "I don't know, Nick. I think so. Let me take you to Kate, and you can ask each other. Come to Chadwick Manor with me now, Nick. Can you ride?" Guy asked uncertainly.

"Yes. All right, Guy. Let's go," Nick said quietly as he reached for his brown velvet coat on the chair where he'd thrown it earlier.

They entered the hall, heading for the main door of the house. Nick had just finished instructing Dickinson, the butler, to have their horses saddled, when a woman's voice, husky with fury, rang out loudly through the hall. "Nick! Where do you think you're going?"

The two men turned to the wide staircase to face the indignant Lady Elizabeth. Guy saw an angry scowl set on Nick's face. His mouth was clenched into a hard line, his blue eyes narrowed threateningly. Nick's voice was deadly calm as he spoke, but there was no mistaking the malevolence in his tone.

"You know I account to no one for my actions. You would do well to remember that, Elizabeth."

And with that, Nick turned on his heel and walked to the door, opened it, and left without so much as a glance backward. Guy quickly followed, not wishing to become the target of the angry barrage of words Elizabeth was flinging at them.

"Most unladylike," Guy observed to Nick, one dark eyebrow cocked in mock disapproval as he banged the door shut behind him.

"Her shrewishness always did overshadow her beauty," Nick replied with a grin as they walked to the stables.

Chapter 52

After Guy Chadwick had gone early that morning, Kate had risen, dressed, then walked the quarter mile to the hospital. She wondered absent-mindedly about the important business that had taken Guy away so quickly. She'd wanted to talk to him about last night. She felt heavyhearted about what had happened between them.

The scent of flowers was heavy in the air. It promised to be a beautiful day. She regretted a little having to spend it in the oppressiveness of the hospital. A message had come to the house that more wounded had staggered in during the night, and Doc Weatherby would be hard put to handle them all, even with help from her, Clara Haggerty, and several other women who came to help whenever they could. Kate quickened her step. She was glad for this work to do. It occupied her fully and left her little time for thoughts of Nick. Her thoughts now were occupied with Victoria Remington and her offer. Kate would speak to Guy about leaving, so he could find a replacement for her. More and more, she wanted to join the Remingtons on their journey to France. It clearly was the best thing to do.

"Morning, Doc," Kate greeted as she entered the barn and hung her bonnet and shawl on the hook near the door.

Old Doctor Weatherby stood up to greet her. He looked so tired. He seemed to have aged years in the past few weeks. Would he ever get the sleep he needed? Kate wondered. Would the stream of wretched, beaten soldiers ever end? She loved Weatherby, loved his wrinkled face and the lines around his mouth that deepened when he smiled.

"Good morning, Kate," Doc Weatherby said. "We've been busy here, as you can see. But I think things are in hand now."

"How many new ones?" Kate asked as her eyes followed his outstretched hand to the newly filled beds.

"Twelve. Came in about four this morning, I think."

"Why didn't you send word? I could have come down to help," Kate asked as she picked up his bag of instruments and a bundle of bandages and followed him to the next bed.

"Didn't need you then. They weren't in too bad a shape. Seems there was a small skirmish up by Regan's Mill, north of here. We lost, but we gave them some lead to remember us by. Right, Sam?"

Doc Weatherby smiled at the man on the cot before him. The man's left eye and the side of his head were bandaged, and his left arm was in a sling, but he grinned broadly. "We'da had 'em beat if reinforcements hadn't come right then. Musta been fifty or sixty of 'em, and us only twenty-five or so."

"There'll be other chances to fight them, on better terms." Kate said encouragingly. She and Weatherby kept walking.

"Got all the new ones patched up best I could, Kate. Mrs. Haggerty was here to help. The others will be needing the usual bandage changes and food. Betta Mead said she'd be over this morning to help you. I'm going to get a little sleep up in the loft. Call me if you need me."

"Right, Doc," Kate said. "Sleep well. Don't worry about a thing."

She picked up Doc's medical bag and began the rounds. Men were starting to waken. There were ten others besides the twelve new ones, and Kate was kept busy changing bandages and checking wounds for most of the morning. Betta Mead arrived and took over in time to feed the men their lunches in her friendly, efficient way.

Kate smiled as she watched Betta. These were good people, Kate thought. Doc, Betta, the men, Guy. It felt right to be with them, to be part of their lives. Yes, they were good, decent people, these Americans. She loved them. And they cared for her in return, accepted her without question of her past or her station in life. They welcomed her among them. She wondered if she'd find this same openness of attitude in France. Or was it part of America's uniqueness?

Kate was checking the new men and had reached the last one. He had his right arm over his eyes, and she couldn't see his face clearly. Thinking he was asleep, Kate started to move away.

"I thought you'd never get to me, miss," he said a little weakly. Something familiar in the voice brought Kate to a halt and she swung around to face Nick Fletcher. No, not Nick. The blue eyes were Nick's, the full mouth, the voice. But the hair was darker, a sandy brown, and the face was younger, no more than eighteen years old. But this man, this boy in a tattered soldier's uniform, looked so much like Nick Fletcher that Kate could only stand and stare open-mouthed.

"Are you all right, miss?" the young man asked, a worried frown replacing his smile.

"I, ah, yes. I'm fine," Kate stumbled, trying to recover herself.

"It's just, I mean, you startled me. You look so much like someone I know. For a moment I thought you were someone else."

"I understand," he said, the smile returning to his handsome face. "For a minute there, I thought you'd seen a ghost or something." He laughed. Nick's laugh.

"I did, too," Kate laughed with him, trying to regain her composure. She changed the subject.

"How are you feeling today?" For the first time she noticed the bandages under his tattered shirt around his stomach. She saw a spot of blood coming through on the right side.

"I'd better have a look at that wound. You're bleeding. Are you in much pain? I can give you some laudanum to help the pain."

She was talking too fast, she knew. But his appearance was so unsettling. She began to unwrap the dressing. The young man shifted uncomfortably. A grimace of pain crossed his face.

"It hurts a little, but it's all right," he said sheepishly. His voice was so like Nick's.

"I'll try to be gentle with this. We don't want you bleeding and messing up things around here," Kate teased, giving him a warm smile. "Mrs. Mead, there, is a real stickler for cleanliness." She continued to unwrap the bandage. "It's only a flesh wound, I see. They can hurt like the devil, though, so don't play brave. I can give you some laudanum to ease it, if you want." She looked into these familiar eyes, so clear and blue.

"With you nursing me, that's medicine enough, miss," he said softly. A charmer, this one, Kate thought, but he has the sincerity his look-alike lacks.

"Flatterer," Kate teased. "For that, you get extra dessert."

His smile widened, but she knew he was gritting his teeth to keep from making a sound as she wound clean strips of cloth around his midsection.

"Some cracked ribs, too?" she asked knowingly.

"Yes. I took a fall down a steep hill when I was hit, and I didn't miss one of the rocks on the way down. Rather clumsy of me."

"Well, try not to move around too much, and you'll be well and out of here in no time," Kate assured him as she stood to leave.

"Miss? Before you go, may I ask you a question?" His face was eager as he propped himself up on his elbows.

"Of course, soldier. Ask away. Just remember, you're not up to any ungentlemanly activity for a while." Kate laughed.

"No, no. Nothing like that," he said quickly, reddening to the tips of his ears. "The man, the one you thought I looked like. Is he someone important to you? Your husband, maybe?"

"No, no. He's not my husband. He's a rogue and a scoundrel," Kate replied. "Probably just like you. But, yes. He has had an influence in my life lately. Not in the sense you mean, however. But you must rest now." She plumped the pillow behind his head, then straightened to leave.

336

"What's your name, miss, if you don't mind my asking?" Those eyes followed every movement as she wound up the remaining length of bandage and put it away in the doctor's bag.

"I don't mind. It's Kathleen Prescott. What's yours?" She hadn't been going to ask. She didn't want to know, didn't want to learn there might be a connection between this young man and Nick Fletcher.

"Mine's Jason. Jason Fletcher."

Kate sat down hard on the cot. So there it was. Another Fletcher. Would she never be rid of them?

"Are you all right, Miss Prescott? You look rather pale,"

"Yes, Jason. I'm fine." Kate's mind raced. Nick hadn't said much about his family in the times they'd been together, only that they were in England and he had several brothers and sisters.

"Do you have a brother named Nicholas, Jason? A brother who looks very much like you?" she asked, knowing what the answer would be.

"Nick? Do you know Nick?" he asked eagerly. He tried to sit up, winced in pain, and settled back on the pillow. "Nick's my brother. He's twelve years older than I am. But people say we look almost alike. I haven't seen him in five years. Is he here somewhere?" He looked around the room worriedly.

"Take it easy, Jason," Kate soothed. "And please don't move around so. You'll start bleeding again. Nick isn't here. I know where he is, though." At least I think I do, Kate added to herself.

"You've seen him lately, then, Miss Prescott?" Jason asked, hope sounding in his voice. "Could I see him? Could I go to him?"

"Now, calm down, Jason," Kate ordered somewhat sternly. "Take a breath and give me a chance to think, won't you?"

"I'm sorry, Miss Prescott," he said sincerely. "It's just that I was beginning to think I'd never find him. A lot of people know of Nick. He's very important in the rebellion. But no one's been able to tell me where to find him. Whenever I'd get any kind of a lead, it would turn out to be a dead end. I've been looking for two years.

You're sure you know where he is?" He looked doubtful. It was clear he worshipped his brother.

"Well, I haven't seen him in about a month, Jason, but I think he's still there. It's not too far from here," Kate explained. She didn't add that he was recovering from being badly hurt. "But don't get any ideas. You're not going anywhere in your condition. I'll send word to Nick that you're here."

Jason seemed to be calming down. He smiled sheepishly at her.

"Sorry to be such a bother to you, Miss Prescott. I know you're busy here and all. I don't want to be any trouble to you."

"Call me Kate, Jason. And you're no trouble," she assured him. "How is it that you haven't seen Nick in five years?"

"That's how long it's been since Nick left home. He and father had a terrible argument," Jason explained, eager to talk of the brother who meant so much to him. "I'd never seen either of them so angry. Most of our money is in textiles, and Father rules over his empire like a king. He wanted all his sons to go into the business with him. Our brother Jarrod stands to inherit the bulk of the estate someday because he's the eldest. But Father would do well by all of us, he assured us, as long as we worked with him. William, the next eldest, decided to study law first, then go in with Father. Nick's the third son, and he'd always been a trial to Father."

"That doesn't surprise me in the least," Kate said with a knowing laugh.

"Nick just doesn't like to conform to rules," Jason defended. "He makes his own. He was suspended from every school to which Father sent him. Only when he was allowed to choose his own school did he complete the courses. He even read law at university for a year, but he decided not to continue. But he always was doing something to keep Father in a perpetual state of exasperation. Gambling, drinking, brawling, dueling, womanizing."

Jason lowered his eyes and flushed pink.

"I mean, ah, I must be painting a terrible picture of him for you," he continued quickly. "But he really wasn't bad, just always needed a new adventure to keep things interesting, he liked to say."

"Don't worry, Jason. You haven't surprised me. He sounds just like the Nick I know," Kate assured him.

He looked relieved. "Nick always was good to me, even though I'm so much younger. He never got along with Jarrod and William. They get along famously together, and Nick always said he felt like the odd man out. Then our two sisters were born after Nick. So when I was born, Nick said he was so glad, he was going to raise me himself. And he practically did, too. He taught me loads of things. About animals, how to shoot, fence, defend myself. I was like his shadow, and he never minded. We used to sleep out in the woods together, and we'd talk for hours about his dreams, about America. He said America would be free of Britain one day, and a man could be and do anything he wanted to here, as long as he was willing to work hard. And he was right, too. He always was right."

A faraway look passed over those blue eyes, and Kate knew he was back home, a boy again.

"No more talking now, Jason," Kate said softly, touching his arm. "You must rest. Nick will be so glad to see you. I'll get word to him as soon as I can."

His hand on her arm stopped her from turning away.

"Wait, Miss Pres—— Kate. I'm sorry. I didn't mean to rattle on so about home. You're easy to talk to, I guess."

"And you're a little bit homesick, I think, Jason," Kate said gently. "Sleep now. I'll be back later. When you are feeling stronger, you'll be moved up to the main house—Chadwick Manor. Mr. Chadwick is a close friend of your brother's. He will see that you and Nick get together as soon as possible, I'm certain."

Jason's grateful smile warmed Kate's heart as she walked away.

Kate left a message for Dr. Weatherby about Jason with Betta Mead. Then Kate headed for the manor. As she walked, she marveled at the phenomenon that was Nick Fletcher. So many people cared about him, admired him. The men on his ship, Henry and Annie Jenkins, Robert and Laurie, Guy, Mr. Franklin. This young brother who hadn't seen him in five years. And, of course, every woman from Boston to Philadelphia, she thought derisively.

Including me, she thought as she walked. I might as well stop trying to convince myself that I can forget him. I've got to see him again, and Jason gives me a good reason to go to Elizabeth's. What if he isn't there any longer? But Guy would know where Nick had gone if he weren't at Elizabeth's. She hoped Guy had returned by now.

When she reached the house, she called for Reynolds, the butler.

"Reynolds, has Mr. Chadwick returned yet?" Kate asked as she took off her shawl and bonnet.

"No, miss. He didn't expect to return until this afternoon."

Kate was thoughtful a moment. Well, no matter. She would leave a message for him and go to Elizabeth's alone. He couldn't object to that. It wasn't as though she were going all the way into Albany again or anything like that. Besides, she thought defensively, she didn't have to account to anyone for her actions.

Kate felt excitement mounting in her. She would see Nick soon.

"Begging your pardon, miss," Reynolds interrupted her thoughts, "but a boy has arrived with a message for you which he says is most urgent. He insists on giving it to you personally."

"A message for me?" Kate repeated, puzzled. "Who could be...? Very well, Reynolds. Where is he?"

"In the parlor, miss."

"Thank you, Reynolds," Kate said as she walked toward the double doors leading to the parlor. There she found a dust-covered, husky lad of about fourteen. He bowed his head, then addressed her with great seriousness.

"Miss Kathleen Prescott? A message for you of great importance. I'm to wait for your reply."

Still puzzled, Kate hurriedly opened the sealed letter. Her blue eyes widened and her heart leaped into her throat as she glanced to the signature. A note from Nick! She was so excited that she could barely focus on the boldly written words.

Dearest Kathleen,

I am in New York and cannot leave now, but I *must* see you. It is important to both of us. Tonight, at the Soaring Hawk Inn.

Yours,

Nick

Kate read the brief letter through again with disbelief. It was so short, almost curt, but that was so like Nick. Dare she read greater meaning into his words? What did he want of her this time? Had he at last realized he loved her, as she loved him? It was too much to hope for, but her spirits soared. She had all but forgotten the messenger until she heard him clear his throat nervously. Kate quickly regained her composure, yet her mind raced. Reason was forgotten. Nick wanted her! And she would bring him news of Jason. She longed to see the look on his face when she told him. There was no time to waste. If she were to make the rendezvous, she must leave at once. How she wished Guy had not gone this morning. She longed to tell him of this, ask his advice. Guy would be furious when he learned she had gone to New York. But there was not time to worry about that now.

"You, what's your name?" Kate demanded.

"Andrew, Andrew Larkin, miss," came the boy's startled reply.

"The man who gave you this message, was he all right? Was he in danger?"

The young man thought for a moment before he replied.

"No, miss. He seemed fine, except that he was most anxious to see that you received this message. Gave me a pound to deliver it as fast as I could," Andrew said proudly.

"I see. Thank you, Andrew. Now go to the kitchen and refresh yourself," Kate commanded. "Wait for me there. I'll join you shortly, and you will escort me to the city, to the Soaring Hawk Inn."

Andrew Larkin stared wide-eyed at Kate. He seemed about to tell her those were not his instructions, but he thought better of it when he saw her determined look. Instead he muttered his assent and followed her wake into the hall.

Kate all but ran down the wide hall, shouting for Reynolds as she went. As he appeared, Kate paused at the bottom of the winding staircase only long enough to instruct him to have her horse, and a fresh mount for the messenger, saddled and ready to leave immediately. Then she rushed up the stairs to change.

In her room, Kate stripped off her blue damask morning gown and put on a tight-fitting forest green suede riding jacket and skirt, with matching suede boots, gloves, and feathered hat. It was a very fetching outfit and she wanted to look her best. She put some belongings into a cloth luggage bag and was in the kitchen urging young Larkin to hurry, before twenty minutes' time had passed.

As she mounted Thunder, the prancing chestnut stallion Guy had given her, she turned to Reynolds, who stood nearby, a look of dismay on his usually expressionless face. Kate handed him Nick's letter.

"Don't scowl so, Reynolds. I know what I'm doing. I didn't have time to write an explanation to Mr. Chadwick. Just give him this when he returns."

Before Reynolds could reply, Kate kicked her heels into Thunder's powerful sides, causing him to plunge down the lane at breakneck speed. Andrew Larkin spurred his horse also and followed as best he could.

Chapter 53

Dusk was just descending as Kate reined in Thunder at the back door of the Soaring Hawk Inn. They had traveled hard and fast, stopping only to rest and water the horses several times and to have a brief meal at a roadside inn. Kate had paid and dismissed the boy when they reached the beginning of the road leading to the inn.

She quickly tied Thunder to the hitching post and bounded through the kitchen door, where she found Henry Jenkins shouting at a cowering cook. Annie wasn't yet back from the market to command the kitchen properly. When Henry saw Kate, he stopped in midsentence and a big grin of pleasure filled his reddened face. Kate ran into his burly arms and gasped laughingly as he crushed her in a bear hug.

"Kate, lass! It does these old eyes a world of good to see you. How've you been all these weeks?"

Henry drew her aside to a quiet corner of the kitchen, where their conversation would not be overheard. The frightened cook looked relieved and quickly disappeared into the storeroom.

"It's dangerous these days for a beautiful young woman to travel alone, what with them cursed redcoats swarmin' all over the place. What brings you to the Soaring Hawk, Kate, lass?"

The smile vanished from Kate's lips, to be replaced

by confusion. Surely Henry knew that Nick had sent for her.

"Why, Henry, I've come to meet Nick. He sent for me at Chadwick Manor, telling me to meet him here. Surely you know of it."

A deep frown furrowed Henry's thick brows. A nagging thought, which Kate had refused to let surface on the journey here, came unbidden to her mind. Something was wrong, but what was it? Henry leaned closer to her. Kate caught the worried note in his voice when he spoke.

"Nick isn't here, lass. I haven't laid eyes on him since we filched him out from under Douglass' nose. You'd better tell me everything that's happened."

Kate was silent a moment as Nick's letter flashed through her mind. Of course. How stupid she'd been to overlook such obvious discrepancies. If she'd been thinking with her head instead of her heart, she would have realized that Nick never would call her Kathleen, much less dearest! He always called her Kate, and he referred to the Soaring Hawk Inn as Henry's place.

"Kate, what is it, lass? You look pale as death!"

Kate glanced quickly around for a sign of anything amiss, all her senses alert. She looked at Henry, her blue eyes wide with alarm.

"A trap, Henry! It must be a trap! I have to get away quickly!"

A commotion coming simultaneously from the front dining room and the back entrance told Kate it already was too late to escape. A thought raced through her mind. Was it the assassin? Would she at last fall prey to his deadly blade? Yet it was not his way to make so noisy an entrance.

Then a half-dozen red-coated soldiers swarmed into the room, leveling their bayoneted muskets menacingly at Henry and Kate. To resist would have been suicide. Even so, Henry stepped in front of Kate to shield her, landing a powerful blow on the jaw of the nearest dragoon. For his valiant effort, he received a crushing blow on the back of the head from the butt of a musket. Kate screamed as Henry fell unconscious at her feet. Then rough hands seized her, pinning her arms behind her, and forcing her roughly against the wall. A gag was wound tightly around her mouth, muffling her screams.

"Well, well, my dear Kathleen," came a sneering voice from the doorway to the dining room, "I knew you would rush to be with your lover Fletcher. Alas, I regret he is not here, but I can assure you he also will be in my hands soon. In the meantime, I shall take great delight in settling the score that remains between you and me."

Kate had whirled her head around to glare at John Douglass. As she looked into his cold, jeering face she was filled with dread. How could she have been so careless?

She struggled against her two captors but succeeded only in having them hurt her. She moaned with pain as she heard Douglass' harsh laugh.

"Easy, men. I don't want you to bruise this pretty piece. I have plans for her. It took me too long to track her down to have her fate come quickly."

He roughly grasped her chin in his hand and forced her head up to look at him. As Kate looked into his cold, gray eyes, her thoughts raced. How had he found her? Had Lady Remington betrayed her? She had made it no secret that Peter was a loyal British supporter. Had Kate put her trust in an enemy? The thought devastated her spirit more than Douglass' leering hatred.

Releasing her chin and letting his finger trace a line slowly down her smooth neck, Douglass brought his finger to rest on the top button of her green riding jacket. Unbuttoning it slowly, he watched Kate, looking for a sign of fear in her wide blue eyes. He saw only contempt and defiance.

"Yes, my dear. Keep that hatred in those lovely blue eyes. I shall enjoy your spirited resistance."

With that, Douglass turned to his leering men and motioned to Henry's unconscious bulk.

"You three," he ordered, "lock this blunderhead in the cellar for now. Then stand guard there and at the entrances. The rest of you bring the prisoner and follow me."

Douglass turned and ascended the stairs, and Kate was dragged, kicking and thrashing, up the stairs behind him. They entered the first room on the right, and

Douglass ordered her tied to the stout wooden bedpost, her back pressed tightly against it, her arms behind her. Kate was startled to see the room already occupied by two others she recognized. Lynette DuPree lounged comfortably on a silk divan. A cold smile spread across her lips at the sight of Kate. She adjusted her position on the divan for a better view of her, straightened her blue velvet gown, and laughed cruelly. Somehow Kate was not surprised to find the deadly Lynette DuPree in the company of John Douglass.

Hensley Forbes also was there. He stood watching Kate with sadistic pleasure. His face was even uglier than she had remembered.

"I have gone to considerable trouble in my attempt to find you, my dear," Douglass was saying. "You have proved to be quite elusive. I'm certain Forbes here will attest to that. You have managed to escape him since London. I did not know about his profession or his special talent when he served aboard the *Newgate*. But then I didn't know about your activities either, did I, sweet Kathleen? Things would have been much different for all of us these past months had I known."

His look of hatred sent a shudder of dread through Kate.

"But that can be remedied easily now. Persistence does win out. Forbes, Mademoiselle DuPree, and I joined forces after your treacherous rescue of Fletcher from the stockade. Together we have made it our goal to find you both. Finally we were able to track you to Chadwick Manor. Your reputation as an angel of mercy in that dreadful hospital for traitors to the Crown has spread far and wide, my dear."

Kate took no comfort in his words except to be relieved to know that neither Lady Remington nor Peter had been the source of her betrayal.

When the soldiers had finished tying Kate securely to the bedpost, Douglass ordered the three of them to wait outside. At the looks of disappointment on their faces, he laughed wickedly.

"Have no fear, lads. I promise you, you'll have your chance with her. But I'll have my pleasure first."

Grinning widely, his men saluted smartly and turned to leave, casting lustful glances at Kate as they went through the doorway. Kate felt sick to the depths of her soul.

"You need have no worry, either, Hensley, my good man. I'll not cheat you of the prize you've been pursuing for so long," Douglass assured the beady-eyed little man who still stood watching intently from across the room. "It will be a superb last revenge on Fletcher, for Kathleen shall lure him here to my trap as the nectar of a sweet flower lures the bumblebee. When my men and I have done with her, Forbes, she is all yours to do with as you wish. No doubt this devious little spy will all but welcome your trusty blade in her conniving heart then. And you can have the honor with that bastard Fletcher, too. I only wish to watch him die."

Kate heard Forbes' evil laugh as he stepped forward a little into the brighter light. His hideous features were twisted into a maniacal smile. Kate gasped in terror as she saw what he held in his hand: a dagger with a gold "X" emblazoned on its black hilt. Her senses reeled as she frantically twisted against the ropes binding her, trying with all her strength to be free of them and this nightmare. But the ropes gave way not an inch.

Chapter 54

Nick was feeling a bit apprehensive as he and Guy turned into the winding driveway of Chadwick Manor. Nick was beginning to feel unsure about being here, and the thought of a last-minute escape through the grassy meadow flashed through his mind as he reined in his mount in front of the house. He hoped the tight knot in the pit of his belly would disappear when he saw Kate again.

But he and Guy had hardly dismounted when Reynolds, who never hurried, suddenly came bounding through the front doorway and down the stone steps.

"Thank goodness you've returned, sir!" he cried, relief showing on his severe features.

"What is it, Reynolds?" Guy demanded impatiently.

"It's Miss Kathleen, sir. She's gone!" Reynolds explained in a worried tone.

"What the devil are you talking about, man?" Guy demanded, his annoyance growing. "Where has she gone?"

"I don't know, sir," Reynolds answered nervously. "A boy came from New York with a message for her, and she left with him in great haste."

Nick, who had been standing quietly beside Guy, now came to life. His instincts warned him of danger, grave danger.

"What do you mean, she's gone? What messenger?"

Nick's eyes were ablaze and the angry look on his face set Reynolds trembling with fear.

"Easy, Nick," Guy cautioned, stepping between the two men. "You'll frighten him out of his wits."

Reluctantly, Nick stepped back. His mind raced. Kate was in danger, and this blithering idiot of a butler turned mute!

Guy turned to face the cowering butler, who never took his eyes off Nick.

"All right, calm down, Reynolds, and try to be coherent. Did Miss Kathleen leave a message for me before she left?"

"Yes, sir. She left this," Reynolds said eagerly, happy to have one answer to Guy's queries.

Guy snatched the envelope from Reynolds and hastily read the brief letter inside.

"My God," was all he could mutter as he quickly handed the letter to Nick. "Who would want to get Kate into the city?" Guy speculated nervously.

Nick had no reply, but instead turned to the still unnerved butler.

"How long ago did they leave?" he demanded, his blue eyes barely visible beneath his frowning brow.

"About two hours ago, Captain, sir," came Reynolds' timid reply.

"They've a good start on us, Guy," Nick stated levelly, now in complete control of his temper and taking charge of the situation. "Get two or three of your stoutest lads to come with us, and have your best stallions saddled. We ride for New York!"

"Right, Nick!" Guy agreed, as he turned to shout orders to the nearby groom. "Bring up Lightning and Gray Boy, and tell Jess, Reuben, and Will to be ready to ride at once!"

At the Soaring Hawk Inn, John Douglass slowly removed the scarlet jacket of his uniform and hung it carefully over a nearby chair. Forbes settled himself in a quilted armchair, gingerly fingering the deadly dagger, the terrible grin still on his face. He whispered something in Lynette DuPree's direction. She laughed and looked at Kate. Lynette's dark eyes were cold and

cruel. It was obvious that these people meant to prolong
Kate's torment. Fear and rage swept through Kate as
she watched Douglass' slow, deliberate movements. She
willed herself to be calm. She must keep her wits about
her if she were to survive. But she could not help realizing her helplessness, and the dread of what was
certain to come almost made her swoon.

Douglass removed his sword from its scabbard. Its
blade glistened in the lamplight as he carefully ran it
through his fingers. His cold, gray eyes never left Kate's
face. For a moment Kate hoped he would kill her
quickly and be done with it, but she knew he would not
let her off so easily. He strode leisurely over to her.

"The sword is an amazing instrument," Douglass
began casually, a sly smile curling his lip. "It can make
quick work of so many things...such as disrobing a
wench."

And with a single precise sweep, he brought the
sword slashing down the threads of her jacket buttons,
sending them flying. He laughed at her sharp intake
of breath as the sword swished by her. The tight-fitting
jacket burst open, revealing her low-cut yellow silk
blouse. For a moment Douglass watched the erratic rise
and fall of her breasts where they showed in the deep
vee of her blouse. How Kate longed to be rid of the gag
that kept her silent. Had she been able to speak, perhaps she could have provoked him into killing her
quickly, before she was forced to endure the degrada-
tion she knew was inevitable.

Douglass slowly walked away to the desk and replaced his sword in its scabbard next to a matching
sheathed dagger. Then, smiling evilly, he came toward
Kate and began to run his finger along the side of her
face, down her neck, and over the mounds of her breasts.
Kate turned her face away, but he grasped her chin and
forced her to look at him. His voice was husky with
desire.

"You are such a lovely creature. I have wanted you
since the first time you came aboard my ship those long
months ago. And now you are mine."

With that he grasped the top of her blouse and the
thin chamois underneath and viciously ripped them
down the front, exposing the soft pinkness of her breasts

to his hungry eyes. Forbes and Lynette laughed wickedly as they watched every movement with eager anticipation. Kate struggled in vain against her tight bonds. The gag choked her as she tried to twist her head free of it. Douglass seemed delighted by her futile effort. Slowly he moved his hands over her breasts and, feeling their softness and the natural tightening response of her nipples beneath his touch, he was overcome by the passion that had been mounting in him. He jerked the gag down from her mouth and brutally covered her lips with his. Kate struggled with all her might, but he pushed his body against hers, pinning her fast against the bedpost and holding her face in his viselike grip to keep her from twisting away from him. Kate desperately tried to scream as she felt his hand move down her body to the side fastening of her riding skirt. His mouth still imprisoned hers, bruising it with the fierceness of his attack. She prayed she would at least faint and escape the horror being perpetrated against her body. But she did not.

Chapter 55

Nick, Guy, and his three men drew up their lathered horses sharply at the entrance to the road leading to the Soaring Hawk Inn. They had barely stopped during the hours of hard riding, and the horses were close to exhaustion. The pain in Nick's side from his wound was excruciating. His skin chafed where the cloth of his shirt rubbed against the still-healing welts on his torso. But this only served to make his senses more alert, his muscles taut and ready to respond to his mental commands. He was oblivious to the pain. His mind concentrated on only one thought: finding Kate.

Inquiries along the way had led Nick to believe that Kate had arrived only about thirty minutes ahead of them. It took all of his will to keep from throwing caution to the wind and riding headlong right to Henry's inn. But, good sense told Nick that whoever had planned this trap was no amateur, and he would have to keep his wits about him and tread carefully if he were to succeed in saving Kate. And save her he would, for he realized now that she had become very important in his life. He didn't want to think of the future without her.

During the long, hard ride, Nick had tried to solve the mystery of the forged letter. All indications pointed to John Douglass. Guy had solemnly agreed. Nick cursed himself mercilessly for having spared Douglass' life when he'd held it in his power so many months ago.

The five men separated, to approach the inn from different directions. The early-evening darkness covered their silent approach, and they were able to surprise and overpower the lounging guards at the two entrances to the inn. Once inside, Nick, Guy, and the bull-like Reuben Peters bounded up the stairway to engage the guards in the hall. They were professional soldiers but could not match the savage attacks from the flashing swords wielded by Nick Fletcher and Guy Chadwick.

In the upstairs room, Douglass, in his lust-filled frenzy, was oblivious to the commotion in the hall. But Forbes and Lynette DuPree were not so preoccupied, and they quickly came to their feet, alert to the danger outside. In the back of her anguished mind, Kate thought she heard Guy's voice shouting above the noise of the struggle with the guards. Her heart gave a leap, and she renewed her fight against Douglass' unrelenting hands.

"We can handle them, Nick! Find Kate!" came Guy's shout from the other side of the door.

Suddenly the door burst open, torn from its hinges by the force of the powerful kick directed at it. At the sound of the splintering wood, Douglass jumped back from Kate and was stunned to see Nick Fletcher burst into the room.

"Nick!" Kate screamed in relief.

Nick stopped dead still, poised to spring, his face livid with fury, his sword dripping blood. Behind him the commotion heightened, but Nick didn't hear it. His cold blue eyes darted swiftly around the room, from Kate to Douglass to Forbes to Lynette DuPree. For a split second, no one moved. Then Forbes lunged across the room to lash at Nick with a sword Forbes hadn't held a moment before. With Nick's attention drawn to his attacker, Douglass took the opportunity to vault for his own blade lying on the desk.

Nick made swift work of dispensing with Forbes. That man's forte was the dagger, not the sword. Nick handled his own steel with unrelenting expertise, and it was only a matter of seconds before Forbes screamed and clutched at his left side, where Nick's blade had penetrated. Nick quickly withdrew his sword as Forbes fell to his knees, dropping his blade with a clatter.

Nick had no time to finish the kill, for Douglass took up the fight and came savagely at Nick. Where Forbes had been a poor swordsman, Douglass more than showed himself to be an accomplished one. He met Nick's calculated blows one for one, yielding no ground, yet not gaining any from Nick.

Kate watched in shocked horror as steel crashed against steel. Her eyes were frozen on the two men fighting a death battle before her. So hypnotized was she that she failed to see Forbes crawling toward the window. It was only as he opened the shutters and used a last surge of strength to climb over the sill that Kate noticed his movement. In an instant, he disappeared from view. It was then that Kate saw Lynette DuPree. She had a small pistol in her hand and was trying to get a clear aim at Nick. But Douglass kept getting in her way. Kate bit back a shout of warning, fearing to draw Nick's attention from Douglass for even one dangerous moment. She didn't know what to do.

The ringing of blade upon blade seemed to have no pause, so intense was each man's concentration on seeing the other defeated. Nick was driven like a madman, yet he made no mistake, never let down his guard to give the now retreating Douglass a chance to strike.

Douglass was tiring fast, but Nick seemed to possess superhuman strength, delivering blow after numbing blow. Suddenly Nick feigned a thrust to the right and Douglass, thinking he saw an opening, made the mistake of lunging for Nick's heart. It was his last mistake. With lightning swiftness, Nick brought his sword up, caught Douglass' blade against his in a jarring blow, and sent it flying across the room to land with a crash on the floor. In nearly the same instant, the point of his blood-reddened blade found its mark deep in Douglass' unguarded heart.

John Douglass stood frozen, a look of shocked disbelief on his face. He clutched at the gaping wound with both hands and pitched forward. He was dead before his body touched the floor.

But Lynette DuPree now had a clear view of Nick,

and she pointed the pistol at him. Kate saw her and screamed a warning. The gun exploded, and Nick fell to his knees, then to the floor. Kate screamed his name. Guy rushed into the room, his own pistol drawn. Lynette threw aside the empty one-shot gun and ran to the desk, where she grasped Douglass' dagger. Instantly she withdrew it from its sheath and raised it back over her head. Guy was her target now. But Guy saw her and fired his pistol. The force of the bullet threw Lynette DuPree back against the silk divan on which she'd been lounging before. Blood trickled down the side of her mouth, and her eyes remained wide open, staring into space. She died as violently as she had lived.

"She'll murder no more," Guy murmured as he turned to his fallen friend.

Nick was struggling to his feet. Guy grabbed his arm to steady him. Blood dripped down the left side of his face. Lynette's bullet had grazed his forehead. He shook his head to clear the cloudiness from his senses, then rushed to Kate. He quickly drew his own dagger and slashed at the ropes that bound her hands and feet.

"Kate, love, did they hurt you?" he asked breathlessly as she fell weakly into his arms.

"Oh, Nick, thank God you came! Are you all right?" Kate cried as sobs of fear and relief racked her body.

Nick crushed her to him, stroking her hair.

"Hush, darling, hush. Yes, I'm fine. They can't hurt us now." He held her tightly.

Guy glanced at Douglass' limp form on the floor, then looked at Nick.

"So it was Douglass. You should have done that three months ago, Nick. It would have saved us all a lot of trouble."

"I know," Nick said quietly, still holding Kate in his arms.

"Nick, Forbes!" Kate cried. "He got away, out the window! He is the assassin, just as we thought. You've got to stop him, Nick, before he gets away again!"

Nick's blue eyes flashed wildly. He'd have the foul bastard this time. Forbes was wounded. He couldn't get far.

"Can you walk, Kate?" he asked quickly.

"Yes, I think so," she answered, taking a tentative step. Her knees were weak, but she knew they would hold her. Nick caught her hand in his, and they hurried downstairs, sidestepping red-coated bodies as they went. Guy Chadwick was close behind. Downstairs, Nick swept up his black cloak from the chair where he'd thrown it when he'd come in and threw it around Kate to cover her nakedness.

"Stay here, Kate," he said as he and Guy dashed for the front door.

Just before they reached the door, Reuben Peters dashed through the entrance from the other way. They all but collided head-on with him. When Nick made to thrust him aside, Peters raised a staying hand to him.

"I wouldn't be going out there, if I was you, Cap'n. The alarm's up and His Majesty's dragoons will be a'swarmin' all over the place any minute now. 'Sides, if it's a certain window-jumpin' weasel you're seekin', look no further." With that Peters brandished the familiar black-hilted dagger that was Forbes' trademark, testing its point gingerly on the tip of his finger.

"The poor bloke broke his leg when he jumped, and he all but squashed me flat when he fell. Why, he was in real agony, hurt and bleedin' like a stuck pig such as he was. Still had enough gumption to pull this nasty little thing on me. It was then I figured it'd only be decent of me to put him out of his misery with the point of me sword!"

They all stared speechless for a moment, fathoming Peters' words.

"Well done, man!" Guy exclaimed, slapping Peters soundly on the back.

Just then, Henry Jenkins came weaving toward them, his head in his hands. Will Benton had heard his bellowing and freed him from the cellar.

"You mean I missed the bloody fight?" Henry cursed as he surveyed the wreckage of his inn. "Damn, Nick lad. Couldn't you have saved at least one head for me to crack?"

"Sorry, Henry," Nick said with amusement. "We'll leave you some next time." Then he grew serious. "Are you all right, my friend?" he asked as he noticed the blood on Henry's hand when he took it away from the back of his head.

"'Course I am," Henry answered gruffly. "Take more'n a musket butt to put me out of commission." He rubbed at the back of his head with a big checkered handkerchief.

"You and Annie'd best go under cover until things cool down. Douglass is dead. And the assassin," Nick stated, again taking charge of the scene. "The alarm's up. There'll be reprisals. You'd best not be around for a while, at least until the city returns to our hands."

Henry nodded agreement as Nick turned to the others.

"The rest of you, let's get the hell out of here!"

With that he grabbed Kate's hand and pulled her behind him toward the back door, where the horses waited.

"Contact me at Dillon's when you need me, Nick! Godspeed to you!" Henry shouted after them as they quickly mounted.

Chapter 56

They didn't rein in their horses until they came to a branch in the road that lead to Duncan's Cove.

"We'll go the rest of the way on foot, Kate," Nick told her, throwing his reins to Guy and quickly dismounting to help Kate from her horse.

"You'd best head for Drurytowne, then double back to Lancaster and lie low for a while, Guy. If Douglass could trace Kate to you, others may, too. I'll be in touch through Dalton at the Fighting Bull Tavern," Nick said as he grasped Kate's hand and drew her to him.

"As usual, we think alike, Nick!" Guy answered, a wide grin on his handsome face. "See you soon, when we'll give these bloody British a reason to respect colonials!" And to Kate he sent a brief salute. "Kate, love, be happy."

Kate smiled warmly. "Good-bye, Guy."

He spurred his horse and was off, his three men following at a gallop. The moon was bright and easily lighted the way as Nick and Kate ran quickly down the road leading to the beach. Nick had sent a message to the *Sea Mist* from Guy's before they'd left to find Kate. Now he hoped his men had received it in time and were waiting for them at the beach. He forced himself not to think beyond that and what might happen if they weren't there.

As they picked their way cautiously down the steep

path, Nick strained his eyes to penetrate the darkness in search of the longboat. They almost had reached the bottom when they heard a low voice call out to them from the underbrush to their left.

"That you, Cap'n Nick?"

"Bennett, you old sea dog!" Nick acknowledged with relief, and a like sigh escaped Kate's lips as Nick helped her down the last few rocky steps to the sand. "I never thought I'd be so glad to set eyes on your mangy face!" Nick said exuberantly as he saw Bennett emerge from the bushes, followed by Ginty Lawson and two others.

"That Miss Kate with you, Cap'n?" Bennett asked, peering intently at the cloaked figure behind Nick.

"Yes, Bennett, it's me," Kate answered.

"But come on, lads," Nick directed. "No time for talking. We've got the British right behind us. Where's the longboat?"

"This way, Cap'n." Bennett pointed to a clump of low bushes about fifty yards down the beach, near the water's edge.

They quickly reached the camouflaged boat, uncovered it, and cast off. The rhythmic dipping of the oars was the only sound breaking the night's stillness. They were just rounding the end of the outjutting cliff for open water when they heard the thunder of horses' hooves on the road that Nick and Kate had just traveled. They heard shouts and horses whinnying as the soldiers reined to a halt, dismounted, and began to descend the path. A few shots rang out when they were sighted as their boat cleared the shadow of the cliff, but they were well out of range of the gunfire. Kate huddled closer to Nick in the bow, shuddering at the thought of what might have happened if the soldiers had arrived any sooner.

As the boat slipped easily through the water around the point of the cliff, Kate felt Nick's body relax. She followed his gaze and saw the welcome sight of the beautiful *Sea Mist,* its tall masts outlined in the moonlight.

Strong arms whisked them on board the ship and, after a few moments of enthusiastic welcome, Nick barked orders to break out canvas and raise anchor. His men sprang to obey him, happy finally to be free of the idleness of the past weeks. They were under way in a matter of minutes, the sleek hull of the *Sea Mist* slipping smoothly through the dark water.

Nick came to stand next to Kate on the quarterdeck, putting his arms around her and pulling her close to him. He leaned down and kissed her long and tenderly, enjoying the warmth and feel of her body touching his. For a long time they held each other, watching the moonlight dancing on the waves.

"Nick," Kate whispered at last, nuzzling the hollow of his neck with her lips. "How did you know where to find me tonight?"

"Our matchmaking friend Guy was dragging me, practically bodily, back to Chadwick Manor, claiming you were pining your heart out for me and that I was doing the same. He insisted we loved each other and that it was about time we admitted it. A pity we couldn't see that for ourselves, Kate," Nick said quietly. "It wasn't until I thought I might lose you to Douglass' insanity that I truly realized I loved you." He was silent for a moment, watching Kate, drinking in the sight and feel of her.

"When we reached Guy's house, Reynolds was beside himself with worry and couldn't give us Douglass' forged letter fast enough. So, with a few of Guy's best men, we rode for the city. You know the rest."

Kate did indeed know the rest, and she shuddered as she thought of John Douglass' planned revenge. She snuggled closer to Nick, relishing the warmth and strength of his hard-muscled body.

"What will happen now, Nick—with the revolution, I mean?"

"Now? The British think we're beaten. Good King George still considers us only a thorn in his royal side. But he and others like him don't understand what Americans are made of. We came here to start a new land, and that's what we'll have. We'll take the best of the old world and forge it into a new free land, the likes of which the rest of the world will envy."

"I want to be part of that new world you're building, Nick," Kate said with quiet conviction. "I didn't think I wanted any more of it. I tried to run away. But I do want to be part of this."

"You are, Kate. You are," Nick told her. He looked at Kate with a tenderness that bespoke the love he'd grown to feel for her.

They kissed again, gently at first, then passionately, cherishing the moment, marking it in the memory of their hearts. Nick pulled away first, stepping back to smile at Kate. Then a mischievous gleam twinkled in his blue eyes.

"But for now, my lovely reluctant rebel, the war must wait a while. I have a need for you that will keep you occupied for some time hence."

Kate laughed. What complete happiness she felt as she put her arms around Nick's neck and drew him down to her until their lips met.

Then Nick swept Kate into his arms and carried her below to his cabin. For Kate, it was like coming home. How well she remembered the hours spent here with Nick many months ago. She let her thoughts focus only on the passions they had known in this cabin, the hunger and desire that had since unfolded into a deep and lasting love.

But thoughts of the past were lost as Nick's nearness ignited the fire within Kate once more. The swinging lantern overhead cast dancing shadows on the rich wooden panels that lined the walls, but Kate and Nick were oblivious to all but one another as they stood together in the middle of the room. He held her close against him and covered her waiting lips with his. When finally they parted a little, breathless with longing, Nick still held her close.

"For a while I thought I'd lost you, my love," he whispered as their eyes met. "What would my life be without you?"

"That you will never have to know, my darling, for I am here, now and always. I love you so. With all my heart and being, I am yours. It is our destiny. We belong together."

And then there were no more words needed between them, only the kiss of love to mark the beginning of forever.